cross fingers

Paddy
RICHARDSON

cross
fingers

hachette
NEW ZEALAND

The author gratefully acknowledges the support and assistance of the University of Otago Wallace Residency during the writing of this novel.

National Library of New Zealand Cataloguing-in-Publication Data
Richardson, Paddy.
Cross fingers / Paddy Richardson.
ISBN 978-1-86971-307-2
I. Title.
NZ823.2—dc 23

A Hachette NZ Book
Published in 2013 by Hachette New Zealand Ltd
4 Whetu Place, Mairangi Bay
Auckland, New Zealand
www.hachette.co.nz

Text © Paddy Richardson 2013
The moral rights of the author have been asserted.
Design and format © Hachette New Zealand Ltd 2013

Designed and produced by Hachette New Zealand Ltd
Printed by Griffin Press, Australia

For Geoff Walker, with many thanks

Prologue

Friday night

He is still Eric as he closes the door behind him and slips out into the night, feeling the sting of air on his face. He breathes it in, watches his breath floating beyond him into the dark.

He needs the chill and darkness, the sharpness of the night. Needs the lights and the weight of heat behind him. Stretched as tight as he is, all his nerves are straining like a jittery animal.

But it's always this way. He'll be better after tomorrow. Saturday's the big one. After Saturday it'll almost be over.

He stops by the letter box, takes the package out and zips it into his duffle bag. He walks along the pavement, softly lit by the street lamps, by the houses close against the fences and the cars swishing past throwing up slicks of light. Into the dark, across the green, then he's pushing through the swinging double doors into the pub and swathed again in the heaviness of heat radiating from the gas fire, the brightness of the overhead lamps.

'All right, mate?' The bartender is standing in front of him.

'A handle of the dark, thanks.'

'Big one tomorrow, eh?'

'Yeah.'

He pays for his beer and takes it to the table he usually sits at, away from the fire and near to the window. He hardly sees the street, though he's staring out at it while he drinks his beer. He comes in here often, they know who he is, know as well what he is and it doesn't matter: nobody says anything. Even when he comes in, his eyes still darkened with residues of make-up, his lips lined and slightly discoloured, nobody says a word. They know him here; he thinks they like him well enough.

And he's still Eric as he goes back out into the night and uses the phone in the box outside, clinking in the coins he picked up at the bank the day before and brought with him. He leans against the wall while he waits for the call to connect and for the phone to be picked up an ocean away. He smiles when it is and he starts to speak, holding one hand over his ear to block out the sounds of the band starting up again in the pub.

'Yeah. Yeah, I'll be OK. Not long now.'

He shoves his hands into his pockets and, ducking back into the town belt, walks head down, thinking about the phone call, thinking about tomorrow but not so tense. The time away and the beer and the talking has taken off the pressure.

A good feeling walking in the silence. The grass feels sodden underneath his feet. He hears the swish and muffled crunch as he treads over mounds of fallen leaves.

He's halfway across when he first hears them, the voices, the footsteps, and is gripped by the realisation that they are coming up behind him. There is the astonishing crack and hurt of the first blow, he flails out with his arms but he's already slipping, falling.

Falling into leaves and mud.

Him. *Eric*. His face, *Eric's* face, in the muck.

He covers his head with his arms against the boots, the boots which come one after another after another, trampling, shattering muscle and tissue and bone.

His mother chose it. Eric. The first had to be James, of course. *Jim.* James was the family name; the first son must have the family name. After that it was given over to the mother to choose.

Eric.

Eric the red. Because his first baby hair was faint, fuzzy red. Even though it later turned to blond, that distinctive white-blond mop. But during those first months he was *her* Eric the red, *her* little ginger-top.

She told him when she was still soft towards him. While he was her favourite.

My Eric. Stooping, smiling, the warm, firm kiss on his cheek, the sharp, dry scent of her perfume.

Her favourite.

8

Eric the red.

When she watched him. The spinning that was flying. Around and again. Around and one more time.

Boots. Smashing, splintering. There is the hot splash and stink of urine on his skin.

But he is Eric still, in the mud and the night and the leaves.

The dog found him in the morning and he wasn't Eric any more but *the body* the man dragged the dog off and vomited beside, *the body* as he retched over and over into leaves stained red.

The body. Car doors snapping shut, cameras clicking over and over in the still of early morning.

It's a nasty one.

The body.

Collected, labelled, braced, sliced; focus and click and click and another one here and click.

The body.

Watching Eric dance.

Eric's body. So beautiful.

The body.

1

I'm in the editing room. The title flashes up onto the screen: *56 Days*. Mike and Tim sit beside me and I watch their faces watch the images I've become accustomed to. The grim-faced police, the dogs, the crouched, dazed woman with blood on her face. The protesters trying to climb fences, trying to rip them down. The singing, the chanting, the placards. The sound of helicopters clap-clap-clappering, the plumes of smoke drifting upwards. All those sad, surreal images moving against the backdrop of our familiar Wellington buildings, roads, bridges. Don Taylor is there. 'We made history, I suppose, but it was a sad way of making it.'

And here are the lambs. Marching at the edge of the police lines, running, zigzagging in and out of the crowds. The white lamb wags a finger at a police officer. They turn around, wiggle their bums at the line of police, wave up at the crowded stands.

And now they're dancing, turning into spinning tops, leaping together, rocketing through the air.

The bright blue sky enfolding and framing them as they spin, spin, spin.

As they spin.

Back to the beginning.

Touch wood, cross fingers, my granddad used to say. Hold off those hovering gods eager to upturn buckets of cold, green slime on your head. Just when things are getting good.

Because they were good, maybe, looking back, *too* damn good. In a matter of days I'd be off on a blissful holiday. Rarotonga. Partially subsidised by the network since it was partially — very partially — work. And I had the best of stories to dive back into when I got back. This was going to be a good one.

I knew there was something of the crusader in me and I knew

from past, bitter experience I had to curb it but I had a particularly warm glow in the pit of my belly over this one. I was going to expose Denny Graham for the total shit he was.

Denny Graham was an ex-cop from Wellington who'd moved to Auckland in the early eighties, bought motels in Mount Eden and got his start by getting around council by-laws and selling the units off separately as 'ownership flats'. He now owned and managed an Auckland-based company which dealt in investment properties. YourWay Prime Investments: 'Your choice, Your properties, Your way'. His company had spin-offs: short-term loans, nightclubs, massage parlours. All of which were still happily humming away while he was doing time for embezzlement.

Murray Turner, Graham's long-discarded business partner, was on the phone. Again. He'd got into the habit of phoning me at any old time and *venting*. Still, even though it took considerable effort, I had to indulge him. I had to be unreservedly tolerant since he was the kind of source journalists usually only dream of. He had clung for years to a virulent resentment of Denny Graham, a resentment which made him itch for Graham to get his comeuppance. He'd worked with him until they'd had the falling out which had left Turner down and broke and Graham blithely moving onwards and upwards.

'It's a fucking joke,' he said, 'him living in that fucking great castle of his. Get this. He's allowed out to do his shopping. All he has to do is phone his probation officer and away he goes down to New World to stock up on his bloody wine and pâté.'

At present Graham was on eleven months' home detention wearing a monitoring electronic bracelet. Turner was right. Denny's incarceration was far from irksome. For most people, the idea of roaming around the four hundred or so square metres of house, enjoying the pleasant vista from the tower and whiling away time in the gym, the pool, the spa and the entertainment room would be the kind of luxury holiday they could only dream of.

'It's a fucking joke,' Turner repeated, 'that sentence. Just a tap on the hand. He gets off with a hundred and fifty hours' community work and he'll get around that one, you wait and see, and $500,000 reparation. That's bloody peanuts to Denny.'

Graham, of course, had had a top criminal lawyer acting for him. He would keep his head down, do his time, if you could call it that, and be absolutely OK at the end of it. Unlike the people he'd persuaded to invest their retirement funds into buying chalets in Rarotonga which had failed to materialise.

'You said you had someone else who might talk to me,' I said. 'One of the women who was involved in the seminars.'

'Dunno about her. Can't make up her bloody mind.'

'What if I contacted her?'

'Not a good idea. If you phoned she'd be scared shitless.'

I laughed. 'I'm not all that scary, am I?'

'Not you, darling. It's Denny she's frightened of upsetting. Give it a few days, eh? We'll get him, girl. What Denny's gone down for's just the tip of the bloody iceberg. There's a whole lot more I can tell you. A whole fucking lot more.'

I made grateful noises and hung up. Yep, this was going to be big. And while I didn't have much sympathy for Turner I was confident he'd give me what I needed.

The couple of times I'd met him I'd come away feeling a bit grubby. His shiny black leather jacket, stringy ponytail, the heavy gold rings on his fingers and the ever-so-chivalrous way he had of addressing my breasts while he talked reminded me of some slimy character straight out of *The Sopranos*. I was fairly convinced that if Graham hadn't done the dirty on him, as Turner put it, he'd still be right there alongside him wheeling and dealing and ripping off susceptible people.

But I needed everything I could get on Denny Graham. He still had a few loyal sympathisers about who were vocal in their disagreement with the charges made against him and his conviction. 'He's done a lot for Auckland.' 'The economic downturn isn't Denny's fault.' I wanted to shut all that fellow feeling right down, show him for what he was.

Because I had the ordinary, everyday, trusting people who'd been badly hurt by Graham queuing up to talk. They'd never get their money back, money which was supposed to be for their security and for their families, money which had taken whole lifetimes of work to save. I wanted to do my bit towards stopping Graham from surfacing out of his 'prison' and bulldozing the next batch of ordinary, everyday people with his next big scheme. If that meant playing nice with the Murray Turners of this world for a few months, I could do it.

Denny had originally made his money out of buying low and selling high in Auckland. He was particularly adept at prising valuable properties from elderly people by offering deals where he would generously swap their sprawling villa for one of his 'brand-spanking-new townhouses'. Graham believed in the personal approach. He'd turn up at some old pensioner's door and sweep them off their feet with his ultra-white, wide-snapping grin and sharp suits. Denny was a real charmer.

I'd met Denny. It was in the early days of *Saturday Night,* the first TV series I was involved with. It was right in the middle of those heady years of the rising property market and YourWay had recently expanded into the holiday home market, buying up land and putting up blocks of holiday apartments. I was in Auckland working on a feature about fairly primitive seaside holiday cottages which had turned, almost overnight it seemed, into million-dollar properties. I was invited out for drinks and Denny was there.

We were introduced. He flashed that famous grin at me and that was all there was to it. Except for the feeling which hit me deep down in my belly as he squeezed my hand and his pale, slightly slanted eyes — *lizard* eyes — scurried up and down my body. My gut instinct was to leap backwards, to thoroughly wash the clammy, cold sensation from my hand. I watched as he moved from person to person, group to group, swooping in on the important people, exhibiting the smile. His hand reached out to pat shoulders. I saw those pitiless eyes flickering, assessing.

There had been whisperings about Denny for years about deals which were questionable if not downright crooked. The retirement apartments that had no soundproofing between the units and, more often than not, had mould growing in the bathrooms and problems with the drains. The holiday cottages that were much smaller than the suggested images in the brochures and had cheap, tacky kitchen and bathroom fittings. And where were the luxurious carpets and tiles? Where were the vast decks? Where was the pool?

'Artist's impression only.' That was the statement on the glossy brochures which covered all the variations, though how Denny Graham got around building specifications was anybody's guess. Those were the kinds of questions I intended asking. It seemed Denny Graham might have had friends in rather high places.

Of course there were buyers who complained but they hadn't read the fine print. Denny was particularly skilled at covering his back — 'It's all there in black and white.' He also tended to build his resorts in places a long, long way from anywhere, the kinds of places where people think they might want to be before they actually are. Seclusion. Tranquillity. *Paradise.*

The Sunshine Coast, for example: 'fifty k's from concern, cares and clatter'. Which actually meant fifty k's away from shops, medical care and, in most cases, beaches. Then there were the Far North Chalets, far being the operative word. For the new owners who might have wanted to protest about substandard building processes, the locations made it difficult to drum up any interest. The media really weren't keen on trekking off to some remote place in Oz, not just for a few leaks and kitchen cupboards that had fallen off walls, nor did solicitors and building inspectors want to travel miles up the Karikari Peninsula.

It was difficult to work out exactly how he got away with it but buyers generally either sold up at a huge loss or got out their deckchairs and barbies and got on with it. New Zealanders are do-it-yourselfers and there'd always be someone they could count on to give them a hand to fix up the electrics or sort out the plumbing for the exchange of a week or so at the bach. And it was a whole lot easier and cheaper to pick up discounted floor coverings and a Para pool than to try to take it through the courts.

New Zealanders don't like to be seen as whiners, they don't

like being made fools of and they certainly don't like anyone else knowing they've been taken for fools. Denny Graham knew that. He knew how to exploit it.

Those who did continue to complain eventually fell silent. That was something else Turner had told me.

He likes to get his own way, does Denny. Denny doesn't like being crossed.

He doesn't like it at all.

I could tell you stories, my girl. Stories about our Denny that'd make your hair curl.

2

I checked the time. I'd set up a phone interview for 2.30 with Gill Ross, one of the many Denny Graham victims. She and her husband, John, had lost around $350,000 to their Rarotongan dream. We were already on first-name terms and I knew them well enough to be certain they'd give a clear account of what had happened.

'Rebecca, how are you?' Gill was a vibrant and intelligent woman, a well-respected former secondary school teacher. She would interview so well and create exactly the impression I wanted. *Graham conned her out of her money? Jesus, what a bastard.*

'Hi, Gill. I just want to run through things we've already talked about. OK if I tape it?

'Absolutely fine.'

'Can you tell me how you and John initially became involved with YourWay Investments?'

'Well, first of all we received an invitation through the mail. I've got it right here. It's printed on lovely, thick, cream paper with italic writing and invites John and me, by name, to a function — I'm quoting now — "celebrating YourWay Prime Investments' good fortune in purchasing a top-quality piece of land in Rarotonga for the purpose of constructing an exclusive community of high-quality villas situated among a paradise of private and abundant gardens".'

'So you decided to go along?'

'Not at first. In fact, I was going to put it into the fire and forget all about it and, my goodness, I wish I had. But enclosed was a brochure and the homes, well, they did look lovely with the decks and the big windows and the pools and palm trees and all that glittering sea. You see, we'd not long been to Rarotonga and we'd loved it, absolutely loved it. We found out later that Graham had targeted couples around our age who'd recently been there.'

'What happened next?'

'We had a follow-up phone call. John answered it. He said the woman who spoke to him was very pleasant and friendly and told him that she and her husband had themselves invested in a YourWay community and were more than happy with the outcome. She said the planned function would be fun, there'd be drinks and nibbles and interesting people would be there and there'd be absolutely no pressure or expectations.'

'That persuaded you to go?'

'We still um-ed and ah-ed a bit. We had absolutely no intention of buying a second home at that point. But then John said, "There's free drinks. What have we got to lose?" So we went. "What have we got to lose?" I'm afraid I've thought back over those words many, many times.'

'Tell me about the function.'

'Looking back, I understand how precisely those things were planned. Just thinking of the people who were there I can see they'd decided to appeal to investors who were moving just beyond middle age and likely to have accrued a reasonable investment portfolio. Well, there we were, all those couples *fortunate enough* to have been *selected to attend* as we were told later. This is after quite a prolonged period when we were treated to some lovely wines and exquisite hors d'oeuvres.'

'Effective marketing strategies,' I said.

'Very effective. Well, after getting just a little sozzled we all sat down and this very tanned and fit-looking couple around our age began their talk — oh, and there was a gigantic screen behind them so we had a series of simply gorgeous images to look at as they spoke. Anyway, the woman came first and she rhapsodised about her *wonderful* home, her *amazing* kitchen, her *fantastic* bathrooms and the absolutely *oodles* of room for the kids and grandkids — that is *if* you wanted the kids and grandkids to stay. Everyone dutifully giggled and then she went on about the pool and the spa and the benefits of the changes they'd made to their lives. I can almost see her there, taking her so-called husband's hand and giving us all a little smile and a wink.' Gill's voice took on a sing-song, high-pitched bleat. '"I'm fitter and slimmer than I was in my thirties and we've never been happier and, um, more *active*".'

'Then it was the man's turn?'

'It was. The sound and durable construction, the low maintenance. All he ever had to do was change the light bulbs. The boat, the golf course, the *freedom*. I could feel John begin to quiver with excitement beside me. We had the big old villa then in Parnell. There was always something that had to be done.'

'Were you starting to feel actual interest in the scheme at that point?'

'Not entirely. It didn't seem quite real.' She laughed a little. 'And it wasn't. The only apartments Graham had built in Rarotonga were for the exclusive use of him and his friends and family.'

'So this couple were just part of the scam?'

'Of course. Anyway, then the couple drifted off into the background and we were addressed by a financial advisor and he absolutely oozed respectability and, to be quite honest, he really did seem to make good sense and that's when we started to take notice. What he said was that for an outlay of from as low as $200,000, investors were assured not only of holidays in luxurious accommodation for the remainder of their lives but a guaranteed income as well. For those who may not choose to live there permanently — though, he told us, more and more YourWay clients were finding it almost impossible to leave their tropical paradises at the end of a stay — those people were able to have their home managed by YourWay Prime Investments as a holiday rental property whenever it wasn't in use by the owners, thus earning excellent returns on their original investment.'

'You thought that sounded feasible?'

'It was starting to. He went on to tell us Rarotonga was not only a beautiful place to visit, it made good sense for New Zealand citizens to retire there. For one thing, it was only a hop, step and a jump away from New Zealand for whenever anyone wished to return, faster than a road-trip between, say, Auckland and Taupo. As well as that, any New Zealand citizen living there would be entitled to full New Zealand superannuation. Rarotonga was an economical place in which to live. A huge saving on power bills, for a starter. Again the dutiful giggles, but I could tell everyone had become more intent on listening. Then he put a whole lot of figures up on the screen which demonstrated how retirement in Rarotonga did actually make economic sense.'

'And then?'

'And then they handed out more glossy brochures and John and I went home and we talked all night. You see, we'd always hankered after a holiday home but there was no way we could afford something anywhere near-decent in a place where we'd like to holiday, not in New Zealand. We'd both fallen in love with Rarotonga and this seemed like a dream come true. The upshot of all that talking was we decided, if it all panned out, we'd sell the house in Parnell and replace it with a small apartment.'

'You would have checked out the contract with your solicitor?'

'Yes, of course we did. What we never considered was the possibility Graham hadn't begun — or would never begin — construction on the project. The plan was we'd spend our retirement living in both Auckland and Rarotonga. So we sold our lovely old family home with its big garden and now we live in a two-bedroom box in the middle of the city. We have no garden, no view and very little savings left.'

'Thanks for talking to me, Gill,' I said. 'I'm sorry this has happened to you and John. It's just so unfair.'

'It's unfair, all right,' she said.

I put down the phone. It *was* unfair. And it had happened to too many people. Far too many.

Denny Graham had been smart. He'd worked out that by the time people are edging just that little closer to old age chances are they want to hang on to, maybe recapture, their youthful energy and good looks and chances are they want to have their dreams *now*. Wouldn't it be so much nicer to enjoy your money in the form of a luxurious villa, architecturally designed and finished to the highest standards? Wouldn't that be so much nicer than having it tucked boringly away in a government-guaranteed investment or some dreary old bank?

Why shouldn't aging couples enjoy the fruits of their labour? And why wouldn't they be tempted by those palm trees, that pool glistening in the sunlight with the perhaps older, but still very attractive, couple stretched out on sun loungers ('outdoor furnishings not supplied') clinking wine glasses and beaming into the camera.

And those gorgeous villas ('artist's impression only'). Investors who had the eyes able to make out the infinitesimal print had been assured that construction on the project had begun. Those who wanted to visit were encouraged to wait until the buildings, pools and landscaping were completed for safety reasons.

The economy fell to pieces and the villas couldn't be built. There were other far more pressing requirements for the investors' money. Denny had his yacht and his own holiday villas as well as the classic sports cars, the SUVs, the Porsches and the houses to maintain. His houses and his women. Denny and his wife Helen lived in a mansion set in half an acre or so of waterfront grounds in Milford. But Denny was a busy boy. There was also the woman in the inner-city apartment and the two or three regulars at the massage parlours.

All that came out around the time of the court case. That was the second time I saw Denny, sitting beside his solicitor in court. His thick gold watch shone against his wrist and his suit was impressive. He appeared composed and untroubled.

'Mrs Brooke, can you tell the court how much money you and your late husband invested in the YourWay Rarotongan scheme?'

'It was $400,000. All our savings.'

His eyes run over her, indifferent, vaguely curious.

Lizard eyes.

3

The phone rang almost as soon as I had put it down after talking to Gill Ross. It was Helen Graham. 'Rebecca? Rebecca, I, I really don't think I can do this.'

Helen Graham was needy. Now that I'd finally managed to persuade her to stop yelling 'Bitch!' at me and thumping down the phone, I'd turned into her new best friend, the only person she 'could really talk to any more'.

'Helen, hi. Just tell me what's going on.'

'I won't be able to do it. Not TV. What will people —? I'm too nervous.'

Her voice was shaking. I'd discovered it was best to let her talk. Just make the right kinds of noises and let her go for it. *God, if I can only get her to front up on camera.*

'If I talk about Denny the kids will never speak to me again.'

It wouldn't be tactful to remind her that they didn't speak to her anyway. Denny's kids knew very well what side their bread was buttered on. Helen now lived in a modest apartment and drove a Toyota Corolla.

She was crying. 'I can't do this. It's all too stressful. I've been . . . I've been through too much already.'

'You have been through a lot,' I said as soothingly as I could manage. 'You've been through so much. But you're very strong and it's some time away before we actually start filming and by then —.'

'That bastard shouldn't get away with it.'

This is the way the conversations usually went. Fragility. Helplessness. Bitterness and wrath.

'He shouldn't.'

'I brought up the kids. I did everything. The house —.'

So arduous with a cleaner, a gardener and a nanny.

'Helen, I know.'

'He had those women. He used to stay out nights. He used to stay away entire *weeks*. I couldn't leave him, I had to think of the children.'

All of whom had been packed off to boarding schools.

'And then he takes everything. People think, oh there's Denny Graham's wife, she'll have come out of it well set up. She'll have done all right for herself. And me *working*.'

Part-time on way-above-average hourly rates as a receptionist at the health clinic of a doctor who felt sorry for her.

'Helen,' I said, 'you can do it. Just tell the truth. That's all you have to do.'

'I'll try,' she said. 'I really will try, Rebecca.'

Naturally Helen feels hard done by. She'd been with Denny nearly forty years, had been photographed over and over again, quietly smiling at his shoulder at the charity functions and the dinners and balls, his intelligent (BA Eng), blonde, slimly attractive, impeccably presented wife. But when it was all made public — Denny's women, the shonky deals, all that deceit — and Helen was forced to acknowledge what she had elected to disregard, she was left with two choices. Either she did her 'stand by your man' routine or she left.

She opted to leave. Helen did have her pride and, besides, she fully expected to be well looked after. What she didn't take into account — surprising since she had lived with him for all those years — was just how much Denny liked to win and since settlements largely depend on who has the best legal representative, he was more than happy to splash out on the best. There were trusts and mortgages and re-mortgages and syndicates and consortiums. In fact, if you were to believe his solicitor, Denny actually owned nothing at all.

In the last interview she'd given before everything blew, Helen is pictured in a double-page article in the *Australian Women's Weekly*, a West Highland terrier (Bobby) on her lap, sitting on a wrought-iron bench. She is dressed in cream linen, pearls and the kind of shoes I'd have to spend around a couple of weeks of my salary to get. Behind her looms the Graham glass-and-steel residence. Around her are gnarled, monstrous trees of the sort usually seen in botanic gardens, set off by dewy white roses and drifting hazes of lavender clipped into careless and burgeoning abandonment. 'We were so incredibly lucky to find this gracious old garden on which to build our home.'

Helen is herself described as 'gracious' and, when asked if she ever regretted not pursuing her own career, she is said to thoughtfully purse her lips. 'Denny is a wonderful man. A self-made man. I've always admired that about him and we have made a very happy life together.'

I actually didn't have a lot of sympathy for Helen.

4

So there I was at my desk working through a list of people I needed to check in with before I left and idly wondering how the Graham story might compare with *How About Me?*, the documentary we'd done about the effects of violent crime on survivors and their families. We'd got a Qantas Award for that one — best one-off documentary. Of course, the Graham doco would be very different, but equally controversial. Maybe it would make it somewhere up there as well.

I wore a blue dress to the last Qantas Awards night — midnight blue, short and sexy, little straps. Maybe I'd go for red next time. Maybe I should take the blue dress with me to Rarotonga.

Rarotonga. Ten days of sun and sandy beaches, warm sea and delicious food. Lounging on deckchairs at the end of every day, sipping an exotic cocktail and watching the sunset.

With Rolly.

Rolly and I had never been away for such a long time before. He'd been dropping sneaky little suggestions that this trip may be significant. Commitment time? Maybe even a ring. A ring and then — *babies*. The blue dress would be good for going out somewhere special, somewhere gorgeously romantic. I'd very happily be proposed to in my blue dress.

'What do you know about the Tour?'

'What Tour?' The palm trees and the sunset had disappeared and Tim Morrow materialised in their place right in front of me.

'*The* Tour. The 1981 Springbok Tour. What do you know about it?'

'Not much,' I said, looking down at my list and putting a question mark beside a name — she could wait until I was back. 'Uh, wasn't there a riot somewhere?'

'Hey,' he said, tapping my shoulder. 'Hey, Rebecca? Remember me? I'm the boss, the important one, the one who makes sure you get your salary. Could I beg just one short moment of your time?'

I looked back up at him and put down my pen. 'OK, you've got my full attention. The 1981 Springbok Tour? I believe I was around four years old at the time and, oddly enough, was neither involved nor particularly aware of what was going on.'

'The thirtieth-year anniversary is coming up next year. We need to make a doco about it.'

'Sorry?'

He spoke slowly and loudly. 'What are your thoughts, Rebecca, on making a documentary about the 1981 Springbok Tour of New Zealand?'

I shook my head. What in hell was he on about? 'Just now,' I said, 'my thoughts are fixed on my long-overdue and well-earned holiday. And after that my thoughts will be entirely taken up with the Graham story which you have approved.'

'Whereas *my* thoughts,' Tim said, 'on that have changed. We'll ditch the Graham story for now and just as soon as you get this long-overdue and well-earned holiday behind you, we'll get going on this one. In the meantime I'd like you to start moving towards it. I want a two-part doco, fifty-minute slots and we'll do it on consecutive weeks to coincide with around the time the Tour ended and just before the start of the Rugby World Cup. Everyone'll be thinking rugby then. So let's say the first one on Saturday August 27 with the next on the following Saturday. Keep this under your hat, won't you? We don't want anyone else getting in on it.'

'You must be joking.' I stared up at him. 'I'm all set up for this thing on Denny Graham. It's ready to go. I've had the worst time getting the names of investors in YourWay and then tracking them down. I've managed to get them to talk about how Graham swindled their money out of them. God, Tim, they *trust* me. How can I possibly tell them the story's been dumped?'

'Not dumped. Put on hold. It can wait.'

'It can't wait. I've finally got Helen Graham talking to me but she's all over the place. She could just as easily change her mind and if I tell her we're delaying, god knows what she'll decide. I've got a good source but, same thing, he might opt out. Tim, I've worked too bloody hard on this to chuck it.'

I heard my voice starting to get way too loud. *OK, Rebecca, down a few decibels.*

'Graham's still news,' I said. 'He's on home detention until around the middle of next year, the same time the doco is supposed to be out. Remember that was the arrangement? But after that no one will want to know. Shit, Tim, you can't do this. That case is important. People lost their life savings because of Denny Graham.'

'It's important, I'll give you that. But it'll keep. A lot of people lost money from property investments during the downturn and it'll be topical for a while yet. This is more important right now.'

'Because a thirty-year anniversary is coming up? How many people care about that?'

'Plenty,' he said. 'Plenty of people care.'

'Please, Tim. Please rethink this. You gave me the go-ahead on the Graham story. We've done most of the research, there's a lot of public interest. Potentially this one is *hot*. Why would we want to do an about-face to work on something that's thirty years old? Apart from the fact that it's totally unfair to pull a story I've already done so much work on, the Tour's been done over and over again. There's no way I'm going to be able to come up with something original. Rehashing old stuff isn't what we're about; you've told me that yourself a dozen times.'

'I want to do this,' he said, 'because I lived through it. It's part of my history and a part of a lot of other people's as well. I want to do it because it affected me. The Tour was why I went to Sydney and couldn't stomach coming home for twenty-four years.'

I took a deep breath. 'Yeah, well. Look, I sympathise. I understand. But is that a good enough reason to take on a topic that's already been done to death?'

I looked down at my list again. I wanted him to just disappear. Leave me to get on with *my* story.

'The Graham story is really starting to work,' I said, 'and I want to keep going with it.'

'It wasn't only me,' he said. His voice was raised. Only slightly, but nonetheless louder than I'd ever heard it before. His face was flushed. Odd. Tim rarely showed any emotion. 'We're too bloody complacent about what happened. A bit of a jolt every so often to remind people that given certain circumstances we're not unshakeable isn't a bad thing. Maybe you're right and nobody cares any more, but they should, they bloody well should, and once you start looking into it you might see why.'

He disappeared behind his office door.

Fuck. What did I do now? Tim was stubborn, so bloody-minded when he got his teeth into something.

There was only one way to shift him. I lifted up the phone. I had to get Graham to talk to me. If I could talk my way into getting an interview with Denny Graham with his home detention bracelet around his ankle there'd be no way Tim would turn me down.

5

I checked the number on my mobile, tapped in the numbers, listened to the dial tone. I felt slightly jittery.

Denny doesn't like being crossed.

I gave my name to the woman who answered. 'I'll see whether Mr Graham is available.'

Mr Graham? He's got his PA there? I held on. I held on a long time.

The jittery feeling was getting stronger. How long should I hold on? Perhaps he was finishing his pool laps or completing his daily workout before he deigned to pick up the phone. Then again, possibly he'd decided not to talk to me and was keeping me on the line as a source of amusement.

'Graham.'

That voice I'd heard during a dozen TV interviews, giving an opinion almost weekly on radio. The clipped, terse businessman's voice.

Denny doesn't like being crossed. He doesn't like it at all.

'Rebecca Thorne here from Zenith, Mr Graham. We're presently putting together a documentary on your company's business interests and I was hoping you may help us with that.'

'Rebecca Thorne, eh? You're doing a doco?' He was silent for a moment. Good. It wasn't often Denny Graham was caught on the back foot. 'Why wasn't I notified about this?'

'I'm notifying you now. We've only just begun to work on it.'

'So who's talking?'

'I'm not able to give you those details.'

He laughed. 'Anyone with a bloody grudge, eh?'

'If you agree to an interview you'll have the opportunity to put your own side across.'

'I know how these things work. You're going to weight this thing, tell the lies, stir it all up to the max. You won't be doing Denny Graham any favours.'

'OK,' I said, 'I'll come clean. We do have people with grievances who are prepared to give interviews but if you agree to come on board you'd be able to give your own version of what happened. You'd be able to say whatever you like.'

He was still laughing, 'I'd like to help you, Rebecca. You look bloody good on the telly. But I think I'll pass.'

The phone clicked.

That was it, then. No fantastic doco. No award. No strutting up to pick up the award in that red dress.

I was so pissed off with Tim. I had Helen, I had Murray, I had past employees who'd been fired for objecting about what was going on. I had the investors, most of whom couldn't even afford the plane fare to Rarotonga any more. I had them all ready and eager to tell all. What should I do?

Maybe while I was away Tim would see how irrational it was to give up a great story for this lame idea he'd got into his head about the Tour. God, *everyone* would be doing rugby stuff next year. The World Cup. Yah-bloody-hoo.

I could just sit on it, not say anything to anyone. As far as Helen and Murray and the rest were concerned, the Graham story was still on. I'd just stick it out. I wouldn't make waves. I'd just wait it out and hope Tim would get over whatever was twisting up his undies. Because despite being pissed off with him now and despite the fact he sometimes annoyed the shit out of me, I'd grown to love him dearly. He could be bruisingly blunt, a bit of a dictator when pressed, but I knew he was on my side. Tim — and Zenith — had been good to me. Two years ago, after I screwed up on the Connor Bligh story — not only had I come out and said a killer was innocent I'd also been instrumental in getting him released from prison — I thought Tim would get rid of me.

Once the announcement was made that Bligh was back in prison and the story blew, Zenith was under siege: 'irresponsible reporting', 'unfounded implications', 'interference in the processes of the law'. Everyone was out to get me and discredit Zenith at the same time.

I had reporters and cameras camped outside my door. Detective Inspector Angus Strode, who had originally been responsible for putting Bligh away, had had a field day. 'Reckless heedlessness of public safety.' 'Wrecked months — years even — of meticulous police effort.' 'The worst case of gutter journalism I've ever experienced.' The previous network I'd worked for were more than happy to report I had 'left under a shadow'.

The easiest thing for Zenith to have done would have been to get rid of me and, in the circumstances, it would have been simple enough for them to work out a way around my contract. When Tim called me into his office that was what I expected, what I'd prepared myself for. I'd decided to go without an argument. I knew my career was gone, that no other TV network or reputable newspaper in New Zealand would take me on, but I had to take professional responsibility for what I'd done. I already had my speech prepared: *Thanks for giving me the chance here. I made a major stuff-up. I can't even begin to tell you how sorry I am. I totally understand I can't expect you to keep backing me.*

'OK, Rebecca,' Tim said. 'How far are we on with this children of immigrants thing you've been working on?'

'Filming's due to begin week after next.'

'You should have it wound up in a month, six weeks?'

'A month should do it.'

He looked at me steadily across his desk. No facing-each-other, demonstration-of-consensus sofas for Tim. He was unquestionably in charge.

My mouth was dry. *Here it comes.* And I didn't want to go. I loved the people I worked with. I loved my job. *Say what you need to and try to get out without crying.*

I barely heard him say, 'So what have you got for me after that?'

'Thanks for —. What did you say?' I shook my head. 'I'm sorry, I don't know what's going on here.'

'What do you mean?'

'With all that's happened, I thought you'd called me in to tell me to pack up my desk.'

'Why the hell would I do that?'

'Because I've stuffed up so badly and I've put Zenith right in it as well. It was because of me that Bligh got out of prison.'

'Rebecca, it was the law that got Bligh out of prison and it was you who put him back in there. Look, you made a bloody fine doco. Sure, you got things wrong but you were acting on what you knew and the fact that other things came out later was just bad bloody luck.'

'But all this shit they're saying about me is dragging Zenith down.'

He chuckled. 'Have you seen the ratings?'

'I haven't looked at any ratings. I can't bring myself to look at any of that stuff right now. You're not telling me they're up?'

'Too damn right they're up. The fact is, all this flak we're getting right now is making people switch over to us to see what all the fuss is about.'

'But haven't I wrecked Zenith's integrity?'

'Through one doco?' He laughed. 'Sweetheart, come *on*.'

'You really want me to stay?' By now I was frantically dabbing at the tears streaming down my cheeks.

'I want you to stay, but for fuck's sake don't cry.'

Yes, Tim had been good to me. Good to and *for* me. I'd learned to listen to what he said. He had an uncanny ability to see instantly what was working, what needed to be done, whenever we were in the editing suite running through film. He had an extraordinary knack for calculating what would come off.

And what did he always say? 'No point in fucking around with stuff that's already been done and dusted. What's happening now, what might happen tomorrow, *that's* what people want to look at.'

So why was he going against his own judgment? Still, I owed him. Owed him a lot.

And he was, after all, the boss.

6

I called in at Mum and Dad's a couple of nights later and ended up staying for dinner. I knew they'd been involved in the anti-Tour movement but whenever it had come up I'd never really listened or asked questions.

'Tim was saying it's thirty years since the 1981 Springbok Tour,' I said, 'and I started wondering how much you two were caught up in all that at the time.'

'The short answer to that is we were very caught up in it,' Dad said, measuring freshly ground coffee beans into his beloved battered and stained coffee percolator. 'Same as anyone who had any interest in what was happening in the country at the time.'

'I think I can remember you going off to one of the protests.'

'We went to more than one,' Mum said. 'The first we went to was before the Springboks were even here. That was in May and there were marches in all the main cities. Thousands of people turned out throughout the country. Then there was another one in July with the same massive turnout.'

'What we wanted,' Dad said, 'was for the government to see how huge the opposition was and to insist that the rugby union call it off.'

'But in spite of all the resistance the government still let them come,' I said. 'How many protests did you go to?'

'I couldn't really say,' Mum said. 'We joined COST, Citizens Opposed to the Springbok Tour. We went to the meetings and joined in most of the protests. You see, every time the Springboks played, there were marches throughout the country, so we were involved most Saturdays, sometimes during the week as well.'

'I can only remember one. Grandma looked after us and didn't I come downstairs and you were all talking? I knew I shouldn't be out of bed so I stood outside the door looking in. You were sitting on that grey sofa we used to have and you were crying.'

'That would have been Molesworth Street,' Mum said. 'I got hit, not badly, but enough to need a couple of stitches. We had to go to A&E and the waiting room there was so packed it was as if there'd been a civil emergency.'

Dad came over to where we were sitting around the coffee table and poured coffee into the little green-and-white-striped cups they'd had for years and handed one to me. 'That was the march following the Hamilton game being called off. 'That's not too strong for you, is it?'

'It's fine,' I lied. Dad is famous for his tarry coffee which keeps you wide-eyed, head buzzing for hours after.

'Molesworth Street,' he said. 'Everyone was incredibly buoyed up after what had happened at Hamilton and we really believed if we could keep up the pressure the government would have to give in and send the Boks home.'

Mum leaned back against the sofa. 'We assembled in Parliament grounds. There were more police than we'd expected and they had dogs. Up until then, the police had certainly been a presence at the marches but they hadn't seemed threatening, more just ensuring things stayed under control. But when I saw those dogs —.'

'I said we'd be all right, that they had them because of the rumours going around that protesters would attempt to get inside Parliament,' Dad said. 'Anyway, COST had been assured police dogs wouldn't be used against demonstrators no matter what the circumstances.'

'We walked from Parliament and headed up Molesworth Street,' Mum said. 'It was all very orderly. The aim was to protest outside the South African consulate. As we got further on we could see rows of police up in front of us.'

'The police started to slow down and linked hands,' Dad said. 'I didn't like what was happening but they didn't tell us to stop, there were no warnings, so we just kept on going. In the end the protesters at the front were packed right up against them.'

Mum closed her eyes. 'The people behind us were moving forward and I thought we were going to be crushed. Then the police spread out and started hitting people in the front rows. People were panicking, pushing and shoving, attempting to get away. Your father was trying to hold on to me but, with the pressure of the crowd, I was so frightened I'd fall and get trampled.'

'I got shoved sideways, across the street,' Dad said. 'I was trying to find your mother but there were so many people and it was winter, already dark.'

'I got hit,' Mum said. 'I could feel blood running down my face.'

I was staring at them. My parents in a brawl? 'You got hit by a policeman?'

'The police hadn't been given the go-ahead to use batons in Hamilton,' Dad said, shrugging. 'The way I see it, some of them were itching to have a go.'

'Though we did hear,' Mum said, 'a lot of them were disgusted by what they'd been asked to do and really shaken up by what had happened. Some of them were so young. They looked like they just didn't have the experience to deal with the situation.'

I looked at them. Mum and Dad are usually fairly animated but I hadn't seen them like this for a while. Mum's face was quite pink and her eyes were bright. 'I can hardly believe this. You two were real hippie protesters, weren't you?'

'I met your mother at a protest,' Dad said, 'against the university prohibiting mixed flatting.'

'Whoo-hoo,' I said. 'You weren't actually advocating mixed flatting, were you? Next you'll be telling me you went on naked marches. What was it? Make love not war?'

'Well, actually, darling,' Mum said.

I plugged my fingers in my ears. 'Too much information. You're traumatising me. I'm your child, remember?'

'Change of subject,' Mum said, grinning. 'Isn't it next week you're going on holiday with Rolly?'

'Uh-huh.'

Mum and Dad didn't exactly exchange glances but I knew they weren't entirely sure about Rolly being *the right one*.

'You've been seeing each other for quite some time now,' Dad said rather too heartily.

'Yep, and he makes me happy,' I said firmly.

'That's all that matters,' Mum said equally firmly.

'OK, so back to Molesworth Street. You got hurt.'

'Not badly but it shook me up. You know, when we were in the waiting room at A&E I heard someone say this was something we had to remember and tell our children and our grandchildren. Well, as a young mum I didn't want to have to warn my children or any future grandchildren about misuse of power, not here in New Zealand. But I had to face it. Policemen and the military are trained to follow orders and if the wrong people are in authority those forces will be used against anyone who doesn't agree with them. It doesn't only happen in other places.'

'We were protesting against repression and the misuse of power in South Africa,' Dad said, 'and here it was, the same thing happening here because we were exercising our rights to lawful protest against what the government was doing.'

'After Molesworth Street,' Mum said, 'I felt somehow dissociated, as if I'd believed in an entirely different reality from the one I was now having to recognise. Up until then I'd been mildly alarmed about the Muldoon administration but after what happened that night I was terrified of what that government was capable of. Muldoon was determined to go ahead with the Tour no matter what happened.' She made a face. '"The Tour has to proceed so law and order can prevail".'

'Which meant,' Dad said, 'we had a government prepared to stifle opposition through brute force.'

'Some people gave up after Molesworth Street,' Mum said. 'We didn't see them any more at the meetings and I could understood why. I was afraid as well and I was very tempted to step back from it all. But in the end I couldn't do that because of all of those people in South Africa who weren't able to simply retreat from what was happening around them.'

'They were trying to frighten us off,' Dad said, 'but they weren't going to do that.'

Driving home, I remembered.

Standing on the front steps with Grandma and my brother Davy seeing Mum and Dad off as we always did. It was in the winter. Late afternoon. Getting dark. Getting cold.

Mum and Dad weren't dressed up like they usually were when they went out together, Dad in his suit, mum in her nice dress. They were all swollen up in big coats. It felt wrong.

I looked up at Grandma and she was smiling yet I felt her hand tightening on mine. Mum and Dad gave us our kisses goodbye and went down the steps, Dad holding on to Mum's hand. I didn't know what made me afraid but I started to cry and call them back.

Mum dropped Dad's hand and came back up the steps. 'It's fine, sweetheart.' She picked me up and hugged me hard. 'Mummy and Daddy have to go out for a while. We won't be long. You'll have a lovely time with Davy and Gran. OK?'

She and Grandma looked straight into each other's eyes. 'You will be careful,' Grandma said.

'Don't worry, Mum. Nothing's going to happen.'

We baked. Chocolate chip cookies and Louise cake because Louise was my second name and so it was *my* cake. 'Why isn't there a Davy cake, Gran, why can't there be a Davy cake?'

'Maybe we can make one up. How about a chocolate Davy cake?'

Grandma had the radio on, a soft background blur, and every so often she'd go over to it and stand close, listening.

The phone rang and she answered it, her back turned as she talked. 'Yes. Yes.

'Yes, I understand.'

Mummy and Daddy weren't coming home for a while but we'd go out and get a treat. How about fish and chips? We drove to Kilbirnie in her car and Davy sat in the front seat because of being the oldest. There were people walking together along the footpaths. Some of them were on the road shouting and waving banners and Grandma drove very slowly, inching along the road.

Then hearing the voices, going down the stairs. Was Mum crying, her hand shaking as she drank that brown stuff out of one of the heavy visitors' glasses? Was Dad's arm around her shoulder and was it his voice I'd heard, raised and angry?

Grandma scooped me up in her arms, stayed beside my bed until I slept.

I remembered the blood on Mum's face and in her hair.

7

I went inside and saw the message light blinking on my phone. Rolly.

'Hi sweetie. Hey, do you realise your mobile's turned off? Anyway, I've picked up the hotel vouchers and the tickets. Can't wait.'

I took my mobile out of my bag. It was off, all right, needed recharging. I plugged it in, put milk into a pot and started warming it on the stove. After Dad's vicious coffee, I was hoping a milky hot chocolate might help me to sleep.

Can't wait. That little bit of sexiness in his voice. It made me smile.

What I couldn't quite get my head around was why Dad, Mum, David and his wife Anna, even one or two of my friends, hadn't warmed to Rolly. Not that they were critical or unfriendly, just they weren't as enthusiastic about him as I'd have liked.

Maybe the fact that he was the press secretary for Doug Harbott, the cabinet minister everyone said would be the next National Party leader, could have something to do with it. Like the rest of my family, I was fiercely Labour, so obviously Rolly and I had different political allegiances. But did we have to agree about everything? Anyway, my parents' greatest friends were true-blue Nationals and *their* political dissimilarities had never made a jot of difference.

Rolly had to be a dream candidate for any future parent-in-law. He was intelligent and attractive (good gene-stock). He dressed well and had effortlessly good manners (socially presentable). He had moved swiftly upwards in a career for which he received an excellent remuneration and owned an apartment (he'll be able to support her). And their daughter was in love with him.

Besides all those obvious pluses, this relationship was so refreshingly steady, so refreshingly open after the last I'd had with my long-and-very-permanently-married lover. In all those years with Joe Fahey, doing anything at all with him had always involved elaborate and convoluted arrangements. But now with Rolly I was able to do ordinary things, spontaneous things: take a walk, watch a film together, jump in a car and head away for a weekend.

It was so *easy* with Rolly. Cheery. Upbeat. Fun. I met him not long after the Connor Bligh saga. I'd believed in Bligh. Believing in somebody you find out has been lying to you all along is hard enough. When the person you've been backing is a multi-murderer, well, let's just say that it was the worst thing that had ever happened to me. Added to that, I'd not long been ditched by Joe. Some days I'd felt so bruised I could barely make it out of bed.

Meeting Rolly was the best thing that had happened to me in quite some time. I'd gone to the press Christmas party at Parliament and the day after that I was on the back of a Harley-Davidson heading out over the motorway. Terror was so much more pleasurable than shame.

Rolly was an enthusiastic lover and very, *very* good-looking. Ten days of blissful holiday stretched ahead. I couldn't wait either.

And, despite this Tour thing being foisted on me it was starting to interest me. Maybe if Tim was still set on doing it when I got back it wouldn't be so bad after all. I sprinkled hot chocolate into the milk and started to stir.

I had a great job. I had Rolly. I had my friends, my family, my gorgeous house. I was so lucky. *Touch wood. Cross fingers.*

In the morning, I tapped on the door and popped my head into Tim's office. 'Still want to do this Tour thing?'

'Let's keep up the niceties around here,' he said. 'Hi Tim. Lovely morning, Rebecca. How are you Tim? Fine thanks, come in and take a seat, Rebecca.'

'OK,' I said, sitting on the seat facing him, 'I get the message. But are you sure you want to go with it?'

'Any reason to think I might've changed my mind?'

'I just thought you might have had an overnight personality change. But you're still the same old obstinate, inflexible, pigheaded Tim we all love?'

'Afraid so,' he said.

I'd been thinking on the way to work that while I knew a little about the Muldoon era, knew anyway that his policies had largely been discredited and the view presently held was he'd had too much power, I didn't know why he'd been so hell-bent on going ahead with the Tour. Nor did I know what happened in Hamilton to make the officials call off the game.

'OK, two questions. Why was Muldoon so eager to go ahead with the Tour? Was he some sort of rugby fanatic?'

Tim looked at me across his desk, narrowing his eyes the way he did when he was working something out. 'Dunno. To be honest, I've never given that a lot of thought. My guess was that Muldoon was a bloody-minded prick who liked people to know who was in charge.'

'OK, next one. Were you at Hamilton?'

He grinned. 'I knew you'd come around.'

'Not much choice when you've got a tyrant for a boss. Anyway, were you there?'

'No, but I can put you on to someone who was and I know she'll talk to you because I've already asked. Jackie Reeve. I'll give you her mobile number. You should try Iris Gibbens as well. A bit of an old trooper, Iris. I've got hers here too.'

'Thanks.' I waited while he scribbled numbers down, tried to ignore his knowing grin. I wasn't going to let him get away with this. Not yet, anyway. I gave him my most seriously displeased look.

He winked back. 'There's a heap of material. The Police Museum in Porirua has a lot. I went there myself last week. I could send Mike up. See what he can pick up for you.'

'Tim, I'm due to go on leave, remember? Next week? I'm trying to finish up a few things before I go. When I get back *I'll* talk to Mike about the research I need done. And maybe, just maybe, when I get back you'll have realised the pointlessness of doing a topic that's already been overdone and I can move on with the Graham story which would actually be a winner.'

'Tell you what,' he said. 'Since you're so keen on beating Graham into the ground we'll keep the story on the books. I promise it'll be the next one and when you've got a bit of slack on the Tour story you can work on it. Be good for this one, as well. If the story out there is our top person is doing Graham, that will keep the Tour doco under wraps. The other networks will be less likely to pinch the idea.'

I stared at him, my mouth wide open. 'Tim, believe me. No one will want to pinch the idea. And, just on the slim chance that I could work two stories at once, does that mean I can rely on getting two salaries?'

His grin hadn't slipped. Not even a centimetre. 'Believe me, I know you're worth it, Rebecca, but you know our budget. Now, how about a teensy smile? I hate it when we fall out.'

8

I put my takeaway coffee and a sandwich on my desk, pressed the play button on my dictaphone and ate while I listened to the interview I'd just recorded. Iris was a sprightly eighty-year-old formidably dressed in a liquorice-coloured coat with a nipped-in waist and cherry-red ankle boots. Despite my doubts about this story, I'd been fascinated by her and by what she'd told me.

Interview: Iris Gibbens. Sister-in-law of unnamed All Black, Tour of South Africa, 1949.
You and your husband were active members of the anti-Springbok Tour movement both during and before 1981.

Oh, yes. When we discovered what was happening in South Africa and how inhumane the system over there was, there seemed no choice.

Could you tell me how you first became aware of the conditions there?

Well, you see, our brother-in-law, Bill's sister's husband that is, was an All Black in the 1949 tour of South Africa and what he experienced over the course of the tour always stayed with him and, eventually, he talked to us about it. I'm not going to name him. I don't want to run the risk of upsetting anyone. People are so proud about having had an All Black in the family.

Can you tell me what he told you?

Well, first of all, he didn't like it that Maori team members weren't considered for the tour. The South African government wouldn't have them and that was that. At the farewell function just before they left, Peter Fraser — the Prime Minister — said that it had been necessary to exclude Maoris from the team through conditions over which New Zealand had no control. No *control*? Even back then, there were many people who were convinced that if Maoris couldn't go then neither should the All Blacks.

But that wasn't enough to prevent your brother-in-law from going?

He was mad about rugby and a good player, a great player, some people have said. He was a young man who'd never been outside of New Zealand and this was to be a huge adventure for him and he didn't want to miss out. They went by ship, stopping at all sorts of places. And of course the Springbok versus All Black games were the ultimate experience for a New Zealand player.

Was he aware of the situation in South Africa before he left?

There was a general awareness that the system was unjust. He told us he went over there with an open mind. He wanted to play rugby and to see the country for himself.

What were his experiences?

First of all, there were no native South African players in the teams they played against. He said whenever they passed through a city the blacks would all be out cheering them on, though. That was because of their name, apparently, the All Blacks. At the games, if the blacks were allowed onto the grounds at all, they were in fenced-off areas behind netting and barbed wire, rather like animals in a cage.

Did he experience other situations of racial inequality?

When they were visiting Paarl, which was a farming area, they were taken to look at one or two of the farms. He said the South Africans were always hospitable, very generous hosts, and they did their utmost to show them around. At one of the farms he saw a young black male tied to a post, his food just out of reach of his hands. The overseer said this would teach him a lesson and he wouldn't make the same mistake again.

The thing that affected him most, though, was they were taken to another large farm in the same area and shown around the pigsties which were utterly spotless and well maintained, a paradise for pigs he said, and then they went on to the native quarters which were mud huts with thatched roofs and no ventilation except for a double door at the front, like a stable door. There was smoke pouring out of one and he glanced in and saw two people cooking over an open fire, no chimney, not even a hole in the roof. All he could make out through the smoke were two sets of white, shining teeth. They were smiling out at him. Those terrible, filthy huts and the people treated as if they had no value, no humanity. Then they were taken back to the farmhouse — a wonderful home with beautiful gardens, all tended by black servants, of course — and given this sumptuous lunch. He said he felt so angry but he had no choice other than to eat and thank them.

Was it primarily your brother-in law's direct experience of apartheid that influenced you to be a part of the anti-Tour movement?

We were certain New Zealand should not be party to that system, and by sending racially chosen teams and accepting racially selected teams here, we were condoning the system. We decided we had to make our feelings known so we were part of the organisation that prepared the petition against the 1960 tour. A hundred and fifty thousand people signed it but the tour went ahead. There was a song going around at the time. 'Fee-fee, fi-fi, fo-fo fum/There's no horis in our scrum.'

'Horis'?

Yes, 'horis'. We weren't exactly racially sensitive in those days.

But the team did include Maori in the 1970 tour.

Maori players who were given the classification of honorary whites. My goodness me, we were actually allowing those racists to poison our own attitudes. Things were getting increasingly worse for the black South Africans and the whites who stood up against what was happening were frequently put into prison without charges or imprisoned within their own homes. It was a police state run by thuggery and fear — and we wanted to play games with them?

And then 1973 was called off.

Norman Kirk had the good sense to prevent that tour going ahead. We saw that as a triumph. But we were back in South Africa in 1976. Then the Gleneagles agreement was signed and we thought no government would go against that. But along came 1981 and despite Gleneagles and despite Soweto, those rotters went right ahead.

I'd loved meeting her, loved listening to her stories, watching how her black eyes crackled and her thin brown hands waved as she talked.

This was fascinating stuff. I was interested but how the hell was I going to drag out some curiosity for this in TV viewers who saw apartheid as something that had happened way back somewhere in the Middle Ages?

I chewed and swallowed. OK, one more before I had to deal with all the emails, phone Helen Graham for one last caring and supportive chat and pack my suitcase. Jackie Reeve. I picked up the phone.

'Rebecca Thorne?' she said, 'Tim said you might call. You want to talk about Hamilton, right?'

'Tim said you were there.'

'I was there all right. I still dream about it. Well, more nightmares than dreams. I was petrified at the time. Wondered if I'd get out of there alive.'

'You thought you'd get hurt?'

'God, yes. I was right there in the middle of the grounds. You know, every so often a film clip comes up on TV and I say to the grandkids, see that hat over there? Well, that's your gran. I do feel proud. Now, how are we going to do this? I've never been interviewed before.'

'What about if you just tell me what you remember.'

I remember — god, I still remember this really vividly — Muldoon came on TV and announced that the government wouldn't interfere and that the rugby union had the right to decide the Tour would go ahead. Sean — he was my husband then — just stared at me. I remember this jolt I felt and this odd feeling things weren't ever going to be quite the same for us.

'It's on,' he said. 'Fuck, Jackie, they've done it. It's on.'

I was keen to march. I hadn't wanted them to come and I was angry that the government wasn't going to stop them. The first game went ahead in Gisborne. They called it the day of shame. Then the next one was us. Hamilton. They said at the meetings it would be a big one. Everyone would be watching to see what happened here.

They'd told us to wear protective layers of clothing and I had on

45

a couple of jerseys and a pair of Sean's long johns under my jeans and a big thick jacket over it all and my hiking boots. I had my new hat. I've always thought of blue as a kind of good-luck colour and I'd bought it especially. As we started marching towards the stadium I started feeling weighed down, far too hot and a bit nauseous — I'd not long found out I was pregnant. But there were so many *people* there, all in their own groups, you know, HART, COST, a Maori Rights group, and just then I felt really happy to be marching there with everyone against something that wasn't right and chanting along with everyone else: 'Two four six eight, Graham Mourie is our mate. One two three four, we will stop this racist Tour.'

People up in front of us were yelling something that sounded like 'Push!' and we saw the fence was down. Sean grabbed my hand. 'Come on, Jackie.' I'd made up my mind to stay away from anything risky but I didn't have time to think and next thing we were following the others. There were police about, but not many. They weren't holding batons, nothing like that. We ran down the terraces towards the protesters standing in a little group in the middle of the field.

I was sweating by the time we made it, trickles of sweat were stinging my eyes, running down my back. Police were trying to stop other protesters joining us and there were the rugby supporters from up in the stands trying to get down. The police were stopping them as well.

I was scared. Yeah, by that time I was scared but I was caught up in it, the adrenalin had kicked in I suppose and, anyway, I knew even if I wanted to leave I couldn't, not without being chased. I looked around me and saw people I recognised, famous people. The Topp Twins and Karl Stead and those lambs were there as well, out in front, making people laugh. Have you heard of them? Two guys who dressed up as lambs, one black, one white. They turned up at most of the games. Anyway, I thought nobody would hurt the Topp Twins or the lambs so we'd be safe.

We were hunched up, close together, our arms linked facing the stands. More people made it across the ground and joined us and, just then, it seemed almost orderly. We were in the middle, there were the rows of police protecting us and then there were all those people in the grandstands and on the terraces. I didn't want to think how shaky it was. I was afraid to look up. There was this vast ocean of angry faces and I knew if that ocean decided to move the police could never hold it back.

Sean and I'd ended up somewhere in the middle of the group and I was feeling jammed in and so bloody hot I was frightened I'd pass out or maybe vomit down someone's neck. I pulled off my hat and started unzipping my jacket and this woman beside me, she was big, you know, a big butch Maori, was watching me. She said, 'Sister, when you get hit you'll be wishing you'd kept them on.' And I thought, '*When* you get hit?' I felt this real clutch of fear. If I got hurt the new baby could get hurt and if anything happened to Sean and me who'd look after Lizzie? She was just a wee thing then, only three. I felt so stupid, so irresponsible. I was trapped there, though. I knew I had no choice but hold on.

Someone started singing 'God of nations' and everyone joined in and the lambs conducted. The crowd was whistling, shouting, stamping; this huge uproar surging down at us, great waves of it and us few in the middle chanting back at them. 'The whole world's watching. The whole world's watching.'

I told Sean I was feeling sick and he squeezed my hand. 'Try not to think about it. You'll be OK.' Try not to think about it?

'Hang on,' someone in front of us called out. 'Hang on. Don't give in.' Then it was like in the *Star Wars* films when the stormtroopers march in with their white helmets and light sabres drawn. It seemed . . . made-up, some weird fantasy film . . . all of these policemen running onto the field in formation with visors covering their faces and long batons in their hands. But I knew it *was* real, it was very real. My mouth went totally dry and I couldn't breathe properly. I was almost retching.

I thought, 'It's the Red Squad. They're really here, they're going to use those batons to bash us, get us off the field and then the crowd will have us.' I said to Sean, 'I'm leaving now.' He grabbed my arm and said I couldn't go, didn't I trust him to look after me? Shit, what was *he* going to do? I looked for places where I could hide, where I could get in among the crowd and blend in. But how could I get there without someone spotting me?

'Move. Move. Move.'

They were circling, edging closer. 'Move. Move. Move.'

'The whole world's watching.'

'*Move. Move. Move.*'

It wasn't some idealistic fantasy any more. This was real and terrifying. All I wanted was to be back at home with Lizzie cutting out biscuit shapes in the kitchen. I smelt smoke and I thought, 'Shit they're using tear gas. Will tear gas hurt the baby?'

'If you wish to leave, leave now. Leave now and you won't be arrested.' I could just make it out over the chanting and the yelling. 'Leave now. If you wish to leave, leave now. Leave now and you won't be arrested.'

'We can go,' I shouted to Sean. 'They're letting us out.'

He stared at me. 'I'm not going. If we leave, they'll win.'

A policeman jogged up to meet me as I came out. He wasn't one of the Red Squad, he was just a, you know, ordinary policeman, I grabbed his arm. I started crying. I told him I was pregnant. He took me through all the shouting and the flying cans. This guy in the crowd spat at me. There was spit running down my face.

I didn't want anything more to do with it after that. Sean went, though. He said he had to think about the people in South Africa.

I said, 'What about thinking about us?'

Only two days until Rolly and I would fly to Rarotonga. I trawled through old news clips. Robert Muldoon, his voice somewhere between a bark and a whine. 'New Zealand is a free and democratic country.' 'Politics should stay out of sport.' Rows of police lined up behind immense coils of barbed wire. A woman police officer supports a man with blood streaming down his face. One policeman holds the legs, another the shoulders, of a young woman, her eyes wide and staring, her mouth gaping open in a scream.

My parents' generation: long hair, wide-legged jeans, how could those woollen hats pulled down over their heads possibly protect them against the lines of police they're eyeballing? In an odd way I envied them; they'd cared enough to take huge risks. Could something like this ever happen again? Could we ever again care so much? Or had this particular conflict slashed so deeply into the country's psyche that people had to fight back?

Why had people been so intensely involved? From what I could see, it came down to two utterly conflicting factors. Factor one: New Zealanders' passionate pride in rugby and all-consuming desire to go into combat with South Africa, our major adversary. Factor two: the equally passionate belief that by playing South Africa we were condoning apartheid.

Two factors that had chafed and swelled and festered into these images on the screen in front of me. The squadrons of blank-faced police, the dogs, the crowds, the woman with blood streaming down one side of her face. A young Maori boy holds a placard high: 'Pardon Me For Being Born Into A Nation Of Racists'.

Yes, they'd cared all right. My problem was: would anyone care now?

9

It was one of those days when the wind is ice-cold and razor-sharp and it seemed everyone in Wellington had decided to come to the airport and leave their cars in the drop-off-pick-up-only zone. The English-challenged taxi driver was unable to understand the concept of, or language for, double parking and pulled up way down in the icy extremities of the parking lane. Rolly grabbed my hand and we ran, pulling our suitcases after us. The doors slid open. We lunged through. The sun-filled days and balmy nights just a few hours ahead of us were very appealing.

Rarotonga had been my choice. Rolly's suggestions for our break away together had involved the kind of activity which caused me severe, though secret, shudders. 'What if we did that mountain-biking tour in the South Island? The Alpine Epic, it's called. I've heard it's fantastic.' And 'I've always wanted to do Tasmania's Overland Track.'

Or 'What if we took the Harley and a tent and free-camped?'

That's his idea of a holiday?

We arrived at a compromise. This holiday would be my choice and next time we'd do whatever he chose. I felt a certain pride: we were working things out the way a couple should work things out. Finding solutions to potentially problematic situations. Acknowledging and adjusting to our differences.

Rolly was more interested and involved in physical activity, and, perfectly understandably, he favoured physically active holidays. Not that I was a complete sloth. I ran — though, according to Rolly, my runs every day along the beach were more in the nature of jogs. My running wasn't designed to beat anyone, not even myself, since I never timed my runs as Rolly had once or twice mildly suggested I might. My running was more the pleasure of feeling the hard, wet sand underneath my shoes, smelling the salt coming off the waves, feeling wind and sun and rain on my face. Rolly's running, swimming, biking were training since he regularly competed in events. But, hey, *vive la différence* as they say. If I had to slog it up Mount Everest on our next holiday, at least I could cheer myself up thinking about the warm seas and sand of Rarotonga.

It started beautifully. Rolly was a Koru Club member; our tickets and bags were effortlessly processed, after which we went to the lounge to drink champagne, eat cheese, grapes and crackers and glance complacently out onto the relentless rain.

Sun.

Days and days of sun.

Our plane was called. Rolly had a whispered word with the check-in staff, showed them his parliamentary card and we were upgraded to business class. I turned off my mobile. That was our rule. No calls for the entire holiday.

Seats that actually had room for your legs. *And* there was a little gift pack. I adore gift packs. Silky socks, a satin eye mask, honey and almond hand cream, a teeny box of chocolates.

More champagne.

We reclined on our seats holding hands, swilling back champagne and nibbling chocolates. We gazed out of the window as the sun turned into a giant orange, dropped into the ocean and the sky turned instantly black. Rolly squeezed my hand.

Singing and ukuleles as we went through Customs, garlands of frangipani slipped over our heads and, thank you God, it was so *warm*. We went out into the balmy darkness, breathing in all those soft lush smells of the tropics as the bus swept us through the night. A smiling woman wearing a sarong met us at the resort — everyone smiled here — and led us through the garden to our chalet.

Pools and palm trees shimmered under gentle lights, the hush of ocean was everywhere. We pulled back the meticulously made bed and blurrily made love on the crisp cool sheets. Woke to the hish-hush of the sea, the warmth of sun coming through the doors onto our own small private deck.

It was perfect. Despite my slight anxiety that Rolly would find the level of activity on the island constraining he appeared immensely pleased to be there. We hired scooters, lined up for our Rarotongan licences, demonstrated that we could drive them in a reasonably straight line, then ventured off for a tour around the island and found ourselves back where we'd come from within less than an hour. But on the way we'd discovered little shops, beaches, places to eat, the main village. We swam and snorkelled. Rolly trekked up into the bush while I luxuriated beside a pool devouring all the books I'd been saving exactly for this and slithering into the water whenever I became a little overheated.

About six every night when Happy Hour started we slipped into the sun loungers that edged the beach, drank our piña coladas and pineapple daiquiris and watched as the sun slipped away. We ate amazing food, enjoyed the kind of sex which leaves you breathless. There is nothing quite like making love on a smooth sheet, in the kind of heat where you delight in stretching out naked, bodies tasting of sun and salt.

It was also fun fulfilling the professional side of the holiday. I'd got hold of the map Denny Graham had provided for his ill-fated purchasers of paradise. We had a little difficulty tracking it down among the scrub and sugar cane but in the end we found a dirt track and followed it to a few acres with a sign dug into the ground. I could just make out the sun-faded lettering. 'YourWay Prime Investments, Private Property, No Trespassing.'

We got off our scooters and stared around. 'For god's sake,' Rolly said. 'Just look at this place. It's the back of bloody beyond. There's no view and the nearest beach is the worst in the whole of Rarotonga. There's no sand.'

'Plenty here, though.' I dug my foot into the soil. 'I can't see too many tropical gardens flourishing.'

'What I can't understand,' Rolly said, 'is why people who bought into this didn't come over and check it out first. How were they so gullible?'

I shrugged. 'The marketing strategies were convincing. There were heaps of photos and brochures. The contracts must have checked out and by the time they'd put down deposits and made progress payments it was too late. Anyway, some of them did come over and still went ahead. Denny had sales people on site and there was a lot of hype over what they were going to do. People had their dream of retiring to a tropical paradise and they got sucked in.'

We trekked over the dry, scrubby land taking photos. I did my top-model routine, posing languorously in front of the collapsing sign while Rolly snapped me.

We heard it clattering over the grooves and potholes before it turned up the drive and stopped. An ancient black Bentley. We could just make out the two large male faces scrutinising us from behind the tinted windows.

'Think it's time we were off,' Rolly said. I took a quick, furtive snap of the car, hopped on my scooter and we drove past them up onto the road. The car was still hunched there like a hefty, murky beast when I looked back over my shoulder.

'Was that a visit from the Raro mobsters?' I said.

'We could've got whacked,' Rolly said, grinning.

'Weird how they turned up, though,' I said.

'Maybe Denny's taken a contract out on us.'

We were both laughing. It had been so bizarre. Who the hell were they? Was there such an insufficiency of crime here that the heavies were sent out to guard patches of overgrown sugar cane?

I popped two photos on Facebook when we got back — the car, the scrub, me in front of the sign — and labelled them 'Rebecca Thorne, investigative journalist'.

'Is this to let everyone know you really are working hard over here?' Rolly said, looking at the screen.

'Just as long as Tim knows it's not all fun and frivolity,' I said.

'Of course not.' He ran his finger down my naked back.

10

We laughed a lot. We laughed and ate and drank wine and had sex. A lot of sex. In a way the holiday was a bit of a test. We hadn't been away together for much more than a weekend before. Neither had we been alone for that length of time.

If it was a test we were passing it with A+ grades.

We'd chosen a small boutique resort on the edge of a long sandy beach where the waves were gently lulling and of the temperature you'd select for a warm bath. The chalet fitted somewhere between 'island' and 'Ritz'. The ceilings were high with wide, dark beams, the floors glossy timber. There were French doors from both the bedroom and the living room onto a deck which perched above our own pool. We'd lie in bed beneath a ceiling mottled by reflections from the water below.

What did we talk about? Nothing particularly heavy. Rolly didn't really do heavy. He'd casually mentioned when we'd started to see more of each other that his last girlfriend was way too intense. Whether or not that was supposed to be a warning to me, I took it as one. Anyway, I'd had enough of angst-ridden conversations. Believe me, a long-term relationship with a married man is enough to cure anyone of *heavy*.

The only (very faint) blemish during the entire ten days was when Rolly became slightly put out one morning when coconut muffins didn't appear at breakfast. 'So have a pineapple muffin,' I told him, spreading my own with butter.

'I like *coconut* muffins.'

His forehead had become rather like corrugated cardboard and I had a sudden unwelcome foreboding. *Is this what he's going to look like when he's middle-aged?* I thrust the thought swiftly away. 'These are very nice,' I said, taking a bite.

'Why haven't they got coconut? They've had them every other

morning. It's not as if we're late or anything.' He looked at his watch.

Does he realise how ridiculous he sounds?

'Would you like me to *force my way* into the kitchen and insist they whip you up a batch of coconut muffins?' I asked sweetly.

'Don't be silly.' More corrugated cardboard.

'Well, then. Get over it.'

He glared at me. I started to laugh, 'For god's sake, Rolly, this is a muffin you're getting your undies in a twist over. A fucking muffin.'

And he started to laugh as well, 'Sorry, but —.'

'. . . I like coconut muffins for breakfast.' I finished it for him. We were both laughing.

Fast-forward to our last night. The flight was to leave at 12.30 am and the plan was we'd have our favourite meal — mahi-mahi in lemon, coriander and coconut cream sauce — at the resort restaurant, take a walk, have a late swim and . . . 'Let's just see what happens,' Rolly said, with a slightly pensive expression in his eyes.

And, yes, I'd decided.

If he asked, yes, I would agree we would move in together. If he asked, yes, I would marry him. I'd lain beneath the soft swish of the overhead fan for the past nights, a soft swish which ended each of its cycles with an infinitesimally faint tick. I lay there thinking of all the pluses, my biological clock tick-tick-ticking along in blissful agreement.

Did we like doing the same things? Well yes, mainly, and anyway, just because you're part of an official partnership that doesn't mean you're joined at the hip for god's sake. I could still do what *I* liked to do with my friends while he carried on training. *Tick*. We got on well. *Tick*. Sex was good. *Tick*. We had mainly similar values. Family was important to both of us. *Tick*.

My family like him well enough. There was room for improvement but it *would* improve once they got to know him better. *Tick*.

He was intelligent. And he was successful. *Double tick*.

We could make a good life together. Rolly was solid. *Tick*.

I could see our future. Rolly, me, two kids and a dog. Possibly a cocker spaniel. Rolly liked dogs. He liked kids as well. And I wanted babies. *Tick-tick-tick-tick-tick.*

OK, what were the negatives? The only thing I could think of that I didn't like about Rolly was his name.

Rolly, in my opinion, was either a dog or a prep-school boy complete with blazer, thick grey shorts and long socks with a coloured ring around the top of them so they stayed up. His actual name was Roger and even though Roger was not a name I was particularly fond of, it would do. In the future, introducing this gradually and with sensitivity, I would call him Roger, perhaps even Rog, until finally he'd get so used to it that he'd start introducing himself as Roger. Or Rog.

Which was better? Rog? Roger?

'Nice to meet you. I'm Rog.' Roger?

I wore my blue dress. I swivelled in front of the mirror. I loved the way the skirt swished and the way the colour looked so great with my tan.

We drank cocktails. We sat at our favourite window seat in the restaurant. Rolly ordered bubbly.

'You look stunning in that dress,' he said. 'So sexy. You know that photo on the net of you at the Qantas? I get it up on the screen sometimes at work. I look at you and feel just so bloody proud.'

I adore compliments. This one, though, felt just a teeny bit uncomfortable. I knew the photograph, I didn't like it and I'd done my best to have it removed. It'd been taken by some shit photographer after I'd had a bit too much of the very good champagne in the hours following the awards being given out. One of the straps of my dress had slipped down and there was far too much breast showing. While it was OK that my boyfriend looked at that particular photograph, it made me feel uneasy thinking anyone else could be looking as well.

'You're back to the Graham story when you get back,' he said. 'Is that going to be another Qantas?'

'It looks like the Graham story will have to wait. Tim's come up with this idea of doing something on the 1981 Springbok Tour. The thirty-year anniversary's coming up.'

The waiter finished taking the orders and brought over our

entrée, stir-fried prawns, to share. We spooned them onto our plates.

'I wouldn't have thought people would have been interested any more,' Rolly said.

'That's what I'm worried about.' I dipped a prawn into the chilli sauce. 'But the people I've been talking to still feel strongly about the Tour even after thirty years so I'm hoping there could be a story there.'

He shrugged and chewed. I felt a sudden slight irritation. 'And people *should* be interested,' I said firmly. 'After all, it's the closest New Zealand's ever come to civil war.'

'How do you mean?'

I put my fork down. 'There was incredibly strong emotion over it. Friends, entire families, in some cases, fell out.'

'That hardly makes it a civil war.'

'The country was divided. The longer the Tour went on, the more violent the protests became. People were hurt, badly hurt in some cases. People involved in the anti-Tour movement were threatened and beaten up. The police force lost control of the situation and the country lost faith in them. There was a strong feeling throughout the country that neither the police nor the government could be trusted.'

Rolly forked another prawn into his mouth. 'I think you're exaggerating the situation. The National government was consistent. They made a tough decision and stuck to it. You could hardly say they couldn't be trusted.'

'Even if their decision essentially isolated New Zealand? Come *on*. Inviting the Springboks to tour was a total breach of the Gleneagles agreement. How could a government that refused to meet the obligations of a treaty we were signed up for be trusted?'

'New Zealand's a democracy. The rugby union was within its rights to invite the Springboks to tour.'

He was interested at last. Great. I liked a bit of a battle. One of the few misgivings I'd had about our relationship was that lightness and easiness which I enjoyed, of course, but sometimes wondered about. Because if this was going to be long term, forever maybe, didn't we have to be able to talk about the serious stuff? That is, if we weren't going to bore each other rigid once the sex and motorbike stopped being quite so electrifying.

'Not if it meant alienating New Zealand as a whole as well as other New Zealand sportspeople from the rest of the world,' I said.

'As a rule, New Zealanders don't like being told what to do, and we're prepared to stand alone,' he said. 'Look at the Lange government's refusal to have nuclear ships here. That isolated us.'

'That's different,' I said.

'It was a decision over what was seen as a moral issue, but because it suited all those liberals who mistakenly imagined that keeping these ships out of our ports was a stand against nuclear armaments and would ultimately save the world, nobody cared too much about it setting us apart from important former allies. But in fact that was a decision which caused us the kind of political and economic grief we're only just beginning to recover from.'

'I don't agree with you, and, anyway, you're talking about entirely different issues.'

'Look,' he said, 'all I'm saying is the people who supported the nuclear decision were probably the same ones who'd been up in arms about the Tour, and in *both* cases New Zealand being alienated from other factions in the world was at issue. But tell me this. Why should politicians take it upon themselves to prevent athletes who've trained long and hard competing against whoever they like?'

'Because an agreement had been signed saying that's exactly what would happen,' I said, 'and, anyway, athletes who had also trained long and hard were prevented from competing in the Montreal Games because of the rugby union's decision to invite the Springboks.'

'But can't you see? If politicians refused to interfere with sport none of that would have happened.'

'How could people ignore what was happening in South Africa?'

'The same way as we ignore a heap of injustices going on in other countries,' Rolly said. 'If we took too much notice we'd have nothing to do with around seventy per cent of the rest of the world.'

'But, in terms of racial equality, what was going on there was at total odds with everything New Zealand is supposed to stand for.'

'Maybe you're right.' He looked around the restaurant and scratched his neck. 'What about a change of subject? Darling, it's our last night here. Let's not waste it by quarrelling.'

Quarrelling? Actually, I'd been rather enjoying what I'd thought of as a discussion. I could feel myself becoming a trifle put out. But I didn't want to spoil things. I was prepared to let it go. After I'd made my point, that is.

'I don't think talking about something important to my work is exactly wasting time,' I said, mildly. 'This has become quite important to me. I hadn't known, for example, how involved my parents were in the anti-Tour movement.'

He smiled at the waiter as he placed plates in front of us. 'It's a long time ago, though, isn't it?'

'I talked to a woman who told me an amazing story about being in the middle of the field at Hamilton. I've talked to the sister-in-law of an All Black who went to South Africa in 1949 and saw how appallingly the blacks there were treated.'

'Yes, what happened under apartheid was appalling,' Rolly said, 'and what happened in Hamilton was fairly major. But apartheid is over and done with and what happened in Hamilton in 1981 has been looked at enough times to be a complete bloody yawn. People just aren't that interested in what was going on thirty years ago.'

'So we should just forget it ever happened? Do you know about Molesworth Street? Mum and Dad were there. Mum got hit. The police behaved like thugs.'

Rolly picked up his fork, carefully put it down again and appeared to contemplate me across the table as if he was having trouble making up his mind. 'As a matter of fact,' he said, 'I do know about Molesworth Street. There was a mob of protesters who'd already had a go at getting into Parliament Buildings and when that didn't work out they decided to do some damage to the South African consulate. They were repeatedly warned not to enter Molesworth Street but they went ahead anyway. It was *them* that were out of control. The police had no choice other than to use batons.'

'There were no warnings given,' I said, 'and the police had dogs.

They were looking for a fight.'

'How I know this, Rebecca, is my uncle was there. He was a senior police officer. Certainly, the police used their batons. It was only for a matter of seconds, but they had to take control of the situation. My uncle is a good man, he was well respected. He had these . . . *mongrels* throwing eggs at him and screaming he was a Nazi.'

'I'm sorry, but my parents were there. They say it was a peaceful and lawful demonstration.'

He looked at me incredulously. 'Are you suggesting you believe the New Zealand police force would beat up their own people without warnings or justification?'

This was getting out of hand. I could see Rolly, the kids, the cocker spaniel and me around the roaring hearth swiftly fading away.

But fuck it, he'd probably want his kids to have dog names as well. *Robbie. Bobby. Dudley. Bruno.*

'Are you suggesting that my parents are lying?' I said with as much ice as I could lay on.

He kept his head down as he cut his fish into small, precise squares. 'Well, somebody is,' he said.

11

We ate silently after that and, since the time before leaving for the airport seemed suddenly a very long stretch ahead, we both chose to have dessert and took a long time selecting and then eating it. After we'd drunk coffee we returned to our chalet. It was nearly eight-thirty.

I took off my dress and folded it. I dressed in a skirt and sweater, brushed my teeth, put the last of my things into my suitcase, zipped it up, wheeled it across the room and placed it beside the door. It was now 8.30 and the shuttle wouldn't pick us up until 11. I picked up my book, fluffed and heaped the pillows into a pile in the middle of the bed and positioned myself against them. Rolly picked up his own book, hesitated, looked at me and went into the living room.

After half an hour or so, he put his head around the door. 'We could have a drink at the bar,' he said, 'or one last swim.'

OK, I thought. Everyone argues. Couples can't possibly expect to agree on everything. Even Anna and David, the most suited couple in the entire world, have tussles, even eruptions. I wanted to be a couple. The ceiling fan swish-swish-swished.

Rolly is a good man. *Tick.* Good-single-straight-men-who-want-to-settle-down are not all that thick on the ground. *Tick.*

Are you going to fuck everything up because of one minor disagreement?

I smiled. He smiled. He came into the room and sat on the bed.

Meet him halfway. Come on Rebecca, don't be stubborn. You can do it.

'Probably I got a bit carried away out there,' I said. 'I'm always a bit like that when I get into something.'

'Well,' he said, 'you did warn me when you told me about the Bligh case.'

Why did he have to bring *that* up? He knew it was a no-go area. I'd felt I had to tell him my side of the story once we started getting

61

serious but he knew I'd had to drink just about an entire bottle of wine to do it. I'd confided in him. But that should have been the end of it.

'Anyway,' he said, taking my foot in his hand and flexing my toes, 'I forgive you.'

It was becoming rather painfully obvious that he wasn't coming anywhere near halfway to meeting *me*.

Still. Annoying habits can be adjusted. Over time, that is. *Tick?*

'I don't think it's a matter of forgiveness, Rolly,' I said sweetly. 'It seems on this particular issue we just happen to have different perspectives.'

'Uh-huh.' He smiled in a way I was sure he was sure would win me over. He began to massage my ankle and calf muscles, to run his hand up onto my thigh.

Yeah, right. Just throw a bit of sex at a problem and it's certain to go away.

I sat up a teeny bit straighter. 'Actually. Look, I have to say this, Rolly. If I didn't feel strongly about what I do, then I wouldn't be able to do a good job, would I?'

'Certainly not,' he said. 'God, your legs are so brown, Rebecca. You really do have gorgeous legs.'

'Well, thanks, but —.'

'I'm sorry we got into all this crap tonight.'

This was his way of coming around?

'Because I'd been planning on asking you to move into my apartment.'

'You want me to move in with you?'

'Well, of course. Yes. We could sell your place. Or rent it out, if you like, until we're sure this will work. Which I'm positive it will. Then later on —.'

'You want me to sell my *house*?'

My house with the rocks and ocean just below? My house with each colour on the walls considered and tried and mixed and so carefully painted, with each cup, each plate, fork, knife, painting, each piece of furniture lovingly chosen and placed? For a stark-white walls, spiky edges, such shiny surfaces they make you blink concrete *apartment?* With traffic so close you could just about put out your hand and touch it?

'You have to admit, my place is more spacious. And it's central. It's more appropriate for us to live there.'

'I like my house. You said you liked my house.'

'I do. It's very . . . quaint.'

Quaint.

'It's charming, of course it is.' He'd noticed the expression on my face and was frantically back-pedalling. 'I love your house, you know I do. We've had some marvellous times there together.' His hand made another run up my leg. 'But there really isn't enough room and it's more of a beach cottage. It's not quite appropriate for us to live in together.'

I particularly dislike the word 'appropriate'. It seems that there is a conviction that to say some behaviour, viewpoint or emotional attachment isn't 'appropriate' will cause any opponent to flush with mortification and instantly evaporate. I have such an aversion to 'appropriate' I find myself responding in an inappropriate manner. And Rolly had used it twice.

'Of course,' he said, still stroking my leg, 'the instant we started a family we would immediately look for something more —.'

'Appropriate?' My voice was a tad sharp. His hand stopped.

'It's what you want, isn't it? You said you wanted a family. Eventually, I mean.'

'I do,' I said. 'But —.'

'I wanted to show you this.'

He pulled out a little blue velvet box from his pocket and snapped it open, exposing a diamond, so large and glittering that it almost entirely eclipsed the other diamonds on each side which were also large and glittering. These diamonds were so bright I could almost have sworn that this was one of my niece Lily's dress-up rings that she loved to cram onto her fingers and swan about with. Except I knew without a doubt these were real.

'It was my grandmother's. I thought we could get it remodelled.'

I stared at it. Can you remodel *people?*

Because I knew as I stared down at those diamonds, which almost any other woman on this globe would have swooned over, that no matter how much that ring was remodelled it would never feel as comfortable as my own chunky silver rings.

Rolly and I simply didn't fit together. I didn't, couldn't, fit into his glass, chrome and diamond world any more than he could fit into mine. We'd had fun together — I'd needed fun after Joe and Bligh and after that final court hearing which had left me wrung out by shame. Rolly meant well. He was a good man. I'd thought I could love him but it was never going to happen.

'Rolly, it's just not going to work.'

'This wasn't the right time to talk about this,' he said, 'I can see that. But, darling, everyone has little disagreements and everything has been really good up until now. For me, anyway.'

He was looking at me so anxiously and I was feeling so utterly bad.

'For me, too. But —.' I shook my head.

I didn't want to tell him I could see those 'little disagreements' escalating to the point where things *wouldn't* be good. Where what furniture we liked, what we liked to cook with, where we wanted to live, where our kids would go to school, would be so fraught with misunderstandings and unhappy compromises that they *couldn't* be good.

He shut the box and placed it on the table next to the bed. 'I'll leave you on your own. Just, well, just have a think about it won't you? I do love you, Rebecca.'

I nodded and smiled up at him. I felt tears pricking up into my eyes.

It was almost time to leave and, while Rolly was in the bathroom, I opened up his suitcase, slipped the little box inside an inside pocket and zipped it up.

We both slept on the plane, somehow lost each other in Customs. He was waiting outside. 'Shall we share a taxi?'

I shook my head and touched his arm, 'No. But, it's been —.'

He interrupted me. 'I'll call you later in the week.'

I watched him getting into a taxi then hauled my suitcase in the direction of the shuttle buses. My throat felt tight and I felt tears rush again up into my eyes. It was hopelessly early in the morning, hardly anybody about and Wellington looked grey and dismal as I stared out of the shuttle-bus window. The only other passengers were a family: harassed-looking mum, distant-looking dad and two teenagers. The girl had the kind of flat-black hair that looks dead and she was slumped in her seat with her arms folded and a decidedly pissed-off expression. The boy had his iPod turned up so loud the sound vibrated out through his headphones. *Boom*-a-ba-ba. *Boom*-a-ba-ba. Sweet little baby boys and girls turn into lumpish clods. So what was I missing?

I unlocked the front door and trundled my suitcase inside. Even though the sun wasn't yet up everything beamed out at me: the ultra-cool pots I'd paid an arm and a leg for on the rack, the photos and paintings on the walls, my snow-globes lined up along the window ledge. And that smell of my house, my own perfume mixed up with salt water and sunshine and lemon furniture polish and lavender soap along with all the other people who'd lived there. I was home.

Mum had left lilies in my big glass bowl on the table and there was a loaf of crusty bread from the bakery and fresh milk in the fridge. I made a pot of tea, cut slice after slice of bread, spread it with butter and gorged. Then I went to bed.

I woke in the early afternoon with the pale sun filtering through the window. I'd slept as I always did after a longish plane trip — heavily, dreamlessly — and I stretched out. My own bed. My own cotton sheets. I lay still for a moment cautiously trying to gauge how I felt. Devastation? Or was it just disappointment? Intense disappointment or merely mild?

It felt more like relief. Would it all hit me later? Would I begin to miss Rolly?

I took a long hot shower, switched on music and phoned Mum. 'Thanks for the flowers. And the bread and milk.'

'Oh, good. You're home. Did you have a lovely time? I didn't phone. I thought you might be sleeping. Or that Rolly —.'

I heard the question in her voice. 'Yes, I did have a lovely time.

I've been sleeping. Rolly's not here, though. Me and Rolly, it hasn't exactly worked out.'

'Oh. I'm sorry.' But was she?

'Everything was fine and then we started talking about the Tour.'

'The *Tour*?'

'It was the first time we'd actually argued about anything. After that, well, let's just say it was all downhill.'

There was a hint of laughter in her voice. 'You're not saying you're another Tour casualty?'

'What do you mean?'

'Oh, just that a lot of relationships broke up because of the Tour. Your father and I went to a dinner party around that time which turned into a full-on brawl. Rebecca, are you sure this is something you can't work out?'

'Yes, Mum, I am sure. I wanted it to work but, you know, I always thought Rolly was kind of a dog's name and I had plans to change it. That says it all, really.'

'Oh, *Rebecca*.' I heard her laughing at the other end.

That's what they all said, one after another. My friends. My brother, David. My sister-in-law, Anna. 'Oh, Rebecca.' How could you have let such a successful, good-looking, *single* man go?

But along with the exclamations of shock and sympathy wasn't I hearing just a smidgen of relief? Had I got it *that* wrong?

I asked David who, like many older brothers, is always more than happy to point out where I've made mistakes. 'Nice enough guy,' he said, 'but there was no magic between you two. Anna and I couldn't work out what you saw in him.'

I opened up my mouth to start listing Rolly's virtues, but I knew he was right. While Rolly was one of those rarities of modern life, a single, heterosexual guy who actually talked about settling down, I'd known it all that time I'd tried to fix us together.

Yes, Rolly and I were yet another Tour casualty and if I felt any regret about him over the next few weeks it was for the things I'd thought we could have had rather than actually missing him.

But, in fact, I felt little regret. I had a story.

12

First day back. I dived into the office early. A note on my desk dated from last Thursday. 'Call Helen Graham. Says it's urgent.' Tim waved cheerily from the other side of the office and came over.

Huh, he wants to get back into my good books.

'Hey, Rebecca,' he said. 'You're looking pretty good. Great tan.'

'Thanks.' I leaned down over my desk and switched on my computer.

'You had a think about the Tour?'

'Uh-huh.' I stared at the screen. Three emails from Helen. What was up?

'And?'

'And I'm thinking about it.'

I'm just a fraction more than average height for a woman. Tim comes up to my shoulder. He has a curved and rotund belly which today was particularly protuberant, overlaid as it was by his favourite T-shirt: 'My Job Is Secure. Nobody Wants It.'

Grinning up at me he reminded me of the illustration in the Snow White book I used to love, of Snow White with a firm expression looking down at Grumpy. I couldn't hold out. I smiled.

'That's better,' Tim said, retreating back into his office. 'You'll be agreeing with me in a couple of months. It's a great idea. It'll be *great*.

I opened Helen's emails. 'I really need to talk to you.' 'Please contact me as soon as you get back.' 'I've tried your mobile but I can't get through.'

I phoned her home number, got a d-d-d-d signal. Had her phone been disconnected? She picked up on her mobile immediately.

'Hi, Rebecca. How was your holiday? Was the weather good? When we went to Rarotonga it rained every day.'

She'd been urgently trying to get me to ask about the *weather*?

'I had a fantastic holiday,' I said, 'and it was hot.'

'Was the hotel nice?'

What was going on? And what was up with her voice? She sounded skittish. Skittish and slightly awkward.

'It was very nice. But how are *you*?' My warm and encouraging voice.

'Well, I'm fine. Really fine. I've . . . Rebecca, I've made some changes.'

'Good changes, I hope.' My hearty voice. What changes?

'I think so. Uh, I'm moving back home. Denny wants to try again. He's been phoning and I've been to see him and we've talked it through. I'm ready to try as well. So I really don't think —.'

She was silent. *Fuck.* I could have shaken her.

'You're not able to be a part of the documentary.'

'No. Well, obviously.'

I swallowed hard. She was going back to that sleaze? 'I hope it all turns out for you.'

'Rebecca, you've been so good to me, listening and everything. I really hate letting you down like this but it's the kids, you see? I hated them not talking to me and I really missed my home and Bobby.'

'Bobby? But I thought he was —.' That was the worst Denny Graham story I'd heard, that he'd had Helen's dog put down rather than let her have him.

'Denny explained that to me. He was keeping Bobby until I got settled in but then he got sick and he had to do what the vet advised. But he's getting me another puppy from the same mother. Denny really has changed, Rebecca. He told me he's done a lot of thinking and —.'

Spare me the details. If you believe that you'd believe anything. 'Look, I understand. Really, it's OK.'

'Denny's not seeing any of those women. He's promised me. I'm not like you, Rebecca, independent and young. When you're in your fifties, well, it's not as if anyone else will want you, is it?'

Is that what it came down to? That a woman's life was defined by whether or not someone wanted her. In that case I was a real sad sack. No boyfriend, not even someone on the horizon.

I wished her luck and clicked off the phone. She'd need luck.

As did I, now that my major feature was disintegrating. Anyway I was stuck for the next few months; I had to somehow try to conjure something fresh out of a story which was way, way past its use-by date.

In the afternoon I drove up to the Police Museum in Porirua and walked around the photographic displays. Protesters haul back wire fences. A woman police officer grapples with a male protester. Plumes of smoke drift up above the crowds. Crowds surge forward holding up banners. 'Boks Go Home'. 'The Whole World's Watching'. A young woman marches, pushing a pram.

Barbed wire. Dumpsters lining roads. Rows of police. Combat gear. Batons raised and ready.

Stunning images, sure, but hadn't they been seen over and over again?

An official photograph of the 1981 All Blacks seated together, arms folded, faces set and grim. Could I do something with that? Ask them what they were thinking all those years ago. Did they question, even secretly regret, their decision to be there?

What about the Springboks in the photograph alongside? Did they have doubts about the philosophy which made them the centre of such upheaval? Were they entirely unaffected by what was happening around them?

Except screeds had already been written about that. By the players, by journalists, by supporters, by critics.

I drove home, opened up the windows to the soft wind and stood at my bench chopping onions, mushrooms, carrot. I cut up tofu, got the oil sizzling and tossed in the garlic.

What was happening in my house when all this was going on? Who lived here? What did they think about what was happening?

What could I possibly do with all those images twisted up in my head? What could I do with what happened during those fifty-six days?

Hamilton? But as momentous as Hamilton had been, hadn't all that been shown and talked about over and over?

'Apartheid is over and done with and what happened in Hamilton in 1981 has been looked at enough times to be a complete bloody yawn.' Rolly, damn him, was right. I needed something else.

The phone rang and I picked it up. 'Rebecca here.'

Someone on the other end listening before it cut out. It had happened a couple of times since I'd got home. Kids having a joke? Someone thinking they might like to burgle my place and checking it out first?

I closed the windows, locked the door.

13

My desk was stacked with printouts, recorded interviews, transcripts. Everyone had a story to tell, a point of view I just had to listen to. What was it about this country and rugby? It was never particularly significant within our family. Dad had played — pitifully, he'd told us — at school. David, on the other hand, had been good at it, good enough to make the first fifteen at his school. But then David was good at just about anything he took on.

As a family, the only conflict we'd ever had over rugby was that Mum hadn't been in favour of David playing. There'd been a number of spinal injuries around the time he was involved and she'd wanted him to give it up. I remember she lost her temper once when he came home, limping and bleeding after a Saturday game. 'It's nothing but legalised thuggery, David.'

And I used to really piss him off, hunching my head into my chest and leaping about making monkey noises, my arms hanging down around my knees. 'Rugger-bugger, rugger-bugger.'

Yet for many New Zealanders rugby is far, far bigger than just a game. Rugby pulsates with nationalism, masculinity: the endurance and courage of our pioneering nation, mateship, heroism. And all of that is intensified in our battles against the Boks. Courageous little New Zealand taking on the brute force of the mighty South African nation. David and Goliath.

The kind of crap I had no time at all for. And yet during the last Rugby World Cup there I was watching the finals. I'd been invited to a bubbly-bacon-and-egg brekkie. I'd thought of having to watch the All Blacks as the entrance fee. They ran out onto the field and lined up in those distinctive black jerseys. Then out it came over the loudspeaker. 'E Ihowa Atua, O nga iwi matou ra.' I felt a bewildering rush of tears.

I picked up a transcript and read it through.

'The Tour changed me. I didn't think the Boks should come. I had Maori mates and I thought it was disrespectful. But Dad, he passed away last year, he thought they should come. When I said I was protesting he said he could see where I was coming from but after Hamilton he was dead set against it. His attitude was you couldn't let a mob force their opinions on everyone else. So we argued and it got quite bad and things changed between us and, to be honest, they were never quite so good.

'The other thing that changed me was what I saw. I'd always thought what went on in other countries, all that corruption and brutality, well, nothing like that could ever happen here. I thought cops were good blokes. But seeing them all kitted out in riot gear with those long batons and the way they came at you, their helmets down hiding their faces.

'The worst of it was the Wellington test match. Downtown bloody Wellington and there's people who'd been beaten up there on the road, this woman with blood running down her face crouched over a kid, trying to protect him with her body. The police. The yelling and the screaming. It was like watching some war zone on TV.

'I just had to get out of it in the end but as I ran I kept seeing things. Like this young kid with his head in his hands and blood spilling out over his fingers bent up and kind of rocking, like when babies rock back and forward trying to comfort themselves.

'After the Tour, I knew we weren't different from anywhere else. I knew that any country can go crazy and anyone can turn vicious. I lost my faith in a lot of the things I'd believed in.'

I made a coffee. And here was another.

'I would have been twelve when New Zealand toured South Africa in 1976. The tests were on at around four in the morning our time and us kids would be under our blankets on the sofa watching with Dad. The last test was in Johannesburg. We had them. We should have got that penalty try. There was no way we shouldn't have been awarded it. But the referee said no. I looked at Dad to see if he was seeing what I was seeing and he had this look on his face like he was bloody near crying.

'I've read a bit and heard quite a lot of talk about that decision. There've been comments made such as the All Blacks had to be beaten during that series because white supremacist rugby was South Africa's way of standing up for apartheid against the world.

'What Dad said was you have to accept it was entirely possible the ref made a mistake. That's the way I prefer to see it as well. Because what I like to remember from all those games we watched together is the drive and the skill and the dedication that went into the game, not all that political bullshit. Seeing the guys out there in their black shirts, knowing how hard they'd worked to be there and what they stood for, that's what was important. Shit, it's a big part of our national pride. It's in our blood.

'I thought about it a lot before they came in 1981 and the decision I came to was that sport had to be protected against politics. I know what I saw that night in 1976 wasn't right or fair. But, what I believed was we should let them come and see how we do it over here.'

I picked up yet another transcript.

'That year, 1981, was the last year of my degree. Chris had already finished his two years of police training and was on the job. Every weekend was the same. Mum would tell us not to hit each other and leave for early morning Mass. Chris would get into his uniform, I'd pad my crotch, put on my thick jacket and hard helmet and we'd both take off.

'Chris and I are identical twins. We don't look nearly so much alike now — I've got a bit more around the belly and he's greyer than me, at least I like to think he is. But back then we were so bloody alike sometimes even we couldn't make out who was who in the photos and we used to have a bit of fun swapping clothes and having people on.

'Those fifty-six days, though, we kept our clothes and our ideas to ourselves.'

I had protesters and supporters wanting to tell me their stories. But which stories should I tell? What should I use, what should I leave out and whom should I believe? Everyone had their own version. Every protester I talked to who'd been at Molesworth Street was adamant there'd been no warnings or instructions. The police told me the direct opposite. 'They were told not to go there. They were told repeatedly so they earned themselves a whack.'

There were so many stories spun into those fifty-six days.

And I was right up against it. There was Merata Mita's film *Patu*, for a start. Bryan Bruce had done *The Tour, Ten Years On*, then in 2004, twenty-five years on, *Close Up* had produced *Springbok Tour Special*. Parts one, two *and* three.

So what was I going to do? *Springbok Tour Special, Thirty Years On*, parts one and two? I could already see the reviews. 'Same old, same old.' I just couldn't go for yet one more nostalgic look back.

Maybe I could focus on a major personality such as Marx Jones who dropped flour bombs on the pitch from a hired Cessna plane during the final test match in Auckland and did six months in prison for it. Except that Mark Sainsbury had done a fairly full interview with him in the *Close Up* special. It seemed that most major personalities had been covered either on film or in print.

I pressed the arrow on one of the short videos I'd downloaded. Hamilton. The group at the centre of the field. Lynda and Jools Topp, Donna Awatere, John Minto, even a couple of long-term friends of Mum and Dad's swaddled up in thick jackets, hats pulled down around their eyes.

The two guys Jackie told me about, the lambs, are out in front chasing each other, winding in and out of the group, and people are pointing and laughing. The black lamb tiptoes exaggeratedly towards a cop who starts to chase him and he's running and another cop joins in but they can't catch him and they turn away to stop more protesters who've broken through the fence. The white lamb runs out to meet the black and they're mimicking the police, marching in unison, and now they're turning around waggling their bums, waving, blowing kisses to the stands.

And they're dancing and while they're absurd in their woolly suits, there's something so brave and so beautiful about them. They turn into spinning tops, leap together, rocket through the air. The bright blue sky enfolding and framing them as they spin, spin, spin.

I called into Mum and Dad's on the way home. 'Just thinking back to the Tour,' I said, sitting down on a kitchen barstool and taking the coffee Dad was holding out to me, 'do you remember anything about the lambs?'

Mum looked up from chopping up tomatoes and red onions at the bench. 'I do. They were quite prominent. They turned up at just about every major game.'

'And they always managed to somehow evade the police and get onto the field,' Dad said.

'Who were they?' I asked.

'Nobody really knew,' Dad said. He tipped olive oil into a jar and started shaking it up with garlic and vinegar. 'It wasn't public knowledge, anyway. Though it was generally assumed they were from Wellington because they were at the general protest marches here. They were at the marches in May and July and at Molesworth Street.'

'They were very clever,' Mum said, putting down the knife and sweeping the vegetables into a salad bowl. 'They had these quite ridiculous routines where the white lamb would try to dominate the black one and end up looking dim-witted. Rather like those chases in the old silent films. They were very skilled, very agile. They must have been either dancers or gymnasts and they wore amazing costumes made out of some sort of fuzzy wool with wonderful plumed tails they used to waggle. Do you remember, Laurie, those masks they wore? This very thick, textured fabric, almost as if it was braided. Bulging eyes, puckered-up mouths. Quite extraordinary.'

'They were gay and they made that very obvious which didn't go down at all well with rugby supporters. In fact, making that so conspicuous was fairly courageous since homosexuality was against the law at the time.' He dribbled his oil mixture into the salad bowl. 'Uh, Rebecca, want to stay to dinner?'

'No thanks, I've got some work I want to get done. Against the law? I didn't know that.'

'Against the law in this country until the 1986 homosexual law reform bill,' Dad said. 'Until 1961 the penalties were life imprisonment, flogging and hard labour. Though that was rather more liberal than execution which was what happened when the law first came in in 1840.'

Mum grinned at me. Dad, being a lawyer, always had these facts at his fingertips and loved to pull them out.

'What about after 1961?' I said.

'Somewhere between a two- and a ten-year sentence.'

'So they were taking a risk?'

'Well, by then, the police tended to let that sort of thing go. Though there was always the threat they could act if they wanted to.'

'And the police did *not* like them,' Mum said, smiling. 'The lambs used to antagonise them. Do you remember, Laurie, that march where the lambs turned up wearing Red Squad headgear and armbands and carrying rubber batons?'

'Maybe there's a story there,' I said. 'Oh, and next question, Mum. Why did you change my cutlery drawer around while I was away?'

'Your cutlery drawer? What do you mean?'

'You put the knives the way you like them. Facing upwards.'

Mum and I have this ongoing discussion. Having properly sharpened kitchen knives is a bit of an obsession with me. I have an excellent steel and I know how to use it. But Mum says my kitchen knives are so sharp it's safer to have them facing upwards, whereas I say facing downwards is the way I like them and anyone who grabs a knife out of a drawer without looking deserves what they get.

'Of course I didn't.'

'Come on,' I said, 'own up. You're always on about it.'

She burst out laughing. 'I am *not* always on about it. Honestly, darling, I really do have other things to worry about rather than your cutlery drawer. You must have done it yourself before you left.'

'But I never put them that way. Oh, well.' I decided to give her the benefit of the doubt. I had been in a bit of a rush when I left and I just might have thrown things into the drawers the wrong way around. 'OK, it could have been me.'

I drove home thinking. Who were the lambs? What happened to them? What had Dad said? It was generally assumed they were from Wellington — so it was quite possible they could still be here, still even be together. In their fifties, maybe sixties.

I poured a glass of wine, hummed along with the stereo as I cooked dinner. My phone pinged. No message. Just the photograph.

The photograph of me at the airport in Rarotonga.

There was no number but I knew Rolly must have sent it. Probably missing me, feeling a bit pissed off with me, trying to remind me we'd had good times together.

OK, Rolly, we did have fun but it's over.

14

'Got a minute, Mike?' I leaned my head out of my coop of desk, computer and chair and called to him across the row on row of similar enclosures cheerily referred to by Tim as our 'offices'. No lolling about on comfortable chairs on company time, not with Tim's eagle eye and spartan fixtures. Funny why I loved him so much.

We were the only ones in the office. Mike Mackey is our researcher who started to work the odd hour or so for Zenith when it first started up but now he's full-time with a couple of part-timers he can call on when he needs to. His research is meticulous; he also has a gut instinct about situations and people. He says this developed during his years working as a cop, and I'd just about trust my life to it. It was Mike who warned me about Connor Bligh: 'The guy's guilty and he's dangerous.' I didn't listen to him at the time and I got into trouble. I'm much more inclined to listen to him now.

He looked up. 'I can spare you a couple,' he said, smiling.

'Want to go and get a coffee? My shout.'

'Hot chocolate?'

Mike also has a very sweet tooth. 'You're on.'

We took the lift down to the café on the ground floor. There were only a few people there — black suits, shiny shoes, newspapers and short blacks — which meant we got the leather sofas with the coffee table beside the gas fire. I bought a coffee for me and a chocolate croissant and a mega-size hot chocolate with whipped cream and extra marshmallows for Mike. He raised his eyebrows as the waiter put it down in front of him. 'This is going to take some time?'

'Mike, you were in the police force here in Wellington during the Tour, weren't you.'

'Yep.' He stirred his chocolate.

'What did you think about the Tour going ahead?'

I held up my notepad. 'You don't mind if I write a few things down?'

'Yeah, go right ahead. Well, it should never have happened.' He popped a marshmallow into his mouth. 'It was divisive for the country and probably the worst thing that ever happened to the police force.'

'Because of the violence?'

'We were in a bloody awful position. No matter what we personally thought, we were under orders to control the protests. I had mates in the force who had family members on the marches. *I* had mates who were protesting.'

'Muldoon made the point that it was a matter of law and order, that you couldn't have one faction of the population preventing others from doing something which was perfectly lawful.'

Mike took a large bite of his croissant. 'Law and order be buggered. Muldoon and his mates didn't have to use batons on ordinary civilians who didn't like what was happening and wanted to make that known. They didn't get spat at and they didn't have to arrest terrified kids. One of the worst things I had to do was try to get a pack of rugby supporters to back off from attacking an ambulance which was there to take injured protesters to hospital. They were trying to force the doors open, slamming into it and trying to turn it over. The couple of women who were inside were petrified. That kind of crap going on for the sake of a few rugby games.'

'Do you think anything positive came out of it?'

'A demoralised police force that no one trusted any more? Another Muldoon government? Families and friendships split? What do you think?'

'Nothing at all?'

'Well, I suppose the blacks in South Africa knew some of us were behind them. The games were all televised, of course, and there was a lot of celebrating there when Hamilton got stopped. You'll know what Mandela said? He was locked in a cell at the time and when he found out the game had been called off he said he felt as if the sun had come out.'

'Nothing good for New Zealand, though?' I asked.

'There are some who would say there were good things,' Mike

said. 'For a start, the Tour showed that New Zealanders would get off their arses and do something when they felt strongly enough. And it motivated Maoris to think about their own rights.'

'But you don't agree?'

He slurped back a gulp of chocolate and patted his lips with a paper napkin. 'No. Because I was right there and saw what it did to people. I may not be much of a theorist but I can't think of any possible good that can come out of a situation where a government uses its law enforcement agency against its own people.'

I stopped writing and looked at him. 'Are you saying you were in support of the protesters?'

'Well, I had a few good friends in COST.'

'You know, you're looking a bit shifty.' I couldn't help but grin at his expression. 'What are you not telling me?'

'I wasn't one of those informers, if that's what you're getting at. But I was against the Tour and, while I had to do my job, my sympathies were with the protesters. Not those ratbags who came out all armed up to have a go, mind, but the ordinary, everyday people who wanted to make their feelings heard.'

'What do you know about the lambs?' I picked up my pen again.

'Not much. At first they were right out there but towards the end they went off the scene.'

'That's odd,' I said, 'I wonder what happened.'

Mike shrugged. 'Things turned ugly. Probably had enough.'

Mum had an almost perfect recall of people and an uncanny way of working them out. Maybe she would remember something more about the lambs, even have her own suspicions about who they were. I picked up the phone and called her office. 'Can you do lunch?'

'Today you mean?' I could feel her frowning. 'A very short one and you'd have to come here. I've got a lecture on company law to give to a hundred or so students at one.'

'I could be there just after twelve. That café we went to last time?'

She was sitting at a table when I arrived. She had the cheddar, rocket and pear-relish sandwiches that I like and our coffees already waiting. Mum is so well organised she puts me to shame.

'I take it you want to ask me something,' she said, giving me a quick hug before I sat down. 'I have to be back in my office by 12.50.' She looked at the oversized watch on her wrist. 'You've got not quite forty minutes.'

'OK, here goes. You and Dad went to most of the COST meetings?'

'Every meeting we could get to. Your father was fairly tied up in the law firm in those days — he'd only recently joined the partnership — and of course you and David were still very young. Why do you ask?'

'I'm interested in the lambs. And since it seems they were based in Wellington, the anti-Tour movement here seems a good place to start.'

'Well, from the beginning COST made itself very visible. There was an office set up in Courtenay Place with a full-time worker and a lot of effort went into the publicity. Leaflets, newspaper and radio advertising, all of that. I daresay the lambs may have turned up to meetings.'

'You had no suspicions about who they were?'

'Not the faintest hunch,' she said. 'Mind you, as I said, we weren't able to go to every meeting. Somebody else might know.'

'Are there other people you could put me in touch with? Maybe someone who was on the committee?'

'There are one or two people I still have contact with. Leave it with me. I'll talk to them and get back to you.'

'One thing I don't quite understand is why COST started up,' I said. 'Why didn't people just join up with HART?'

'There was quite a bit of bad feeling around about HART. It wasn't warranted, but there'd been negative publicity which had built up over the years, some of it focused on Trevor Richards. He was the former leader. The general perception was a new organisation would attract more people who may have been reluctant to join in with HART.'

'What kind of bad publicity?'

She raised her eyebrows and smiled a little. 'Richards was accused of having communist sympathies. There were theories being put forward that HART was using racism in South Africa and rugby between the countries as a justification for causing havoc to promote anarchy and take down the government. Accusations were made that some of its members were terrorists who intended using violent methods. There was one particularly nasty rumour that there were plans to blow up Mount Cook Airlines if the 1972 Springbok Tour went ahead.'

I couldn't help but laugh. 'A communist takeover? *Here*?'

'Back then it wasn't seen as anything to laugh at,' she said. 'McCarthyism and the Cold War weren't that far behind us and, in fact, we were still very much influenced by the reds-under-the-beds syndrome. Muldoon certainly bought into it. You know, when I was in my last year at primary school I remember our teacher showing us on a map how, if we didn't stop them, communists would move down through Asia and eventually get to Australia and New Zealand and take us over. I had absolutely no idea what a communist was but, from the look on the teacher's face, I certainly didn't want to meet one.'

I couldn't quite believe this. 'You were actually scared?'

'I was until I got home and told your granddad and he laughed his head off.'

'But you're telling me people actually believed that crap?'

'Well, that teacher undoubtedly did. You've got to understand that communism for many people back then represented an enormous threat. The accusations that HART was a covertly communist organisation were so damaging that people who were against the Tour going ahead were reluctant to join because of its reputation.'

'I'd really like to talk to people who were at the inaugural meeting.'

'I can help you with that, and I'm sure the people you talk to will be able to give you other contacts.'

'I'm stuck,' I said. 'Everything I've considered has already been done. The lambs could be interesting. But I don't know that I could base a whole two-part documentary on them, even if I could find out who they were.'

'You seem interested in COST,' Mum said. 'Maybe you could do something with that.' She looked at her watch again. 'Just about time I was off. Uh, have you talked to Rolly at all?'

She said it idly but I felt her glance slide over my face as she said it.

'Why are you asking?'

'David says he keeps running into him.'

'They do happen to work in the same building, Mum.'

'It's a very *large* building.'

'What are you suggesting? That Rolly's stalking David?'

'Of course not. It's just that David told me he keeps running into Rolly and he seems very eager to ask after you. What you're doing, things like that.'

I shrugged. 'I suppose it's fairly natural he would.'

'No regrets?'

'God, no. I think it was fairly much doomed from the start but the biological clock got right in the way and I couldn't see our rather obvious differences.' I laughed, 'Anyway, you know me, I may jump into things boots and all but when I jump out again I'm gone.'

Mum gave her most deeply theatrical sigh. 'Rebecca the ballerina, Rebecca the Olympic Games gymnast, Rebecca the —.'

'World-famous concert clarinettist. Mum, I get it.'

When she had gone I ordered another coffee and treated myself to a lemon tart. Mum asking about Rolly had reminded me of the photo he'd sent me. Actually two photos — another had come through just before I'd driven over here. Me again. Rarotonga again.

I pulled out my mobile and looked at it. I'm standing on the deck wearing my blue dress. We're about to go out for dinner. *That* dinner.

What was he up to? Maybe I should phone him. Then again, probably not. Best to leave it alone, let him get over it.

But Mum was right. COST *was* interesting. Maybe I was on to something; if I focused on the anti-Tour movement in Wellington I would be doing something no one else had done. I could start from the beginning, the founding of the organisation, the personalities involved, the growth, the marches, the politics. I could follow through from its conception to the end of the Tour.

I'd talked to enough people and read enough to understand that COST was fairly unique among all the other anti-Tour groups throughout the country. As Mum and Dad had told me, the association prized itself on being highly organised and disciplined. I'd talked to a previous member who was more than a little disparaging about what went on in Auckland, which, he said, was completely lacking in the control and restraint instilled from the start in Wellington.

'That Auckland lot lost sight of what they were protesting against. Some guys came armed with metal piping and there were others tearing palings off fences and having a go. There was crazy stuff going on there and the whole thing went to hell. It surprises me nobody got killed.'

On the other hand, COST was a tight unit and had a strict ethos of non-violence. Peaceful demonstration. Passive resistance. Maybe I could compare COST with other non-violent campaigns. Gandhi. Parihaka.

I ordered another coffee — I just about had time for it — and started to get ideas, questions, names down on my laptop. First episode: the start of COST, the marches, Molesworth Street. I could look mainly at the Wellington test.

And the lambs? Had they been at the meetings? Did they turn up separately, remaining silent and inconspicuous or did other protesters know who they were? It could be they weren't even associated with COST, preferring to remain mavericks, moving in and out of the bounds of the protest movement.

How could I find out? Who should I talk to? I stared through the large window, trying to think it out — and saw Rolly. He saw me, hesitated, stopped by the door then moved towards me, an awkward expression on his face. I glanced at my watch. Shit, I'd been so caught up I'd lost track of the time. I leapt up, manoeuvred my way around him. 'Sorry, so sorry, Rolly, but I really have to go.'

I'd set my next interview for three, in Willis Street. *Please, God, let me find a park.* I managed a swift duck-in just as another car backed out, tried to look innocent as the woman glowered at me from the SUV she had all poised to launch into that exact spot. *Anyway, driving that great oil-guzzling thing is bloody ridiculous in the city, bad for the environment.* I raced down the street, took the lift to the fifth floor.

I'd been curious to meet Tony Carlisle, one of the most vocal and active dissenters of the seventies and eighties. He'd been prosecuted for throwing tomatoes at some minor, never-to-be-heard-of-again MP at a Waitangi Day celebration and later for burning a flag at an anti-Vietnam War demonstration. And when Germaine Greer had said 'bullshit' and 'fuck' while addressing a feminist symposium in Auckland in 1972 he'd been on his feet cheering and was subsequently dragged out struggling and yelling ('Bullshit bullshit bullshit! Fuck fuck fuck!') by three cops.

He'd been right up there, in fact, in just about every dispute there'd been over the time: Vietnam, Bastion Point, the Treaty, and he was one of the major voices against New Zealand's sport association with South Africa. *And* he'd been a member of COST.

I got out of the lift into one of those wonderfully sparse chrome-and-glass outer offices — the long silvery reception desk, the tinted glass coffee table, the black leather chrome-footed chairs. What will happen when the fashion changes? Will there be a glut of chrome and tinted-glass tables and leather sofas waiting for poverty-stricken people to pick them up for nothing at the Salvation Army? I remembered overhearing a woman in an upmarket design shop, her voice trembling with forlorn longing, 'If only I hadn't thrown out Mum and Dad's banana seats.' I gave my name to the receptionist, who lifted the phone and then motioned me towards the door of an equally sparse office.

I held out my hand. Was *this* the figure in the famous photograph; the raised, clenched fist, the penetrating eyes, the open, angry mouth? 'Amandla! Amandla!'

The knitted hat, bushy mop of hair, beard, had been replaced by the number-one haircut trendier men of his age adopt when they want to persuade everyone they've lost their hair on purpose. Still, it looked good on him. Especially with the grey linen suit and black silk turtleneck. If I didn't know anything about him I would have instantly assumed that Tony Carlisle had been a lifetime, paid-up member of respectable and upright society.

But the grin was the same flare of wickedness and charm. That same charm and wickedness that had made him a natural focal point of interest for media. And who could forget that voice blaring out through the loudspeaker at an anti-Tour march in early 1981, 'One two three four, who will stop this fucking Tour?'

Yet another prosecution. Obscene language in a public place. New Zealand was still so prudish in the eighties and Carlisle had not minded getting into a bit of strife. A couple of nights earlier, I'd watched a debate on the old Thursday night *Close Up* from the archives. Tony Carlisle and Robert Muldoon. There were other people there as well but the Carlisle/Muldoon skirmishes were legendary. Eventually Muldoon refused to be in the same room as him, let alone talk to him.

People were afraid of Muldoon. Everyone said it; someone I'd talked to had told me when Muldoon was around the air stretched taut like a rubber band about to snap. But on-screen, Carlisle appeared to be one of the few who didn't seem troubled by him.

In this particular debate, the camera was mainly focused on Muldoon who held the floor — maybe even the network was afraid of him — while he explained why the government had not, in fact, broken the Gleneagles agreement, since a clause had subsequently been added which gave the ruling bodies involved justification to allow individuals the right to participate in sports with representatives of apartheid. After that, he launched into his 'individual freedom' and 'sports and politics must be separate' routine. Any attempt by the interviewer to ask a question or by any other participant to interject was tersely dismissed. 'I'm here to make important points clear to the citizens of New Zealand.'

It was all going well. So well that he treated himself to one of his lopsided grins before slogging onwards: 'This government's refusal to ban the Springboks from playing here allows our New Zealand citizens the right to choose for themselves, the right of individual consciences. The stand of this government is anti-authoritarian.'

And then came the interruption, this time impossible to ignore.

'Ha-ha-ha-ha-ha-ha-ha!'

The camera swung in on the other participants — a priest, a police representative, a woman on the HART executive — all, until now, sitting stiffly at the table, water glasses at the ready, looking, as my granny used to say, as if they had apples up their bums and lemons in their gobs. Their faces burst into unrestrained grins.

'Ha-ha-ha-ha-ha-ha-ha! Anti-authoritarian, Mr Prime Minister? Anti-authoritarian? *You*?'

That acerbic, wicked grin. Muldoon stood and walked off the set.

I reminded Tony Carlisle of that interview as he waved me towards a leather chair.

'Yeah,' he grinned. 'For a long time after that, it was always, "Oh, you're *that* Carlisle." They repeated the clip so many times it became embarrassing. When Muldoon finally got put out, they used to play it alongside the one where he was pissed and announced the snap election. What I said wasn't even clever but everyone seemed to think it was hilarious.'

'You were the real genuine revolutionary back then, weren't you?'

'I'm not what you expected?'

I shrugged. 'People change. I didn't know what to expect.'

He sat down, stretched out his legs. 'Want a coffee?'

'Thanks, but I've just had one. I suppose I am a bit surprised but, then again, did you ever envisage a future where you'd be a media consultant?'

'Probably not. I had a slightly overdeveloped social conscience in those days. Which is still there, mind you. I do my bit, just in a different way now. Back then I was prepared to take a few risks and the media latched on to me. I didn't care about people abusing me because I was some long-haired layabout with a big mouth so long as I had my say.

'It's the Tour you're interested in, isn't it? Well, over the time of the Tour, it got so I couldn't cross the street without some mad bastard getting me in his sights and aiming his bloody car at me. People knew who I was and when you have packs of yobs wandering about looking for a fight I was the one to pick on. But I guess all of us eventually get a bit too old for that kind of thing. I'm not so quick or good at sidestepping as I was.'

'Was it rugby supporters who hassled you?'

'Yeah, and the police had a few goes at me. Used to haul me in, try to teach me a bit of a lesson just so I'd know who was boss. Funnily enough, I had a big lesson not long after the famous Muldoon debate.'

'Are you, in all seriousness, telling me that the police used to pull you in and threaten you? Come *on*, we don't live in a police state.'

'All I'm saying is from time to time police kept me at the station for questioning and gave me a bit of a slap-around so I wouldn't push them too far.'

'Didn't you complain?'

'Who to?' he grinned. 'The police? You've got to understand that back then Muldoon ruled this country and he got away with it. The *country* let him get away with it. Muldoon was quite prepared to destroy anyone who got in his way and he had the media right under his thumb.'

'How did he do that?'

'Intimidation. Any journo who got on the wrong side of Muldoon, well, if he was tough enough to survive the singling out and harassment — and believe me, harassment by Muldoon was like being mauled by a Rottweiler — he'd be banned from press conferences and denied access to government information. Then if he was still hanging on, his editor would most likely be pressured into letting him go. He'd most likely end up in Feilding reporting on the agricultural shows and local fires, that is if he was lucky enough to ever get another job.'

'I can't believe editors would put up with crap like that.'

'OK, examples. He publicly ordered Tom Scott — and he was one of the best political journalists around — out of the press gallery. Then there was Simon Walker, one of our top TV interviewers. He questioned Muldoon on claims he'd made about New Zealand being threatened by a Soviet naval presence in the Pacific. After that interview his career in New Zealand was over, thanks to the gutless bastards that ran TVNZ.'

'They got rid of him because he asked questions?'

'Walker challenged Muldoon and he wouldn't back down. Muldoon couldn't take it. I'll never forget that savage, clipped bark he had. "You're not going to set the rules, my friend." Terrifying if you let it get to you.'

'You obviously didn't.'

'He never took me seriously. Not really. I was small fry and he could've stomped on me easily enough if he'd wanted to. A few pointed questions and threats and I'd have had to ease off.

'My brother's gay, you see, and back then he was a teacher.'

'So?'

'So he was living with his partner. So what they were doing was illegal but, worse than that, my brother, this *deviant*, was in charge of innocent children. A word to *Truth* and he would have been without a career. Muldoon made it his business to know about his opponents.'

'What I don't understand is why Muldoon was so determined to go ahead with the Tour.'

'That's easy. He knew the next election was going to be close and he had to have the regional pro-rugby voters on his side to win. That shows how ruthless the man was. He was willing to risk what amounted to civil war to ensure he kept his leadership. He did it too. By one seat.'

'You were in COST, weren't you?'

'Yeah, I was. I was never much of a joiner but I could see if we were going to get anywhere with the Tour it had to be through a united stand.'

'Were you on the committee?'

'God, no. Too much of a loner for that.'

'Do you remember the lambs?'

He grinned and nodded. 'Yeah, yeah I do. Those two were fantastic. A real laugh.'

'Were they at the meetings?'

'If they were I didn't know about it. I'd have loved to have a yarn with them.'

'You don't know anyone who might have known who they were?'

'Sorry, can't help you with that one.'

I drove home. Right into the middle of late-afternoon traffic, dammit. I slowed down, keeping my eyes on the car in front of me.

The Muldoon government. Those ugly, brutal tactics. But he'd been popular. Rob's Mob. And even if it was by only one seat, he'd got back in. Did people actually buy into that 'law and order' bullshit?

A silver-grey Volvo that looked like Rolly's passed me on the nearest lane going in the opposite direction. I glanced up into the rear-vision mirror. TOPSKI. Most definitely *not* Rolly, who would probably prefer torture and even death than be seen driving a car bearing a personalised plate.

Rolly. The latest addition to my list of failed relationships. I could put him right there just above the biggest mistake of them all. Joe Fahey, my very-much married man.

I wanted a man. I wanted a baby. Babies, in fact. I was thirty-three. Tick-tick-fucking-tick.

Any regrets? Mum had asked. Right now I could have been awaiting the return of those redesigned and remodelled diamonds. I could have been organising an 'intimate and picture-perfect' wedding on 'the soft sandy shores' of the beach at our resort in Rarotonga.

Oh, yes, I had flicked through the brochures. A floaty dress. Bare feet. Frangipani threaded through my hair.

Weren't you just a teeny bit intolerant? Does everything have to be on your terms? Your house? Your life?

But I couldn't imagine letting my house go. Too much had happened there, too many memories.

Becoming, being Rebecca Thorne *Saturday Night*. Losing my job. Starting at Zenith. Joe holding me through a stolen night. Saying goodbye. Connor Bligh. The night on the deck when it all ended with that click of the gate. Through all those triumphs and losses, through each new beginning, my house has held me close. How could I live without the faraway lights on the water shining out into the dark, without my ocean whipping and thrashing around me?

If I really was too awkward and set in my ways to have the man, maybe I should just have the baby. Simply select one handsome, healthy and intelligent specimen from off the net.

I was feeling sorry for myself. Babies. Men. Why could I manage everything else perfectly well yet miss out on what most women seemed to so effortlessly achieve?

Still, I'd managed to score an interview for the next day with Oliver Neil who'd been involved with setting up COST. I turned into my carport. Tricky, I always had to concentrate. I got out of my car, picked up the loaf of bread from the passenger seat — and saw Rolly.

He was directly across the road. He met my gaze. I heard his car engine start up.

I stood watching for a moment as his car drove off. Maybe he was returning my DVDs, the couple of books he still had. But why hadn't he stopped when he saw me?

I checked my letter box. Nothing.

I unlocked the door. It was all so odd, so out of character. Rolly was predictable. Rolly was level-headed. So why in hell was he sending me photographs? Why was he outside my house?

I went into my bedroom, pulled on jeans and a sweater and prowled around, checking the bedrooms, opening the wardrobe doors, looking around my study, scrutinising the desk, drawers, trying the doors onto the deck, making sure they were locked. Everything looked the same, but my house felt different. Something felt wrong.

Was the bathroom door half-open when I left this morning? Were the papers on my desk exactly like that?

This was crazy. I was getting myself all screwed up. I filled a glass with wine, had a couple of gulps, turned on the news.

I'd only talked to him once since we'd been back from Rarotonga and that had been hurried and uncomfortable. I wasn't all that good at talking to past lovers; there never seemed much left to say. *Sorry it didn't work out? Sorry I hurt your feelings?*

He'd left a couple of messages. I should have phoned him back. Maybe there was something he needed to talk to me about. I had to admit, I'd acted carelessly. In fact, quite badly.

Why had he been parked outside my house? Maybe he was on his way to the airport and he'd just stopped in on the chance I'd be home.

But that didn't explain why he hadn't spoken to me. Even if he was in a hurry he could, at least, have waved.

It disturbed me. Far more than it should have. Not so much seeing him there, which was strange enough, but the expression on his face as I looked up and saw him. Startled. Almost furtive. *Definitely* weird.

I stared at the TV news, then David came on and I relaxed as I listened. He'd been asked to comment on Wellington schools which had opted out of the new National Standards system and he was voicing his support. 'Most of the students in these schools have English as a second language. It's unreasonable that they should have to meet the same kind of benchmarks as kids who are native speakers. This is a system devised by people who've never taught and know nothing about grass-roots education.'

David was starting to make his mark and when Labour made it back into government, the talk was he'd have a top portfolio. He was articulate and well-informed, knew how to listen and when to speak, and he had a way of drawing people in, making them feel he was on their side. And, my god, he looked good. In his dark jeans and soft grey sweater, my brother was very handsome. Maybe he'd make Prime Minister. I could see David and Anna and the kids as the New Zealand equivalent of America's First Family fantasy: ultra-good-looking parents, cute-as-buttons kids. Charismatic. Bright. Talented. In fact, totally fucking gorgeous. Good thing I loved them far too much to hate them. David would continue to do well, I knew it. But I didn't want them turning into a Kennedy family, public property, vulnerable. I couldn't bear to have them exposed to the kind of criticism families in the public eye endured. I couldn't bear to see them hurt.

I poured more wine — only half a glass — and kept an eye on the news as I threw a sliver of butter and some fish into a pan, squeezed in lemon, made a salad, cooked rice.

I turned off the TV, opened up my laptop, started making a list of questions I wanted to ask the next day.

COST's first meetings. Where did you hold them? How were they advertised? Who turned up?

The questions were there, banked up in my mind ready to pour out and I tapped them quickly onto the screen. My head had cleared and I was feeling good about the project; I'd narrowed it down, found something that hadn't been done before.

Let's hope Oliver Neil has a good memory, that he can speak well, that he won't freak out on camera, that he actually will agree to be on camera.

I was working as I always did, in my study, at the vast table that is my desk, covered with what is actually an orderly clutter of files, clippings and the odd scribbled note. I like to work with the curtains open to the ocean and the sky. While I was assembling my questions everything had darkened and the planes taking off from the airport turned into flickering lights. The waves hummed and slapped below me and the wind, which had just sprung up, whacked against the house.

This was going to be a good interview. I knew it. Now that I had my story, I knew exactly what I had to ask and Oliver Neil was exactly the right person to give me the answers.

The phone rang. I picked it up. I heard someone breathe. The line cut out.

Wrong number?

15

Usually I sleep well. I absolutely know my house. I know, for instance, that the solid timber door which leads from the little foyer to the front steps judders in a strong wind, making a muffled thud-thud-thud, despite all the fix-it methods Dad or David or I have tried. It was the original door and I won't replace it so I live with it. I know also that the gate from the deck to the rock slabs leading down to the beach squeaks and clangs but I won't replace that either because it was that gate which saved my life when Connor Bligh tried to kill me. It's staying because it deserves to, because it's a reminder of what I got myself into, a warning that I must never get in so deep again.

But that night each thud, squeal and clatter jolted me awake. The sounds and shadows I had learned to trust seemed foreboding and there was a new sound, something I couldn't work out. A dragging, shifting sound that joined the others whenever the wind picked up.

And then the morning swept in red and gold and the wind dropped. I've always had too much imagination, always allowed myself to be scared of the things I can't see rather than be wary of those I can.

I met Oliver Neil in Betty's Kitchen. I hadn't been there before but, according to Oliver, Betty's had the best cheese scones to be had in Wellington. I'd offered to drive up to Waikanae — he and his wife had just retired, he'd said on the phone, and had recently moved up the Kapiti Coast. 'No, I'll meet you,' he'd said. 'We're having this new kitchen put in and a deck built on the front and the noise is so bloody awful I like to get away from it.'

He didn't have nearly so much hair and what he had was grey but I recognised his lanky legs and arms, his long, slightly mournful face, from the photos and film clips. He stood up and shook my hand and we ordered our coffees. He asked for a cheese scone and then dug out every scrap of butter from the packet to smear all over it. 'We don't have butter at home,' he said, 'and we don't often have cheese either. Cholesterol.'

He took a deep, wide bite and sighed loudly. 'Jesus, that's good.'

I opened up my bag, got out my list of questions and dictaphone. I must have had a slightly puzzled expression because he grinned at me. 'You're disappointed. You expected to meet an anarchist and you end up talking to some sad old bugger who's sneaking cholesterol behind his wife's back.'

I laughed. 'I'm not disappointed, not at all. But I was looking at some photos of you last night and you looked so *fierce*.'

'I was.' He took another mouthful of scone. 'Fuck, this is so good I'm going to have another one. Maybe two. I'm meeting an old mate for lunch around twelve, we're going to have a few beers, quite a few, and then I'll pour myself into a train and snore drunkenly all the way home. Bloody marvellous. Now. What do you want to know?'

'Well, first of all, what if you tell me about the beginnings of COST. I understand you were involved from the start?'

I got back into the office just before lunch and turned on my recorder. I'd succumbed and bought one of Betty's scones and, dammit, they were good. I took bites as I transcribed the interview. I was happy at last. This was all good stuff. Oliver Neil was more than willing to say what he'd told me on camera and he was the kind of guy any audience would find likeable.

I was in HART then I was involved in starting up COST. The thinking at first was with enough pressure the Tour wouldn't go ahead. Public opinion was swinging against it and HART came up with the idea of nationwide anti-Tour demonstrations on May the first. The main point of the first meeting of COST was to set up the May Mobilisation Committee in Wellington and promote the demonstration. People turned up and we elected an executive committee. I was on that until I moved down south around the middle of August.

Tell me about that first meeting.

Right. Yeah, well, it was held in the Wesley Lounge, that's in Taranaki Street, somewhere around February 1981. There'd been a few posters around, people on the HART mailing list had been contacted as well as church groups, women's organisations, any group we could think of that might be on the same wavelength. Around a hundred, a hundred and fifty people turned up. If I had to come up with a label, at that point I'd say COST was mainly white, middle-class intellectuals. There were a lot of students from Vic, people from HART, and I recognised quite a few from the Vietnam War protests I'd been involved in. That first meeting ran very smoothly. We elected the committee, appointed a full-time worker and made the decision to get the office in Courtenay Place.

What did you talk about?

We needed to get people interested in marching in May so we talked about getting some publicity rolling. For a start, we had to make people aware that COST actually existed, but we also had to make them sympathetic enough to our cause that they'd show. The feeling at the meeting was not only did we have to make what was really happening in South Africa absolutely clear, we also had to persuade people that playing rugby with a Springbok team would have huge ramifications for New Zealand.

What happened after that?

We decided to have what we called plenary meetings every Monday evening. They were open to whoever wanted to be there and, as time went on and the Tour got closer, more and more people turned up. The committee met Wednesday nights as well so I suppose you could say it was a fairly demanding commitment from the start. First of all we planned the May 1 march and after that we organised another mass demonstration for July 1. We were hoping the government would see sense but, at the same time, we had to plan for the possibility of the Tour going ahead and during that time we became incredibly organised. It was like a military deployment. We had marshals assigned to oversee and control ranks of ten protesters. We worked out and practised techniques, marching with arms linked then splitting and turning in opposite directions, stuff like that.

Tell me about that first march, May 1, 1981.

All I can say is it was a fucking triumph. We had no indication of how it would go; we were shit-scared it would be a massive flop. We had more and more people turning up to the plenaries and there were people coming into the office offering help. But whether the march would be supported, we just didn't know. We hoped — at the most we hoped — somewhere between fifteen hundred to three thousand people would turn up and then there were fifteen fucking thousand turned up in Bunny Street. Christ, we couldn't believe it. There was this *mass* of people with their placards waving above them moving through the city to the Civic Centre. Christ, I felt proud. To be a part of that, part of bringing that together. I thought if the government doesn't take notice of this . . . Muldoon's *got* to take notice of this.

But he didn't. It didn't fucking matter to him that thousands of New Zealanders were against the Tour. The only notice he took of it was to build up a military-style police force. As far as the government went, we were pissing against the wind.

There would have been a police presence there and, I suppose, rugby supporters?

Any rugby supporters who turned up were way outnumbered and didn't make an impression at all. Police were there keeping an eye on things but they fairly much kept out of it.

What about your impression of the police in later marches?

Up until Hamilton my own impression was that the police were mainly fair. They did what they had to but there was a feeling they weren't entirely against us. In fact, they weren't that big a presence. The day the Hamilton game was on two thousand of us marched from Lambton Quay onto the motorway and blocked it and there were only twenty-six cops as escort. Then, of course, we heard the match had been cancelled, and we were bloody ecstatic. It had been a good march; Trevor Richards was at the front and there were families, kids, older people out and we'd done what we thought was the impossible, we'd occupied the motorway and then we had the news from Hamilton. What we thought, walking back to the Cenotaph, was that the Tour was over and judging from the reactions of the cops escorting us they weren't too unhappy about what had happened. But after that the whole scene turned really ugly.

As in the Molesworth Street march?

As in the Molesworth Street march. That was the turning point. There was a shift in police tactics and it came directly from Muldoon down through Ben Couch, the Minister of Police. Bob Walton, the Commissioner, had held back on using batons against protesters occupying the pitch in Hamilton and he'd been savagely criticised for it.

Was there a change in the meetings after Molesworth Street?

I left not long after that, went down to Christchurch and joined up with the group down there. But the few I went to after Molesworth Street, yeah, there was a change. For one thing we lost a few supporters but they were more than replaced by people who were pissed off with what had happened and decided to join us. The main thing was we knew we had to protect ourselves effectively so there was more time given to how to do that — protective clothing and hats, what to do in an attack, stuff like that. We got a whole lot more defensive.

Can you tell me anything about the lambs?

They were crazy bastards.

Why do you say that?

What we needed back then was people working as a team. A couple of committee members challenged them once or twice when they were on the Wellington marches. Told them to stop the fucking grandstanding and front up. All that dressing up and pissing about, that was Auckland, never us.

You didn't know who they were?

No, and that's another thing I didn't like. What I think is if you're going to stand up for something you don't hide behind masks, you get out there and put your face and name behind it.

They didn't make contact? Didn't turn up to any meetings?

One of my mates — Johnny King, I'll give you his number and you can talk to him if you like — told me one of them did make contact before the Wellington test, said they wanted to do what they could on the day. There was all this cloak-and-dagger crap — no names given, all that shit — but they did have a job to do and, guess what, they didn't bloody show. Never showed again as it turned out.

Never showed again. What could have happened? Maybe they'd just simply lost their nerve. I phoned Johnny King who said, yes, he'd talk and was available Friday afternoon around 2.30. I wrote down his address. All good. I was getting somewhere.

I checked my emails and found one from Gill and John Ross, the couple from the Denny Graham story: 'Dear Rebecca, Sorry to be the bearer of bad news but John and I have decided we won't be available for your programme after all. On reflection, we feel it's best to put all that behind us.'

Fuck. But they'd been so keen. Should I phone them? I picked up the phone, put it down again. Maybe wait. They might reconsider after a month or two. But this was exactly what happened when you put a story on hold. People pull out and, dammit, by the time I got back to Graham there might not even be a story.

Which made me think of Murray Turner whom I hadn't managed to contact since coming back from holiday. I tried his mobile again. Turned off. I tried his home number. No answer.

Mike peered at me across the multitude of cubicles. 'You all right? How's it going?'

'The usual. One door shuts and another one slams.'

He laughed. 'Not that bad, surely?'

'Maybe not. I think I've got my Tour story. Remember we were talking about the lambs? I've got this gut feeling they could add something extra to this. I want to track them down. Could you find out what you can? All I know is they probably lived in Wellington in 1981.'

He raised his eyebrows, 'The usual wealth of information. I'll see what I can do.'

I stood up. 'I'm seeing your friend Don Taylor this afternoon. Better not be late.'

'He'll look after you,' Mike said. 'He's a good guy.'

Don Taylor had been a cop stationed in Wellington over the time of the Tour. He lived in Tawa in a split-block home with pristine lawns and gorgeous roses along the fence line. He came out onto the concrete terrace and held out his hand as I walked up the path. 'Rebecca, isn't it? Come in,' he said. He pushed back the net curtains bunched around the sliding glass doors. 'Bloody things. June insists on having them, says people can see in and if you let too much sun in it'll wreck the carpet. I suppose she's right. Anyway, sit down. Can I get you a cup of tea?'

I sat down and he sat across from me in the matching gold dralon-covered La-Z-Boy. 'I'm fine, thanks. Mike told me you've not long retired.'

'Five months, twenty-three days.' He smiled self-consciously. 'June says I've got too much time on my hands and it's about time I got myself off to golf or bowls.'

'You miss being a cop?'

'I'd be lying if I said I didn't. Mind you, it was time to go. The old blood pressure was right up, things were starting to get me down. Not many cops stay on into their sixties. It's a tough business.' He shook his head. 'Tougher than it ever was.'

'How long were you in?'

'Just over forty years. I went into Trentham — that's where we trained back then — not long after I left school.'

'You liked being a cop?'

'Some times more than others.'

'How was it being a cop during the Springbok Tour?'

He grinned. 'Well, I agreed I'd talk about it so I suppose this is where we get down to business. To be honest, I didn't like it much at all, but at the same time there was a job to be done and this is the way I saw that job.' He began to count the points off on his square, large fingers. 'One, we had to protect people's right to protest in a lawful manner. Two, we had to protect other people's rights to be able to move around on footpaths and roads in the usual way and to watch a rugby game if that's what they chose to do. Three, we had to protect property. Four, we had to protect the protesters from rugby supporters and, five, we had to protect rugby supporters from the protesters.'

'That sounds fairly simple and straightforward,' I said, grinning back.

'If people hadn't started playing silly buggers it could have been a helluva lot more straightforward.'

'Silly buggers?'

'Silly buggers.' He leaned back in his seat. I could tell from his expression, from his voice, the kind of cop he had been. Reasonable, fair, down-to-earth and absolutely on the side of law and order. I could also tell by the way he was looking at me that he wanted me on that side as well. 'Look, if people want to march down the street to show that they don't agree with something or other, that's their lookout just so long as it doesn't interfere with other people. But when it comes to sitting in the middle of a motorway or blocking up a major road tunnel and stopping folk from going about their business, us cops have to do something about it. As far as I'm concerned, that's not lawful protest.'

'Your sympathy wasn't with the protesters?'

He shook his head again. 'I wasn't on anybody's side, I was just doing my job. Look, anyone has the right to their opinion and the right to make that opinion known. What I didn't like was these smart farts that were behind it all, persuading ordinary folk who genuinely were against the Tour to do crazy stuff that put them and everyone else in danger.'

'Who were these, uh, smart farts?'

His face was flushed. 'There were a lot of them around in those days, commies mainly. Protesting against everything. Just wanting to take everything down.'

'Why would they want to do that?'

'God knows. Spoilt young buggers didn't like authority.' He stood up, opened the doors and the window above his chair, pulled a pack of cigarettes out of his shirt pocket and lit one up. 'I'm not supposed to inside but one won't hurt. Where was I? The protesters, they got themselves into some dangerous bloody situations. If you have people aggravating other folk, breaking down fences and climbing up towers, someone's going to get hurt. There was all this talk about police brutality but we were put in a no-bloody-win position. We had to stop protesters from causing bedlam and from getting themselves damaged as well.'

'They were reckless?'

'You can say that again. If you've got a handful of protesters trying to stop forty thousand people watching a rugby game they're putting themselves at risk. If we hadn't protected them somebody would have been killed and that's for certain.'

'How would you respond to accusations that police acted brutally?'

He sucked hard on his cigarette. 'They were the other lot of silly buggers, weren't they? That Red Squad, they had the idea they were above everyone else, thought they could get away with anything. The Blue Squad, they were doing the same thing, but nobody heard of them. They did their job properly, that's why.'

'Why did you say the Red Squad thought they could get away with anything?'

'Just forget I said that.'

'But —.'

'No, I mean it. All I'll say is there were faults on both sides. But us ordinary cops, we were the meat in the sandwich. Sure, we had those new long batons but that was all we had to protect ourselves. I had mates, in Auckland especially, got hammered. Pelted with eggs and paint, rocks, had their cars turned over. Got attacked with meat-hooks, four-by-twos with nails hanging out of them, anything the bastards could rip off fences.' He took another long draw on his cigarette and made a scoffing noise deep in his throat. 'The Mongrel Mob were there along with all the other gangs. Thugs who couldn't even show you where South Africa was on a map were right there in the middle of it because it gave them the chance to have a go at the cops.'

'What about in Wellington? Did that happen here?'

'Not so bad down here but it was bad enough. Every time there was a game on you thought, "Here's another bloody scrap." The longer it went on, the tougher it got. We had it down from the top: "You'll protect the country no matter what." Didn't matter what you felt about it, it had to be done. So we'd be standing there, hoping like hell we wouldn't have to use the batons and getting all this rubbish from the crowd about being Nazis. *Nazis*. Listen, the Tour was the only point in the whole time I was a cop I could have bailed.'

'What made you keep going?'

'I knew in the end it'd be over. Fifty-six days. I used to cross them off on the calendar.' He went over to the kitchen bench at the far end of the room, stubbed out his cigarette and poured water down the sink to wash it down.

'Good thing June's not here. I'm not supposed to smoke for one thing, and if she saw me getting het up she'd be on about the blood pressure. Now, how about that cup of tea? June made us some biscuits.'

He brought over a pot of tea, pretty rose-coloured cups and saucers, milk in a jug, chocolate chippies on a flowery plate, all set out on a tray. He poured, handed me a cup and saucer and I helped myself to a biscuit. 'I hope bringing all this back hasn't upset you,' I said.

'No, no. It's good for me,' he said, finishing one biscuit and reaching for another. 'I'm not sure about this retirement lark. Getting fat and lazy. Good to have a talk.'

'You'd talk on camera?'

'Oh yeah, sure. If you wanted me to.'

'Any particular memories you'd like to talk about?'

'One I still have a bit of a laugh about. It was in the earlier part of the Tour before it got nasty. There was a march on and a couple of other cops and me were blocking off one of the streets off Lambton Quay. Well, we were standing there, just watching the march go by, nothing happening, and then a whole bunch of protesters split ranks and came running towards us. Seeing there were only the three of us, there wasn't a helluva lot we could do other than order them back, though they didn't take a scrap of notice. But we had this young cop with us, fairly new, you know, all set on making his mark and he went tearing after them, then came back, all hyped up, yelling out he'd arrested one and what should he do with him? Well there we were, dozens of protesters, no back-up, no cars, and he was trying to hold on to this one guy. So I yelled back, "Well, bloody un-arrest him then!"'

'Nice story,' I said. 'I'd like you to tell that on camera. Anything else?'

'This one happened to one of my mates, Gary Williams. He was a good cop, straight up and down, would have done anything for anyone. Well, his wife and her family were among the protesters and, while he never said anything, I knew his sympathies were with them. Anyway, this particular time we were all lined up, I was on one side of the road, he was on the other and we had our batons drawn because that was the order. It wasn't long after Molesworth Street and feelings were running high and these two women protesters, excuse my language, but they were out-and-out bitches. They took a particular dislike to Gary, don't know why, but they started taunting him, going up close as they could, calling him a butcher. "How does your mum feel about you being a butcher? What about your wife?" He got out of the force not long after that. I knew it would happen. He was a good cop but I could tell by his face what happened had wiped him out.'

'Another good story.' I placed my cup carefully on the saucer.

'I just want you to know there was more than just one side to this,' he said, 'and the police weren't the bad guys. Not by a long shot.'

'Can you tell me anything about the lambs?' I said. 'I understand they were based here in Wellington.'

'They were a bit of a laugh,' he said. 'Bit of a nuisance as well. Don't know anything other than that.'

There was a photo album on the coffee table between us and he gestured to it. 'Have a look if you like. I kept a bit of a record of what happened. It was one of the more interesting times of my career, even if it was one of the toughest. I had a mate who was one of the official photographers. He gave me a lot of what's there.'

I leafed slowly through the pages. Scenes I'd become familiar with. The masses of people and the banners. *Stop the Tour.* Candles flicker in the vigil outside Parliament. Wellington Airport just before the test: lines of police in full riot protective gear, the airport's crash boats ready, the fire engines moving onto the tarmac, cars and motorbikes positioned at the exits. A woman holds a banner: 'Judas Airline'.

I paused over a line of policeman, backs straight, batons ready, faces taut with tension. 'That's you, isn't it?'

'Yeah. Good-looking bloke, wasn't I?'

'Not bad. A bit grim, though.'

'It was a grim time.'

I looked down at the photograph and back at him and he chuckled. 'I know what you're thinking. How can that silly old bugger sitting around wondering what to do with himself be that young cop looking like he's all set to clobber someone?'

'I can't believe you'd have wanted to clobber anyone.'

'I didn't but there were times I had to do it. We all mellow a bit with age, you know. Look at Muldoon. Probably the most feared man in New Zealand at one time. He ended up back with Thea in Auckland growing lilies.'

I looked down at the photograph again. 'Isn't that Denny Graham?' I pointed to the face.

'That's Graham, all right. How do you know him?'

'He's my next documentary.'

'Well, you better come back for that one as well. I can tell you a lot of stories about Denny.'

'I'll know where to come. What sort of stories?'

'Bad ones. Graham was a right bastard. He left not long after that was taken and I can't say anyone missed him. I saw in the news he'd got himself into a spot of trouble and that didn't surprise me. Wondered how he'd stayed out of it so long.' He tapped the photograph. 'You know, all this we went through over the Tour, it's taught in schools now. Universities as well. We made history, I suppose, but it was a sad way of making it.'

We made history, I suppose, but it was a sad way of making it. I liked that. I'd get him to say it for the camera.

I shook Don's hand, thanked him, went back to my car and pulled out from the street. He'd been absolutely right. I couldn't reconcile the man he was now with the cop in the photo. That man in the La-Z-Boy: round, a bit jowly, twinkly blue eyes, looked like any granddad. There were photos on the china cabinet of him with little kids sitting on his knees. There'd been the wedding photo as well. June had dark hair and a sweet face beneath the waft of veil looking up at him smiling with such love. I wondered what she thought as he went out in his riot gear. Did she ever think about him hurting people? Did she ever wonder if he'd come home?

16

I drove home thinking over what he'd told me. 'If we hadn't protected them someone would have got killed. We were the meat in the sandwich. If you've got a handful of protesters trying to stop forty thousand people from watching a rugby game they're putting themselves at risk. A sad way of making history.'

I could have him somewhere near the beginning saying that, maybe even use it as the title. But was it too long? And was it catchy enough? I went into the kitchen, opened the fridge and stared into it. I desperately needed to shop; there was absolutely nothing there that shouted 'Eat me!' or even 'Cook me!' There was a four-day-old bag of salad greens, two eggs, a tomato and a scrap of cheddar.

An omelette? I didn't feel like making an omelette, nor did I feel like eating an omelette. I'd had an invitation for drinks that night. Josie Morgan — I barely knew her but she'd left a message. 'I'm having a few people for drinks and wondered if —.' You get a lot of invitations like that when you're in the media. Most of the time from people who want to latch on to you because they think you're someone they possibly should know.

But maybe I would go. I replayed the message. 'It's Josie here. Josie Morgan? I met you last year at the Zenith Christmas party.'

The address was in Hataitai. Not too far away. Anyway, what did I have to lose? I could go, check it out, leave early if I wasn't having a good time and I could pick up a kebab at the Egyptian Palace on the way home and solve the omelette problem. Except I'd have to change my clothes, tart myself up and I was tired. Could I be bothered?

'You *should* be bothered,' my inner voice told me. 'You should get out more, meet new people. It's just too easy for you, going to work every day, working nights, seeing family and the same old friends.' What did I read in that crap magazine at the dentist's? 'If you keep on behaving as you're behaving, you'll keep right on getting what you're getting.' Yet another cliché to add to my already lengthy repertoire.

I went into my bedroom, looked in the full-length mirror and, OK, what I was wearing, my new skinny jeans and black T-shirt, was fine. I really didn't have to change my clothes.

Margo. 'Where've you been? What've you been doing? Have you met anyone?'

Margo, who'd had such a lovely, safe, stable relationship for the past five, safe, lovely, stable years. Margo, who told me they were planning on getting pregnant within the next twelve months. 'Have you thought about the internet?'

Now that I'd ditched Rolly, all that would be starting up again. But, who knows? This could be it. I'd walk into Josie Morgan's house and there he'd be. Mr Perfect.

Yeah, right. Still, I ran my hands through my hair, puffed it up with product, changed my earrings for the new long black sexy ones. Lipstick, a jacket and heels, And yeah. Yeah, I'd do.

The house was easy enough to find. As Josie had said in her directions, you can't miss it, look out for the grey villa, a big number 62 on the letter box. There were a few cars outside and I had to drive further up the road to park. Trekking back down the hill in heels wasn't easy, nor was tramping over the shingle drive, my shoes sinking into the dampish ground beneath the thin layer of stones.

The door was open. I tapped and peered in. The music was good, Hollie Smith, and there was the sound of fairly animated voices so someone was having an OK time. A woman came to the door and I recognised her from the party. Josie. I remembered she was a journo, a freelancer, and she'd done a bit of research work for Zenith. She was little and quite pretty in a pale skin, blue eyes and blonde kind of way. Quite pretty and very animated. 'Rebecca! It's so fabulous to see you!'

'You too! Thanks so much for inviting me! What a gorgeous house!' Etc.

I followed her along a hallway into the living room where we paused while she poured and handed me a brimming glass of pinot gris. I turned around — and it was girls' night. Dressed up to the eyeballs, huddled into tight little bunches, waving wine glasses, they were going for it. '*Did* you? *Did* he? Oh *really*. Oh my *god*.'

Believe me, I love women. Some of my best friends are women. But en masse with a few glasses of wine under their belts, they *bray*. Maybe I do too among friends, but fifteen or so women all dripping glitz and braying — I just wasn't in the mood.

I looked down at my glass. It was very full, the sort of oversized glass that you sip over an hour or so along with a reasonable number of nibbles to blot it up. If I tossed it back on an empty stomach I'd be too pissed to drive. And, anyway, I *couldn't* toss it back and immediately leave, not without seeming rude.

I looked around. There was no one I recognised that I could attach myself to and indulge in a bit of gossip with. One or two of the brayers eyed me, taking in what I was wearing, then immersed themselves back within the huddle. I turned to Josie who was now chattering excitedly to a tall woman — henna hair, tight black jacket and pants — who had just emerged from the kitchen carrying a tray of the type of exquisite savouries so teeny-tiny you can't actually taste or even feel in your mouth. 'Did you? *Did* he? Oh *really*. Oh my *god*.'

'Rebecca, do you know Suz? Suz, this is Rebecca. Now I must just go and —.' Josie vanished into the kitchen, leaving us to make conversation.

Suz was beaming at me.

'You're Rebecca Thorne, aren't you?'

'Yes I am.'

'You did that thing about the Bligh case, didn't you?'

This was why I avoided going out among strangers. Her expression was *avid*. But I gave her the advantage of the doubt. Suz was most likely a perfectly pleasant woman who had erroneously imagined I liked to talk about all that.

'Oh, that was ages ago,' I said in my slightly cool, definitely uninterested voice, terminating eye contact and gazing vaguely around the room. That generally worked when people brought the subject up. Anyone with any sensitivity at all could not possibly have failed to understand it was a subject I didn't care to discuss. But Suz wasn't having any of it.

'But it must have been so interesting.' Her smile was rigidly fixed and she was actually quivering with — what? Intrigue? Curiosity? 'I mean you met him and everything, didn't you? Like, you believed he was innocent, didn't you? You were the one, really, who actually got him out.'

'Not entirely. Uh, Suz, what do you do? You're from Wellington?'

But on it came. 'He got what he deserved, though, didn't he? In the end? They got him for the other murder as well, didn't they? That woman's boyfriend? So . . .'

I fixed my eyes on her, didn't say a word. I've found that, on the whole, people, however rude or senseless, generally shut up if you remain utterly silent.

Change of tack. This woman was persistent. The smile dropped, the voice lowered to an 'I'm actually a very caring and understanding person' register. 'I really, really understand. It must have been awful. Didn't he *threaten you*? Look, if you would like to talk to someone . . .'

She was pressing something into my hand. Her card. What the fuck *was* this woman, a counsellor or a crystals therapist or a fucking clairvoyant?

I took a swift glance downwards. 'Assistant editor: *Je* magazine.'

She was working for *Je*? No wonder she was desperate. I almost felt sorry for her. I looked back down at the card. 'Suz Brownie.' Brownie. Sickly sweet. And very, very bad for you.

Though I gazed back at her with my very best blank-and-frosty look, my 'last chance before I completely lose it at you' look, I had an almost irresistible instinct to giggle, the utter craziness of me actually thinking I should come to this drinks thing, thinking it would be *good* for me and could be *fun*. That I might meet, for god's sake, an actual man.

But she was still babbling on. 'People should know your story, Rebecca. I can understand why you wouldn't talk at first, you must have been just so raw. And fragile. But couldn't now be the time for closure?'

'Raw and fragile?' I said sweetly.

She was making progress at last. She'd obviously got me alongside. 'Mmm. Raw. And so devastated. When you — you know? — believe in someone and they let you down? It must have been so depressing.'

Not nearly so depressing as doing a crap job for yet another crap magazine that's about to go down the tube, darling.

I put my glass down. I smiled. She smiled back.

'Raw, fragile, devastated *and* depressed? Well, you certainly have me thoroughly worked out, don't you?' I said breezily. 'But, you know, I really have to go.'

I put down my glass, edged my way past her and through the brayers. And saw Rolly.

Rolly was walking through the doorway into the living room and aiming directly towards me.

Rolly?

I knew Josie knew him. I knew she'd worked with him way back some time. I'd even seen them talking together at the Zenith Christmas party. But what in the hell was Rolly doing at a girls-only party?

I didn't want to be in a social situation which included Rolly, especially not one where people were crammed into a very small space. It wasn't exactly the kind of situation where I could catch his eye and casually smile or wave — he was less than three metres away. I'd been all set to discreetly slink out but now it would look as if I was going because he'd turned up. But, dammit, what did it matter what anyone thought? I crossed the room rapidly, waving vaguely towards Josie and mouthing something which was supposed to mean 'Thanks but I have to go', and took my bag off the hook in the hallway.

I'd probably beaten my record for the shortest time ever at a party. I negotiated the drive in my heels again and was halfway up the road when I heard bounding feet coming up behind me, felt somebody catch me by the arm. 'Aren't you going to say hello?' he said jovially.

I swung around, pulling away my arm. 'You're bloody stalking me, aren't you? You were outside my house. You've been phoning and hanging up. It's you, isn't it?'

All the frustration and fury at Suz and at Bligh and at fucking *life* was there in my voice which was loud and shrill and startled even me so much I actually wanted to call it back and modify it into something much more normal and rational. But that tone of voice was out there and I'm not good at backing down. I stood there glaring at him.

He sprang back, looking slightly alarmed. 'Of course I'm not stalking you.'

'Then how come you're here? How come someone I barely know invites me for drinks and you just happen to turn up as well?'

He looked away, started to pull at his ear. I knew that particular gesture. It was his 'I'm decidedly uncomfortable' sign.

'I've known Josie for ages. I didn't know she was having drinks tonight. I just dropped by.' He was still pulling, wouldn't meet my eyes. *Yeah and so why are you edgy?*

'Don't give me that shit. You put her up to this, didn't you? You asked her to invite me. So what do you want?'

'I don't want anything,' he said, 'other than for us to behave like reasonable adults and say hello to each other from time to time. I really can't see why you're being hostile. Remember, it was you who broke up with me.'

'Just stop sending me photos, OK?'

I darted another intensely evil look at him, turned my back and walked off. He'd looked shocked, in fact plain stupid, standing there staring at me with his mouth open. Well, let him be bloody shocked. Maybe he'd leave me alone now.

Egyptian Palace had already closed. There was a Thai takeaway a few blocks further along but the queue was so long and I'd so completely lost any semblance of good humour I drove past. Fuck it, I'd starve.

When in hell would people stop asking me about the Bligh case?

I parked in my carport and went inside. Put on some soothingly soft jazz, poured wine, poached the eggs, put them on top of buttery toast and curled up on my sofa with a plate and a glass.

Rolly's *face*. I giggled a bit to myself.

Get a grip, Rebecca. If you carry on like this you'll have no friends whatsoever. Maybe a bath.

By the time I'd soaked myself in my bathtub filled with semi-hot water and a good dollop of bath salts and finished off another glass of wine, I'd giggled quite a bit more.

Raw, fragile, devastated and depressed. The expressions flittering across Suz's face — that truly awful, false, cloying concern followed by perplexity then panic as she came to the realisation that she really hadn't handled this well.

And Rolly. I *had* sounded fierce. I'd have guaranteed that by now he'd be counting himself fortunate that his grandmother's ring remained intact and could be remodelled for a future, pleasanter and more moderate woman.

I dried myself. Flannelette jammies, my nice, thick towelling robe, my big, warm bed and the book I'd been saving. *Who needs a man?*

Sometime in the night I woke up. It was always like this when I was in the midst of a story. There were too many ideas running around in my head to sleep properly; I thought too damn much. And that noise was there again. I'd noticed it just recently. Something loose, something lifting, dragging, maybe in the ceiling or on the roof. It's what you get with older houses, Dad always said, a few extra creaks and squeaks.

Tomorrow I had the interview set up with Janine Blair, there was the meeting with Tim in the afternoon, then there was Johnny King to see, my car was due for a warrant and I had to pick up my jacket from the dry cleaners and. And. There'd been something niggling at me, something at the back of my head.

I'd taken out my jacket, the grey one, to be cleaned. The grey jacket beside the black-and-white jacket and then the skirts and dresses. The dresses. It always stood out among the mostly black other stuff. I always noticed it.

Where is my blue dress?

I turned on the light, got up and opened up the wardrobe. I hadn't noticed it because it wasn't actually there. Had I hung it up in the guest bedroom? Oh *shit*, had I left it behind in Rarotonga? I'd taken it off, folded it and — dammit — I was positive I'd put it in my suitcase. But had I hung it up when I got home? I couldn't remember.

I prowled around the house, checked the laundry, chests of

drawers. It wasn't in the house, it wasn't anywhere. I switched on my computer and sent off an email marked urgent to the resort we'd stayed in.

OK, it's your favourite dress, but it'll turn up. You probably left it behind. Just calm down.

I switched off the lights. Willed myself to go back to sleep.

Around 4 am the information that Rolly still had a key to the front door wafted into my consciousness. How in hell had I missed that? I got up, heaved a heavy chest in front of the door, ensured for about the third time that night that the French doors were locked and the windows shut, and got back into bed.

Was I completely bloody paranoid or did I actually have something to worry about?

'You look stunning in that dress.'

But for god's sake, this was Rolly.

'So sexy.'

Rolly would not come into my house and steal my dress.

'You know, there's that photo on the net of you at the Qantas? I get it up on the screen sometimes at work and I look at you and feel just so bloody proud.'

I knew Rolly. Rolly would never, ever behave as weirdly as that. Would he?

I'd phone him. First thing in the morning I'd phone and ask for my key back. But, in the unlikely event that Rolly had turned into the stalker from hell, how could I be certain he hadn't made a copy?

'So sexy.'

OK. The most sensible solution was to go ahead and have the lock changed. Anyway, it was still the original lock, probably not secure, and maybe if the lock was changed the front door would stop shuddering. Problem solved. I'd phone a locksmith in the morning.

I finally drifted into sleep around 5 am partly because I was exhausted and partly because it had started to pour with rain and I'd decided that Rolly, however much spite and hostility he harboured towards me, would be unlikely to consider an attempt on my house in this kind of weather.

And so I overslept, got into the office late and earned myself a few black marks from Anne, who punctiliously juggles her roles as Tim's PA plus receptionist plus general overseer of everything. She darted out of Tim's office, her hair, clothing, make-up as always impeccable and her voice sharp. 'Your 9 am interview has been waiting a good ten minutes now, Rebecca.' I poked my head inside the door, introduced myself, apologised profusely and asked if she'd like coffee.

'Tea, please.'

I made a pot of English Breakfast and took it along to the broom cupboard referred to as the 'interview room' on a tray with our nicest cups and saucers and a jug filled with real milk. We even had some reasonably fresh Shrewsbury biscuits. I had a long list of names of people who had marched against the Tour but this was one I particularly wanted to talk to since, when I'd phoned about a possible interview, she'd told me she remembered the lambs well.

I left the door slightly open — there was no window and we had to breathe after all. I poured the tea and placed it on the table in front of her. 'Janine, I really am so sorry I'm late.'

'I don't mind at all,' she said. 'I haven't been in a television studio before. It really is quite exciting.'

'Do you mind if I record this?'

'Not at all.' She waved her small, white hands at my recorder. 'Go ahead by all means.'

'When I spoke to you,' I said, 'you told me you remember the lambs. Can you tell me why?'

She smiled. 'Curiosity, mainly. I'd been a dancer myself — I was teaching ballet by then — and I saw they were very capable dancers and wondered who they were.'

'Did you find out?'

'No, I never knew.'

'You told me you noticed them at the earlier marches in Wellington.'

She took a biscuit and sipped her tea. 'I didn't go to any more after Molesworth Street. As a ballet teacher I had to be physically fit and I couldn't risk being injured. But I saw the lambs at the first march in May. Bunny Street, that was. They were among the first to arrive and they were near the front as we chanted and sang and marched through the city to the civic centre. They were at the front in Marion Street, as well, on the July march.'

'Did you ever speak to them?'

'I never got close enough to either of them. They seemed a very tight unit. I don't remember seeing them speaking to anyone else.'

'So you really had no idea who they were?'

'I did suspect that one of them was a past student but I made some enquiries and found out he was overseas at the time. By then, though, I'd become quite fascinated by them. They were very good dancers, very skilled, and even after I'd stopped going on the marches myself I watched out for them on television.'

'You were particularly interested in them since they were dancers?'

'There was that,' she said slowly. 'They danced beautifully, but most of all I appreciated the risks they took to make people laugh during a very unhappy time. They did their best to defuse dreadful situations. The Red Squad, for instance, well, you'll know how terribly seriously they took themselves and how threatening they were all kitted out in their gear, but when the lambs were behind them mimicking the way they marched they didn't seem quite so frightening. I would imagine the lambs would have taken quite a few knocks from police and rugby supporters but they were always out in front keeping people going when things started getting grim.'

'Would you classify the lambs as an important component within the whole anti-Tour movement?'

'Oh, I would. They were utterly dedicated to it. They were at every major game — Gisborne, Hamilton, New Plymouth — then they followed the teams right down to Invercargill, through the South Island and back up again.'

'But they dropped out just before the Wellington test?'

'You know,' she said, putting down her teacup, 'that's something that's always mystified me. I mean, they were at the airport on the Friday afternoon. After that, nothing. What was the story behind that? You don't know, do you?'

'You're saying they were at the airport on the day before the test?'

That was something I hadn't known.

'They were right there but after that they seemed to have disappeared. What could have happened?'

What could have happened? I looked up at the clock. A couple of hours to write up the interview and make a few phone calls before my meeting with Johnny King. But first I had to make absolutely sure my house was secure. I'd almost convinced myself as I opened up my curtains to the daylight, showered, grabbed some coffee in my so-familiar house and driven along the so-familiar streets that this really was crazy, it was all in my head. But Sensible Rebecca kicked in with better to be on the safe side, better safe than sorry.

So Sensible Rebecca started phoning and five locksmiths later there was one who would be able to be at my house at 4.45 that day. Fantastic. I'd be able to sleep free of the fear Rolly could be sneaking in and stealing my dresses.

My mobile rang. 'Rebecca? It's Josie.'

Josie? Setting-me-up-with-Rolly Josie?

Unfriendly and standoffish voice. 'I really don't have much time right now, Josie. Perhaps I could call you back.' *As if.*

'Rebecca, all I wanted to say is, well, I'm really, really sorry about last night. Rolly said you were offended about him being there. I just wanted to tell you it was a total mistake. It was supposed to be just a girls' night, you know, and then he turned up quite by accident.'

'OK. It doesn't matter.'

'Suz said you and she were having a really good talk but then you saw Rolly and got upset and left. I'm so sorry. I wouldn't *ever* want to upset you.'

'Let's just forget it. I really do have to go.'

'Rolly's in a bit of a state about it. We really do want to stay friends with you.'

What was she going on about? Neither of them were my friends.

'Rolly said you thought he'd put me up to inviting you. I want you to know that definitely wasn't the case.'

Could I bring myself to hang up while she was still talking?

'Because it actually was Suz who wanted to meet you and I'd just hate it if something was getting in the way of you two getting together and talking. She thought you seemed quite interested in talking about, you know, Connor Bligh.'

What? 'Josie, believe me, Rolly turning up did not get in the way of Suz and me getting together. That's just never going to happen.'

I clicked off. Was she insane or just plain stupid? She was exactly the type of journalist I loathe. Devious, scheming, using people for what they could give her — and brainless enough to admit to it.

Johnny King was a silversmith who had a gallery and workshop on Cuba Street. He put his Closed sign out and I spent the first half hour or so drooling over exquisite necklaces, bangles, rings and to-die-for earrings. 'Closing down like this can't be good for business,' I said, picking up my so-far favourite earrings: arcs of silver with tiny black pearls embedded inside. They looked like baby pea-pods.

'It's all right,' he said. 'I'm starting to sell quite a bit of my stuff online now. Try those on if you like.'

'I don't dare,' I said, glancing at the price tag.

'Put them on. See how they feel. Jewellery should feel right as well as look right.'

I removed my dangly plastics and slipped them into my ears. He narrowed his eyes and looked at me. 'Yeah, not bad. Keep them on while we're talking.'

'Oliver Neil said you'd be a good person to talk to,' I said.

'I got to know Ollie when we were both in COST. We still see quite a bit of each other.' He grinned. 'We have lunch and a few too many beers together whenever he gets into town.'

'Ah ha,' I said, getting my dictaphone out of my bag. 'You were the mysterious partner in crime he was about to meet up with.'

Interview: Johnny King. COST member.
You were part of COST from when it was first set up?

Yes. Once the announcement came that the Tour was going ahead there was a lot of anger against the government and the rugby union who didn't give a toss about anything other than rugby. I personally felt very good about being part of a movement where people felt the same as me and were prepared to stand up for that.

Oliver told me the early COST meetings were orderly and well controlled. As more people from various disparate factions joined, did they remain that way?

We had Lindsay Wright in the chair and he was a fantastic negotiator. But, yes, as you would expect, there were disagreements as COST grew and the Tour went on and things got tougher. What was decided at the Palmerston North game, for example. We were met by the Red Squad with their batons drawn and our leaders had to decide whether we'd push forward or retreat. They decided it was too bloody dangerous to try storming those brutal bastards and we backed off. Afterwards there was a lot of flak flying around accusing COST leadership of losing its guts.

Who was critical of the decision?

The Auckland groups, mainly, but at the following meeting on the Monday night here there was a lot of anger expressed by the more radical members who'd wanted to take the fuckers on. At the same time, a lot of people, including me, were happy with the decision. The ethos COST was built on was we were tactical rather than confrontational. If there was a reasonable likelihood of marchers getting hurt, we'd step back.

I understand there was some police infiltration into the meetings.

Yeah. One in particular, I remember, was this young woman who started turning up to the plenary meetings. She said she was from New Plymouth and had come to Wellington to look for work. Why I first noticed her, though, was because of what she had on her feet. I've always had an eye for detail, I suppose, and if something stands out in some way it catches my attention.

So [laughing] she was wearing snakeskin stilettos?

In fact, the most awful ugg boots with matted sheepskin around the top. Very nasty. I couldn't help looking at them whenever we were in meetings. I used to wonder how she could bear to wear them at all, let alone in public. And then I also started noticing she asked a heap of questions that didn't have a lot to do with what she was involved in. And I started noticing how she was always hanging around committee members and asking more questions, that she was, in fact, unusually inquisitive. So I told people what I was starting to suspect and we tried to work out a way of busting her.

And did you?

We — the committee that is — waited until she was hovering around and then we went into the kitchen and shut the door, as we used to when we wanted to talk something over. Everyone kept on talking fairly loudly while I sneaked over and yanked open the door and there she was right outside. Well, it was all fairly unpleasant. We accused her and she cried and denied it and we threw her out. This is what made me laugh, though. A few years later I was in Masterton and I picked up the local newspaper and there she was on the front cover. The community bloody police officer.

Still wearing her ugg boots?

They'd been replaced with nice, shiny lace-ups.

I've heard the odd rumour that there were members of the police force who were sympathetic to your position and were prepared to pass on information.

Yes, that did happen. Just after Molesworth Street I got a call from someone saying his brother was a cop and wanted to help us. We set up a meeting and he said he'd do what he could so long as it didn't mean doing anything which would put his fellow policemen in any danger. We used to meet on Fridays in a garden shed and he'd tell me what he knew about what the police were planning. We had this code for contacting each other and we used to leave messages in plastic bags in a letter box. Great stuff. Took me right back to 'Boy's Own Adventures'.

I've been told Muldoon and his government were prepared to use bully tactics to suppress resistance to decisions and policies. Do you know of any threats made to COST, either to individual members or to the organisation as a whole?

Nothing direct but there was a lot of crap that went on. People being phoned and threatened in the middle of the night, that kind of shit. But who would know where that came from?

Can you tell me anything about the lambs?

Why do you ask?

I've been told they were expected at the Wellington test, that they had a job to do but didn't turn up. If protesters were being bullied and threatened, I can't help wondering —.

If there was a bit of pressure applied for them to stay away?

Yes. Perhaps the police found out who they were. Do you know anything?

The feeling at COST was they were unreliable and so when they didn't turn up on test day people were pissed off but not really surprised.

Yes? But you haven't really answered my question.

Do I know anything? I don't. Not really.

Not really?

All I know is the night before the test a young guy crossing the green belt at Thorndon was attacked and there were rumours.

You think he could have been one of the lambs?

I don't know for certain but it's possible.

What was his name?

I don't know that either. His name wasn't made public when it happened, one of those 'family members have not yet been notified' situations, and then if it ever was published I didn't see it.

What happened to him?

He died.

I turned off the dictaphone. Johnny King was watching me intently. 'I've been looking at you,' he said, 'while we've been talking. Those earrings aren't right, not for you. On the other hand . . .' He opened a drawer and dropped another pair into my hand. Long silver strands threaded with soft blue gemstones. 'Sapphires. I think they match your eyes. Hold them up. Did you know the Persians believed the Earth was an enormous sapphire and the sky the reflection?'

I held them up to the light. 'No, and I didn't know you could get pale blue sapphires either.'

I walked over to the mirror and threaded them through my ears, trying to ignore the price tag. They *did* match my eyes. Dammit, I'd missed out on a ring. I deserved them. I got out my credit card. 'How long have you been doing this?'

'I suppose it's a bit of a cliché but the Tour really did change me. I'd just qualified in law when I joined COST but after all that I wanted nothing to do with it. So this is what I do. I try to make beautiful things.'

I walked out onto the street. There was a café nearby and I ordered a large flat white, sat at the seat nearest to the window and watched the people going by while I waited for the screech and bubble of the coffee machine to subside and my coffee to materialise.

A young guy crossing the green belt at Thorndon was attacked. There were rumours.

The coffee was good. Creamy at the top with a fierce blast of caffeine underneath. I picked up my mobile and called Mike. 'Remember I asked you about the lambs? Someone I just interviewed, well, he told me a young guy was beaten up and died on the Friday night before the test.'

'And you're assuming he could have been one of the lambs?'

'It's possible.'

'Name?'

'I don't have a name. It happened in the bush area near Thorndon if that helps at all.'

'No promises but I'll see what I can do.'

The locksmith turned up, told me I was doing the right thing changing the lock, this was the sort of old, worn-out rubbish anyone could break into in less than a couple of minutes, and I was lucky I hadn't been robbed.

He drilled, swore under his breath, drilled and swore and muttered and screwed things in, told me if I wanted to be sure of the house being safe I should have him put on one of these new kinds of chain-locks while he was there, much safer than this old one which would snap if you put even a little bit of pressure on it.

I said he could. He gave me keys, demonstrated repeatedly how both the lock and the chain-lock worked, explained as if to a slow-witted child why I should never leave a key under bricks or bins or in an unlocked garage since criminals always knew exactly where to look and I should be extra careful living as I did close to the street.

OK, this was one of those protective granddad types who truly believed any young woman living on her own needs painstaking instruction on the art of caring for both her house and her person. That, combined with him being some sort of born-again locksmith, made him extra vigilant. I knew he was well-meaning, I knew he wanted to be helpful, but did changing a lock really have to take almost two hours? I was due over at Anna and David's for dinner and I wanted time for a play with the kids before they went to bed. But eventually he was gone and my house was suitably protected.

I phoned Anna. 'I'm on my way.'

'Great. I haven't even thought about dinner yet. Nina's been so grumpy and —.'

'What if I pick up takeaways?'

'You are such a darling. Indian? Mild chickpea curry for the kids.'

I pulled on my jacket, picked up the bottle of wine I had ready on the table, locked the door behind me according to instructions. And my mobile beeped.

I'm lying beside a pool. Our own private pool in Rarotonga.

So very private that I am naked.

17

I got into my car, backed out, my heart still thumping. Should I phone the police?

And say exactly what? My ex-boyfriend phones my house and hangs up when I answer? My ex-boyfriend is sending me photos?

How many? Three photos. Four, possibly five, calls.

It didn't seem all that serious.

But a naked photo. I imagined explaining *that* to a policeman across a desk at the police station. I'd see that little shift in his eyes. *She poses naked for her boyfriends?*

I saw my ex-boyfriend parked in his car across the road from my house. He turns up to parties I go to. My ex-boyfriend has stolen my dress.

One party. You don't know he stole your dress. You don't even know he's making the phone calls.

I called in at the nearest Korma Sutra then headed across town. Anna had just started back working part-time at the law firm she was with but Wednesday was one of her days off. She was sitting on a sofa reading to Nina, her extra-adorable one-year-old. Lily was playing some sort of complicated game which involved her ever-expanding Sylvanian family of small bears, rabbits and badgers going on holiday in a caravan and Ted was making star shapes with playdough and a cutter. Those kids are so cute, so clever and so perfect in every way that I tell myself even if I never have any of my own I've got them.

'Hold this one.' Anna held out Nina who obligingly held out her arms and grinned. 'I'll pour the wine. I'm *desperate*.'

I glanced at myself in their most recent acquisition, a mirror framed with a thick band of turquoise green that caught the light from the window. Bloody hell, they always find such gorgeous things, they have such impeccable taste. And there was me, pale, fraught, my hair needed attention and —.

'Oo-ooh,' I said as Nina took my finger and bit down. 'Another tooth?' I gathered her close against me. That heavy, comforting, small, round body resting against me. The smell of her, her little shell ears, the wisps of white-blonde hair. 'I love babies.'

'You wouldn't be quite so entranced with that tooth if you'd been up with it all night,' said Anna. I watched as she poured wine into two gleaming tulip-shaped glasses. She was dressed in grey trackies, a pink singlet top and with her fresh face and hair pulled back into a ponytail she looked about fourteen. Unlike anyone else I knew, Anna had babies and immediately emerged as trim and stunning as ever.

Anna sipped her wine and looked on as the kids and I played games and read stories and I painted Lily's toenails with the new 'real-red' polish I'd just bought, on the lengthily negotiated contract between Anna, Lily and me that she would wear socks and shoes to school the next day instead of open-toe sandals. David came home and we ate and the kids got bathed, more stories and the house was finally silent. David poured wine. Anna and I reclined on the sofas.

'I'm wiped out,' I said. 'I don't know how you do that every day.'

Anna's eyes were tightly closed. 'Neither do I,' she said faintly.

'And she always appears utterly composed and beautiful,' David said, handing over our glasses and winking at me.

'Yeah, right,' she said. 'I need a haircut and . . . actually what I need is a full-blown makeover.'

'I'll put out a Trinny and Susannah alert,' I said. 'Get them to make an emergency trip to New Zealand. They can do me at the same time.'

I glugged my wine back. Nicely anaesthetising. I held the glass in the air and tipped it back and forward at David. 'I saw this woman doing this at a waiter at a café in Auckland once. Terribly obnoxious but it had the desired effect.'

'Mine too, please, darling,' Anna said. 'I was completely alcohol-deprived all the time I was pregnant and feeding Nina so I deserve a night of total indulgence.'

David grinned and refilled our glasses. 'I take it you're staying the night?'

'Please.' I loved staying the night in their guest bedroom with the nice sheets and the nice soaps in the bathroom, and in the morning the sun sneaking in through the blinds and the kids rushing in and jumping all over me.

'We haven't seen all that much of you lately,' David said. 'What's been happening? How's this Tour thing going?'

'I'm enjoying it. I think it's starting to come together.'

'Good. That's good.' David looked and sounded distracted, 'Uh, listen, I've got to ask you this. What's up with Rolly?'

Shit, what else was going on? 'Why do you have to ask me?'

'I keep running into him and whenever I do he looks furtive as hell.'

I just did not want to get into all this. 'It can't have anything to do with me. It's been over for weeks.'

Anna was watching me. 'You look upset. Has something happened?'

What do they say? A problem aired is a problem shared. Maybe it was time I told someone. 'Look, it's probably nothing but I keep running into him as well. I, well, I saw him parked outside my house and then he turned up at this party I was invited to.'

'That's odd,' Anna said.

'It's probably all just a coincidence, but he sent me some photos. It was confusing because his number didn't come up but it must have been him.'

'What sort of photos?'

'Just me in Rarotonga. You know.'

'Anything else?' David, this time.

'I've had a couple of phone calls where someone's listened and then hung up.'

'This could be serious,' Anna said. 'If you get another phone call like that you must have it checked out.'

'It might have nothing to do with Rolly,' I said. 'It could be someone getting a wrong number.'

'Wrong numbers *and* photos?' David said.

'I don't like this,' Anna said. 'I've had quite a bit to do with relationship violence. Some people really can't cope with being dumped and they turn nasty. I know Rolly's very controlling.'

'I wouldn't go so far as to say that.'

'What about that time you were going out and he asked you to change out of the trousers you were wearing and put on a dress?'

We'd been going for drinks and dinner with 'my colleagues', as he always referred to them. Never 'Mary and Jack and Richard' but 'my colleagues'. Whatever had I seen in that man?

'Yes, but I hadn't realised we were going to Logan Brown,' I said.

You look stunning in that dress.

Anna raised her eyebrows.

'OK, I suppose you're right, he was a little controlling. He was used to things going his way. You know, only child syndrome and all that.'

'What about when they didn't?'

I thought about him sulking when the coconut muffins failed to materialise for his breakfast in Rarotonga. 'He got a bit miffed. It wasn't anything bad.'

'Rolly saw his life all set out with you in it. You've pulled the mat out from under him and he can't let it go.'

You look stunning in that dress.

'Anna, I really don't think. I mean, this is *Rolly*.'

You know, there's that photo on the net of you at the Qantas? I get it up on the screen sometimes at work and I look at you and feel just so bloody proud.

'I don't think you're taking this nearly seriously enough.'

So sexy.

I was starting to feel panicky. I took a couple of deep breaths, tried to clear my head. Anna looked tense and her voice was shrill. Anna wasn't *like* this. What was going on?

'The thing is,' David said, 'we've had a couple of calls as well.'

'Someone phones then hangs up?'

'Not straight away.'

'Have you had them checked out?'

'They've come from call boxes.'

I couldn't get my head around this. 'I can't believe Rolly would do that.'

Anna looked hard at me. 'I've got a friend who's been involved with the Robertson case in Auckland. You know the one where the guy murdered his ex-girlfriend?'

'Yes, of course I do.'

'Well, there we have Gary Robertson, a seemingly normal and successful young man, who just could not deal with the end of a relationship and so he kidnapped and strangled the girl who'd rejected him.'

'But we're talking about Rolly. He could never be dangerous.'

'Yes and if anyone had had a conversation like we're having before that man murdered his girlfriend that's exactly what they would have said. "But we're talking about *Gary*." People can never believe that kind of thing can happen.'

'I just don't believe —.'

'What do you really know about Rolly? What do you know about his other relationships?'

'Hey,' David said. 'Hey, let's stop this right there. There's probably nothing going on but we should be careful. If there are any more phone calls for either of us, we'll take it to the police. And, Rebecca, if Rolly contacts you, just be very cautious about what you say to him and if he comes around it might be safest if you don't let him into the house. Now, let's all just try to relax.'

We were silent.

'I'm sorry,' Anna said. 'But please take care, that's all. Promise?'

'Promise,' I said.

'More wine,' David said, 'and let's watch that DVD I picked up last week. It's supposed to be funny.'

18

Mike looked up as I walked into the office. 'I've got something for you, my mate,' he said, coming over to my desk. 'Take a look at this.'

He was looking fairly pleased with himself as he handed me the folder. 'Photographs at the scene, reports of the initial crime scene, transcripts of media releases, forensic pathologist's report and the coroner's report. In fact, the complete works.'

'Mike, you're a gem,' I said.

I opened the top file. Sat down quickly.

'Shit, Rebecca.' Mike looked embarrassed and extremely apologetic. 'I should have warned you. You develop the stomach for that kind of thing when you've been a cop.'

I looked down again at the photographs, trying to take them in, at the same time trying to breathe myself out of the woozy, sick-cold feeling creeping across my skin.

A body. Face down. Arms clenched around the head.

'Looks like they really put the boot in.' Mike was watching me carefully.

The lower part of the torso and arms, the backs of the hands and legs were dappled and ridged by livid bruising.

There in the darkness. Boots and fists. One after another after another.

I looked more closely. The photographs had been taken in early-morning winter when light was limited and the images were hazy despite the flashlights which would have been used. But.

'What — what in the hell is that?'

Mike cleared his throat as I stared up at him. 'He was, uh, he was sexually assaulted.'

My hands flew up to my face. 'It's —. My god, there are some sickos around.'

128

'Yeah, it's a bottle. That's how he was found when the police were called. But that does make it unlikely this was linked to him being one of the anti-Tour lot. This was a mob of thugs, no question about it.'

I closed the file. 'I think. I think I'm going to have to look at this later. Did you come up with any evidence this guy could have been one of the lambs?'

'It seems he was. It's all in the report. Des Horton at Central Police Station told me. He was one of the cops called after he was found.'

'What made him so sure?'

'It all tied in. He fitted the profile; they found out from his family he was around the right age, he was a dancer and he was gay. Then the fact that the lambs never appeared again was a giveaway.'

'They tracked down his family?'

'Yes. He had a wallet with his driver's licence in his pocket.'

'Did you talk to Des Horton about the family?'

'Des said he'll tell you what he knows. We go way back, he's a good bloke, and he said to just give him a call,' Mike said. 'Rebecca, did you look at the name?'

I looked back at the folder. I'd been so fixated on the photographs it hadn't registered. 'Eric Woolley,' I said.

'Looks like the guy had a sense of humour.'

I took the police file home with me at the end of the day and put it on my desk. Then I occupied myself with the type of cleaning and tidying tasks which are so tedious and barely necessary that I hardly ever do them. Folding, dusting, wiping, polishing, sweeping. Avoidance behaviour.

I'd seen other photographs; bodies stabbed, shot, strangled. But this body. This sad, ruined body.

Does everyone have that fear? You're on your own in the dark, you hear something. Someone else is there. Somebody is following.

I ate while I watched the news, then I went into my study, opened up the folder.

'The body of a young man, understood to have been the victim of a serious assault in the early hours of Saturday August 29, was discovered in the Thorndon Reserve area at around 6.30 am.

'The victim, described as a Caucasian in his early twenties, of slim build and average stature and wearing a black woollen hat, dark green jacket and jeans, is understood to have suffered severe head injuries from the attack.

'Detective Constable Scott from Wellington CID described it as an assault of a very serious nature and would like to hear from anyone who was in the Thorndon park and reserve area on the evening of Friday August 28 or the early hours of Saturday morning. Police are unable to disclose the identity of the victim until family members have been notified.'

I spread the photographs across my desk. He is lying at the side of a track leading into the reserve. The ground around him is blurred with murky puddles and the trees and bush appear weighed down, sodden. He is spread-eagled, dark splotches across the buttocks and legs, arms and hands. Then the close-ups, the blood pooled and coagulated around his head.

Another deep swallow of wine. Another deep, hard breath inwards.

The photographs included in the forensic pathologist's report show that his body has been cleaned and his head shaved. The skin on his forearms is so lacerated that in some parts it is torn away and there are deep, raw gouges along his spine, on his legs.

As Harry said, they really put the boot in.

I read through the report. Multiple lesions, three broken ribs on the left side, rupture of the left kidney, head wounds. Cause of death: internal bleeding.

Despite the bruises and swelling it was easy to tell by the shape of his face and delicate features that Eric Woolley had been a beautiful young man.

Where had he been that night? What had happened? Had he been walking home from visiting friends or a late dinner, taken a short cut across the park and they'd been there? Had they been in a pack? Gay bashers out to teach some fag a lesson?

I wondered what he thought when he saw those moving shadows there in the dark?

Probably they're harmless enough, just keep on walking, head up, shoulders squared, keep on walking.

Or should I run? Should I start running now?

Can I outrun them?

If I shout, will anybody hear?

Did they call out to him? Or did they just come at him with their fists and their boots, this 'gay-boy', this 'other'. What is it that closes off the recognition of shared humanity? How can you hurt a stranger?

When did he know he was going to die?

I scanned back through the report. Blood alcohol content, 0.02.

Maybe he'd had a couple of drinks in a bar, met up with the wrong guys who followed him, beat him up and shoved a bottle up his arse to let everyone know how much they hated queers. Anyway, whatever happened that night, the possibility that Eric Woolley had been beaten up by cops or rugby thugs was fairly much shot.

Still, the lambs were a great story and while one was almost certainly dead the other most likely was alive. I phoned Des Horton next morning and asked if he'd talk to me. He told me to come right over to Central Police Station: he was available for most of the day.

He came out of the office holding out his hand. Another policeman who looked like everybody's granddad. I wondered if he'd whacked anyone with a baton in 1981. He took me into the cafeteria and handed me a mug filled with tea. He had a file under his arm and put it down on the table. 'You're one of Mike's mates, working at the TV place, aren't you? He talks about you a lot.'

The mate who got involved with the Bligh case and caused a lot of trouble? (Always told her she was barking up the wrong tree, but would she listen?) *That* mate?

'Nice things I hope,' I said lightly.

'Oh, yeah, thinks the world of you, Mike does. Now aren't you the one —.'

My stomach clenched. *Here we go.*

'I had the idea you were doing a story on Denny Graham. Mike was talking about it. Quite a yarn, that, and as far as I can see there's a helluva lot more to it than came out in the trial.'

'I'll be getting back to the Graham story later in the year but this documentary has to come first since this year is the thirtieth anniversary of the 1981 Springbok Tour.'

'Hope you're not going to make us lot look like sadistic brutes.'

I laughed. 'Not much chance of that with Mike keeping a close eye on what I'm doing. Anyway, the cops-as-sadistic-brutes angle has already been covered. That's why I'm trying to follow up on the lambs. Mike said you're certain Eric Woolley was one of them.'

'Yeah, I'd just about swear to it.'

'You never found who killed him, did you?'

He stirred sugar into his tea. 'No. It was a bad time to get murdered.'

'Sorry?'

He shifted uneasily in his chair. 'I suppose that makes me sound like I'm one of those cold-blooded cops people go on about. But it *was* a bad time for a murder to happen because the killer would have had a far above average chance of getting away with it.'

'I'm not sure what you mean.'

'There were a lot of people out on the streets: the anti-Tour lot, rugby supporters, thugs looking for a scrap. Then we had just your ordinary, everyday crims thinking they could do whatever they had a mind to because of us cops being overworked and pulled in every direction.'

'Are you saying there was a higher crime rate over the time of the Tour?'

'Put it this way,' he said. 'When you've got your entire police force focused on keeping law and order because all hell has broken out, other things get put on the back burner. Woolley was killed the night before the Wellington test. We were tied up with ensuring Athletic Park was secure for the test itself and we had the Boks billeted underneath the stands because it was decided it was the safest place for them to be, so we had to protect them. We had skips and barbed wire surrounding the entire area and men patrolling it twenty-four seven. That's where our resources were going.'

'How did you read the attack on Eric Woolley?'

'My gut feeling was he ran into a pack of louts, just one of those wrong place at the wrong time scenarios.'

'Did anything come up later to make you think there could've been other possibilities?'

He shrugged. 'Nothing that contradicted my first impression. We went through all the usual processes and tracked him down to a bar in Thorndon. He'd been there until around 10.30 or 11, talked to the barman and a couple of guys, then left on his own. After that, we lost him. Nobody saw him on the streets and he didn't go home.'

'What about the guys he was talking to?'

'They were musicians who played around Wellington and they'd chatted briefly with him about the music scene. No mention of the Tour so any idea he'd been rattling on about it and riled someone up was shelved. Those two guys went home to their wives in both cases and their stories checked out.'

'No chance their wives weren't telling the truth?'

He looked mildly put out. 'Uh, Rebecca, we do know how to run an enquiry. But no. One of the wives actually came to pick them up and came into the bar to let them know she was there. Two bar-workers and three people who were there verified the story.'

That was me told off. 'Sorry, Des. Maybe there's a frustrated detective inside me somewhere.'

He laughed. 'That's OK, but we have a lot of people come in here thinking they could do our jobs better than we do ourselves. Must be all these crime programmes they watch on the telly. Quite frankly I'd like to see them have a go.'

'So you have no indication of what happened after Eric left the bar?'

'Not a thing. There were no reports of fights or noise around the area. Mind you, where he was found was fairly far back from the road. We looked into all the usual places — family, people known to him, people who'd worked with him. Came up with nothing. Which took me right back to my view he'd decided to walk across the town belt and got attacked. Cutting through there was the quick way home.'

'Where did he live?'

'He had a flat in one of those big old homes they have around there. Nice place.'

'You talked to people he worked with?'

'That drew a bit of a blank. He was a dancer and he'd been working overseas but over the past year or so he hadn't been doing anything regular, just the odd gig here and there. Do you want another cuppa?'

I shook my head and watched as he went over to the counter, poured himself more tea. He was tall, stood very straight in that almost military way policemen hold themselves. *Good cop, bad cop.* What kind of cop was Des Horton? The kind who'd haul someone he recognised as a radical off the street and slap him around as a bit of a warning?

Dammit, this story was getting to me. But how could I know he was telling the truth, that he wasn't protecting someone?

'You said he lived in a flat,' I said as he sat down again. 'So there must have been other people around. Did they know anything?'

'There was only one other living in the house. The owner. Caspar Stone.'

'What can you tell me about Caspar Stone? I presume you talked to him as well.'

He put down his cup. 'Well, I'd say, totally off the record, that Caspar Stone was the other lamb and more than likely Woolley's lover. Though Woolley had a separate apartment within the house which Stone went to some lengths to demonstrate — Woolley's clothing in the wardrobe, food in the kitchen cupboards, things like that.'

God, this was *great*. This was exactly what I'd been hoping for. When I got back to work I was going to kiss Mike. I was going to buy him king-size hot chocolates every day for an entire week. 'Did you ask Caspar Stone if he was the other lamb?'

'We asked but he refused to tell us.'

'You didn't search his place to find out?'

'Being one of the lambs wasn't against the law. We had no reason to search his place.'

'I suppose you had to look through Eric's flat, though. Did you find a costume?'

'No, and his flat was gone through thoroughly to check there were no threatening letters or whatever. Stone was always helpful about letting us in.'

'So —.' What else should I ask? 'Do you know what Caspar Stone was doing the night Eric was killed?'

He shook his head. 'Rebecca, we did our job. Stone had a tight-shut alibi. Anyway, he was wiped out by what had happened. When we turned up at the house the first time, he broke down when I talked to him and in this game you get a feeling for what's genuine feeling and what's not. His was.'

'Did you talk to him much about Eric?'

'Yeah, a bit. To tell you the truth, I felt sorry for Stone. I went round there one day and he'd been drinking. Told me Woolley was the love of his life and always would be.'

'How about Eric's family? What can you tell me about them?'

'Auckland. Very wealthy, as a matter of fact. Old money. Hadn't had anything to do with him for some years.'

'Nothing to suspect —?'

He was grinning. No doubt he was laughing at me. 'Not a thing. The case was cut and dried. We knew what had happened, only thing we didn't know was the bastards who'd done it. The coroner's report came in as death by misadventure.'

'What happened to the case, then?'

'Still open. We did what we could. Fact is, we got told we were spending too much time on it, taking into account everything else that was going on. Once the body could be released to the family, James Woolley — the father — turned up and arranged a cremation.'

'There was no funeral? There *must* have been animosity between Eric and his family.'

'Which, believe me, we looked into. They'd been estranged for quite some time. He was gay, didn't want a bar of the family business, they disapproved totally of his lifestyle etc etc, but it was very evident that, while there was definitely bad blood between

135

them, that had nothing to do with this murder.'

'Other than Eric's father, did you meet any members of the Woolley family?'

'I went up to Auckland, spoke with James again as well as his mother and then I talked to the older brother and sister-in-law.'

'What did you make of the parents?'

'The big house and posh accents are about all I remember.'

This was like pulling fucking teeth. 'So what did they say?'

'His mother said they'd always given Eric the best but he'd chosen to go the way he had.'

'And had to take the consequences?'

He nodded. 'That about sums it up.'

'No grief, no remorse?'

He shook his head. 'Not that I could see.'

'What about Eric's brother?'

'Jim Woolley. Evidently, the family's blue-eyed boy. He said he hadn't had any contact with his brother since he left Auckland and while he was saddened by what had happened he couldn't help us with information. I got the impression there wasn't much love lost between them.'

'Jim Woolley's wife?'

'Isobel — I'd never met an Isobel before. She suited the name, very upper-crust and flawless, if you get the picture. She said she'd been fond of Eric, she'd admired his talent as a dancer, but she hadn't had anything to do with him since the rift. She asked to be excused as she was driving the children to school.'

My gut instinct was telling me something else must be lurking around behind all this. How could someone be murdered in a public place without anyone seeing or hearing anything at all? What was being hidden? 'Who said you were spending too much time on it?'

'Up there.' He jerked his head upwards. 'The powers that be. We were let know our priorities, first, second, third and fourth, were law enforcement for the country over the time of the Tour. By the time that was over any leads were long dead.'

'You *did* have leads?'

'Nothing we could put our finger on. We questioned a few bully-boys known to us but we didn't have anything on them.'

'So you came up with nothing at all?'

'Zilch. Not a thing anywhere we looked. We just had to let it go. And, looking at how we found the body —.' He glanced quickly at me.

'You mean the bottle?'

'Yeah. Gay bashers, that's what it was about.'

'What about Caspar Stone? Is he still alive?'

'No reason to think otherwise.'

19

On the way back to work I called in to the flat Murray Turner shared with other twice- or thrice-divorced, middle-aged, down-on-their-luck wheelers and dealers. Whenever I'd tried phoning him over the past weeks his answer phone had been on and he hadn't returned the messages I'd left. I needed to let him know the Graham doco was still on, just put on hold for a month or two. I also wanted to make sure he'd still talk.

His sleazy mate with the bleached yellow hair answered the door. Muzz wasn't there.

'When will he be back?'

'Don't know if he will be.' He was looking me up and down as he talked; protracted delays on breasts and legs. 'You his girlfriend?'

'No. Are you saying he's moved out?'

'Some of his gear's still here.'

'So what makes you think he won't be back?'

'He left in a hurry.'

'Did he say where he was going?'

'No, sweetheart, he didn't.'

Dammit, Helen was out and now it looked as though I'd lost Murray as well. Still, by the time I started back on the story he could be back and Helen could have decided Denny was, in fact, the bastard he was. I went back to work, hugged Mike and gave him a voucher for a week's worth of Jumbo-Chocs.

I needed to find Caspar Stone and talk to him, then I'd get in touch with Eric Woolley's family. I was certain there was much more to Eric's death than Des Horton had told me.

Was I getting sidetracked? This doco was about the Tour, not some unsolved thirty-year-old murder. But it was about the lambs as well and if I could somehow find out more about what happened that night . . . Wasn't it an amazing coincidence that Eric had been killed the night before the test? And wasn't it slightly odd that the police investigating his murder had been diverted away to more 'important' proceedings?

Caspar Stone was easy to find. I simply looked on the online White Pages and his name came up twice — once under 'Caspar Stone, Design', which turned out to be a shop in Cuba Street, and again under his home phone number in Tinakori Road. I phoned the business number and he agreed, after a little coaxing, that he had known Eric Woolley sometime around the eighties.

'I'm presently putting together a documentary about the 1981 Springbok Tour and I understand you and Eric Woolley were involved in the anti-Tour movement.'

'I really can't help you.'

'I understand you and Eric were the so-called lambs who had a strong presence at many of the protest marches?'

'Wherever did you get that idea?' He was beginning to sound decidedly tetchy.

'From what I've been told, you and Eric Woolley —.'

His voice snapped out, interrupting me. 'Miss Thorne, you're wasting your time.'

OK, so I had to get a little more assertive. I told him I was presently investigating the lambs' role in the anti-Tour movement for my documentary, that I knew he and Eric Woolley had lived together and that I would reveal what I suspected, that he and Eric were, in fact, the lambs. Furthermore, I'd discovered Eric had been murdered just before the Wellington test, and I intended disclosing that as well. 'I'm giving you the opportunity to tell your side of the story,' I said.

He sighed. 'Miss Thorne, there is no *side* to this story. Now if you would forgive me, I have work to do.'

'If you refuse to talk to me I will divulge what I already know and I *will* divulge your name.'

He won't want his name associated with something as sordid as the murder of his lover. Bad for his personal reputation, business as well.

139

*Design shops aren't doing so well now the economy's turned, he won't
want to take the risk of having his name out there.*

'Miss Thorne, I never talk about that particular interval in my life
or of Eric Woolley for that matter.'

We'll see about that.

'In that case, I'll simply have to give my own interpretation of
what happened.'

He was silent.

'I'm willing to come and talk to you whenever it's convenient,'
I said.

His voice was brisk. He would be home at 5.30 the following
evening. He gave me his address and rang off.

This was the grief-stricken man Des Horton had felt so sorry for?
OK, I suppose most people would assume that hearts tend to heal
over a thirty-year time span and the person you spoke of long ago as
the love of your life could now be forgotten. But he had sounded so
indifferent and unfeeling.

Joe had been the love of my life. I couldn't imagine speaking so
coldly of him, even thirty years on. But I was doing fine. Just *fine*.
He'd chosen to stay with Michelle. I'd been an add-on, a bit like
disposable income — it can give you a nice little treat but it's not
entirely necessary.

Back to my story. What did I have? There were police prepared to
talk. I had Tony Carlisle and I had former protesters like the woman
I'd interviewed just that morning who, as a twelve-year-old, had
marched with her mother. I pushed the play button on my recorder.

She was on the ground, her eyes rolled back in her head, there
was so much blood I thought she was going to die. Dad was up in
the terraces.

Well, she didn't die. All that blood turned out to be just a
superficial wound. The ambulance people told us cuts to the head
always bleed the most.

The worst wound, if you like, was what opened up in my parents'
relationship after that. When Dad got home they had this huge row.

What the hell was she doing taking a kid to a bloody protest march? What the hell was *he* doing supporting a racist system? I can still remember Dad yelling at Mum that she was a sanctimonious cow who put her bloody principles before her own kid's safety. They split not long after that. It wasn't only the Tour, of course, but they'd muddled along well enough up until then.

All the 'he said, she said', the government, the cops, the protesters stuff was engaging, it did provide insight and fascinating social commentary — but I needed the lambs, something to lift this out of the also-ran division. I'd been manipulative, pushy even, with Caspar Stone. But I'd had to be. I needed my story. I'd had to toughen up over the past few years.

Mike came into the office and stopped by my desk. 'How's it going?'

'I've got a heap of information. I'm just not entirely sure what to do with it.'

'All you have to do is stick it all together.'

'Ha *ha*.'

The red light was flashing on my phone when I got home. I eyed it warily. What Anna had said kept coming back to me. 'All the warning signs were there. He kidnapped and strangled the girl who'd rejected him.'

I pressed play. 'You have one message recorded at 3.30 pm.' I felt my body tense then ease as Margo's voice sang out at me. 'The NZSO's doing the Mozart clarinet concerto next Friday. It's your favourite, isn't it? Give me a call and I'll pick up the seats. My treat for your birthday.'

My treat for your birthday. And, yes, it was my favourite, my total favourite, ever since Mum and Dad took me and David to a matinee performance of it around the time I was thirteen. After which I'd insisted on learning the clarinet, torturing myself and everyone else within listening range trying to get some kind of reasonable sound out of that thing.

141

Margo was treating me. My birthday was coming up. Everything was absolutely fine, everything was *normal*.

The lost dress, the phone calls, Rolly outside the house, at the party; all were odd, certainly, but surely couldn't be linked. Probably the calls to Anna and David's house were made by some pissed-off constituent. *Anna is getting a bit stir-crazy at home with babies. Her imagination must be working overtime.*

Back to work, back to the doco bright and early in the morning. I opened up my computer, started trawling through emails. 'Beautiful day,' Mike called over from his desk.

'Yes,' I said. 'Really good.'

'How're you going with this info about the lambs?'

I stared at the screen while I talked. 'I've got something to go on now. I was hoping to come up with this super-dramatic revelation about Eric Woolley's death being connected to his anti-Tour activities, but it looks like that's a no-go.'

'How many docos come up with a super-dramatic revelation?'

I looked over at him. 'Not many. That's why I was hoping to do it.'

'Maybe you're better steering away from revelations.'

He was grinning ever so slightly and I knew exactly what he was thinking of. Connor Bligh. OK, I could take shit from Mike and I owed him. If it hadn't been for him Bligh might be long gone rather than in the prison cell where he deserved to be. And I might be dead.

'Look, Mike, if Eric Woolley *had* to go and get himself killed the night before the test why the hell couldn't he have got the SIS or a mob of rugby thugs to do it?'

'Rebecca.' He was starting to chuckle.

'Very thoughtless of him. I had it worked out. I had him all set up to be the sacrificial lamb. I could really have done something with that.'

We were both laughing by then. The phone on my desk rang and I picked it up. I was still laughing. 'Rebecca Thorne here.'

A pause. A long, drawn-out, soft-breathing pause. Click.

My mobile dinged and I snatched it up. A photo. I'm standing outside Don Taylor's house, my back to the camera. The sliding doors are open and Don is shaking my hand.

'What's wrong?' Mike was staring at me.

I attempted a smile. 'Nothing. It's nothing.'

It had rained all day, dreary trickles for a start-off with a swift follow-up of some serious competition in sheer strength and volume between our drive-everyone-crazy Wellington wind and sheeting torrents of rain. And just in case all that wasn't enough, we'd had a freakish thunderstorm. I got to Thorndon with my windscreen wipers going flat out and drove slowly along Tinakori Road peering through gushing rivulets at letter boxes, trying to decipher the numbers.

Caspar Stone's place was a sprawling two-storey weatherboard set way back off the road. There was a high iron fence along the front with electronic gates. Gates which remained securely fastened when I drove up to them.

Fuck. I parked further down the road, hauled my umbrella out of the boot, opened it up and aimed it and my body towards a path running up to the house. I unclipped the gate with sopping, fumbling fingers, pushed through it and sheltered beneath the dripping trellised portico while I got my umbrella, which by now had turned itself inside out, under control, then hurtled up the drive, propelled by my wind-filled umbrella and the best speed I could manage in heels.

My hair was drenched, rivulets streaming down my face and neck. I'd *dressed* for this meeting. What they used to refer to as power dressing. A little suit. A crisp shirt. The heels. Which were now squelching heels.

'Ah.' The door had opened. 'The ever-glamorous Miss Thorne.'

The man standing in front of me was as streamlined as a greyhound, all lean ribs and long legs, with dark eyes lit, it seemed, by an expression of savage glee.

I held out my hand. He took it with a show of politeness and an almost imperceptible shiver of distaste. 'Why ever didn't you drive up to the house, Miss Thorne?'

'The gate was locked.'

'That's odd. Oh —.' He raised his finger to tap below his left eye.

What? I raised my fingers to my own left eye, dabbed, withdrew them and observed the grey watery smears.

'I always consider,' he said, 'waterproof mascara the safest option.'

He stood back and ushered me into what I would imagine would be called a vestibule and was almost as large as my living room, gingerly hung up my umbrella which drooped suddenly, dripping onto the smart black-and-white mosaic tiled floor, then gestured me forward. 'Just along the hallway, Miss Thorne. Last door to the right.'

He was following me down a vast and endless dark wood-panelled hall, so murky I could barely make anything out. *Why doesn't he turn on the lights?*

Thank god, there at last was an open door. A door which opened into a beautiful room — soft chairs, thick rugs, a painting glowing above the blazing fire. I was freezing, shivering with damp and cold. I couldn't wait to get in front of that fire. I paused but he tapped my arm, waved me onwards. 'Up there, Miss Thorne, to the right.'

The curtains were pulled shut. The room was dark and very cold. I blinked trying to see through the gloom. *What in hell was I doing in this weird place with this horrible man?*

The door clicked behind me and the lights snapped on flooding the room with bright, brash light, lighting up the walls with — *faces.*

Faces coming out at me, parchment and yellow and grey. Some like dried skin, some like ancient yellowing ivory. Gaping mouths and tufts of dead hair and teeth. Spiked teeth, brown teeth, rows and rows of teeth beneath hollow eyes.

I cried out and reared backwards, almost colliding with Caspar Stone who was so close behind me we were almost touching, so close I could feel his breath against my neck.

'Are you at all interested in masks, Miss Thorne? I hope you are.' He waved me to a sofa and sat on the armchair directly opposite me. 'I thought you may enjoy seeing my collection.'

He was so elegant sitting there, one leg crossing the other, observing me. Dark jeans, a soft grey, close-fitting jersey, hair clipped very short, a tiny silver ring in his left ear.

Was he laughing at me? If I couldn't get the advantage here, maybe I could at least claw back some sort of parity. I sat up straight, gave him my best let's-be-friends smile. 'Rebecca,' I said. 'Please call me Rebecca. I don't know much about masks. Can you tell me why they interest you?'

Could you tell me why anyone would choose to have those hideous faces staring down at them?

'There are many reasons, Miss Thorne.'

Hopefully my smile had remained warm and was also conveying keen interest and curiosity.

He cleared his throat. 'I'm sure you're aware that throughout history masks have been employed for all kinds of purposes. To appease the gods, to protect the wearer against evil spirits, to hide from one's enemies. Particular masks give the wearer supernatural powers to accomplish feats which are normally impossible.'

'Some of these appear very old.'

'Yes,' he said. 'Some of these *are* very old. If they could speak, Miss Thorne, I wonder what they would tell us.'

Nothing I'd particularly want to hear. I wanted to close my eyes, shut out those skull-like heads, those long bony antlers, the black, blind eyes. 'Do you, uh, know the stories behind them? Is that why you like to collect them?'

'Only a few. One of the reasons I enjoy them is because of the secrets they conceal. Rather in the same way that we appropriate our more contemporary facades to hide behind. Would you agree with me, Miss Thorne?'

His voice was slightly husky as he leaned towards me, his eyes scanning my face.

'I'm not sure what you mean.'

'Surely you understand. Even as I face you now, I can't help but wonder if this so very obviously attractive young woman wearing her Karen Walker suit and rather superb Johnny King earrings is quite as she appears? Is this all there is to her?' He raised his eyes to the walls again. 'Oh, but then, you are very young, aren't you? Perhaps when I was young I had more reason to hide away than you do, and more reason to think more. After all, here you are, a physically appealing, *normal* young woman.'

'I'm not altogether sure about normal.' I said it quickly, jokily I hoped.

'But of course you are. Isn't it *normal*, after all, for an ambitious young woman to insist she visit an old man so she may jab and prod at his deepest secrets? Now tell me, Miss Thorne, looking around these walls, which mask would you select as your own favourite?'

I felt the heat rushing across my face and I wanted to run out of the room like the pathetic bimbo he obviously thought I was.

Right, he hates me, but what's the choice here? Apologise for my rudeness and back out gracefully, or do I stay with it? I need what he knows, he's the only one who can tell me. So stick it out. And don't cry. Don't you dare fucking cry.

I scanned the walls, jabbed my finger upwards. 'That one.'

The mask I was pointing at was crafted from what looked to be very pale jade. The eyes were slightly curved and the mouth turned upwards into what appeared to be a frenzied grin.

'Oh, but that's not one I'm terribly fond of, I'm afraid,' he said. 'Though it is one of my more valuable pieces. Chinese. A funeral mask. It signifies death, Miss Thorne.' He looked directly at me as he said it and my heart juddered. Was he telling the truth or simply trying to unsettle me?

'Mr Stone, I've obviously offended you. I realise I shouldn't have been so demanding when I asked you to talk to me but —.'

'But?' He leaned back in his chair and surveyed the walls as if he didn't have the remotest interest in my answer.

'But as I explained to you, I'm making a documentary about the 1981 Springbok Tour. The lambs were a very strong part of the anti-Tour movement and nobody's told their story.'

'And you, Miss Thorne, have decided this is the story *you* should tell?'

'Yes.'

'Why?'

'Because it's an important story and I'm certain I can do it well.'

'And so — let me get this clear — this certainty you have that you can do it well makes it acceptable for you to use any means, blackmail or whatever, to ensure that I'll talk about something which is both very personal and painful to recall?'

'Mr Stone, I'm just doing my job. It's clear to me that you and Eric Woolley were the lambs. It's become even more apparent now I'm here.'

He raised his eyebrows. 'Why do you say that?'

'I recognise those.' I pointed just above where he sat. 'They're the ones you and Eric wore.'

Two masks placed side by side. Creamy white, made from some sort of thick, coarse fabric with round holes at the eyes, wide slashes at the mouth.

'Are they?' he said. '*Are* they? I would have said they were Iroquois. Iroquois corn-husk masks.'

He looked at his watch. 'You'll have to excuse me. I have dinner guests arriving.'

'I wanted to talk to you about Eric Woolley.'

He was behind me, shepherding me down the hall. 'I told you, Miss Thorne. Perhaps you weren't listening. I never speak of Eric.'

I was desperate. 'Des Horton said you told him Eric was the love of your life.'

He took my shoulder in one hand and propelled me firmly through the open door out into the rain. I remember that sensation, the hardness and coldness of his fingers. 'And how, Miss Thorne, could you possibly imagine that I would speak to someone like *you* about that?'

147

20

I drove too fast through the rain, got into my house, shut the door behind me and cried.

I'd changed into a person I didn't like, a horrible person, a hard person: demanding, manipulative, grabby and superficial. Janet Beardsley, from my last job, popped into my mind — that glinting calculation in her eyes as she summed you up: *what can I get from you and how can I get it?*

This job. This industry. That awful party I'd been invited to just because Josie had sized me up and worked out I could be of use to her good friend Suz. *So let's get her over here, give her a great big drink and see what we can get her to do.* No doubt there'd be some kind of pay-off down the line for Josie as well. And I was just as bad.

Who could I talk to? Who would tell me honestly if I'd turned into Janet Beardsley? Not Margo, my best friend. Not David who was actually far *too* honest. Not Anna, who was too kind.

'Mum?' I was still crying. 'I have to change my job.'

'What? Rebecca, whatever's happened?'

'It's changing me. I'm turning into an evil person. I don't even like myself any more.'

'Absolute nonsense.' Her brisk, let's-be-rational voice. 'Tell me what's gone wrong.'

I told her everything. How I needed the lambs so I'd put pressure on Caspar Stone to talk. How I'd thought he wouldn't want bad publicity because of his design shop and she laughed. 'I don't know Caspar Stone personally,' she said, 'but I do know he's very wealthy. I'd imagine the shop is just for personal interest.'

'He said I'd used blackmail to get him to talk to me. He made me feel so *bad*. This job . . . I'm scared it's turned me into an utter bitch.'

'No it hasn't. I agree with you that you went too far this time but you know that and it's made you realise what you don't want to be.'

'Well —.'

'Darling, you've had a bad day. Just try to put it behind you. Have an early night. Maybe a bath.'

Mum's remedy. A bath and an early night. David and I used to laugh at her, tease her. If anyone got cross or upset we'd jump right in ahead of her. 'A bath and an early night.'

Still, she was right. I felt chilled, shivery. A hot, deep bath, lots of my new lemony bath balm. I *was* tired. But although Mum's remedy usually worked I hardly slept. Each sound, each gust of wind had me sitting up staring anxiously around the dark room. When I closed my eyes I saw grinning mouths, tufts of hair and eyes.

Eyes. 'A funeral mask. It signifies death, Miss Thorne.'

Why had he agreed to see me? If Mum was right and the shop was just for his personal pleasure then he had no reason to protect his business interests. Had he agreed because he wanted to have the opportunity to put me in my place? Had I been so rude, so pushy that was what he decided I deserved?

At some point there was a thud somewhere near the house and I went to the window and looked outside. The light was odd that night. There was a harsh, yellowish glint to the sky. I turned on the lamp above my bed, read for a while, fell asleep, the book still on my chest. I dreamed of faces looming out at me, chattering and sniggering.

A funeral mask.

A funeral mask.

It signifies death, Miss Thorne.

I ran along the beach early in the morning then, before I left for work, sat at my desk and wrote Caspar Stone a letter, handwritten on the thick creamy paper Margo had brought me back from London. I thanked him for seeing me, for showing me his collection of masks and telling me about them. I wrote that the mask I had assumed for my negotiation with him did not represent the person I either was or wanted to be. I apologised for my lack of respect and aggressive behaviour.

I sealed and addressed it and posted it on the way to work. It was the best I could do. I'd been all of those things I'd vowed way back in journalism school I'd never be. I wanted to make amends.

I sat down at my desk, switched on my laptop. Back to work. *OK you fucked up but you've apologised so get on with it.* And while I didn't have anything super-dramatic, no sensational revelations, I had interesting people with interesting stories, their own stories of a time which had been significant, not only to themselves personally, but to New Zealand. I kept hearing it: 'The closest we've come to civil war.' 'The closest we've ever come to anarchy.'

I would give some attention to the lambs. Even if I had stuffed things up with Caspar Stone there were others I had interviewed who were keen to talk about them. I would disclose the evidence that Eric Woolley was one of the lambs and, although I'd make it clear the attack which led to his death was, according to evidence, a random, wrong-place-wrong-time event, I would talk about how both violent and non-violent crime had escalated over the time of the Tour because of the extra pressure on the police force and because there were more people out on the streets with a grudge.

I could give the example that after the Hamilton game was called off gangs of thugs went down to the university campus and beat up any student they could find out on the streets because, they assumed, it was students who were behind the protest which had stopped their game. There were others as well. I'd look for some specific to Wellington. I was cheering up. I would make this work.

Mike came in carrying a large brown envelope which he handed to me. 'Police photographs, Wellington,' he said. I opened it up and took them out. I was beginning to recognise the rallies: Bunny Street, Marion Street, Wellington Airport, Ewen Bridge in Lower Hutt, the motorway. 'Fight apartheid. Stop the Tour. Stop the Tour. Stop the Tour.'

'Anything interesting?' he said.

'These are good,' I said. 'I'll definitely use some of them. Hey, this is Napier, isn't it?'

A huge banner held up by five grim-faced marchers. 'Ka whaiwhai tonu matou. Bind together, work together, fight together.'

'Yeah,' Mike said. 'Maori All Blacks against the Boks. There was bad feeling about that game. A lot of Maoris believed that having their team play the Springboks signified that Maoridom condoned the Tour.'

'I was talking to one of the leaders of the Maori protesters,' I said. 'She had very good reason to feel bitter about that team playing. Her grandfather had been the leader of the Maori All Blacks who played against the Springboks in 1921 and after the game the Springbok captain refused to shake his hand.'

Mike watched as I turned to the next photograph of protesters outside the Napier hotel where the Springboks had stayed. I knew there'd been a ferocious, though short, confrontation there between protesters and police. The lambs were there, arms locked with other protesters facing the police only inches in front of them. Maybe I'd use it.

We were both caught up in the photograph, staring down at those faces; the anger, my god that rage, and as always, I felt that rush of shock and disbelief. *This happened here, this happened in my country?*

I laughed suddenly and Mike gaped at me.

'Sorry,' I said. 'I promise I'm not going crazy. I was just reminded of what a past member of COST told me. One of the favourite games his kids played at the time was "Protesters against Police".'

'Just about says it all, eh?'

I turned the photo over and we both looked down again. 'That's Denny Graham, isn't it? I saw him in one of the photos at Don Taylor's place as well.'

Mike leaned over the desk for a closer look. 'Yeah, and that's Don there.' He pointed to a face. 'That's Pete Greenwood, dead now, heart attack a few years back. And, believe it or not, there's yours truly.'

'Really?' I looked closer, 'Handsome, weren't you? You haven't talked to me yet about the Tour. What about if I interview you?'

'Nope, and don't ask me again.'

'Oh, come on, Mike. Anyway, tell me about Denny Graham. Don Taylor described him as a real bastard. Did you work with him?'

'Not if I could avoid it.'

'What was he like?'

'He was a right bastard, like Don said, and he had just one interest which was the advancement of Denny Graham.'

'But you didn't have much to do with him?'

'Only the one time, really, and that was during the Tour. Quite a few of us went over to Nelson to give the local boys back-up and Graham was with us.'

'And?'

'Nothing much. Just threw his weight around. He was a bully at the best of times.'

'Don said he left the police not long after the Tour ended.'

'Yeah. That's when he went up to Auckland and made a lot of money very quickly. A lot of stories about how he made it, too.'

'Do you believe the stories?'

'Put it this way, I'd put more trust in Namibia winning the World Cup than I ever would in Denny Graham. When he was in the police force he was grilled a few times over things that happened but nothing ever came of it.'

'What sort of things?'

'The stories going around were that he had a tendency to use extreme force, turn a blind eye for the odd sexual favour and that he was willing to take paybacks. One specific story I heard was he persuaded a couple not to press charges after their place was broken into. There was a kid involved who lived just around in the next street. This couple said they saw him outside the house as they packed up the car for a couple of nights away, then when they came home the back door had its glass smashed out and some cash and all the alcohol in the house was gone.'

'So what happened?'

'The kid's fingerprints were inside the house. There was no doubt it was him. This couple was all set to press charges then they backed right off. They both turned up at the station and told the police officer on duty they weren't going ahead with it and they wouldn't give evidence against the boy if the police pressed charges independently. They came up with some cock-and-bull story he'd visited them some time or other and that was why his fingerprints were there. When pressed a bit they said if it was this kid — and they really weren't sure any more — they wanted to give him a second chance. They said they'd come to the decision themselves, no one else had been involved in making it, but the cop on duty said they seemed anxious, almost frightened.'

'You think Graham might have pressured them?'

'The parents were wealthy and sure as hell didn't want their little darling in trouble with the law.'

'Doesn't that kind of thing get looked into? It's not as if we're living in Russia or the Middle East.'

'Of course it gets looked into. That is, if there's some sort of proof or a complaint and, in this case, there wasn't. Everything was fine and dandy on the surface. I had a feeling the boss had a talk to Graham about it but he left shortly afterward anyway, and there weren't too many tears shed over him going, I can tell you.'

'It's a good Denny Graham story. Maybe you could find out the name of the couple for me? I might talk to them when I get back to him. That is if I ever make something out of all this.'

I waved my hand at my desk and Mike backed away. 'Well. Good luck with it, mate.'

I looked down at the photograph again. A bit of puffiness even then around his cheeks and eyes — from all accounts he'd always been a boozer. His face was square-chinned, too good-looking; the kind that you fall heavily for when you're fifteen and don't know what's good for you, the kind you learn later to run away from as far and fast as you can.

I could tell you some stories, girl, about our Denny.

21

Interview: Mary Stratton. COST member.

I remember going to Palmerston North with a real sense of purpose. It was the game after Hamilton and we hoped to stop it and the government would give up and the Tour would be over. At the same time, we'd learned by then what the police and the rugby crowds were capable of. I had a friend who'd stayed on the field in Hamilton after most of the others had moved off. He had thirteen stitches in his head and was still in a bad way. After that there was Molesworth Street.

So we knew this wasn't going to be like when we'd blockaded the motorway and the police had stood back, simply making sure nobody got hurt. The main aggression there had come from the drivers and passengers in the cars which were being held up, people shouting at us through the car windows and abusing the police for not having the courage to clear us off the road.

Everything had turned around by the time of the Palmerston North game. We were aware that Police Commissioner Walton had had his hand slapped over the way he'd handled things in Hamilton and Prime Minister Muldoon had set his law-and-order campaign in motion: 'The New Zealand police force would uphold the country's stability at any cost.'

The tactics for this match had been decided at the plenary meeting. The idea was a group of us would keep police busy by getting in and occupying the showgrounds while another got inside the park and onto the field. Then the news was passed on by one of our sympathetic policemen that police numbers for the game would be fifteen hundred. To make matters worse, the information sent through was that long batons would be used and dogs set on anyone who attempted to force a way through police lines.

The thinking in COST was that the situation needed to be brought out into the open. So a press conference was called and committee members met with reporters and film crews and told them that a peaceful protest was planned and protesters had no intention of breaking through police lines.

But whereas we'd dressed for cold weather in hats and jackets when we marched to the motorway, this time we dressed for protection, padding up with polyester and cotton beneath our thickest jackets. I remember people were joking together when we met up in Courtenay Place, showing off what they were wearing and punching each other's arms and legs and shoulders to see if the blows and thumps could be felt. Quite a few were wearing hard helmets. People who'd been in Molesworth Street had that experience fixed firmly in their minds. There was a lot of apprehension in some of the faces around me.

We set off in cars and vans. We'd been warned there'd be police searches and road blocks along the way but the drive through went without any hitches. HART and COST and MAST — Manawatu Against the Springbok Tour — were all there. Once we got together it seemed as if each group had different ideas about what should be done. There were some who felt even moderate protest was dangerous and, on another level, there were those who wanted to go right ahead and try to break through police lines. COST, of course, had already given an assurance we wouldn't do that and we couldn't go back on it, not without playing right into Muldoon's hands by showing we couldn't be trusted.

In the end, we set out to the park and there were around five thousand of us by the time we got there. We'd had the usual swearing and name-calling from the crowds lining the footpaths as we marched but people had joined us as well. You asked me if I remember seeing the lambs that day and, yes, they were there. They were just in front of me at one point running in and out of crowds of rugby supporters moving towards the grounds. I heard one of our marshals say, 'Those grandstanding bastards are here again.' I know the committee didn't like them but for the rest of us they lightened things up and we could see how brave they were.

We first saw the Red Squad as we approached the entrance to the grounds. I was close to the front, close enough to see their faces and, it might seem odd that I remember this, but they were so well-groomed, so scrubbed and polished, their moustaches appeared to be fastidiously clipped, clipped down to the last hair, it seemed, and somehow that made what was happening worse. I can't quite explain why it affected me but perhaps I was reminded of war films where the Gestapo is always immaculately turned out.

We heard the command, 'Red Squad visors down.' The media was directed out of the way and then the rugby crowd who'd been shouting and cheering, egging them on in fact, were ordered to move on into the park. 'Red escort group draw batons.'

I was frightened. It seemed to me the media and rugby supporters were intentionally being removed so they could attack us without witnesses. That may seem far-fetched, but I was positive that no matter how vicious their behaviour, they'd get away with it. That's how it had become. This government had trained the police force to make war on ordinary citizens.

The voice came over the loudspeaker. 'As you can see from the front of the march there is nothing peaceful about it. Move. Move. Move! *Move!*'

They were advancing on us, visors down, thrusting their batons forward. One of the reporters hadn't moved out of the way in time and the sound of that inward gasp as he was hit and the moan of pain as he went down ricocheted along our lines.

They stopped about ten feet away from us. I wondered how much a bit of cotton wadding and a few tin hats would stand up to that brute force. Someone behind me began singing. 'God of nations, at thy feet, in the bonds of love . . .' I tried to join in but the words cracked up in my throat and came out as a sob. I didn't know the man standing beside me but he grabbed my hand and squeezed it. 'We'll be all right,' he said. His face was grey.

'Hold your lines. Hold your lines.

'If I tell you to go it will be rapid action.'

I was convinced that if anyone made a wrong move they'd be on us. Even the lambs were silent. One of them — the black one, I think it was — started to make a move towards the blockade of police then obviously thought the better of it. You could physically feel the tension and hostility. There was a policeman in the front row who had his eye on him and you could sense how much he wanted to let loose with his baton.

Well, we stood our ground for some time but finally we just had to back down and leave. There was a lot of criticism later but it was the right decision. We had to go. The police were wound up. You could feel it, that itch to lash out with those batons, almost like there was some animal there rubbing up against you, ready to tear into you with its claws.

So we left. Our marshals lined up, bravely forming a barrier between protesters and the lines of police and the whole demonstration rotated around in front of those police lines. There were five thousand of us and we chanted and sang as we went past.

We were a miserable lot heading back to Wellington. The people in our van mainly agreed those in charge had made the right decision. We told each other all the right things, that pulling back demonstrated our self-control and respect for the law, that the country would see that the government was prepared to set its police officers on innocent people.

But we'd set out thinking there might be some way of getting onto the rugby grounds and stopping that game. We fell silent after a while and I believe we were all thinking the same thing but didn't want to say it. We would not stop the Tour now.

I felt that kind of exhaustion that hits you after you've had a bad shock. I'd been frightened, *so* frightened. I'd believed I'd be injured and I'd tensed my body ready for the blows and hurt which I'd thought certain to come. I needed that silence in the van to come back into myself again, to convince my body I was safe.

Those rows of well-scrubbed and carefully clipped young men with nothing in their faces stayed with me throughout that silent trip back to Wellington and for a very long time afterwards. For me, those young men represented the kind of government-controlled forces which will mindlessly carry out orders, no matter what they are. I'd not thought I would see their kind in New Zealand.

I ran the length of the beach, looping up into the dry sand, pushing myself. *Those young men represented the kind of government-controlled forces which will mindlessly carry out orders, no matter what they are.*

Her face had changed as she told me, had become uneasy, almost fearful. It was almost as if she was back there, no longer the fifty-plus woman in the Paula Ryan black coat, silver bracelets around her wrists, but the young woman, her mouth dry, her heart racing.

My body was hurting. *Concentrate on the breathing. Heel, instep, ball of your foot, heel-instep-ball-of-your-foot.* I was panting, felt the dull jab threatening to become a stitch in my side. I hadn't been running enough, not nearly enough. *Watch for what's under your feet, careful not to fall, heel-instep-ball-of-your-foot and breathe.*

'I'd not thought I would see their kind in New Zealand.'

I had to be impartial, take the police, the protesters, the rugby supporters, *all* opinions into account. But *I* had not thought I'd see anything like that in New Zealand. I'd have been around fourteen when we'd done the two-week module on the Tour in school, of an age when anything that'd happened more than a couple of months ago was boring and irrelevant. I'd looked at the pictures of posters and banners, the photographs of marches and skimmed through the assigned readings. The major thing I'd got out of it was they'd had terrible hair-dos and awful clothes and what they were protesting against had all been fixed up anyway.

But what I'd disregarded then I was now painfully aware of. Our own government had placed New Zealand in a position of shame and discord with other countries. It had armed, trained and set the country's police force onto citizens who were asserting their legal right to protest. It had assembled a smear campaign, releasing a list of fifteen 'radicals' in leadership positions within the protest movement who were said to have been identified by the SIS as being aligned to the Communist Party, the implication being that the protest movement was being manipulated to create havoc and revolution in the country.

Isolation. Propaganda. Violence. *It could never happen here.* How many people have said that, for how many years, and in how many countries? *Not here. Not us.*

I got back home panting hard, dripping with sweat, stood under the shower for a good ten minutes washing it all away. *It's a story. Don't let it get to you.* I was meeting Margo in an hour. My birthday treat. Marco's for a glass of wine, bread, cheese, a dollop of pâté. That was our ritual. Marco's, the concert, Za-Za for lemon cream pie and coffee afterwards.

Margo and I adore our concert nights. We dress up: killer heels, little bags, best dresses. We buy the same seats, round to the left of the circle and front row so you get a good view of the orchestra. I love it all: the orchestra tuning up, the leader coming in, the way the conductor's coat-tails swish as he moves, the black jackets, crisp white shirts, black bow ties, the lights catching up the sequins and gleam of velvet.

So there I was in my little black dress, lulled by crusty bread, creamy pâté and a glass of luscious pinot gris and transported far, far away from police and batons and injustices. The concerto started. I was transfixed.

My clarinet teacher had said I could have been quite good, that I had reasonable musicality and with perseverance . . . All of which pleased me so much now because instead of all the years of work and the nervous anxiety I'm sure musicians experience despite their patina of cool, I could relax and allow my head to soar, my eyes to close and to fill up with tears as I listened to those notes which meander and twist, plummet and ascend in loneliness and longing, grief and joy.

There was an eruption of clapping intermingled with foot-stamping and bravos. I sat there limp and saturated while people sidled past us out for the interval.

'I don't really want to go out,' Margo said. 'I'd like to just sit here and think about it.'

'I don't even know if I want to listen to anything else,' I said. 'That was . . . God, that was stunning.'

'The Dvorak will be good, though. Uh, isn't that Rolly over there?'

I looked over to where she was indicating. Front seat, right side of the circle. He knew I loved the Mozart clarinet concerto. He knew I'd be there. He picked up the programme from the seat beside him and looked down at it.

'I didn't know Rolly liked this type of music,' Margo said. 'I've never seen him at a concert before.'

Could this be a coincidence? Another coincidence? *What do you really know about Rolly?*

'Is he by himself?' Margo was squinting over at him, looking as though she wanted to wave.

'Just pretend he's not there, OK?' I said.

'What's going on?' She turned her head to look at me.

'Nothing. It's, well, he keeps turning up.'

'What do you mean?' Her eyes were wide. 'Like where?'

'Just places. And once. Well, I saw him outside.'

'Outside your house, you mean?'

Some people just cannot cope with being dumped and they turn nasty.

Margo was staring at me now, her mouth open.

'It's nothing. Really, Margo, it's fine.'

'Rebecca —.'

The buzzer called people back in, the lights went down and the conductor came back in. I hardly heard the symphony. Though I didn't look towards Rolly again, I felt his presence there across from me in the dark.

We went to Za-Za, ate our slices of lemon pie and I persuaded Margo that I was absolutely OK. Rolly turning up, well, it must all be some sort of weird chance thing and, on the very slim chance that it wasn't, he'd stop it soon enough anyway. And if he didn't I promised her I'd deal with it. I dropped her off at her house and drove home.

Did I leave the kitchen light on?

I unlocked the door, peered inside then edged in, locking it behind me. The lights of a car swept across the window as it turned and headed up the street towards the city. I turned on the living-room lamps. I turned on all the lights and prowled around looking in odd corners. Had I left that coffee cup there, those spoons turned that way up?

You're OK. Everything's OK. You're letting yourself get spooked.

I switched off my mobile, kept my bedside light on until I was almost asleep.

He kidnapped and strangled the girl who'd rejected him kidnapped and strangled the girl who'd rejected him kidnapped and strangled the girl.

The girl who'd rejected him.

The photo of Anna and David and the kids? Hadn't it been shifted?

Stop it. You're OK.

Everything's OK.

At some point in the night I woke to hear the phone ringing. I heard my voice asking the caller to leave a message.

I listened to the silence before the caller clicked off at the other end.

22

I woke up late, rushed through my shower, pulled on clothes. Make-up, shoes, bag, keys. And the phone. The red light flickering. *Why the hell should I let a phone frighten me?* I pressed the play button. 'Rebecca Thorne here.'

That long silence. That click.

What should I do about this? I didn't have time for all this crap. I had an interview set up for 9.30 and it was already quarter to.

But I had to deal with it. Maybe I should go to the police after all. But the scenario still seemed so terribly lame. 'I think my ex-boyfriend's stalking me, he was outside my house, he was at a party, at a concert. I think he may be calling me and hanging up. Not actually outside my house but parked opposite and, yes, there is a grocery store there. And the party was hosted by a mutual friend and there were hundreds of other people at the concert and, no, I really don't have any proof it's him who's phoning.'

The dress? I couldn't mention the dress. I hadn't received an email back from my enquiry at the resort in Rarotonga so, in the end, I'd phoned them. They were looking into it.

All right, then, let's fill out the forms. 'Rebecca Thorne? The Bligh case?'

I backed my car out of the drive. I'd just phone him. Ask him what the hell he thought he was doing there last night. Really have a go at him.

I would simply phone Rolly. Who would simply deny he was stalking me. And wouldn't contacting him be giving him what he wanted? Wouldn't it be proving to him I was giving him thought and attention? What had the websites I'd looked up said? 'Do not engage in further discussions with the stalker. Do not argue with them. Do not negotiate with them. Ongoing communication will reward the stalker and lead him to maintain contact.'

What should I do?

Maybe I'd talk to David. And if I talked to David, he'd tell Anna and she'd get even more upset. And if I talked to Mum she'd tell Dad and he'd tell David and, *fuck*, this was all too bloody hard. I had an interview to do. That was what was important. I had to focus on what was real.

Rolly would go away. In the end, he'd go away.

Interview: Harry Taonga Williams. COST member.

For me, the Napier protest — that is the protest against the Maori All Blacks game — was the most significant. Already the Springboks, a team representing a government which denied dignity and equal rights to the indigenous people of its country, had been officially welcomed to New Zealand on the Poho-o-Rawiri Marae in Gisborne and Maori, whose marae it was, been denied entry. Our intention in going to Napier was to make it clear that there were Maori who opposed this Tour and were shamed by a Maori team playing.

There was a feeling of disappointment that there was only a small Wellington representation in Napier. The mood among Maori who travelled there was of dissatisfaction with our COST companions who had not come with us when we had supported the movement so vigorously. However, that resentment was soon forgotten as we sat down, both Pakeha and Maori, from Wellington and from Auckland, with local people to plan the day's proceedings and tactics.

A small group of us was commissioned to visit the Maori All Blacks at their hotel. While my mind told me that speaking to them would not persuade them against playing and our words might further harden their resolve, in my heart I hoped that at least one might reconsider.

I had a certain sympathy towards these players. I myself had been a representative rugby player and knew the hours of training, practice and sacrifice which take you into a top team. I understood too that craving for the challenge of playing against outstanding players. However, my final judgment was that these players were both selfish and short-sighted. Is a game, however notable, a reason to betray your brothers and sisters who are daily oppressed and mistreated?

We found a place near the windows of the room where they were staying. They were cleaning their boots, preparing for the game. When we called to them they immediately pulled the curtains across to shut out the sight of us.

But they could not shut out our voices and I believe they carried our words with them out into the field, carried them long after that game was over. 'By your actions you are misrepresenting your people. By your actions you are supporting apartheid. By your actions you are betraying your South African brothers and sisters.'

We then joined the main march which had assembled at the hotel hosting the Springboks. The small group of us there were surrounded by pro-Tour locals. 'We don't want your sort here.' 'Get back into the hole where you belong.' 'Black bastards.'

We hadn't experienced such hostility before but despite the belligerence our march was peaceful and without incident. As we moved towards the ground we were joined by others along the way who joined in with our chanting and singing. 'Kia kaha, Kia kaha, Ka whaiwhai tonu matou.'

We came to a stop in the middle of the main street and faced down the Red Squad, one after another addressing them, not as the collective mob which gave them their identity and strength, but calling them by their names. The effect on some of these men was clearly evident, two in the front line being so markedly wounded by our words — 'White man's lackey. Black man's traitor' — that they were moved into the back lines.

At the end of the day we returned to the church hall where we presented a koha to the local people and were, in return, farewelled before we began our journey back to Wellington.

For me, that day in Napier remains a benchmark in the Maori movement for justice and equality. It proved, without question, that we could unite as a people and protest in a controlled and effective manner. During this demonstration none of our people were hurt, there were no arrests, no violence. We made our feelings, as Maori, evident, calling on our heritage of discourse and oratory to demonstrate to both New Zealand and to the world that we opposed this team representing the apartheid system being here.

That day I felt proud to be Maori, whereas there had been times before in my life I had been made to feel ashamed. The Springbok Tour was my starting point of assessing for myself what being Maori in Aotearoa was and could be. It was at that time I recognised I must make a stand against racism in my home and that I embraced and began to use my middle name. 'Taonga' was from my mother. As a child I was made uneasy, even embarrassed, by that name. It was a Maori name. Nobody else in the classroom had a Maori name. Teachers would trip over this name, mispronounce it and my face would flush with heat as other children sniggered.

My mother told me Taonga means 'treasured person' and now I use this name, always, in remembrance and in pride.

I'd watched him on TV debating and asserting Maori land issues. I knew that after 1981 he had entered university, studied law and then used his qualifications and skills to serve his people. He was approaching seventy now, still an imposing presence, very upright, that thick white hair, the fiercely intelligent, watchful brown eyes. He was dignified and polite but his reputation suggested he could be uncompromising and very, very tough.

I'd asked him if he recalled seeing the lambs on the march in Napier and he'd waved his hand as if swiping the question away. 'They were there.'

I pushed a little. 'You didn't approve of them?'

'We were marching for a cause of great importance. We didn't want their lightweight antics.'

'So what did you do?'

'We asked them to leave and when that didn't happen, we distanced ourselves from them.'

'How did you do that?'

'We marched, as always, in groups of ten. If they joined a group, the rest of the team wheeled around and went to the back of the formation and left them on their own. We wanted to demonstrate they were not a part of us.'

'Although they were marching for the same principles?'

'This was primarily a Maori protest. It was important that we conducted ourselves with dignity.'

How many people had disliked the lambs? From what I'd gathered they were mainly out of favour with COST committee members. 'Bloody grandstanders'. And the rugby supporters, well, maybe there was a bit of a love/hate thing going on there. A bit of a laugh, real entertainment, 'those queer bastards'.

They weren't only anti-Tour, they were gay *and* they took the piss out of rugby. As for the police, they took the piss out of them as well. There was the photograph that had turned up in just about every newspaper in the country. A squadron of police marching in unison followed by the goose-stepping lambs.

Yes, there were people who disliked them; maybe disliked them enough to beat them up if they got the chance. But as for the process involved in first identifying who they were and then following them and murdering one when he was alone and vulnerable — it seemed far too much of a stretch even for my imagination. I probably had all the mileage I was going to get on the lambs. I'd stuffed things up so badly with Stone there wasn't much chance he'd talk to me again and no one else seemed to know anything. Still, they fascinated me. I'd pull down images when I had the odd spare moment, watch the video clips.

And there was still Eric Woolley's family. It was worth a try. Telecom White pages.

Woolly for you
Wild and Woolly Yarns
Woolley, James. Remuera
Woolley, James. Devonport

Woolley, James, and Woolley, James. Easy enough, though I very much doubted either of them would want to talk to me.

But I'd try. Parents first. *Here come the usual accusations of muckraking, digging up dirt.*

'Are you there?' A lace-doilies and Royal-Doulton-tea-sets voice.

And *my* sweetest and most sincerely deferential voice. 'Good morning. My name is Rebecca Thorne. Am I speaking with Mrs Woolley?'

'If you're from the cleaning agency we're not happy and I'm simply not prepared to give you another chance.'

'Mrs Woolley, I'm sorry, I don't represent a cleaning agency. I work for Zenith Television. I'm putting together a documentary on the 1981 Springbok Tour and I'm hoping I may be able to talk to you about that.'

'The what? Who is speaking?'

I repeated the details slowly.

'I can't understand why you should possibly want to talk to me. Is this one of those surveys? I'm very busy and —.' Her voice was deeply suspicious.

'Mrs Woolley, I've contacted you because I understand your son was active in the anti-Tour movement and I was hoping you'd perhaps remember some of the details of his involvement.'

'Jim would never have been involved in that kind of nonsense.'

I closed my eyes. *Prepare for the onslaught.*

'I was hoping to talk to you about your son Eric.'

'*Eric*?' There was the kind of stunned silence you can actually hear down the phone.

'Perhaps if you'd rather not speak to me your husband might agree to —.'

'Heavens, no. James is in la-la land.'

I waited. I expected her to hang up but instead her voice had softened when she spoke again. 'I haven't heard Eric's name in years. He's dead, of course.'

'Yes, I know.'

'I was angry with him. We all were. He told us he was *that* way, he was a queer — he refused treatment for it, you know. James blamed me. Letting him have his way over those wretched dancing lessons.'

I couldn't quite believe it. I was actually getting somewhere. Should I ask questions or stay silent, let her talk on?

'The way he died. James didn't talk about it. But it was that man.

That dreadful man.' I heard her breathing shallowly at the other end. 'If it hadn't been for him none of it would have happened. Eric would have, he would have come around and seen sense. That man was responsible for my son's death.'

'You mean Caspar Stone?'

'I gave him the choice, that man or his mother. He was always my favourite. The boy broke my heart. I pretended he'd died, that was the only way I could cope.'

She was silent again.

'And then he did die. James said it was for the best. "Iris," he said, "what kind of life could he possibly have had?"'

That old-ladies' voice, stiff-upper-lip and a nice little G&T at the end of the day. So refined. So *chilling*.

'I'm not sure what you mean, Mrs Woolley.'

'You see them everywhere now, don't you. Deviants. Making a spectacle of themselves. It makes me sick. Better for my boy to be dead.'

I thanked her, clicked off my phone. Mike had glanced up a couple of times from his desk and now he was watching me.

'Shit,' I said. 'Oh *shit*, Mike. What people do to each other.'

'It's why I prefer dogs,' he said.

'How could any mother say her son is better off dead?'

'You were talking to Eric Woolley's mother?'

'I thought for just one minute she actually was this sweet old lady who'd loved her son. Then she started telling me how they'd cut him off and he was better off dead because he was a deviant. I just can't fucking believe what I just heard.'

And I burst into tears. God, I'd done some awful stories, heard terrible things, but this was the worst.

Mike was there in a second, wrapping his arms around me. 'Come on, mate, you can't take it to heart.'

'This boy dying all alone with a bottle stuck up his arse and his mother thinks it's all for the best? All the hurt and lies and —. What sort of world are we living in? I just can't bear it.'

'Ssh, shh, come on, Rebecca. You've been working too hard.'

I drew back from him, grabbed a handful of tissues from the box on my desk, blew my nose and wiped my eyes. 'Sorry. I'm sorry. I just lost it.' I tried to smile. 'No wonder you prefer dogs.'

'This is getting to you isn't it?' he said.

'I haven't been sleeping all that well. I've been . . . It's probably nothing, but I've been getting these weird phone calls.'

'What sort of phone calls?' His eyes were on the alert.

'Someone ringing, then hanging up. It's a nuisance more than anything.'

'Have you checked it out with Telecom?'

'I thought I'd wait and see if it happened again and then I got too busy and —.'

'Do you want me to look into it for you?'

'I should do it,' I said. 'It's just, I haven't quite got around to it. I can't possibly expect you to.'

'Course you can. No trouble. I might have more luck finding out what's going on. I can still pull a few strings.'

'Well, that would be great. But look, I'd better tell you. It's this ex-boyfriend. He's been hanging around.'

I told him what had happened, told him it was probably nothing, probably coincidence, probably my imagination working overtime. But.

'But you're not easy about it? I'll see what I can come up with on the phone calls and if you get another one or have any more trouble you're to call me, right?'

'Well, OK.'

'Don't you worry. We'll sort it out.'

I wrote him a list of the dates and approximate times the phone calls had come, ending with the one from the previous night. I knew it was probably too late to do anything about them but I felt better. *Mike is older than me, bigger than me, he's been a policeman, he'll know what to do.*

I took a leisurely lunch at Za-Za: corn fritters, bacon, avocado salad and a cake. I was tired, I'd let things get on top of me.

So. Regular runs and I would start cooking properly again and I'd have some early nights. It was time for me to accept that I had as much as I needed, or was going to get, about the lambs. I had enough material to make a good doco. Not out of the ordinary and neither would it expose entirely fresh material. But it would be rock-solid. I'd do it well.

Less stress, I told myself as I finished the very last morsel of chocolate banana cake. Less stress. From tomorrow. Because today, this afternoon, I just could not let it go. Because what I needed to know was did *everyone* in this family feel relieved Eric was dead? Did everyone believe he was better dead rather than bringing shame down on the esteemed Woolley name? Was there no one in this family who felt regret or sadness?

I suppose it was curiosity mixed with outrage that drove me on. I knew it had very little to do with the doco, that I probably wouldn't be able to use anything of what I might find out. And I knew I was doing exactly what I'd told myself over and over: don't get personally involved.

But I *so* wanted to pierce through all that smug respectability. I wanted the Woolley family to feel *something* for Eric even if it was only that this bitch from the media may reveal something which could cause them embarrassment.

That dreadful man. That man was responsible for my son's death.

Sorry, Mrs Woolley, it was you. You and your dreadful family.

This time I pressed in the numbers for Woolley, J, Devonport.

'Hello.' A tinkly, bob-and-diamonds voice.

Isobel Woolley? Des Horton said that she had expressed a 'fondness' for Eric. Maybe I'd be more likely to get something from her rather than her husband.

'Am I speaking to Mrs Woolley?'

'Yes.'

I breezed through the pitch. Name. Workplace. Research into. 'You see, what I'm hoping for is a human angle, to let viewers see the people behind that great mob of protesters they're used to seeing whenever the 1981 Tour gets mentioned. So, Isobel — it *is* Isobel isn't it? — when I found out that your brother-in-law was part of the anti-Tour movement, I wondered if you'd be able to fill in a few of the blanks?'

'This is *not* Isobel.' Although the voice remained tinkly there was now a coating of ice.

Oh *fuck*. Proceed with caution. 'I'm so sorry. But it *is* Mrs Woolley? You are married to Jim Woolley?'

'I am.' Glacial.

'I'm terribly sorry but I seem to have mistaken your name but, uh, do you have any memories of Eric Woolley?'

'No. I do *not* have any memories of Eric.' The tone was flat, hard, tinkles withdrawn. I heard a fragment of frantically whispered conversation then a man's voice cut in.

'This is Jim Woolley. Who am I speaking to?'

My perky/appealing voice. 'Rebecca Thorne, Zenith, researching for the thirtieth year of the —.'

'You're the one who's been bothering my mother. An eighty-year-old woman looking after an invalid. I hope you're proud of yourself. No comment and don't bother my family again.'

Click.

Arsehole. And I hope you're proud of yourself for disowning your own brother.

I couldn't let it go. Who else? Who would talk to me?

Sounded as though Isobel had been replaced. Ex-wives are often good to talk to. In my experience, ex-wives are often itching for the chance to pour out all the ex's and the ex-family's secrets and scandals, just longing to set all those skeletons rattling and jangling out of cupboards.

Woolley, I. Hillsborough.

Not Remmers or Devonport. Was that a sign the settlement wasn't enough to keep her in the circumstances she was accustomed to? Maybe she wouldn't be too reluctant to haul open those cupboard doors and let those bones come rolling on out.

'Isobel Woolley. Please leave a message.'

I hung up. No point in leaving a message as a warning I was

trying to make contact and give her the chance to hang up when I phoned back. But I'd found her.

I checked my watch. Nearly three o'clock. I had an interview at three-thirty. Time to go.

Interview: Member of the Red Squad. Anonymous.
You can use what I say, but I refuse to be identified. It's not I'm ashamed I was part of the Red Squad but it's not something I talk about, either. It carries a stigma, like soldiers who went to Vietnam, putting their lives at risk and doing what they had to for their country then got abused at the end of it.

The Red Squad was set up to accompany the Springboks over the fifty-six days of the Tour and to do its bit towards keeping order within New Zealand during that time. There were fifty-four of us selected, then we were divided into two squads of three sections and underwent an intensive preparation course at Papakura Military Camp. We'd been given the task of protecting the Boks and defending the law and order of this country and we had to have the means to do our job. Much of our training was in the use of the Monadnock PR-24 baton, which became commonly known throughout the country as the long baton. It was twenty-four inches long, made of aluminium with about a six-inch wooden handle attached at right angles towards the end of the baton. Quite an effective weapon in both defence and attack. We were coached in what was called rapid action, which was a kind of high-speed prodding using the baton. It also included using the short end of the baton, making downward slashes aiming towards the collarbone and also using the short and long end of the baton at a fast pace striking the head.

I can see what you're thinking. These big men with their bloody great batons breaking collarbones and smashing up heads. It's always that way. We were the bad guys, we were the fascists and racists trampling all over those peace-loving protesters. But I tell you right now, that's not the way it was. The guys in the Red Squad with me weren't killing machines, they weren't a savage pack of brutes let loose to smash up mums and dads and kids.

Look, *we* had kids, most of us, anyway. We were an ordinary team of blokes with the same cares and fears as anyone else and the idea that it was some sort of contest between good and evil and we were the bullies dishing it out is bullshit. Those so-called peaceful protests turned into a whole lot of lunatics destroying other people's property. If they were intending to be peaceful, why did they turn up wearing hard hats and carrying weapons? What about them chucking rocks and bricks and bottles?

You asked me to talk about what happened at the test in Wellington. We knew it was going to be a big one. We knew the protest movement was going all out to stop the game and there'd be a concerted effort to get into Athletic Park.

We felt the pressure as soon as we got into Wellington with protesters at the airport and cars and motorbikes at every airport exit ready to follow us. We fooled them, though. The Red Squad headed to the St George Hotel where we were staying, while the Blue Squad escorted the Boks to Athletic Park where they were billeted under the grandstand. There'd been bomb threats and we reckoned that with the barbed wire and barricading around the park and police patrolling it was the safest place for them to be.

We were in a fairly good position considering the fortification of the grounds and the available manpower. We had a rock-solid — impenetrable, we thought — barricade around the park and an extensive police presence including dogs and trainers.

On the day of the test we were called to the southern end of Rintoul and Luxford streets. There were over five hundred protesters wearing heavily padded clothing and helmets and carrying wooden shields. That mob was out for blood. The noise was unbelievable — the chanting and yelling and above it all you could hear those marshals. 'Go to the edge of the law and beyond. Go to the edge of the law and beyond that.'

I could feel the adrenalin kicking in and, my god I'll admit to this though I kept hold of it, pure bloody anger. What they were yelling at me and my mates. 'Nazis. Fascist bastards. Scum.'

Scum? They knew nothing about who we were. Nothing.

Then their Brown squad got into action. They were your hard-core radicals, many of them known to police long before the Tour got under way. They began to chant; you could feel them winding themselves up for confrontation. They did their haka, eyeballing us all the time. Then they started to advance.

'The police will use their batons if you attempt to breach our lines. If you attempt to breach our lines the police will use their batons. Some of you will be severely injured. The police will use their batons if you attempt to breach our lines.'

Then they were running at us. I felt my hand tightening around my baton and even though it was cold and pissing down with rain, I felt myself sweating.

About two feet away they stopped and sat down. They knew they couldn't break through our lines. I started to relax a bit. We'd won.

Then a few of them broke away and ran through properties, breaking down fences and trampling through gardens to get into Waripori Street which runs along the outside boundary of the park. We knew it was possible they could breach the barricade around the park so that lot got herded up and steered back into Rintoul Street. But when the militants saw them coming they saw it as the opportunity they'd been waiting for and started egging them on, urging them to press on ahead through the barricades into the park and with the numbers there — there must have been around a thousand protesters — they could have shoved their way through the turnstiles and onto the grounds.

The order came. 'Long batons, move.' We proceeded forward — 'Move. *Move. Move!* — prodding with our batons. The mob went crazy either trying to shove their way into the grounds or to get back outside the barricades.

The whole thing ignited. Packs of them started running at our lines and began hurling rocks and bricks and bottles.

'If you don't stop throwing missiles a police advance will be ordered. Long batons, move.'

Police around us were being attacked with knives, smashed with iron bars and while some protesters were hurt, some badly, I swear that the physical force we used was restrained and entirely appropriate in terms of the violence we were faced with. The action we took was brief and we held them back. They knew they'd been beaten and hit back at us by showing off their knocks and wounds to the media and complaining about police brutality.

There were accusations that protesters sitting peaceably on the ground in Waripori Street had been kicked and batoned and bashed by police. Those accusations are untrue. No peaceful protester was intentionally hurt. Another allegation was that a Red Squad officer had been heard to shout over his megaphone, 'Take no prisoners. We are not taking any prisoners.' While I can't totally deny that since I wasn't there, I am able to say that, given the discipline and control displayed by Red Squad officers and what other people told me, that was a lie. Just as I'm convinced that stories of Red Squad members losing control and having to be held back from beating protesters also were lies.

Yes, protesters were injured. All I can say is, they were warned. Over and over again, they were warned. Nobody who heeded those warnings would have been hurt and while the police manoeuvres may have surprised and shocked some citizens watching the scenes from the safety of their homes, we were there and we were threatened and our brief was to maintain law and order. Ordinary New Zealanders asserting their rights to attend a rugby game were threatened by a mob who'd fitted themselves out for a battle. They were the law breakers. It was our job to stop them.

As it was our job to ensure protesters were protected from the rugby crowds which streamed out into the streets after the game. We didn't get any thanks. 'Filthy fascists go home.'

23

I was back in the office listening to the tape and literally rubbing my hands together. As well as persuading a Red Squad member to give me his account of what had happened on the Wellington test day, I had an utterly contrary version of the events from Jane Devlin, one of the protesters.

I'd done my best to coax him into a debate on camera; his story against hers. What could be better than a stand-off between a Red Squad member and a protester? As I'd expected, he'd refused. But there was still time. I'd give it a few more goes. I was sure he'd liked me. When I'd first made contact with him he wasn't having a bar of it but he'd eventually warmed up enough to agree to talk. But even if he didn't agree I could do a voice-over with film clips, follow it immediately with Jane talking on camera.

I was buzzing. This was going to be *good*.

Interview: Jane Devlin. COST member.

We were in Waripori Street. The ordinary police were there and then the Red Squad turned up. They started moving towards us, all the time yelling through loudspeakers. 'Clear the street. Clear the street. You are not allowed to be here. Clear the street. Clear the street.'

But their warnings were utterly false. They were only giving them because the rule was they had to give a warning before using their batons. The truth was we couldn't get out because they'd blocked off the end of the street. It was absolutely clear what they were doing. Their intention was to beat us up.

They moved in, bashing and shoving people down the embankment on one side of the street. The people around me sat down and I did as well. I didn't think they'd hit us if we were sitting down and, you know, I was still naïve enough to think they wouldn't hit a woman, not if she was just sitting there, doing nothing to get in their way.

But they came at us kicking and lashing out with their batons. I rolled into the protection position we'd learned at the plenary sessions, curling up my body, shielding my head in my arms. I was absolutely passive, I was no threat to them whatsoever, but I still got smacked over the body and the head.

I'd never in my life been hit by anyone and I felt absolutely helpless and terrified and *outraged*. It bloody hurt, they really *hurt* me. I could see even the protesters who'd stood up and were trying to move off like they said they wanted us to do were being knocked down. There was this deafening sound of whacking and people screaming and the shouting over the megaphones and the clatter of helicopters just above us.

I was thinking, 'I'm a teacher, I'm a mother, this can't be happening. This can't be happening to me.'

In the end we were allowed up. We got into a line and police shoved and pummelled us as we made our way towards Rintoul Street. People were crying, some had blood running down their faces. I glanced back at the police and their faces were absolutely blank. I can't exactly explain to you what it was like but it was as if they didn't see us as people at all, we were just a pack of animals they were herding down the street.

Watching and listening to them, I'd have sworn they were both telling the truth. So who was lying? Though what really mattered was I had these wonderfully conflicting accounts. I looked at my watch. Just past 6 pm, time to try Isobel Woolley again.

'Isobel Woolley's phone. Please leave a message.'

I listened carefully. What did her voice give away? She wasn't exactly warmly greeting her callers or imploring them to leave their messages. I tried it again. A well-bred voice, the kind of rounded vowels I tend to associate with Christchurch — though why it's well-bred to sound more English aristocracy than the Queen I fail to understand. Did she sound imperious or slightly tense?

I was wasting time, trying to read something into a voice. What had I told myself just that morning? Regular exercise, food, sleep.

Cut the stress levels.

Time to go home. My fingers moved to switch off my computer. I glanced down at the news headlines: 'Murder Follows Calls from Stalker'. I clicked onto the screen, scrolled downwards scanning through the columns. Police called to address in North Shore. Body of eighteen-year-old woman. Multiple stab wounds. Reported calls from stalker in days before death. Body found by flatmate.

I switched off quickly. Probably some poor kid who'd plastered herself over Facebook, maybe on 'Find Friends'. Which was what kids did all the time except it left them so exposed and vulnerable to any wrong guy who took a liking to them.

'Murder Follows Calls From Stalker.' I picked up my laptop, my dictaphone, a couple of articles I wanted to read and zipped them into my backpack. The office had cleared out: I was the last one there. I locked the office door behind me, stepped into the lift down to the carpark. I opened the door into the stairwell which led down into the carpark.

Why doesn't the lift go right down into the basement? Shouldn't someone complain? Isn't it a safety issue?

I hesitated beside the door. I hate carparks when they're nearly empty; the echo as your heels hit the concrete floor, the sudden swish as a car unexpectedly rounds a corner and you're dazzled by the lights as it passes you.

Body found. Multiple stab wounds.

Multiple stab wounds.

I crossed quickly to my car. I was almost running, my eyes darting all around the building, one corner to another, to another, another, and when I'd made it across those acres of concrete into my car and locked the doors I rested my head in my hands for a moment. I was shaking slightly and my mouth was dry.

That poor girl died. She died.

But what's happening to me is totally different. It'll all turn out to be nothing. Absolutely nothing.

I drove up over the ramp, slipped my card in, the barrier lifted and I was on the kerb waiting for a gap in the traffic. A car swished past, a grey Audi.

Rolly's?

Was it Rolly?

There are at least a thousand silver Audis in Wellington. Get a grip. Home.

I slipped off my jacket, pulled the curtains, poured a glass of wine. I checked the time. 6.45. Maybe she'd be home by now.

And this time it was Isobel herself. OK. Onstage. *Rebecca Thorne. 1981 Springbok Tour. Research. Anti-Tour movement. Eric Woolley.*

'I don't understand why you've contacted me.'

They never *do* understand. 'I believe Eric was your brother-in-law.'

'Well, yes, he was. But I had absolutely nothing to do with the anti-Tour movement. The family was pro-Tour.'

'It's not so much the Tour but Eric I was hoping to talk to you about.'

'I hardly knew Eric. It was only when Jim and I were first married. He was quite a bit younger and he and Jim didn't get on terribly well. To be quite honest, I hardly ever saw him.'

'A police officer who talked to you shortly after Eric's death told me you seemed fond of him.'

'Well, I was. He was very outgoing, had a good sense of humour, he always had me laughing. Jim always said he was a total show-off but I didn't see it that way.'

'He was a bit of a comedian?'

'I suppose you could say that. He and I did get on well, when we saw each other, that is. Jim and his father were always so bloody pompous and Eric'd make these sly little remarks and he'd kind of slide his eyes towards me to see how I was taking it. They weren't malicious comments, just taking the mickey.'

'Any specific reasons why Eric and Jim didn't get on?'

'Oh god, where would I start? They were totally different, what's that expression — like chalk and cheese? That's what they were like. Jim was conventional and quite reserved and Eric was the opposite. He was a dancer, as you probably know, and he never had an entirely stable job, just went from one to another and then he'd eventually turn up at home. Flat broke some of the time. Jim didn't like it and neither did his father. Inconsiderate and irresponsible. I can almost hear them saying it.'

She was certainly chatty. 'Jim thought Eric was a bit of a user, do you think?'

'A user. Immature. Reckless. Selfish. All of those and more. I think —.'

I waited, then prompted her gently. 'You think?'

'I might be getting into a bit of amateur psychology here but I do think a lot of how Jim felt about Eric was because Iris, their mother, clearly preferred Eric. James favoured Jim and Iris favoured Eric was the way things were. Until everything fell apart.'

'What happened?'

'It was like one of those Victorian melodramas where the disgraced daughter is driven out into the snow. You know, "Never darken my door again." Except in this case it was the disgraced son.'

'Disgraced?' This woman was every journo's dream.

'A blot on the Woolley name. He was gay, you see. Shock, horror.'

'They didn't know?'

'Well, if they didn't they were blind as well as stupid. It stood out a mile. Everyone knew. Not that anyone said anything. Eric had gorgeous thick hair, very shiny and a beautiful natural blond, and he always had it quite long and that's what Jim and James used to go on about. Not that he was gay but that his hair was too long.'

'How did it all come out?'

'Eric told them. That was the sin, of course. Once he told them they actually were forced to face it. He'd met that guy he lived with. Cas something.'

'Caspar Stone?'

'That's right. Eric told his parents he was gay and he was living with a man.'

'And?'

'All hell broke loose and he was banned from their house and ours. I'd not long had our son and there was no way in hell Jim's deviant brother was getting near his precious baby boy.'

'You're joking.'

'No. Listen, homosexuals attack little boys. They can't be trusted, according to the lore of the Woolleys.'

'Do you remember two guys who dressed up as lambs and protested against the Springbok Tour? Did you know Eric was one of them?'

'I suspected he was.'

'Jim never mentioned it?'

'Jim never mentioned Eric full stop. Mind you, it would have driven Jim and his father James mad if they'd known. The disgrace to the family —.'

'You never saw Eric again?'

'Uh.' I heard the hesitation in her voice. 'I always wanted to but that would have meant going against Jim and his family and that was more trouble than I wanted. I expected there'd be a reconciliation eventually and I would see him again. But that didn't happen. That's the way it is with that lot. Once you're out, you are out.'

I heard the bitterness in her voice. *This woman is amazing. All she wants is an audience.*

'I take it that you're out as well now?'

'That family. If they get their knives into you —.'

'You sound upset.'

'Darned right I'm upset.' Her voice was shrill, on high-speed. 'It's so ironic it'd almost make you laugh. Eric meets someone he wants to be with, right? They're both free, no ties, not hurting anyone but he gets thrown out. Then Jim gets involved with this slut, half his age, and, guess what, it's *me* being chucked out. It's *me* that no one's talking to any more and it's *me* that finds out Jim and his father have locked everything up in a trust. So the houses and the assets are all tied up and I'm supposed to feel grateful that I get almost enough to buy myself an ex-state home in Hillsborough. She moves into the house I cherished all those years and, guess what, she's already pregnant and she has twins and those little bastards are entitled to as much of the family trust that I was partially responsible for building, as my own kids are.'

'Nasty.'

'I shouldn't be telling you all this. You don't want to hear. But all I've ever done for myself is working part-time selling clothes in Smith and Caughey's. Isobel's "little interest" and it was, I happen to like fashion. But Jim always came first, Jim and the children and the house and now I'm sixty. Sixty and I've got a mortgage. I've still got the job but god knows how long that will last and if it does it looks like I'll be doing it for the rest of my life. I've got nothing while Jim and that bitch —. That family is evil.'

'Can't your solicitor do something?'

'Nothing to be done, he says. The Woolley family have their fingers in pies all over town, best not to cross them if you're a solicitor and you know what's good for you. I should leave Auckland, just get away from it all, but my kids are here, my grandchildren. I don't want to leave them.'

'Isobel, I'm really sorry. That's so unfair.' I paused for a tactful moment. 'Just one last question. How did the family react to the news of Eric's death?'

'There was a death notice in the *Herald* and that was pretty much that.'

'No tears?'

'You must be joking.'

I put together my favourite vegetable curry, poured a glass of wine and sat in front of the windows. There was a thin layer of mist floating above the sea. It was still light enough to make out the airport on one side, the sweep of land on the other. The waves were churning up froth, seagulls were free-sailing, one of the ferries was moving out past the horizon.

I could have known from the arrogance and condescension in Jim Woolley's voice that he was exactly the kind of cold bastard to discard his wife of many years and replace her with a later model with a bit more pep and gloss.

Hadn't I wanted Joe to do that? To leave Michelle?

But we'd loved each other. It was different with us. We were in love.

Isn't it always different?

I whirled my wine around in the glass, watched it slosh and tip up the sides. It was a luscious colour, this pinot gris I'd just discovered. Pale golden, the colour of almost ripe pears.

It was different with us. We were in love.

Strange how 'different for us' always ends in the same way. Either you or someone else badly damaged.

I looked back out towards the sea and sky. Almost dark. My *own* house, my *own* wine and food I had chosen for *me*, my evening stretching out ahead to spend exactly as I chose.

Maybe it's better this way. This way you depend only on yourself; you don't get discarded. This way you don't get hurt.

I ate and cleaned up, made a cup of tea, turned on my recorder.

Interview: Graham White. COST member.

I went down to Nelson for the August 22 protest there with about fifty others. Some of the marshals went with us. COST sent them to help the Nelson HART group with organising the day's activities. Others from COST would have gone as well but the transport wasn't all that easy and nobody wanted to get arrested that far away from Wellington, not with the test only a week away.

There were a couple of things that happened in Nelson before the game. Protesters broke up a council meeting because of the mayor agreeing to give the Springboks an official welcome. The other thing made us laugh and the police look stupid — they blew up one of the South African journalist's typewriters because they thought it was a bomb.

On the Friday night before the game we caused a bit of mayhem. Some of us got into the Rutherford Hotel where the Boks were staying and set off the fire alarms. There was full-on pandemonium, everyone rushing about and sirens blaring. When all the other protesters arrived the Boks and the Red Squad and police and all the other guests and the hotel staff were downstairs in the hotel lobby.

We gave them the full blast. The Boks for being there, the Red Squad for being the fascists they were, and the hotel for letting the country down by hosting them. We also had a bit of fun paying calls throughout the night with hooters and sirens and rubbish-tin lids. I doubt anyone staying in the hotel got a lot of sleep that night.

We went back at 7 am the next morning and camped outside, keeping up a constant round of singing and chanting and speaking. We had a go at stopping the bus taking the Boks and the police to the park but it was a no-go and quite a few people got bashed and knocked over by the riot squad. Around midday Trevor Richards and Hone Tuwhare turned up and talked to the crowd and then we marched — there were about a thousand of us — down Trafalgar Street until we broke into three groups.

I was with the group who went to the Maitai River. It bordered the park and on that side the park was fairly much unguarded. The river was up, though, so there was no way we could have walked over. A few, me included, thought seriously about swimming across and we went in up to our knees but then gave it up. It was bloody freezing being the middle of winter, and it was swift, not worth the risk, and anyway we would have needed more than a handful of us to get onto the grounds and stop the game.

The phone rang. Margo. Excited, giggly, obviously dying to tell me something. 'Guess what?'

'No idea.'

'Come on. Guess. I'll give you a clue. We're drinking champagne.' More than a couple of glasses going by her voice.

'You're pregnant.'

'I wouldn't be drinking if I was *pregnant*, would I? We're *engaged*.'

'Oh. Congratulations.'

I hoped Margo would not detect the lack of full-on enthusiasm and excitement in my voice. Engaged? They'd been living together practically from the time they'd left school. Why the hell were they getting engaged? Engaged was *so* mid-twentieth century. It was hope chests and flowery china and waiting for years and years with a tiny sliver of diamond chip on your finger while you paid off the section. I was never, ever getting engaged.

Rebecca, be nice.

'That's fantastic news. When are you —?'

'Getting married? That depends a lot on when we can get in somewhere. We were thinking the Brookland Lodge, but apparently it's booked months ahead. Oh, darling, Jeremy's brother's on the other line so —.'

'OK. We'll talk later.'

'I need to ask you something. I'll call you right back.'

Dammit, it was getting late, I had a busy day tomorrow and I wanted to finish this up and get to bed early. I turned the tape back on.

Where we were situated, not too far from Trafalgar Park, in full view of the rugby crowd, we could certainly make ourselves heard. We held our banners up high and kept up with the chanting and singing. There was one song I remember. I'm not much of a singer. It's 'John Brown's Body' if you don't get it.

The Springboks are the heroes of the Afrikaner tribe,

They would feel at home in Molesworth Street with batons by their sides,

Barbed wire's their national symbol and apartheid is their pride,

So send the racists home

We will stop the Tour to-ge-ther

We will stop the Tour to-ge-ther

We will stop the Tour to-ge-ther

And we'll send the bastards home.

I was smiling. He'd been so bursting with eagerness as he'd sung it to me but he was right. He wasn't much of a singer.

The phone rang. Margo again. 'Rebecca? Listen, you will be my bridesmaid, won't you? I'm only having one and it has to be you.'

Oh fuck. I'd already been Anna's bridesmaid and Julia's bridesmaid and Sarah's and Amy's and Liesle's. I'd already crammed myself into too many too-tight, too-shiny, too-downright-awful dresses.

'Well. I'd love to. But are you sure? I mean, what about your sister?'

Please, God.

'No, it has to be you. I'm asking Sara — that's Jo's daughter, remember — to be flower girl so that covers that one. But listen, Jeremy's brother knows someone who thinks he can get us into this absolutely gorgeous new place in Martinborough. It's a vineyard and they've just opened it up as a wedding venue. Isn't that exciting!'

'Fantastic.'

'I was thinking about an all-white wedding? But that's been done so many times? So, I might wear that ivory colour, it'd look much better with my skin tone, and I was thinking of a kind of light coffee colour for you.'

Great. I'm going to wear a brown dress.

'Sounds good,' I said. 'Hey, let's catch up and celebrate really soon, OK, and we can talk about it.'

'I'll be able to show you the ring by then. We're going shopping tomorrow. Jeremy was going to surprise me but he was worried I might not like what he chose and, after all, it's something I'll be wearing forever, isn't it?'

Haven't you looked at the statistics?

I hung up. God, I was turning into a bitter cow. But I was busy and, of course, I was pleased for Margo and Jeremy, I loved Margo and Jeremy and, of course, I wanted to hear all about their wedding stuff. Just not right now.

I turned the machine back on.

After the match we went back to the Rutherford Hotel. The police were there in force and I think they'd had enough of us and they laid in fairly solidly with their batons and shoved people around and there were a few injured.

You asked about the lambs and, yes, they were there. They'd gone with another group to the other side of the park and they'd done their usual acting the fool stuff, chasing each other and marching after the police. They made it part-way up the barbed-wire fence and started blowing kisses at the rugby crowd. Not everyone liked what they were doing but you couldn't help laughing at those two.

Something I thought of, though, to tell you. Well, afterwards, while we were outside the Rutherford and the police were getting stuck in, I saw this cop —.

The phone rang. I snatched it up. Margo telling me she wanted me in a pink crinoline with a bonnet?

'Hello.'

Someone breathing. Breathing and listening. Someone checking I was home?

'Rolly, you've got to stop this. You've got to stop this right now or I'm calling the police.' I smacked down the phone and checked the time. Nearly eleven. Too late to call Mike.

Telecom. I had to deal with this *now*. Muzak. 'Your call is important to us.' More muzak. I slammed it down, pulled up the Telecom website.

'If you have or are receiving nuisance calls you are not alone. Telecom receives 3000 complaints a month and operates a specialised call centre to assist.

'If you are receiving calls that you consider to be a nuisance Telecom may be able to assist. However, we are only able to investigate if it is causing serious problems and calls/text messages are occurring on an ongoing basis.

'You can contact the Telecom Call Investigation centre on 0800 809 806 during the hours of 8 am–5 pm Monday to Friday (excluding statutory holidays).'

Right. If I received any death threats I now knew to inform my threatener to get back to me between eight and five and to make sure it wasn't on a Saturday or Sunday or Queen's Birthday Bloody Weekend.

I turned the machine on again.

I saw this cop. He had his helmet down covering his face. I noticed him because of the way he was moving, real fast, holding his baton up like he intended giving someone a hiding. He was shoving his way towards the black lamb. I thought the white one would have seen the cop heading towards his mate because he was right in the way, but he couldn't have because he took off in the other direction.

The cop had almost got to the black lamb. He had his baton held way above his head and it was so bloody obvious what he was going to do with it I could almost feel that baton crunching down on my own head. I yelled out a warning, 'Get out of the bloody way, mate!' Not that anyone could have heard anything above all that noise.

Then the crowd surged backwards, shoving everyone with it, and the black lamb looked over his shoulder and saw the cop coming for him. He turned around and yelled something at him, he was waving his arms and yelling, and then he turned and started leaping and ducking and diving through the crowd.

I turned off the recorder. I was tired. I washed my face, rubbed in moisturiser, pulled on my pyjamas and opened my wardrobe to hang up the jacket I'd left on my bed. I reached up for a coat hanger and there it was. My dress.

My blue dress.

I started to shake.

24

It's odd how we rationalise things. Though maybe not so odd — nobody wants to believe a stranger has slipped into their house, opened up their drawers and cupboards, touched their things.

It was near the back of the wardrobe. It was hanging beside the blue sweater which is just about the same colour. Hanging between the blue sweater and my black woollen coat which swamps anything close by.

It wasn't in its normal place.

I've been so busy I just haven't noticed it was there all the time.

It couldn't be anything else. Nothing like that could happen.

Not to me.

Anyway, nobody could get in. I've had the locks all changed.

I got into work early enough to talk to Mike before anyone else got there. 'I want to put something to you, as a cop. Just hear me out, OK?'

'I'm all ears.' He folded his arms.

'Right. As you know, I've been doing interviews and in four at least, people have mentioned police behaving aggressively to the lambs.'

'Now that doesn't surprise me. They were bloody pests. They knew how to work a crowd and they'd rev up some of the rugby supporters to the point that it was even harder for us to control them. They were right out there in terms of opposing the Tour and to top that off they were overtly gay at a time gay pride hadn't even been thought of, not in this country anyway. There they were dressed up, dancing around and flaunting what they were.'

'I've been told they lightened things up and made people laugh.'

'They might have made some people laugh but they made a lot of others bloody angry. As well as all the outrage about the Tour, we had people getting up on their high horses complaining about the risk to public morality. These men were flagrantly breaking the law so why weren't they arrested?'

'Could you have arrested them?'

'And have gay-rights riots as well as anti-Tour? You must be joking. Those lambs made a bad situation worse and it was up to the cops to somehow keep a set of circumstances that they'd set up themselves from turning incredibly nasty. They were a problem and a few of the guys were fairly vocal in voicing the opinion we should let the crowd have a bit of a go at them so they'd no longer *be* a problem.'

I stared at him. 'They were that keen to get rid of them?'

'Far as I'm concerned it was just talk. But look, I can see there's something you want to say so just tell me what you're thinking.'

'Uh, I know you were a cop and I know you were a good one. But I've seen the pictures and the video clips. Some cops behaved brutally during the Tour. Whether the pressure got too much for them, I don't know, I can only imagine what it must have been like —.'

'But cops chased protesters when all they wanted was to get away and they hit and kicked protesters who were sitting on footpaths and left them injured and bleeding. Is that what you're saying?'

I looked at his face. His expression was grim. I loved Mike. He was one of the best guys in this world and I didn't want to hurt or insult him, but. 'I am saying that.'

He sighed. 'Well, I'm saying it too and I'm ashamed of what happened. There were guys I knew who went too far, some of them even my mates. I know what you're saying is right and I don't like it but that's what happened.'

'I know you're going to think this is far-fetched but I want you to think about it carefully. What if someone from the police, maybe more than one person, *really* got pissed off with the lambs?'

'And decided to get rid of either both or one of them?' Mike was shaking his head. 'No.'

'You said they made a bad situation worse and some cops wanted to let the crowd loose on them.'

'And they could have done that and got away with it as well. If a few cops got together and decided they really wanted them off the scene, it would have been easy enough to stand aside and let it happen.'

'But the lambs had a lot of support. I've talked to people who loved them. If they'd been badly injured during a protest there could have been more bad feeling against the police. There may have been even more of a swing against the Tour as well, if the lambs were perceived as martyrs. Everyone who watched TV knew who they were. They were seen up and down the country as highly talented and funny. Even kids watched out for them. If they'd been injured, the media would have had a field day. Maybe it would have been rugby supporters who hurt them but the police would have got the blame.'

'So better to get them on their own. Is that what you're saying?'

'On their own and removed from anything related to the Tour. And Mike, Des Taylor told me when he was looking into Eric Woolley's death he was made to feel by people above him he was wasting his time, that his first priority had to be the Tour.'

'So the police got rid of Woolley and then covered it up?'

'Well, yes.'

'The first thing you need to remember, mate, is that this is real New Zealand and not a New York crime novel, OK? I'm not laughing at you, but cops here make mistakes, sure, but we don't go out and kill people even if they are getting on our wicks and we sure as hell don't cover up murders. The next thing is, this killing had a very obvious sexual element to it and that puts it in a whole different ball game from someone killing Woolley because he had a personal grudge against him.'

I was determined to stand my ground. 'Yeah, but whoever did it might have used that bottle to make it *look like* the attack was sexually motivated.'

Mike shook his head again. 'The attack was vicious. Eric Woolley was kicked to death and raped. This wasn't some cop with a chip on his shoulder, this was a pack of homophobic animals.'

'But —.'

'Forget it. You're barking up the wrong tree. Now, any more of those phone calls?'

'Uh, there was one last night.'

'Last night? Why didn't you phone me?'

I knew I'd get that reaction and I knew I was burying my head in the sand over it but it was too much trouble. I wanted to get on with what I was doing. There was an explanation for all of this. I'd made a mistake about the dress, the phone calls were from kids having a laugh and —. Dammit, now Tim was in the office as well with his ears all pricked up at the sound of slightly raised voices and heading directly for us. 'What's up?'

'Your T-shirt for a start,' I said.

Tim, at the ripe old age of forty-seven, had married for the first time in what would be generally termed a whirlwind romance. Thank god that Gina, the object of his affection, was equally besotted. And now, their six-month-old, Reuben — born, I'd swear, within nine months of their very first meeting — was regularly paraded through the office by his unashamedly adoring father. Reuben's T-shirt yesterday had the words 'Carry Me! I Can't Walk' stretched across his plump little belly and, yes, he *was* cute. Tim's T-shirt today was similarly stretched but differently worded. 'Carry Me! I Can't Work.'

Tim grinned. Looked at Mike. Stopped grinning. 'What *is* up?'

'It's nothing,' I said.

'It's a bloody long way from nothing,' Mike said. 'Rebecca's been getting phone calls where the caller hangs up. Quite a few of them, in fact, and she told me she'd let me know if and when she got another one.'

'All right. I got one last night but it was late and I didn't want to disturb you.'

'Could this be work-related?' Tim was looking worried.

'I told you to phone any time,' Mike said.

They were both standing over me, scrutinising me. 'I tried to ring Telecom,' I said trying to stare them out, 'but you can only contact them between 8 am and 5 pm.'

'Could it be anything to do with what you're working on?' Tim asked. 'The Tour story?'

'I doubt it. The Tour's long over, there's still some bitterness but I don't think that would extend to what we're doing. The people I've talked to have been keen to talk about what happened. I haven't struck anyone who's seemed aggressive.'

'You've got no idea who's doing it? What about things you've worked on before this?'

'There's an ex-boyfriend,' I said. 'I seem to keep running into him.

But, well, you've met him. Rolly. He's just about the last person you'd suspect of doing anything like this.'

'How can anyone know what someone else is capable of?' Tim said. 'You hear it all the time. People saying they lived next door to some psycho and he was so quiet they can't believe what he did.'

'I told her the same thing,' Mike said, 'and I've seen it time and again.'

'You're both overreacting,' I said.

'I've just been reading this one.' Tim said. 'Is *this* overreacting?'

He bent down, manipulated the touch pad on my computer, brought up the latest news flash.

Murder Victim Named

Following the discovery of a body in a bedroom of a North Shore apartment last week, police have now named the victim. She is Anya Katherine Davis.

Miss Davis's body was discovered by her flatmate. Miss Davis had expressed fears about a person she believed was stalking her in the weeks previous to her death.

Detective Senior Sergeant Alan Parkinson said a post-mortem examination showed Miss Davis had suffered 'savage' knife injuries to her neck, face and lower abdomen.

Police are continuing with their enquiries.

There was a head-and-shoulders photograph. Anya Davis had long dark hair. She was smiling. She was pretty. Her shoulders were bare and tanned.

An interview with her flatmate was positioned just below the main story: 'She said when she first got the calls she was like, "Who is this? Stop calling me, OK?" But then she got worried because this guy kept texting and calling her and she didn't know who he was. She didn't answer the texts and she'd hang up right away when he called but he wouldn't stop. She was scared he might be following her.

'She was really freaked out.'

'I think you should go to the police with this,' Tim said.

'According to Telecom directives you only go to the police if someone threatens you or swears at you or uses sexually explicit language. This is probably just a couple of kids taking some random number and having a bit of fun at my expense.'

'Yeah, and a couple of kids are randomly sending photos?' Mike said.

'Photos?' Tim asked.

'That's stopped,' I said. 'I haven't had any more.'

'I'm going to get onto this right away,' Mike said, 'and, Rebecca, you've got to phone me if it happens again. Phone me when it happens, doesn't matter what the time is. Got it? Now promise me.'

'Mike, I *promise* that if I get a call at 2.30 in the morning I will phone you.'

'And at any other time.'

'And at any other time. Now, if you two will excuse me, I'll get on with my job.'

I made a point of appearing busy looking something up on my computer and they drifted away. My dignity was very badly injured. First by Mike who'd been amused by my well-thought-out theory concerning Eric Woolley's death which he obviously believed was inspired by second-rate thrillers, and second by the two of them coming over like Victorian patriarchs. They'd banded together against me, treated me like I had no sense.

Those two as my minders? It was almost laughable. I tower over Tim and I absolutely guarantee that if the need arose I could run a lot faster and punch harder. And while Mike is big and has been fairly tough in his day, he's thirty years older than me.

I can look after myself.

I'd looked after myself perfectly adequately for all of my adult life. I did read newspapers and listened to and watched the news. Hell, I *was* the news, some of the time. I wasn't some sheltered innocent. I knew very well bad things happened. Which is why I was frightened.

I was frightened because this was something I didn't understand and couldn't control. When I was little I was scared of the dark — until I understood it was the same room, the same house, except without the light. I stopped being frightened when Dad bought me a torch and I practised turning it on and off, seeing the room first in light and then in darkness. After that I was OK. I knew the torch was there. I had the control.

So how to control this thing?

I didn't want Telecom or the police to take control. I wouldn't have given Mike the control if I hadn't been so busy and preoccupied. What were the choices? I didn't want to change my mobile and home numbers or to have an unlisted number. There were too many people who had to be able to get hold of me. And what had that website about stalkers suggested? 'Don't change your phone numbers because it will only give your stalker an extra challenge.'

Think it out. From now on, whenever I was at home I would let the answer phone pick up any calls. If the caller's number was withdrawn on my mobile I wouldn't answer. If I got any more photos I would delete them immediately.

'Do not reveal shock or anger. In most cases this is what the caller wants.'

Whoever was doing this wouldn't hear my voice again. If they didn't hear my voice, maybe get some kind of kick out of the effect the calls had, they'd stop.

From now on, I would always leave the office when someone else was leaving and go with that someone else into the carpark. I'd lock my doors as soon as I got into my house. I'd keep my windows closed, pull the curtains and blinds shut. Probably all that was over-vigilant but at least I'd feel safe.

Maybe I should carry a rape whistle and a can of hairspray. I'd heard you can virtually blind someone with hairspray if necessary. And I could hide weapons around my house — a hammer in the bathroom, a knife under my bed.

Probably that was taking it a bit too far.

The dress was a mistake. It had to be. There was no other explanation.

Next problem. Was my theory that Eric Woolley's murder could have been related, after all, to the anti-Tour movement totally implausible?

25

Caspar Stone's shop offered the type of artworks which could cause any brave soul venturing to peer into those fastidiously composed windows to reel backwards to the safety of the footpath. It was only a very brave or very rich passer-by who would presume to cross over the threshold.

I glanced then gaped at the large display window which was backdropped in heavy cream satin. At the centre was a carved wooden sculpture of a naked male figure raised up on a pedestal. Above it a sole spotlight cast a low soft sheen that made the dark wood glow. Each muscle in the torso, the thighs, the calves and upper and lower arms was distinct. The hands were elegant, the fingers long and slender, appearing to be grasping for something. The eyes were blindfolded.

It was the kind of art which repelled rather than drew you close, then wrenched you back to gaze. Inside, the *objets d'art* were displayed on velvet-covered tables and against white walls. I wanted to stroke my fingers over the child carved from jade, smooth out the legs drawn up so tightly you could almost feel that tight constriction on the chest. I wanted to ease those arms which shielded the head and soothe away the expression of suffering.

Caspar Stone watched me from behind his desk. 'Miss Thorne. How lovely to see you. Are you looking for anything in particular?'

Oh, I'd simply adore a Fabergé enamel cross pendant. Or maybe a Victorian mourning brooch.

'I was hoping to speak to you,' I said.

'As you can see I am very busy.' He looked back down at the papers in front of him. I was dismissed.

Time for shock tactics. I marched up to his oak Edwardian desk and slapped a photograph in front of him. 'This is what they did to him. Aren't you interested in finding out who it was?'

He glanced down. I hadn't chosen the worst one. This was head and shoulders only.

He looked at me. Nothing other than a drowsy kind of blandness. Did this man ever feel anything? 'Really, Miss Thorne, even in terms of the present-day media which is renowned for rudeness and forceful behaviour, I can't help but admire your brashness and stridency. You are perfectly free to browse, but I'd much prefer that you remove both yourself and this unpleasant photograph and allow me to continue with my work.'

I drew myself up. I'd allowed myself to be patronised by two men today and I wasn't letting it happen again. 'The police said Eric Woolley was murdered by a group of thugs they never happened to find,' I said. 'Haven't you ever thought it was rather convenient that these so-called thugs took out someone who was making the police's job increasingly difficult?'

He looked over the paper on his desk, scrawled his signature at the bottom and took another from the pile beside him.

'Come *on*,' I said, 'talk to me, please. I'm on your side.'

'I have no desire to have an amateur girl detective on my side.'

'This,' I said, 'is the man you said was the love of your life.'

'At a time when I had not yet come to the understanding that one experiences many loves over a lifetime. One love goes away, another comes along. It's the way life is, Miss Thorne, as I'm sure you will have realised many, many times. Now if you would please excuse me —.'

'There were police who hated you and Eric Woolley, police who wanted to stand back and let the crowd have a go at you. Police like, like Denny Graham.'

He turned his eyes away from the pages in front of him and looked at me. Had I earned myself a flicker?

'You must know about Denny Graham.' I was starting to babble. I had to somehow keep his attention. 'It's been all through the newspapers and over TV how ruthless he is. He was a cop back then. Everyone I've talked to has said he was crooked. With cops like that around, don't you think there's just a chance Eric's murder wasn't some random attack?'

197

He opened his diary and leafed through the pages. 'Tuesday. 7 pm. At the house.'

'I'll be there.'

That fleeting expression in his eyes. *Denny Graham.* Did that name mean something to him or had he just softened slightly? Or had he picked up I actually cared about this, that this had become more than just a story to me?

Because I'd come to think of Eric Woolley, rather than as a victim who would earn me a bit of mileage for my story, more as a young man passionate enough about a cause to put himself on the line. A young man who had died horribly and alone. Whom the police hadn't been concerned enough about to make the effort to investigate his murder. Whose family hadn't cared enough for to give even the dignity of a funeral. And now, thirty years later, he was an overlooked police file, a dirty family secret, ditched and buried. Yes, I cared that a gifted young man had been cheated out of his life by evil bastards who'd got away with it.

Another interview. Ten minutes to get there.

Interview: Wellington COST member. Anonymous.

I was on the list Muldoon gave to the press. According to him, the SIS had compiled and disclosed the names of fifteen extremist activist radicals who were in control of the anti-Tour movement and he'd decided to release those names because of the danger to the country; the danger being that all of us on the list were using the anti-Tour movement to drive the country into anarchy.

In other words, us commies had seized on the opportunity presented by the Tour to steer all those thousands of meek protesters into collective disobedience. This, of course, would end up in a revolution which would knock down the government and democracy and there we fifteen would be, at the end of our dastardly plot, rubbing our hands together over the great Marxist conquest.

I wasn't, in fact, a lefty, though some in the movement were. Just like some were Catholics or Presbyterians or Lodge members or belonged to the Maori Women's Welfare League. What we were didn't matter so long as we kept the move against the Tour and apartheid foremost in our minds.

Obviously, I'm Maori. I was marching for black rights. It made no difference who was standing beside me. Didn't matter what the motivation was. What mattered was doing what was right.

Someone phoned me up, 'Hey bro, you're on the list.' It gave me a bit of a jolt. Big Brother watching. But Muldoon singling out us so-called troublemakers had just about the opposite effect to what he'd wanted to set up. It made for more commitment rather than less. For one thing, the idea that fifteen of us were conning all the rest of them was just plain silly. At the same time it was insulting for all those who turned up week after week for the meetings and marches and that made us all that much stronger, closer. Another run-off was others joined who said they'd been in two minds about demonstrating but now they'd seen Muldoon was prepared to use 'reds under the beds' scare tactics, they got right behind us. There was an American couple used to come to meetings. They said what made them immigrate to New Zealand in the first place was McCarthyism and the Cold War. They said we had to stamp it out here before it ignited.

You asked if I ever felt threatened, other than the shit we got during the protests. Well, we did have a Molotov cocktail thrown at the house. Not really up to much — it landed on the lawn, popped a couple of times then fizzled, a bit like a fireworks display on a wet night. I filled a milk bottle with water and ran outside and put it out. But the worst of it was we — me and my wife, Marie — got phone calls. 'You're dead you nigger bastards', that kind of bullshit. We always pulled the phone cord out after eleven o'clock but I remember one night we forgot and it woke us up at around 3 am. The kids started crying and Marie was so bloody angry she ran out into the hallway and yelled into the phone, 'Would you bastards just leave us alone?' Then I got angry with her.

'They phone because they want to make us angry and scared. They want a reaction and look what you've done, you've given them exactly what they bloody want. Now they'll never leave us alone.'

'I want out of this. Out. It's putting us in danger. We're putting our babies in danger. Don't you care?'

I remember both of us standing there in the hall screaming at each other, both close to tears. The stress'd really got to us. Took a long time to get over that.

After the Palmerston North match all our efforts and planning in COST was turned towards the test and, as the days passed, the tension grew, you could almost feel that pressure coming in on you at the meetings. There were a lot of decisions to make. We still had the after-effects of Palmerston North, the bitterness hanging over from COST members who believed we'd lost our nerve there and, while the aim was clear — we all wanted to stop the game — there were clashes over strategies.

Why did we come to the decision that the thrust of the campaign on the day would be to block the roads to Athletic Park and prevent spectators and players getting in? Well, what we saw first of all was the unfeasibility of trying to get around ten thousand protesters into the park. But mainly it was motivated by safety issues. We'd already seen the lengths police were prepared to go to and we felt responsible for the people who were joining us. We didn't want a blood-bath.

But many at the meeting saw the occupation of the park as the best way of stopping the test and they were hell-bent on trying. They also saw this decision as another cop-out, another case of the executive losing nerve. We finally came up with a compromise but there was a lot of shit flying around before it happened. We'd support an attempt on the park by two teams.

The strategy we finally came up with was people would assemble in Kent Terrace on the morning of the test and be divided into sections — Orange, White, Pink, Green, Yellow, Blue — which would be used to block both the motorway and all roads leading to Athletic Park. At the time the game was due to start all the groups would go to the park, thus drawing the attention and activity of the police, giving the two groups making a move on the pitch time to make their attempt at occupying it.

You asked about the lambs. Well, it was unofficial and strictly under wraps but this was the one time they did get onside with us. Before that they'd been mavericks, turning up, doing their thing and leaving, no communication with anyone. This time, though, they made contact. We never met them, didn't know who they were even, but we knew we could use them in the plan. They were supposed to get into the park and create a diversion at the time the two groups inside and outside were attempting to storm it. The idea was the lambs would piss the police off, get their attention, and that would be yet another distraction from what was happening on the other side of the park.

Why did the COST leaders go into hiding the week before the test? Well, it wasn't because of any specific intimidation but we found out through our sources that the police saw this test as the biggest threat they'd be likely to come across. At that point we were still only halfway through the Tour and if this game didn't go ahead there was still the possibility of stopping it. The news was the cops were going all out to prevent that happening.

So we hid because we thought there was a strong likelihood they'd arrest leaders on trumped-up charges which could make a shambles of the plans and organisation for test day. It caused a lot of complications for marshals since communicating and making final decisions had to all be done second-hand. Quite a bit of cloak-and-dagger stuff going on.

It was also bloody difficult for us with the test only a matter of days away and the adrenalin pumping. I was wired. Couldn't sleep, hardly ate over those last days we were in hiding. It was how it was for most of us and as well as the test coming up every one of us had lives which had to be put on hold. Some of us had kids, most had partners. Those who had kids, more often than not, had partners who also were involved in the anti-Tour movement which made for more problems because who was going to look after them? We'd set up a crèche and that worked up to a point but I knew some of the people there with me were worried about their families and the effect all this time and focus on the anti-Tour movement was having on them.

Marie and I finally decided the best choice in our case was for her and the kids to go to her family in Rotorua until after the test. She didn't want to be in the house on her own and her family was putting on the pressure. She was pregnant and her mother was afraid she'd get hurt. Marie was scared for me and she thought I'd done enough, she wanted me to back out now the baby was only a matter of weeks away. Her family was angry, thought I was putting the protest movement before her and the kids. I never thought of it like that, weighing one up against the other, coming up with what was most important, but all that, Marie, the coming baby, her family, weighed heavily on my mind in those days we were in hiding. I wanted to be out there in the midst of it all and to be home with Marie and the kids. To be honest, I thought the idea of hiding away was overcautious.

I was proved wrong when the cops raided the HART and COST offices the day before the test. What resulted was a total shambles mixed up with real danger. A total shambles because the police botched the raid by getting a warrant for only the HART office, so all that the COST members in the other office had to do was to lock the doors on them.

But the danger happened when protesters just beginning the march from Civic Square on Friday night got wind of the raid on COST and started moving towards our office. What I was told was that as the march headed up into Courtenay Place, Francis Wevers, the marshal in charge of the march, was tackled by four policemen and dragged away injured and struggling. The crowd pitched forward. People were angry and upset and there wasn't any control with the key leader gone. There were so many cops shouting into megaphones the marshals couldn't be heard. The sound level was multi-decibels.

'If you do not move you will be arrested. If you continue to be disorderly there will be more arrests.'

'Shame shame shame!

'Shame shame shame!'

Then the Red Squad turned up. We'd been told that the purpose of both the Red and Blue escort squads was for the protection of the Springbok team and the grounds and games, yet there they were in full force. They walked alongside the marchers, visors down covering their faces, moving those bloody batons back and forth, ramming aside anyone who got close, shoving marchers across the street. 'Move move move. Into line, into line, into line. If you do not do so you will be violently resisted. We will repel you with violence.'

We knew without doubt the Red Squad's presence there that night meant any rules and assurances we may have relied on were worthless. They were in for the kill and test day was tomorrow.

Back home with the doors locked, the curtains drawn. Three calls on my answer machine. 'Would you be interested in updating your insurance?'

'Hi, it's Jess, just wondering if —.'

The silence. The breathing. The click.

The silence and the click.

Get over it, Rolly. Just get over it.

Should I phone Mike?

They phone because they want to make us angry and scared. They want a reaction.

I sat at the table listening to the recording of the interview as I ate. 'We knew without doubt the Red Squad's presence there that night meant any rules and assurances we may have relied on were worthless.'

What had Des said? 'It was a bad time to be murdered.'

A good time for killers, though. Especially good for killers with all the resources and concealment that officialdom would allow at a time of extreme unrest.

'They were angry and they were in for the kill.'

There were police infiltrating meetings. Although the lambs' role on test day was supposed to be a secret, it could have been leaked.

'The police saw this test as the biggest threat they'd be likely to come across.'

They had to win this one. If they lost it they'd have the fury of Ben Couch and the wrath of Muldoon on their heads. To say nothing of the rest of the country seeing the police force as a bunch of ineffectual buffoons.

Why not eliminate the risk factors? What better camouflage than a uniform, what better mask than a visor?

26

I was in the editing room watching interviews for Part Two and trying to figure out ways of fitting them together. I had plenty of film footage, stories and photographs but they were a mass of jigsaw pieces waiting to be assembled.

Interview: Anna Steveley. Protester, Blue Section.
I was against the Tour from the start but I kept quiet about it. I had a father and a husband and two sons who loved the game and with them it was always the 'politics and sports shouldn't mix' angle. But I had a growing sense of unease about what was happening. The Springboks represented a corrupt system and, watching and reading about what was going on, it seemed to me they'd brought that corruption over here with them and it was infecting our own country. I held off doing anything until the test and then I couldn't wait any longer.

I dressed in just about every layer of clothing I could fit over my body, put on one of John's padded jackets over all of that and pulled out an old motorcycle helmet from the garage. John and the boys were going to the match. I told them where I was going. I said it might be best if we didn't talk about it and then I left.

I was scared and exhilarated at the same time. I'd come to the decision on my own and I was carrying it through entirely on my own as well. I felt free in a way I hadn't in years, possibly since before I was married.

There was a massive crowd at Kent Terrace and, you know, I found it all quite thrilling. All those people on the streets, the banners and the chanting. I went down the back of the lines where I thought I could just blend in. What I didn't understand was that Blue Section — the section I'd inadvertently put myself in — was to be used to block roads closer into the city and we were likely to meet the police and rugby supporters earlier than the sections who were moving towards the motorway and other areas. I recognised Trevor Richards. He was marching at the front of our section and I thought that might mean trouble. I thought about switching sections then I told myself not to be such a coward.

We were marching past the Caledonian Hotel and rugby supporters drinking outside started yelling abuse at us. I was expecting it but the reality was, well, just awful and then they started throwing things, beer glasses, even jugs. People were being hit, then a man, not too far in front of me, got hit in the face and he was bleeding. There was a lot of blood.

The police who were trailing us didn't help but a traffic officer turned up and used his radio to get an ambulance. The next thing that happened was they attacked Trevor Richards and then the police got into it as well, kicking and using their fists, trying to haul him away.

By then my exhilaration had gone and I was just plain frightened but I was determined to stick it out. We got to the intersection beside the Basin Reserve and sat down. I joined in with the chanting and singing and got back part of my nerve. Whatever happened afterward, whatever happened to me, I had this very strong feeling I should be there doing exactly what I was doing with all those other people who were prepared to stand up for what they believed in.

It's odd, looking back, but I became almost mesmerised sitting there. The sun was trickling through the grey sky and, despite the coolness of the day, I was warm, all bundled up as I was in layers of clothes. Warm and, somehow, calm. We were singing to the 'Amazing Grace' tune and just at that moment I was more concerned about hitting the high notes than the police surrounding us. At that point I felt almost safe.

'No Tour, no Tour
'No Tour, no Tour
'The people say no,
'Send them back, send them back.'

Then we were directed to the intersection of Rintoul and Riddiford streets and that was where all hell broke loose.

Interview: James Cross. COST member, Green Section.
In 1981 I was a third-year student. I was in COST right from the start; joined with quite a few of my friends. On test day I was in Green Section which was mainly made up of students from Victoria, members of the Anti-Apartheid Club like I was.

Green Section split once we got to Adelaide Road, with around half of us staying there to block Adelaide. I went on with the remainder to the Rintoul-Riddiford Street intersection. There was a barrier of dump bins at the end of Rintoul Street and a line of police standing in front of them. We walked right up to them and sat down, jamming the intersection, and did a bit of singing and talking and ate our sandwiches. Everyone was reasonably laid-back.

I had my issues over the sitting-down strategy. I understood why COST had settled on that — it presented an image of a peaceful group of protesters, police couldn't easily move or arrest seated protesters, and any violence would be picked up by cameras. It was easier to bash people when everyone was milling around and you couldn't be seen so easily. But it made me feel defenceless and vulnerable. My fear was those rugby bastards would plough in and start kicking.

I was wrong about that but, as things turned out, it wasn't the worst that could have happened. A police bus came towards us up Riddiford Street, stopped nearby and ten, maybe more, cops got out. Then this guy turned up and started trying to shove his way through the seated protesters. He was punching and kicking, trampling over people and, instead of just a couple of cops grabbing him as they easily could have, they huddled together into a group, joined arms and all of them dived in after him.

It was a set-up. There's absolutely no doubt in my mind. The cops wanted a reason to get into the group and so they used an undercover cop to give them one. This guy had simply taken off his helmet, put a long coat over his uniform and charged in. Which gave them the excuse to get right in there, shoving and kicking and kneeing. Anyone in their way got dragged off. They were so aggressive — they forced demonstrators up against a shop window and it shattered and then people were getting cut and trying to get out of the way of the boots and the fists and the glass.

I was kicked a few times, once in the side of my head. I tried to get up but I couldn't. I was completely hemmed in on all sides. It felt like I was going to suffocate down there. I curled up with my arms around my head trying to protect myself. Some of the people around me were standing, the cops were shoving them back, and I thought I'd be trampled.

In the end I half-crawled, half-staggered out. I sat at the side of the road dazed and barely conscious of the blood pouring down the back of my neck.

Interview: Brent Ussher. COST Member, Yellow Section.
Yellow Section was responsible for keeping a presence at the Shaw Savill Lodge where the All Blacks were staying. We gathered there early Saturday morning and kept the police occupied by moving up and down the roadway. There were two arrests — one of our guys was arrested for standing on the lawn and another for pointing out to one of the cops he wasn't in line. Right: standing on the grass or making fun of cops was against the law.

After the All Blacks left the hotel we had a bit of fun with the cops by heading off towards the airport, then we reconvened with the other part of Yellow Section which had been blocking Constable Street and stayed there until we got the call. Reinforcements were urgently needed at the intersection of Riddiford and Rintoul streets.

What we walked into was a bloody disaster area. Cops were shoving people across the road clearing the footpaths. There was a lot of shouting and screaming and people hurt. Once the footpaths were cleared the police lined up along the side, letting rugby supporters through and bashing any protesters that got too close.

Interview: Anna Steveley. Protester, Blue Section.
By the time we got to Rintoul Street the police had cleared the footpaths and rugby supporters were walking through to the grounds. Beyond the footpaths there were people hurt and bleeding, some sobbing. Others were raging at the police.

The marshals got us all sitting down but it wasn't like when we were sitting by the Basin Reserve. We were on edge, charged up with tension. For me it seemed surreal, like I was watching a film that somehow I was a part of. There were helicopters clattering above us, then that bank of blue uniforms. I'd never been on the wrong side of the law in my life and I smiled tentatively at a policeman. I'll never forget that blank, grim face which looked back at me.

Some rugby supporters started jostling us and trying to start up brawls. The police must have decided the road needed to be emptied but they came at us with no warning. They simply linked arms, ran at us and leapt in — they called it the 'flying wedge' method, I believe — stamping on and kicking and hitting out at anyone in their way. A woman in the row next to me was hit by a boot and left unconscious on the ground after they backed away.

We were running away but as we came around the corner we saw more of them beating two women who were lying face down on the ground. Some of them went for the cameraman, punching him in the face, ripping the camera out of his hands and tearing out the film. Then I felt this whack to the back of my head and I fell face downwards on the road.

I remember thinking through the shock and pain, this can't be happening. Not in Wellington. Not here. But I wasn't frightened any more. I was too bloody angry. It was the unreasonableness that got to me, that and the out-and-out brutality. I stood and went right up to one of them and yelled he was a disgrace to his country. I called him a fascist. A Nazi too.

I got arrested, spent a night in the cells. It's something of a family joke now and it's certainly been something to tell the grandchildren. The story of Nan going to prison is a real favourite. But it's something that's never left me. We were peaceful, lawful protesters, sitting there, defenceless on the road yet we were savagely attacked by fellow countrymen acting for a democratically elected government. It changed me. I was less trusting after that and I became a lot more politically active and aware. I came to the realisation that day — that night, too, sitting in a prison cell — that you have to speak out for the things you believe in and that's all there is to it.

I'll tell you something else I learned that night in the cells. While I was sitting there I found a ballpoint pen in the pocket of my jacket and I kept my hand on it. If any police officer had come near me and tried to shove or hurt me I think I would have put his eye out or at least given it a good go. It made me realise how far perfectly civilised and sane people will go if they're pushed hard enough.

I stopped it there. I needed to think about that. 'It made me realise how far perfectly civilised and sane people will go if they're pushed hard enough.' Anna Steveley was small. She was perfectly groomed from her sleek, grey hair to her immaculate leather shoes. I could not possibly have imagined her gouging out a police officer's eye. Yet when she told me that I'd believed her. I'd believed her because of the steel in her voice and in her eyes.

So many stories.

It was just after six o'clock, almost mid-winter, starting to get dark on the streets outside. I was at work later than I'd decided I should stay but I always got more done once the place started to empty out. If protesters in the eighties were brave enough to risk police batons and boots, then I was surely brave enough to take myself out of the office and across a carpark. The calls and hang-ups were still coming but now that I'd worked out how to deal with them they weren't such a problem. I was certain that hearing my voice, hearing the discomfort in my voice, was what Rolly was after.

If it was Rolly. I hadn't seen him in weeks. It *could* have been someone else. There were plenty of people around who could have a grudge, maybe felt I'd misrepresented them, been unfair. It could even go way back to cat-show fiascos, natural remedies for slimming, breast enlargement/breast reduction, cures for penile dysfunction, the Speagle (spaniel cross beagle) breeders I'd done stories about years ago in my last job.

But I'd taken charge. Whoever was doing this would eventually get bored and stop.

I was ravenous. I'd been working all day, hadn't stopped for lunch.

My head felt slightly swimmy from all the caffeine I'd taken in. I needed to pick up something to eat. Something nice and lots of it. Maybe I'd call in at the Malaysian place on the corner. Or at the Japanese. Though what I wanted was something that would fill me up. Japanese didn't do it for me.

I went into the main office, put on my coat and picked up my bag. Indian would be good. Samosas for a start. With that gorgeous sauce they made at Korma Sutra. Naan. Garlic naan. That hot creamy chicken I had last time, what was it called? Indian food, definitely, was what I needed. God, I was hungry.

I closed the door behind me and heard the lock click into place as I stepped into the lift. Or palak paneer. And what were those little stuffed pastries I'd had once. Kachori? Yes, kachori. Kachori and probably palak paneer and I just had to have those potato patties. Aloo ki tikki.

Through the door and onto the stairs. 'Aloo ki tikki.' I wondered if New Zealand food sounded in any way exotic and tempting to Indians. Apple pie. Roast lamb. Pork chops. Pavlova. Kumara. I supposed pavlova and kumara sounded quite appealing, even a teeny bit exciting. But nothing like palak paneer. Nothing like aloo ki tikki.

My heels were clacking on the steel steps. *Pavlova. Aloo ki tikki. Apple pie.* I heard the door open above me, heard the footsteps behind me. I turned my head, saw the face.

I felt the hand on my shoulder.

I tried to grip the railing as I felt my foot trip, my body pitch forward, and I was tipping, falling down, down, landing on my hands which were stretching out in front of me trying to cushion my fall.

I landed heavily on my knees and hands. *Fuck, my wrist. Is it broken?*

Footsteps behind me, clattering down the stairs. I was half-dazed. *Can I get up?*

There was a face above me, bleached out under the pale lighting. Looming above me. Moving closer.

A car engine started up, headlights switching on as it drove towards us, bearing down, lights bouncing across steel girders and empty concrete. Brakes squealed as it stopped. I recognised the two women getting out as the cleaners for our offices. Pink overalls, one with frizzy hennaed hair, the other the kind of blonde people used to refer to as platinum.

He was bending down. He was holding out his hand. 'You OK?'

Platinum pulled out her mobile. 'Shall I call an ambulance?'

I took a breath, hauled myself up on my knees and pulled myself up, ignoring his hand.

'Are you sure you're all right?'

'Who in hell are you?' My voice bounced and echoed around the walls. It sounded like a scream.

'I'm Jason. I work up there.' He pointed towards the stairs. 'For Labyrinth.'

Labyrinth was the design company that occupied the floor directly beneath Zenith. From time to time we had Friday-night drinks with them. This man was large, his black jacket stretched over bulky shoulders, his dark hair long and slightly greasy. This man looked like a crim.

'I know the people at Labyrinth and you don't bloody work there.'

'I've only just started. God, I'm really sorry. I didn't mean to startle you.'

'You pushed me down the fucking stairs.'

The two women were watching, mouths gaping. 'I can be a witness,' Platinum said. She was obviously right up there in the courtroom drama stakes. 'Should I call the cops?'

'I didn't push you,' he said. 'Why would I do that? I don't even know you. I'm really sorry, I was probably moving too fast and gave you a fright. When you looked back at me I could see you starting to trip and I tried to grab hold of you.'

I stared at him. Now that I was a little more calm, I could see he was quite ordinary-looking, a perfectly ordinary-looking rather large man wearing jeans and a jacket. He was gazing directly right back into my eyes with an expression of extreme concern.

Why *would* he push me?

The three of them were staring at me as if I was a crazy woman.

My tights were torn, my knees grazed, one of them bleeding and my wrist was throbbing. I felt humiliated and in pain and then, *fuck it*, I started to cry.

'What if I drive you to After Hours?' he said. 'Get you checked out. That cut on your knee might need stitches.' He was looking at me with such distress I had to believe it was genuine.

'It's OK,' I said. 'I'm fine. It was a bit of a shock, that's all. I'll just, I'll just get into my car and go home.'

Henna and Platinum appeared reluctant. They were shaking their heads and making 'tsk' noises. Either they were disappointed that a real-life drama was dissolving or they truly believed I was too demented to be allowed to carry on without help.

'Is she all right?' Henna turned towards Jason. 'What if she's in shock? Should we let her drive if she's in shock?'

'She might have concussion.' Platinum looked hopefully at me. 'If she's got concussion she could black out.'

'I really think we should get you to a doctor.' Jason stepped forward holding out his hand and I moved quickly backwards. 'Don't touch me,' I said sharply. I fixed my eyes on Platinum and Henna. 'What I want is for you to just stay here and watch while I get in my car and go. Will you do that for me?'

They nodded, staring nervously at me as I backed away.

Acting a bit weird, eh?

I unlocked my car, got in, drove up over the ramp, sobbing slightly. Dizzy. Dizzy from pain and shock and lack of food. Maybe I should stop. Call Mum and Dad or Anna and David. They'd pick me up, feed me, look after me with paracetamol and bandages.

How hurt was I? I slowed the car trying to focus on my injuries. I wasn't bleeding profusely and my head had only suffered the slightest bump. My wrist hurt but it wasn't quite so bad now. Unlikely it was broken.

What I really needed was food, a hot bath, a warm bed, followed by an early night. I needed to be home. I'd order in Indian food, take a bath, go to bed. The dizziness had passed. I was OK. Korma Sutra delivered. I'd get the whole works. Samosas, palak paneer. A naan.

Kachori. Aloo ki tikki. And I'd eat it in bed.

I got myself inside, turned the heat pump on high. I looked at my watch: 6.50. I'd order the food to come in an hour's time. That would give me time to soak my bruised and battered body and warm up. I was shivering slightly. Maybe it was the shock and hurt but suddenly I was freezing.

I ordered online, filled up the bath. One large medicinal glass of wine. I lowered myself tentatively into the water.

My wrist throbbed, my knees were swollen, already turning slightly blue. I *hated* falling over. Maybe it was because I was taller than average and there was further to go. Maybe it was because I was a wimp. I was terrified of pain.

I liked to swim because there wasn't anywhere to fall. And running was fine. As long as you watched out where you were going you stayed upright. Skiing or skating — forget it.

Anyway, obviously, apart from a few bruises and a cut knee I was all right. But I'd overreacted and I'd *so* embarrassed myself. Abusing strangers. Bawling.

I closed my eyes. *Don't think about it. I've been under pressure. I can find this Jason person later in the week and apologise.*

I floated for a while, had another wine, put on trackies, T-shirt, my red fluffy socks and dressing gown, turned on the TV and lay on the sofa.

The car stopped outside and the doorbell rang. I was ready for that food. I opened the door.

I opened my mouth and screamed.

27

Whenever I have the sort of nightmare that becomes so terrifying I have no option than to scream, all that issues from my mouth as I wake myself up is a forced, almost inaudible groan. But this scream would have done a diva proud. It spiralled around and above us, soaring, shrill and penetrating.

He grabbed my shoulder, shoving me backwards through the door. *Stop it. Get inside.*

The screams were coming thick and fast, one after another, like a scale of screams ah-ah-ah-ah-ah-ah-aaaaaaaaah. He shoved me into the kitchen and I was lashing out with my fists and feet.

His face was bright red, he was yelling at me. 'For Christ's sake, calm down, Rebecca!'

Calm down, when he'd come to kill me? No fucking way I was going to calm down and let him get on with it.

He drew his right hand back. I punched him as hard as I could. Felt the crunch as my fist smashed into his nose.

Someone comes bursting through the doorway. Someone with bare brown arms and biceps. Someone who drops a red plastic satchel as he hurls himself across the room and tosses Rolly onto the floor and holds him in a headlock. I'm shaking so hard, my heart is hammering, my throat raw and tight from the screaming.

Rolly's nose is spurting blood.

'Get him off me. Get him fucking off me.'

'What's going on?' Biceps gave Rolly's arm a bit more of a twist and stared up at me.

'He attacked me. I opened the door. I thought it was the takeaway and he *attacked* me.'

'Should I call the cops?'

How often is it that you hear *should I call the cops* more than once in one day?

214

'Don't call the cops,' Rolly was squeaking. 'It'd mean my job. I can explain this. Let me get up. You're breaking my neck.'

The guy looked enquiringly at me.

'Can you make sure he hasn't got a knife?' Echoes of every horrific crime I'd read about, seen on TV, were raging through my head.

'Of course I haven't got a bloody knife,' Rolly said. 'Let me up.'

I stepped back, making sure I was close enough to the door to run.

Rolly stood up and looked at me. His nose was bleeding heavily, his black-and-white-checked button-down shirt smeared red. 'I want my grandmother's ring.' He spat it out between his clenched teeth.

'*What?*'

'I tried to call you but you wouldn't answer, would you? I wanted to be tactful. That's why I didn't come in when you saw me in my car outside the house. I drove away because I realised it might be too soon and you'd get upset.'

'I —. *Upset?*'

'I've been going out with Josie. It started just after we got back from Rarotonga. I wanted to tell you. I thought I should give you some time.'

'You started going out with Josie *right after we got back*?'

'All right, it started sooner than it should have but it's not a hanging offence, Rebecca. Whenever I've seen you or tried to explain, you've carried on like I'm the son of Dracula. For god's sake, all I wanted was to move on and now you've *broken my fucking nose.*'

'I saw you at the concert —.'

'I was with Josie. Josie likes music.'

'You were going to hit me.'

'You were bloody hysterical. I was trying to calm you down.'

'But you've been phoning me and hanging up. You've been stalking me.'

'I have *not* been phoning. I have *not* been stalking you. Josie and I are in love and I'm sure that when I ask her to marry me, as I'm planning, she'll say yes. I want to give her my grandmother's ring. Which you have.'

'No I don't.'

'Yes, you do. I showed it to you in Rarotonga and you kept it. It's worth a lot of money and I want it back.'

I stared at him. 'But I put it in your suitcase. In the pocket, that little one at the side. You know the one. The zip's hidden so you don't actually know it's there?'

'The *what*?'

'All you needed to do was ask me.' Suddenly I was laughing, laughing so much I sounded hysterical, laughing so much I could hardly stay upright. 'So sorry. Your nose —.'

A final seething, blistering gaze and he was striding to the door, slamming it loudly, vehemently, on the way through.

I was helpless. The laughter was coming in waves, spasms. My whole body was shaking with it.

'Hey, Xena?' Biceps was starting to laugh as well. 'All he wanted was his grandmother's ring.'

'Oh my god. I might've broken Rolly's nose.'

'He's called *Rolly*?' Biceps was snorting with glee.

'Yes.' I had tears streaming down my face. 'He's got a dog's name.'

'And a *broken fucking nose*.'

'How could I *do* that? I'm mortified.'

But I didn't feel mortified at all. There'd been an intruder in my home and I'd annihilated him. As well as that, I'd acquired a new friend. I was pleased to learn that Biceps was actually named Matt — a strong but friendly non-dog name — and he had finished his evening duties so was more than happy to share a late dinner and a glass or two of wine now that was over. Matt had the kind of twinkly and amused eyes I particularly like. His hair was thick and dark and floppy. And he had the greatest smile.

So that evening, in my dressing gown and fluffy socks, my face scrubbed and my hair still wet, I ate samosa and palak paneer, naan, kachori and aloo ki tikki and drank wine and laughed with one of the most interesting and attractive men I'd ever met.

Despite my injuries, I felt definitely jaunty as I limped into the office. A condition of one of his former occupations was that Matt completed a first-aid course and so he had deftly strapped up my left wrist and bandaged my knee.

Mike looked up vaguely as I passed his desk then took a second, much sharper look. 'What the hell happened to you?'

'I fell down the stairs going to the carpark.'

He stared at me. 'You what?'

'I was walking down, not thinking about what I was doing and this guy came up behind me in a hurry and I was startled and tripped.'

'What guy?'

'Mike, you really don't have to look at me like that. It's nothing. Honestly. I already feel bad enough about what happened. I accused him of pushing me when all he was doing was trying to stop me losing my balance.'

'What guy, Rebecca?'

I was getting a little tired of Mike's fatherly concern. 'His name is Jason. He's just started work at Labyrinth. He saw I was about to trip and he reached out his hand to try and catch me. End of story.'

'How do you know he's telling the truth?'

'Why wouldn't he? Anyway, I checked out the names on the office door as I went past and his is there. Jason Harvey, OK?'

'You having any more of those calls?'

'No.' Just a teeny white lie to get him off my case.

'How's the doco coming on?'

'Good. I'm starting on Part Two and I've just about finished the interviews.'

'You found anything more on the lambs?'

I smiled sweetly at him. 'I've stopped fantasising about solving cold cases if that's what you're concerned about.'

I walked to my desk, sat down and switched on my computer. Halfway through the morning I relented and bought coffee and muffins to share with Mike. He was a good guy, a little overvigilant, but he'd been very kind to me. He couldn't help coming from a generation where men take charge and protect helpless females. I didn't need protection but it was nice he wanted to look out for me.

In fact, today I felt generous and compassionate towards everyone and everything, so much more in tune with the world than I had in a long time. I was happily receiving texts from Matt who now called me Xena. How amazing to discover we loved the same TV programmes. *True Blood, Mad Men, Glee. Xena.*

'Your little friend is dying Xena. How does that make you feel?'

'Good.'

So between the editing suite and making adjustments to my script I was playing the Xena game and trying not to giggle too much. The rule was no looking up the net.

'I tried to give you Olympus. I tried to give you everything but you stabbed me in the back.'

'We just didn't want the same things.'

Interview: Harry Heta. COST member, Brown Squad.

I was certain the only way to stop the test was to get in and occupy the grounds and I was fairly vocal in expressing that from day one. For that reason I was part of the Brown Section: the 'hit squad' as we came to be known.

There were around two hundred and fifty to three hundred of us, just a small group, but when we first started marching we were escorted by a mass of police. The word had got out we were the ones who needed watching. So we divided up and the police dwindled away — probably thought we weren't such a threat after all — and then we joined up again.

The plan was to get up onto the bank on Waripori Street, break through the wire barricade then come down onto the park from the southern side. We made our dash; every one of us sprinting as fast as we could, climbing up and jumping over fences and gates and tearing across lawns and gardens in the drive to get up the bank. Of the ten people who got up there, a couple almost made it by climbing over the wire-mesh fence while others were trying to wrench it down using ropes or having a go at it with wire cutters.

There were helicopters clattering around right over us and no doubt they would have let the police on the ground know what was happening on the south side of the grounds because they came running. We'd been so close to making it I could have bloody cried.

If we'd had only a few more seconds we'd have got in there.

We regrouped in Waripori Street. Both ordinary police and the Red Squad were there, some of them cutting off the end of the street, the rest bearing down on us. And then I heard it: 'Take no prisoners. We are not taking prisoners.'

I'd taken a hit on the head and I thought I might be out of it, imagining what I'd heard, but I checked with others who were there that day and those were the exact words. 'Take no prisoners.'

We sat down. We wanted to show them we were defenceless, non-aggressive. They just bowled right in with their batons and boots, knocking anyone who tried to get up back down on the ground. Some of them were out of control, hitting out again and again. I saw one Red Squad member grab another's arm trying to hold him back.

They herded us into a line, the ones of us who could still stand, and we were driven like animals towards Rintoul Street.

Interview: Dave Wallace. COST member, White Section.

Sit down on a road and wait for the bastards to have a go at you? There was no way. No bloody way I was doing that.

White Section's plan was to get onto Athletic Park through MacAlister Park and stop the game.

We walked, jogged, ran, through scrub and grass up to our knees as well as the mud — the rain was just pissing down. The police were behind and helicopters hovering over us. We got down through the scrub onto MacAlister and three people ran forward and cut the barbed wire. The game had started. There were police in front of the wire, but not that many. When we cut through they started attacking with their batons but by that time we'd picked up lengths of wire and were using them as defensive weapons, swinging them in front of us.

We got the wire down. There was a clear space between us and the police. But instead of pressing through, the marshals held us back. They wanted to give protesters who were exhausted a chance to get back their energy.

We moved again, marching towards the police, spreading across the park. There were three lines of us, three of them. We knew we could make it through. The Maori among us stepped up and performed a haka.

Then the rest of us shifted as well, moving slowly forward, standing there, shouting at police, eyeballing them. We waited for the order from the marshals to advance. Stood there, the rain running down our faces, fucking freezing, and the order never came.

I was so fucking pissed off but probably, looking back, they were right not to make the call. By the time they'd got in reinforcements, people would've been badly hurt. We found out later what happened in other places.

The moment we could have made it through was when the wire came down. People were drenched and exhausted, I'll give you that, but some of us could have done it.

You asked about the lambs. They were supposedly all geared up to make a diversion that day. They were to join up with our people already in the park and when we came through the wire they were meant to be provoking the police, getting their attention. That was the only time we'd relied on them for anything and they didn't show.

I still feel bitter about that day. We lost the opportunity. Standing there with that bloody game going on and the crowd roaring, I felt so angry, so bloody powerless. But, then again, *was* it failure? What's the defeat in five hundred men, women and kids, row on row of them, old people, young people, linking arms, singing and crying and chanting? A rainbow of hats and coats and helmets beneath the rain. 'Amandla. Amandla.'

He came over well. Looked good with the sort of face that works on camera: strong features, dark intelligent eyes, thick hair shot with a bit of grey. His voice was strong and compelling and rich.

'It was the only time we'd relied on them for anything and they didn't show.'

Because one of them had been kicked to death and left lying in muck and blood. Because the other had lost his mate. What had happened, what was the truth? Perhaps I'd find out more when I talked to Stone.

I finished up early and drove towards Thorndon. Despite my promotion to Xena Warrior Princess, I was nervous. Caspar Stone made me very nervous. He didn't engage like ordinary people do, didn't smile when you expected him to, and if he didn't want to answer a question he simply remained silent. Unnerving.

Still, I had to take on board that a part of that was quite possibly a reaction to the way I'd initially approached him. I'd provoked him and that, I *hoped*, had aggravated his peculiarly cranky behaviour.

And he had actually invited me back to his house. Maybe this time he was prepared to talk.

If he was difficult I could take it. I was a big girl. *Xena*. I grinned.

This time the electronic gates were wide open and my car slid over the curb and up the long drive. I parked outside the house, looked up and he was standing there on the veranda, looking down. So far so good.

'Welcome, Rebecca. Come on up.'

The steps were a little tricky with my stiff and somewhat painful knee but when he saw I was limping, he held his hand out, immediately solicitous. 'You've had an accident? Oh my dear, do come in. We'll get you comfortable.'

Was this the same Caspar Stone? He took my arm and veritably hoisted me down the passage. I felt the concentrated strength in his arm and shoulders.

'Really, I'm fine.'

'Nonsense, let me help.' He ushered me into the room I'd spied last time — soft lights, a blazing fire, oversized, cosy-warm armchairs around a low coffee table. 'And look at your poor hand. What *have* you been doing to yourself?'

'I slipped. Not really looking where I was going.'

He stood over me, frowning slightly. 'I've got a sauvignon chilling but perhaps you'd prefer a brandy? Much better for the nerves.'

I laughed. 'My nerves are fine. A sauvignon would be great.'

Either he'd had a complete character change or this was Caspar Stone's nice twin taking over. I looked around. No masks. *Thank you, God.*

This room was pure sumptuous elegance. Soft greens, pale lemony creams and delicate textures: velvets, grainy linen, silk. So many beautiful things placed together, all in a magnificent harmony. A row of ceramic bowls, one like a volcanic crater, edges of dark grey dipping into a depth of brilliant blue-green, shimmered from a satiny oak sideboard. Quirky pieces merged with classic. Oranges in a black wicker basket glowed; the curtains fell and trailed perfectly onto the satiny timber floor. A couple of Hoteres, a Woollaston, an Angus, a McCahon and a Sydney shone out from walls the colour of birds' eggs.

'I suppose everyone who comes here tells you what a beautiful room this is,' I said as he came back into the room carrying a tray.

He put the tray — black, lacquered and embossed, bearing glasses, a bottle of Cloudy Bay, a platter of crackers, cheeses, grapes — down on a small, carved table. 'It's a room which has tended to ripen,' he said.

He poured the wine, handed a glass to me. Despite the sofa being so obviously suited to lounging back and engulfing yourself in, he sat very upright on it, his feet planted on the floor. 'This,' he said, waving his hand at the wine and platter, 'is somewhat of a peace offering. I'm afraid I was rather impolite when you were last here.'

'I'm afraid I was rather impolite to you,' I said.

'Well then,' he said abruptly, holding his glass out and clinking it against mine. 'Let's put that behind us. What do you want to talk about?'

'Well,' I said, 'as I've told you, the documentary I'm presently working on is about the 1981 Springbok Tour and I'm focusing on the Wellington anti-Tour movement and looking at the part the lambs played.'

He nodded.

'And, from what I understand, Eric Woolley was one of the lambs and he lived here.'

'He had his own apartment within this house.'

'And he was your partner at the time?'

'I loved Eric very much.'

I'd actually coaxed out Caspar Stone's *human* side?

'Have you noticed this?' He pressed a light switch on the wall beside him and a soft spotlight lit the painting above the fireplace. It was the head and naked upper torso of a young male dancer. He was turned to one side, his face directed away from the viewer and the light above the painting accentuated the pallor of the skin. There were three small dark moles on his forearm, chest and neck close to the chin. His collarbone protruded above the muscle and bone of his chest. The sweep of pale flesh, chest to hip, was fluid and graceful; his body was slender, taut with muscle.

His eyes were deeply shadowed, his nose and ears small and neat and his lips were thin and delicate, so red they seemed almost black. His hair was thick and straight, slicked back from his face and almost white, shocking somehow against the darkness of the background which was concentrated levels of darkness, deep sandy brown merging into stony grey, into the inkiest blue.

'It's Eric, of course,' he said. 'I had it painted the first year we were together and we put it up above the fireplace the day we moved in here. I've considered moving it many times. Having it in such a central place, well, it's a constant reminder of what I lost and of all those years of living and opportunities that had been taken away from him. But, somehow, he belongs there.'

His face appeared stricken as he gazed upwards. What could I possibly say? That the portrait was remarkable, beautiful, moving? Any observation seemed so feeble in response to this painting which was almost fearsome in its intensity. And I felt so sad for him.

'I don't know what to say,' I said. 'I feel as if I'm intruding. I can see how much you miss him.'

'Ah, but it's Eric I feel most pity for.' He leaned back on the sofa. 'I assume you want to know about him. You're a journalist. You want to discover what you can.'

'Yes I do. But —.'

'But?' he held up his hands palms upwards.

'I don't want to upset you.'

'Ah, a journalist with a heart.' He smiled at me.

'I'm sorry,' I said, 'I hate to ask you this but are you in agreement that I can use what you tell me?'

He looked at me silently for quite some time, obviously mulling over what I'd asked, then nodded. 'I refuse to be filmed and my name must not be mentioned. If you agree to that, and remember, Rebecca, a verbal agreement is binding, you can use what I say.'

'Can I use this?'

I took my dictaphone out of my bag. He shook his head. 'I'm afraid you'll have to take notes.'

I took out my notepad. 'How long were you and Eric together?'

'Five, nearly six years. We met in Sydney. I was dancing with a company he auditioned for. We were over there a while and then we came back to Wellington. My mother died and this house became mine.'

'Did you continue dancing?'

'Eric did. By then, I was almost forty and dancing requires even more training and dedication once the body becomes older and there were other things I wanted to do. This house, for a start, needed attention. Besides that, I was in the rather fortunate position that I didn't have to work. When Mother died I was the only beneficiary.'

'When did you come back to Wellington?'

'The end of 1979. In 1980 Eric took contract work dancing and I oversaw what was needed to be done on the house. As you can see it's large. My mother couldn't have cared less about it, she was barely ever here, but I'd always loved it and it became my project and my passion — as it remains. In 1981, and I presume this is what you primarily want to know about, Eric and I were very much averse to the Springbok Tour going ahead and decided to put our energies into doing whatever we could to support the anti-Tour movement.'

'People I've spoken to, COST and HART members that is, have said you weren't involved in their meetings and strategies.'

'We used to turn up to the odd COST meeting but more to find out what was going on than anything else. Nobody recognised who we were and we used to sit apart at the meetings to make sure of it.'

'But why weren't you involved?'

'A very simple answer.' He smiled again, finished the wine in his glass and offered the bottle to me. 'No? You're driving? Well then, a half-glass?'

I nodded. The warmth of the fire, scrumptious wine, treasures shining out from every highly polished surface. It was all so lavish, like a room from one of those stately homes you visit in Britain and tiptoe cautiously around the areas barricaded off with little waist-high fences made from posts strung together by silken cords, peering in. Except I was on the inside, lolling against a velvet armchair, one of those Lenox wine glasses in my hand. *Lady Mary and Xena Warrior Princess in twenty-four hours.*

'Very simple. Eric and I kept very much to ourselves. We had our own friends and like us they were gay. Back then it *had* to be that way.'

'Because of the law?'

'Of course. As long as one remained silent and hidden, the police would leave you alone. But if you made yourself known, the fact you were homosexual made you an instant target. We knew that protesting against the Tour could be that step which got us into trouble. So we decided we would not involve ourselves with anyone, or any organisation, who would know about us and lead to the law knowing about us.'

'But you were almost overt about your homosexuality at the games and marches. The police would have seen that —.'

'*Almost* overt, Rebecca. We stayed well within the law and it was always in the public eye. What we did certainly teased the police but what could they have arrested us for? Running after each other? Throwing our arms around each other? Chasing policemen? It was nothing and we always managed to disappear very quickly afterwards. We'd have bags stashed somewhere and we'd nip in, haul off our costumes and masks and walk off separately. We could have been anyone.'

'So you weren't involved with the official protest movement because you wanted to keep a low profile as far as your identity went?'

'We suspected there would be police infiltrators at the COST and HART meetings and recognition could have meant trouble. Besides that, Eric and I were somewhat free spirits. We preferred to work for the movement in our own way. We were able to go to any game or march we chose to without being bound by any particular organisation's strategies and plans.'

'I understand you were at almost every match. Until Wellington.'

'Yes.'

'But, I understand from COST members that you *did* have a definite role to play in the Wellington test which involved working with one of the COST sections.'

'It was Eric's idea. He set it all up. We were to provide a diversion along with other COST members who were in the park at the time that White Section cut a way through the barbed wire barricading Athletic Park from MacAlister. But Eric was dead by then, of course.'

'What happened that night?'

'On test day we had to be in touch with White Section so we'd know the exact time the diversion was needed. The arrangement was we'd pick up our part of a walkie-talkie from a letter box the evening before the test. We had friends staying here — dancers we'd worked with in Sydney — and Eric said he'd go on his own. He said he'd walk across the reserve, pick it up and probably call into our local for a beer.'

'What time did he leave?'

'Nine, nine-thirty? Around that time, anyway. I stayed up for a while with our friends then went to bed. I didn't realise until next morning he hadn't come home.'

'Did you phone the police?'

'There was no point. He was an adult male and they would have laughed at me. Besides which, that could have earned attention we didn't want.'

'So what did you do?'

'I phoned around friends and I waited. Then I heard the report on the radio that a young man had been assaulted nearby. I knew it was Eric. I phoned the hospital. Nobody would tell me anything. I wasn't his next of kin or even a relation so I had no rights. Then the police came around to ask questions. That's when I found out he was dead.'

'Did you have any contact with his family?'

He put his glass down and very deliberately filled it. 'I phoned his parents' house immediately. I wanted to see him and to know the arrangements for his funeral. His brother answered and told me that neither he nor the rest of the family had any intention of speaking with me about this "matter", as he called it, and I was not to attempt further contact.' He shook his head. 'What could I do? I had no rights whatsoever. I went to the hospital. I thought some kind soul might allow me to see him in the morgue but, if I can believe what I was told, they'd already taken him away. They'd performed an autopsy and he was gone. "The body has been released to the family." It was almost as if he'd been some package which had been collected from a pick-up depot.'

'Did you agree with the police's assumption that his attackers had randomly come across Eric and killed him?'

He sighed. 'I had all sorts of theories. One of them was that the police had somehow set it up. But the more I thought it through, the more I tended to agree the police were telling the truth.'

'But he had become a real nuisance to police. So had you.'

'They might have roughed him up a bit — or me, for that matter — to take him out of circulation for a while. But to intentionally kill him? I had to ask myself whether it was feasible that anyone would deliberately and calculatedly murder Eric and the answer had to be no. Anyway, nobody knew for certain we *were* the lambs.'

'You said, though, that you were intending working with COST for the Wellington test. Did anyone there know who you were?'

'Eric did all the negotiating.'

'Didn't you say there were police moles at their meetings?'

'Well, yes.'

'Doesn't it seem strange to you that Eric was killed at a time when he was most dangerous to the police? They were afraid of losing control. Some of them were brutal. Men like Denny Graham.'

He looked directly at me. 'You mentioned that name before.'

'He was a bent cop, got out of the police force not long after. Went up to Auckland. He's been in the news quite a lot over the last year. For fraud, among other things.'

'So.' Caspar made a pyramid with his fingers and looked at them. 'What could this Denny Graham possibly have to do with Eric's death?'

'What I was thinking is someone *like* Graham could have developed a grudge against him.'

'But you don't actually have any evidence for that?'

'Well, no.' I knew what I was saying was vague, even slightly idiotic, but he continued to smile encouragingly at me as I trailed on, then he put his glass down and silently looked at me. 'Let me give you some advice. All you have are suspicions and suppositions. The sensible and safe path to take, my dear, is to put those aside and get on with the task in hand.'

I looked back at him. 'I understand "sensible" but I'm not sure what you mean by "safe".'

'Getting on the wrong side of the police, Rebecca. Can you expect that to be an entirely safe position, knowing what you've found out and with the suspicions you have?'

'I don't understand.'

He hesitated. 'I would imagine that in your career being friends with the police is very important.'

'So is finding the truth of what happened.'

'Perhaps you're right.' He stood up. 'It's time, I'm afraid, for my solitary dinner and a little work afterwards. It's been very pleasant speaking with you.'

He walked me through the front door and onto the veranda. I held out my hand. 'Thank you.'

He shook it. 'Friends now,' he said. 'And please remember what I said about taking the sensible and safe path.'

He stood on the veranda watching as I began climbing down the stairs to the path below. 'Take care going down, won't you?'

28

I was at my desk. I'd transcribed the notes I'd made and was jotting down ideas. I had a date later with an Indian-food delivery man and a bottle of wine, but there were a few hours till he got here and there were things I wanted to clarify in my mind.

First of all, of course, I had no intention of taking Caspar Stone's advice. It was my job to scrape together whatever I could out of this. I already had great stuff: the interviews, TV clips, personal photographs former COST members had given me. What I was putting together would be different from the same-old-same-old that viewers had seen five years on, fifteen, twenty, twenty-five years on and in all those docos and articles which had sprung up in the past thirty years. At the very least, I'd achieved a new slant on a topic which had been almost milked dry.

Because the lambs had faded away from the public eye before the last matches, nobody had ever really looked at them before. I'd found out who they were, I had fantastic film clips and photographs and if I could imply even in the most nebulous way that the death of one of them could be linked to his involvement in the anti-Tour movement, this would be a coup.

And while I had enough to do exactly that, I wanted to get closer, find out as much as I possibly could. I was scribbling down the ideas as fast as they came. 'Who killed Eric Woolley? Rugby supporters, gay bashers, police, random thugs, government agents, family.'

Underneath were the pros and cons. I drew arrows if there seemed any links between them. For example, I'd linked 'gay bashers' and 'random'. Eric was slight, beautiful and with his thick mop of blond hair would have stood out in the pub, walking along the street or across the park. He could have walked into a gang of thugs, as the police concluded, or he could have been followed by gay bashers looking for a bit of fun.

There was no evidence that he'd been set on by rugby supporters. He wasn't recognisable as one of the lambs. The mask had covered his face and head — he could have been anyone. Of course, there was the chance he'd been identified and his name circulated but that was a long stretch.

Government agents? The police? While I'd have the story of the year if I could connect the government and cops with his killing, I couldn't help but come to the conclusion that this pushed the boundaries of credibility.

I'd had quite a bit to do with people who worked in the police force — Mike, for one — and there was no way in the world the guys I knew would hunt someone down and kick him to death, no matter how much he'd irritated them. Caspar was more than likely right: 'They might have roughed him up a bit — or me for that matter — to take him out of circulation for a while.'

But to kill him? It made no sense.

The family? OK, they'd done the Victorian 'never darken my door again' thing but why would they murder him?

Which brought me right back to the random gay-basher theory. But there was something more. I felt it. In my gut I felt it. Something I didn't know, maybe wasn't seeing.

My mobile dinged. Matt. 'On my way.'

My stomach lurched, tipped over, tingled.

Come on, Rebecca. I'd met him only the night before and here I was inviting him into my house again. I was allowing this to move way too fast. I wasn't some hormone-driven teenager, I was a grown-up woman who should be cautious, careful. I should keep my distance until I knew him better. 'Sensible and safe.'

So what was I doing dashing off to the bathroom mirror, putting on lip-gloss, checking out my hair, spraying on a teeny bit more Coco Chanel Mademoiselle and undoing the second button of my shirt to display a very slight hint of cleavage?

Because he was fucking gorgeous. That was why.

Two glasses of wine, one *Xena* episode and a whole lot of talk later I was stretched out on my sofa with him close beside, holding my bare foot in his hand, explaining and demonstrating the principles of foot reflexology by gently pressing the pressure points and describing the parts of the body they related to.

'Oooh,' I said as he ran his thumb over my heel. 'That feels a bit tender.'

'That's your lower back,' he said, kneading. 'It's telling you sitting over a computer isn't making it happy.'

'How do you know all this?' I said, closing my eyes.

I could hear his grin. 'One of my many life skills.'

'Don't tell me you used to be a faith healer.'

'I didn't used to be a faith healer.'

'My god,' I said, 'that feels so *good*.'

'This is your ears and this is your jaw. This is the top of your shoulders and now I'm moving down to your elbow.'

Who cares about my elbow?

I draw my body up so I am crouching beside him. He gently takes hold of my shoulders. I have my hands on those hard, curving biceps and I am kissing his mouth. Little kisses which turn into slow and long, turn into me losing myself in his soft, full mouth.

We shed our clothes and move to the rug in front of the fire. Our bodies are lit and warmed by flames. We kneel together, touching, kissing. His body is smooth and hard and perfect, his mouth is on my neck, on my breasts. His hand slides down my spine to my waist, around to my belly, to the tops of my thighs, between my legs and then he is watching me, watching my eyes as he moves his hands to beneath my buttocks, lifts me forwards, begins to move inside me. My legs are wrapped around him. I want to scream, shriek and bellow with pleasure, want this to go on, on, on.

To have this so simply, so effortlessly, so entirely by chance. To find him and to have him here.

We slept easily, his hands around my waist, mine curled around his arms. I woke to him breathing close against my neck, to the glorious musky smell of sex and man. We made love, showered together. He made coffee, I made toast.

He hooked my hair back with his hand, kissed my neck and then my mouth before he left. 'I'm going to Christchurch later on today,' he said. 'I'll be back after the weekend, OK?'

I kissed him back. 'OK.'

I flew into work a little late, a little flushed and definitely more relaxed than I had been in a very long while. I worked in the editing room for most of the next day. Part One was fairly much under control: clips and interviews which gave a walk-through of the All Black/Springbok rivalry and the politics, essentially the background to 1981, then moving into the Wellington anti-Tour movement and the setting up of COST. That would be followed by the May 1 Mobilisation and the mass demonstration on July 3, the occupation of the Wellington motorway which coincided with Hamilton, then Molesworth Street. I was bringing in the lambs into this first section, the photographs, clips, people talking about them. Part One ended with COST's involvement in the demonstrations at Palmerston North, Nelson and, finally, Napier.

It was working. Enough action to catch and keep attention and I was more than happy with the interviews. I'd been lucky there. Everyone who spoke was articulate, passionate even, over what they were talking about. They sounded and looked great. Best of all, you could tell this wasn't a half-forgotten, minor incident in their lives. For most of them it was big, almost as if it was something momentous that had happened to them very recently instead of thirty years ago. You heard these middle-aged, even elderly, people talking and that staunchness, that *fire*, blasted right out into the camera.

Interview: Irene Costello. COST member, Pink Section.
'The people's flag is palest pink, It's not as red as you may think.'

I still have the leaflet and I still have the hand-knitted, pale pink balaclava I wore that day. I found it in an op-shop. I remember grabbing it out of a bin and laughing out loud. It was such a find.

The smear of blood is still on the side, faded to a pale rusty brown now. I never washed it. Never wore it again, either.

I wonder if other people have relics their children or grandchildren will toss out one day, screwing up their noses. 'Why would she want to keep *this*?' And I wonder too, does everyone have that segment of their lives they return to again and again both consciously and in their dreams? We were so united, so committed. I've never felt so strongly about anything since then. I laughed so much that year, and I felt so fired up, so angry, and I drank a lot, smoked a lot of dope, had a lot of sex. Jesus, I was alive.

Yeah, I was one of the commies Muldoon was so twisted up about. Along with most New Zealanders, he saw socialism as the worst kind of evil. All he had to do was suggest communists were behind some cause or dispute and the whole country'd be up in arms. It's how he swept in in 1975. That dancing Cossacks ad on TV really did it for him.

I suppose I'm still a commie. At least, in my heart and soul. Maybe I still fancy myself as that young woman with the pink balaclava marching and chanting and waving a banner. I remember one of the first rallies we had and Andrew Molotsane — he was a South African trade unionist — was there speaking and he said that every year in South Africa eight billion dollars' worth of gold is taken out of the mines and every year 50,000 children die from starvation.

Doesn't that make you think? Babies dying because they don't get enough to eat while the rich bastards gather their gold? That's why I marched. Racism was a part of it but oppression of the workers was at the heart. In my book, skin colour wasn't so much the issue as the subjugation of those workers. They needed to keep those black people down so that they'd have no choice other than to give them what they wanted, which was cheap labour. If you've got an endless stream of bargain-basement workers keeping up your industries and making your beds and keeping your house clean and cooking your food and looking after your garden and your kids, well, you've got it made, haven't you? Especially when those workers happen to be instantly and conveniently identifiable by their appearance. And if you've got a conscience you can tell yourself you're giving them jobs and stopping them from starving. It's a good system so long as you're one of the ones on top.

It's still happening. Funny how that Gap T-shirt is so pricey seeing what kids in China made it for, eh?

The Pink Squad's task on the morning of the test was to jam up Rintoul Street and Adelaide Road. We sat outside the bottle store there, blocking the entire footpath and the road. We had rugby supporters trying to force their way through and there was a lot of shoving and yelling and then when more police were called in things turned nasty for a while, but we were used to that by then. I'd already taken a few clouts. The first time it happens it knocks you back a bit but you couldn't let it stop you.

Closer to kick-off, our task was getting to the park and diverting police attention from Brown Squad who by that time would be making their attempt on the park. There were three rows of police standing by the dumpsters being used as a barricade and what we did was charge at them until we were about two feet away then stand around eyeballing them for around ten minutes. Finally we sat down facing them, chanting and singing.

So we were sitting there and there was at least three metres between us and the police. Our marshals were persistently making the point that none of us was to make an attempt on police lines. Nice and calm, you know? As long as we stayed nice and calm everyone would be OK.

At the same time, Red Squad officers were hyping things up, yelling and prancing about behind the lines. 'Rapid action! Rapid action!'

Then Brown Squad was driven back into Rintoul Street. They looked beaten. Not only physically — you could see it in their eyes. They told us later they'd been only seconds away from getting through the fence and onto the ground.

Still, they were jogging as they came towards us, despite the hammering they'd taken from the Red Squad following behind. They weren't just being let through Rintoul Street, they were being driven down it. Anyone who hesitated was shoved or prodded in the back by some Red Squad bastard. Pieces of shit, those guys.

To join the rest of us, they had to be let through the formation of police already there. The officer in charge's command clearly indicated that was what should happen. 'Fall back. Let them through. Let the two groups link up. Fall back.'

For a moment, it seemed the police line was stepping back and allowing the Brown Squad to go through and join us on the other side. They were starting to move forward when, without any warning, the police streamed off the footpath and started battering those nearest them. They were bashing them, ramming those batons into their stomachs and their chests, thrusting them into their backs. And the sound of it, I'll never forget that. The screams, those batons like whips cracking, boots hitting the ground, thudding into bodies.

Fuck. The *panic*. There was a woman. Hysterical. On her knees moaning, 'God save us. Please, God, save us.' There were people trying to get away, blood running down their clothing, some unconscious on the ground. The worst thing for me was when I saw a Red Squad member stamp down onto someone's hand, worst because it was so obviously cold and considered. He'd already knocked this woman over, he'd hit her hard with a kind of underarm motion with his baton and she fell backwards and was sprawled there winded on the ground, her arms spread out, trying to get back her breath. I saw his face as he very slowly and deliberately raised his leg up and stamped down with his full weight on her open hand.

The Red Squad was out of control that day. This was not the disciplined troop of professionals they tried to make themselves out to be. They were kicking and bashing protesters who were on the ground and clearly no threat. They were chasing and knocking down people who were only trying to get away.

I don't know how long it went on for. I remember hearing Red Squad officers calling the men back, telling them to re-form into lines. That was when that frenzy of terror and panic turned to rage. People began to chuck whatever they could get at the police lines. Bottles, pieces of wood, whatever was around. The marshals were calling for calm and order. Brown Squad joined us and we stood there chanting.

Shame on you

Shame on you
Shame Shame Shame

Tom Poata, one of the Brown Squad marshals, stood between the police and us, trying to calm the situation. 'We know that the whole world is watching. We know our black brothers and sisters in South Africa are watching. Our sacrifice has been a small price to pay. Kia kaha. Kia kaha.'

Powerful stuff. The interviews were great, the images fantastic: police with batons raised above a cluster of protesters sitting in Rintoul Street, protesters in thick jackets and crash helmets dragging barbed wire back against a backdrop of the dark bush edging MacAlister Park, rows on rows of helmeted police spreading way out to the skyline, eyeballed by row on row of protesters.

Part One wasn't too far away. Part Two still needed pulling together. I had six weeks. I could do it. I had enough to make it work and, so far as the lambs' role was concerned, I could take Caspar Stone's advice. Safe. Sensible. I could simply offer the facts of Eric's death: he was kicked to death in a Wellington Park, the night before the Wellington test. Let the audience make its own assumptions.

The cold, hard truth without explanation or embellishment may be more effective, anyway. Images. The lambs dancing, mocking the cops. I could track down actual photographs of Eric, his face, images of him as a professional dancer. Just show those with a voice-over.

Was it enough?

29

I left the studio just after five and walked down Lambton Quay. I was due to meet Anna at Chow. Girls' night out. We always ate at Chow and shared the same food: flat beans, pork rolls, prawn dumplings, fish cakes. We'd have a good old goss over early dinner and follow it up with the sort of girlie movie where you either weep copiously or giggle hysterically. Tonight was *Sex and the City*.

She was already sitting at a table when I got there. She got up and we hugged. 'Just got here. I haven't ordered anything yet,' she said.

'Let's have a wine first. My head's buzzing. I need to just sit for a few minutes.'

'What's going on?'

'Oh, this doco.'

A waiter came over and we ordered our glasses of wine.

'Going well?'

'I think so. I've got some great material.'

'It's a fascinating time in our history.'

'It is that.' I leaned forward. 'But it's more than that. What happened should be remembered and seen as a kind of warning of what can happen when a government has too much power. The kinds of bully tactics that were used, attempting to defame protest leaders, equipping police with weapons, training them to use violence against their own people. That's so dangerous.'

'Well, yes, it is but —.'

'But it's a long time ago? Did you know that just a couple of weeks ago Ross Meurant told the *Herald* he'd lied at a police investigation at the time? Not only did he say he'd lied, but he also said he'd rigged an identity parade to protect one of the Red Squad members who he knew was responsible for beating up protesters. You know he justified it? He said he'd been right in doing what he did. This is a guy who went on to be an MP and, so far as I know, nobody's really picked up on it, nobody's said, shit this is *wrong*. We've become apathetic.'

'Not back then, though.'

'No,' I said. 'Not back then.'

The wine arrived. 'Well,' Anna said. 'Well, cheers. It's good to see you so enthused over something again. I haven't seen you like this since —.' She flushed slightly.

'Since Connor Bligh?'

'Yes. Sorry.'

Anna and David had warned me over and over about the Bligh case. Getting too involved. Not seeing, as David put it more than once, 'the wood for the trees'. I looked at Anna and noted a similar, though carefully disguised, expression of caution.

'Don't worry,' I said. 'It's nothing like that. I've not become personally involved with a murderer this time. If I was still on the Denny Graham thing and was sitting here telling you he was an innocent man who people had somehow got entirely the wrong idea about, *then* you'd have something to worry over.'

'Denny Graham,' she said. 'There's a piece of work.'

'Well, I know that. But this sounds like you have some inside information.'

She sipped her wine. 'Just something that's come up at work.'

Anna had only just returned to part-time work and I knew she was taking a lighter case load. So why and how was she involved in something connected to Denny Graham? 'Can't you tell me? In total confidence? I promise you —.'

'Oh, well.' She put down her glass, began to run her finger around the edge of the stem. 'The media's sure to get hold of it, anyway. One of my clients claims Denny invested in a number of massage parlours she has here in Wellington. She says she goes way back with him, they were friends, whatever that means, when he was living here and she came to him with her idea of themed massage parlours and he financed the deal just before he left. According to her she gradually paid back the loan, which was set at a hefty interest rate. She had nothing other than the idea and the banks wouldn't play ball. She said Denny told her the interest rate had to be high because of the risk he was taking in investing. She says she paid him back ten years ago but he's now claimed she has no rights over the properties, he still owns them and he's selling and taking all the money.'

'But there'd be a contract.'

'According to her, Denny and his lawyer set all that up. She just signed the papers and was foolish enough to trust him. She was so keen to start the business she didn't take the care she should have and she doesn't even have a copy of the original contract. Anyway, Denny's been threatening to send around the heavies to get her out and her partner rather coincidentally got beaten up in a carpark last week. Ended up in hospital. Very nasty.'

My mobile pinged and I picked it up. Matt. I grinned. A beaming face with clapping hands.

'Who's that from?' Anna was looking curiously at me.

'Oh, just this guy I met.'

'When did you meet him?'

'Three days ago.'

'Come on,' Anna said. 'More information, please. Where did you meet him? What does he do?'

'I met him at my place. He was delivering a takeaway Indian meal and that's what he does.'

I love my sister-in-law, but she went to Woodford House and, by the expression on her face, that private-school background continued to have a powerful influence on her. 'He delivers *takeaways*?'

'Yes.' I was enjoying this.

'So.' She was obviously trying to get her thoughts together. 'So you ordered a takeaway and —.'

'And he turned up.'

She was incredulous. 'You invited him in?'

'Not exactly. He invited himself in because he thought I needed saving from Rolly.'

'*What*?' Anna said. 'OK, *Sex and the City* is on hold. I'm ordering food and more wine and you're going to start from the beginning.'

So I told her. About Rolly. About his nose and Josie and his grandmother's diamond ring and by the time I finished, Anna's private-school decorum had long evaporated and we were whooping with laughter and wiping away the tears running down our cheeks.

'But this man, Rebecca. This Matt. You're *seeing* him?'

'Why ever not? He's gorgeous and he's fun and he's interesting.'

'But. Well, the men you've been out with in the past have, well, have had, uh.' I saw she was struggling to find something tactful to say.

'Ambition?' I suggested.

'Well, yes.'

'He likes what he does,' I said with a smile.

She was looking rather worried. 'It's just, I thought you were keen on, you know, settling down.'

'I am.'

'But.'

'Anna,' I said, 'don't get heavy on me. I can work out things for myself. Have another wine? Please?'

We drank far too much wine, talked, giggled, and finally fell into taxis. On the way home I scrolled down the icons on my mobile, pressed send. A little round face, one eye closed in a saucy wink.

'So you ordered a takeaway and you invited him in?' Anna's face. I loved her dearly but her *face*. 'Rebecca is getting herself involved with a takeaway deliverer?'

Actually Matt was just a little more than a delivery boy, not that I was going to let that one out, not straight away. At the age of nineteen he had left school and turned up at first-year lectures along with all his friends. Marketing, management, accounting, economics. He'd lasted the first week then gone truck-driving, fruit-picking, house-painting, whatever turned up. Eventually he'd trekked around overseas and ended up in India washing dishes in a restaurant. Then he'd done a tad of cooking himself, got interested and come back to Wellington. He'd borrowed money from whoever would lend it to him, imported an Indian chef and set up the first Korma Sutra — OK, he'd said, the name wasn't exactly sophisticated but it was *catchy* — in Petone. And it boomed. He now had three Kormas in Wellington, four in Auckland, a couple in Christchurch. He liked to be hands on, which is why he'd been in the Newtown restaurant when my order had come in. All the delivery vans were out, he was on his way home and so —. In fact, Matt was a bit of a mogul. But that was my secret.

He was also very funny and *very* sexy.

I unlocked the door to my house, switched on the lights. No messages on the phone, nothing shifted, nothing missing. My house looked and smelled exactly as it had when I left in the morning. There'd been no messages, no photos since Rolly had been sent on his way. Maybe it had been him all along, just a rejected boyfriend venting a bit of spite. And who else could have sent the photos?

Anyway, whoever it had been, it seemed to be over.

30

I checked my emails. Another couple informing me they had 'reluctantly' decided they were unable to speak about their dealings with Denny Graham. They wished to 'move on'.

Denny Graham. I kept coming back to him. He was crooked way back even when he was a cop. From what people told me, even when he'd been swimming along in the tide of respectability there was always that undertow of fishy deals. 'Her partner rather coincidentally got beaten up in a carpark last week. Ended up in hospital. Very nasty.'

What did I know about his earlier life? He'd left the police force towards the end of 1981, gone up to Auckland and made money out of property deals. A lot of money.

But what had Anna said? Her client had told her he'd financed the massage parlour business before he went to Auckland. So where had that money come from? Even if she'd started at the lower end, just with one property, a place in mid-city Wellington with the added costs of setting it up wouldn't have come cheap.

Perhaps he'd got the money from the bank, charged her a higher interest rate? I had a quick scan through lending policies in the eighties.

How would he have borrowed a sum like that? It wasn't nearly so easy then to take out a loan and interest rates were heading up towards twenty per cent. At the same time there was the possibility he'd sold his house in Wellington in preparation for his shift to Auckland and that had financed the business. I pulled up the profile I'd created on Denny Graham and checked through the timeline.

Born 1948. Grew up in Porirua. Not much likelihood, then, of family money. Married August 1973. Owned 9B Farr St, Hutt Valley. Shifted to Auckland, December 1981. Purchased 22 Ajax St, Takapuna.

How did he go from owning a house in the Hutt Valley to one on Auckland's North Shore plus buying commercial property in Wellington in a matter of months? On a policeman's salary?

I flipped the pages. Who was Denny's lawyer?

I scanned through the newspaper cuttings from the trial. My god, how had I missed this?

'Mr Graham is represented by the firm Woolley, Barnes, Jacobs and Frances.'

I tapped on Tim's office door beaming my sunniest smile. 'Rebecca,' he said, looking up from the computer screen and frowning slightly. 'What can I do for you?'

'Have you got a moment?'

'I suppose. The kid's been up the last few nights with his teeth coming through. I'm way behind.'

'The kid'? Usually it was a besotted 'Reuben'. Tell him the good things first, coax him into a better mood. 'The doco's coming together really well. It was a fantastic idea and everyone who's had a look thinks it's going to be great. But I really need to go to Auckland.'

He was still frowning. 'What for and how long?'

'Just to tie up a few loose ends. Two days? We could stay on if it takes longer.'

'We?'

'I want to take a cameraman.'

He pursed his lips. 'I need to know a lot more than that if we're budgeting a cameraman in as well.'

'It's this angle I've got.'

'What angle?'

'On the lambs. One of them still has family living in Auckland I need to talk to.'

'Why?'

'Uh, background.'

His frown had turned into a veritable scowl. 'Let me get this straight. You want to take a cameraman up to Auckland to get background on someone who plays a very minor role in this doco?'

'But he's definitely involved.'

'What's this angle you're talking about?'

'It's a bit of a long shot but I've got a few questions related to Eric Woolley's murder I want to follow up on.'

He stared at me then slowly lowered his head to his desk and began to thump on it with his forehead. 'No. No. No. *No.* Absolutely and emphatically no. You are *not* employed to investigate a murder. You *are* employed to make a documentary. Understand?'

'Look, if I'm right about this it'd blow anything else that's been done about the Tour right out of the water.'

'The purpose of this doco is not to blow anything out of the water, as you put it, but to produce an informative, truthful documentary. Are you hearing me, Rebecca?'

'But —.'

'No buts. You are *not* going to Auckland.'

I scowled back at him.

'Right?' he said.

'Right.'

'Well, then,' he said. 'I'm glad that's settled. Now let's go out and get some coffee and cakes. I, for one, deserve a treat.'

I followed him out. This was the problem with Tim. He said no to something you really wanted to do and then spoiled you so you couldn't possibly hate him. He spent half an hour with me, telling me how fantastic this doco was going to be and how fantastic I was. In other words, schmoozing me into good spirits and obedience.

I knew that the conclusion to these Masters in Manipulation tactics would be a final warning and there it was. 'You don't need to do anything fancy,' he said, patting my arm as we walked back into the main office. 'What you've got is good solid stuff. But you have to make sure you don't lose your focus. Auckland is *out*. Don't ask me again.'

'Good solid stuff.' That sounded about as fascinating as a hefty slice of doughy steamed pudding. I waited until he was safely behind the closed door of his office and then pulled up the Air New Zealand website. Wellington–Auckland. Departure 6.30 pm Friday. Auckland–Wellington. Departure 6.30 am Monday.

Perfect. I tapped in my credit card number. What I did in my own time and with my own money was my own business.

I phoned Isobel Woolley from home on Thursday night. While she wasn't entirely delighted about the prospect of seeing me, she didn't say no. The others I'd just front up to. While knocking at a door and pleading for whoever answered not to slam it in my face wasn't a part of the job I enjoyed, the element of surprise was usually the best approach.

And if everyone other than Isobel refused to speak to me, well, at least I'd enjoy a weekend in Auckland. I found a good deal on a hotel in the CBD, arranged to pick up a rental car at the airport. I could shop in Ponsonby, have lunch in Devonport, maybe take the ferry to Waiheke on Sunday, do a vineyard and walk along a beach.

My mobile rang. My favourite Indian-food deliverer. 'I can't get back till Tuesday, maybe even Wednesday,' he said. 'How about coming to Christchurch for the weekend?'

'I'm afraid I have other plans.'

I heard his grin. 'Are you so brave that you fear someone caring for you?'

'You look like a gentle soul. That's rare in a man.'

'So, Rebecca, do you really have other plans or are you just reluctant about spending an entire weekend with me?'

'I'd love to spend the weekend with you,' I said. 'But I really do have other plans. I have to go to Auckland for work.'

'Dinner next week?'

'Well —'

'What if I took you out for a slap-up meal with real Indian cooking?'

'Absolutely yes.'

Thursday. I was in the editing suite when Tim popped his head around the door. 'Don't forget we've got the invite tomorrow for drinks downstairs after work. It's the two-year set-up date for Labyrinth and I want everyone there, show them a bit of support and collegiality.'

'You didn't tell me,' I said. *Fuck, I can't tell him I'm due on a plane to Auckland at 6.30.* 'Uh, I've got a date.'

Was he looking at me suspiciously? 'We're talking around five o'clock, Rebecca.'

'OK. Only, half an hour, though. It's an early date.' I'd pack my bag the night before, take it to work with me and head out to the airport after the drinks to make it in time for the requisite thirty minutes before the plane took off. It'd be a bit of a rush but I could do it.

'See you there, then.' Was he looking at me oddly? I wasn't all that good at lying, even evading the truth. My mother again. 'I can deal with anything, Rebecca, except lies. If you don't know the truth, you can't possibly know what you're dealing with.'

While I hadn't exactly told lies about being with Joe Fahey those years we were together, I'd become adept at withholding the truth. When all that had come out in the media she had been so angry with me I'd almost thought she'd not forgive me. 'He's married to my friend. A friend who's presently battling with cancer. How could you have been so selfish?'

I shook my head. I didn't want to think about that. I didn't see or speak to Joe any more, nobody mentioned him to me. All I saw were occasional mentions of him in newspapers, the internet, TV news. I didn't know how he was, how Michelle was. I used to know everything about him. I'd loved him. It was time to let all that go.

I turned back to the interview I was watching.

Friday. Downstairs sharp at 5.00. There were bottles of bubbly and a chocolate cake with a large 2 on it on a table in the middle of the main office which was filled with people from Labyrinth, from the advertising agency office on the third floor, as well as us from Zenith. Good. I'd be able to sneak out without being missed.

I looked around. I'd expected to meet up with Jason which could be embarrassing. I'd thought about phoning him and apologising but other things had got in the way. Anyway, this could be the chance to say I was sorry and prove I wasn't usually crazy.

I kept an eye out for him and chatted to people I knew. Someone clinked a spoon against his glass. Damn, there were going to be speeches. I couldn't politely leave right away but I'd slip out as soon as they were over.

'Labyrinth had had a tough start. The economic downturn. Businesses like ours folding. Had some setbacks. But the energy, creativity and drive of this talented group of workers. Optimism. Expansion.'

I was half-listening, waiting for him to finish.

'Bringing in new talent. Like to introduce Jason Harvey. Been with us a few months now. Fine addition to our team.'

Jason? The guy everyone was smiling at was short, skinny, nerdy, fair hair clipped close to his head and wearing a suit. The speech ended, people started eating, drinking, talking, moving around again. I turned to Anya who'd been with Labyrinth over the past two years. 'Anya, this might seem a slightly weird question but do you have two guys called Jason working for you?'

She looked slightly confused. 'No. Why do you ask?'

'Nothing,' I said. 'I must have got it wrong.'

It was 5.40 already. I dived down the stairs into my car, drove fast to the airport, left my car in overnight parking and raced into the terminal. Carry-on luggage. Gate 9. Onto the plane. I put my bag in the locker, snapped on my seatbelt, settled into my seat and closed my eyes.

What the fuck is going on?

31

I woke up in downtown Auckland in an ultra-king-size bed. My room was silent and anonymous with cautiously neutral walls and furnishings, a wide-screen TV set attached to the wall. Last night I'd enjoyed a long bath in the white-tiled bathroom, skin treats, bath treats, shampoo and conditioner arranged on the glass shelf. 'Hand-crafted in New Zealand.' I'd eaten in the hotel café, swum in the heated pool, bathed and slept. Slept like a baby though my experiences of David and Anna's babies suggest they hardly sleep at all. Slept like a log, perhaps.

Anyway I'd slept and now I was in a safe room, light coming in through beige blinds and the sounds of traffic way, way down below me. Lights flaring out through the dark all that way into town on the motorway from the airport. Horns blaring, cars braking, passing fast. All those cars.

Who was coming up beside me? Who was behind? Who was following? Who was Jason?

I pulled on the fluffy, white compliments-of wrap and went to the window. The harbour was blue and bright, the glass-and-steel buildings around the hotel gleamed in the winter sun. Yachts skimmed across the water, their white, red and deep blue sails billowing. A ferry headed towards Devonport, froths of milk billowing up behind.

I'll turn this into a holiday weekend. Shopping and nice lunches. Swims in the pool.

A young man was kicked to death in a park thirty years ago. But he was nothing to do with me. He wasn't worth all this persistence and energy. Or danger.

Is this about Eric Woolley? Am I getting too close?

But how could it be about Eric? The calls started as soon as I got back from Rarotonga.

I'd have a holiday, go back to Wellington, tell the police what had been happening, put it in their hands.

But could I trust the police?

'Getting on the wrong side of the police, Rebecca. Can you expect that to be an entirely safe position knowing what you've found out and with the suspicions you have?'

Had Caspar Stone been warning me? Did he know something, something he wasn't able to tell me?

Who could I trust?

I'd buy something nice to wear to dinner. A new little dress and shoes. I loved Auckland shops. Then I'd go home, begin the final work on the doco. I'd have dinner with Matt. I'd have dinner and make love and laugh and talk with Matt next week. I would get on with my life.

'What you've got now, Rebecca, is good, solid stuff.'

'The sensible and safe path, my dear.'

'The sensible and safe path.'

But how could I let this go?

Isobel Woolley lived in Hillsborough in an ex-state house in a street filled with other ex-state houses: tiled roofs, brick or weatherboard cladding, perched at the front of large sections. Most had additions and changes with larger windows, sliding doors, rooms and decks added on, but still appearing somewhat modest, still those solid and durable homes that had been built for working New Zealanders in the fifties and sixties.

I stopped outside the address Isobel had given me. Tiny and pretty, the pale bluish-grey facings suited the colour of the dull red brick and French doors that opened onto a small bricked terrace. The garden had shingle paths, lots of flowers crammed into the beds.

She answered the door immediately. 'Rebecca?' She was smiling. A little nervously, I thought.

A living room, the kitchen tucked behind a bar. Polished floor boards, pale walls, bright paintings, a big shaggy rug, comfy well-worn chairs and a sofa. Books and lots of cushions. The room smelled of the coffee spurting in the bright green percolator on the stove.

'Your house is charming,' I said, sitting in the chair she'd pointed me to.

'Well,' she said, 'it's mine. I'm gradually making it into what I want it to be and I don't have to put up with any crap here. Coffee?'

'Thanks.'

She handed me a mug. 'You want to talk about Eric, I suppose.'

'Yes. Anything you can remember.'

'The Woolleys should never have had a son like Eric,' she said. 'He was different. Sometimes I used to think they'd picked up the wrong baby from the hospital.'

'He was *that* different?'

'He looked like Iris but in temperament he was different. He was most certainly made to feel his difference and that he had no chance of meeting the Woolley standards. My theory is that in the end he stopped trying to please everyone and went in exactly the opposite direction. He was the family's black sheep.' She smiled a little. 'So he certainly stayed in character.'

'He tried to *displease* them, you mean?'

'He seemed to shut off as far as they were concerned. He was dancing over in Sydney for quite some time and he hardly kept up any contact with them at all.'

'Did you and your husband keep in touch?'

'I did more than Jim. Eric used to send the odd postcards and clippings of the shows he was in. He knew I was interested.'

'So you were friends?'

'We were quite good friends. At that point, anyway. But we hardly ever saw each other, it was only the odd letter. Then after he got back to New Zealand and came out, well, that was that. I was part of the family and —.' She held out her hands, palm upwards.

'Did you feel it would have been disloyal to keep in touch?'

'Well. Yes.'

I looked closely her. Was she avoiding my eyes? Isobel Woolley didn't give the impression of a woman who would be an easy pushover. Or had that flinty expression in her eyes, and the sharpish edge to her voice, been an add-on after the divorce? 'Are you saying while you were married you were kept firmly beneath the Woolley family thumb?'

'I was dependent on my husband and I really didn't have that much of a say about what went on.'

'You're not saying your husband would have thrown you out if you'd continued to have contact with Eric?'

'Of course not, but it would have made things difficult.'

'So you had no contact with him after the family quarrelled?'

'No.'

'I don't want to upset you,' I said, 'but there are issues surrounding Eric's death I'd like to talk about.'

'What do you mean?'

'Eric was one of the lambs. We've already spoken about that. But it seems quite a coincidence that the night before the Wellington test, someone who had developed a fairly high profile in the anti-Tour movement and had a significant role in the forthcoming test was murdered.'

'What are you suggesting?'

'I'm not suggesting anything. I don't really *know* anything. But —.'

I had no reason to trust her with what I'd found out but maybe she knew something. She was my last hope. 'But it seems to me there were a number of people around at the time who would have been very pleased to have Eric out of the picture.'

'Police, you mean?' Her eyes were wide open and fixed on me.

'There are other possibilities.'

'You don't —. You couldn't mean the family?'

'What if the family knew Eric was one of the lambs? Wouldn't they want to avoid the kind of scandal and public embarrassment that could generate? Their own son flaunting not only the fact he was gay but also his left-wing, anti-government principles? How would that have gone down?'

'Eric was murdered by a mob of louts.'

'His mother told me he was better off dead.'

She shook her head. 'She couldn't have meant it. This is insane.'

'Have you ever heard of or met Denny Graham?'

'That guy who's been in the news, you mean?'

'Yes. Were you aware he was represented by your ex-husband's law firm?'

'No. What are you implying?'

'After the Tour, just after Eric's murder, Denny Graham came into a lot of money. He also had a lot of help, it seems, after he relocated to Auckland.'

'Listen,' she said. 'The Woolleys may be thoroughly unlikeable but I can't believe they're murderers.'

32

The next stop was St Vincent Avenue, Remuera. The house and garden were enclosed by a thick stone wall, trees billowing up above it. A wide, wraparound veranda, double doors into the main entrance and a set of stained-glass windows, a sunburst of syrupy yellow, ruby red and blue. I rapped the large, brass door knocker.

'Yes? What is it?' Her voice was at exactly the right pitch to make underlings quiver.

'Mrs Woolley? I'm Rebecca Thorne. I've already spoken to you on the phone and I'd like —.'

'Get off my property or I'll set the dogs on you.'

I didn't much like the thought of being pounced on by vicious animals so I walked briskly back through the gate and ensured it was closed firmly behind me. I lingered — I *was* curious — and the door opened. A tall, stringy woman with stiff grey hair stood in the doorway peering around. An overweight dachshund appeared soon after followed by his twin and they waddled out into the garden.

So much for the killer dogs.

'Hi, Mrs Woolley.' I popped up from behind the fence and waved. She looked astounded then cast a malevolent look in my direction as she shut the door. Probably my only bit of fun in a day which was swiftly becoming less and less promising. Next stop Devonport.

People complain about driving in Auckland, the awful traffic, the jams, but on this clear blue winter's day with a scrap of sun coming in through the windscreen and the cars humming around me, well, I loved it. You turn up the music and get on with it. OK, Auckland's a bit brash, a bit big, but I like the edginess of it, all those people and the banks of hills and the harbour.

The northern motorway; look out for a gap in all those cars swishing past, get into the right lane, watch for exit 420 Esmonde Road or god knows where you'll end up. It's easy to get lost in

Auckland but that can turn into an adventure. Chances are you'll come across a market or a great café hidden away somewhere.

'I'm going to Jackson and that's a nat-u-ral fact.

'I'm going to Jackson ain't never coming back.'

Albert Road.

'Yeah go to Jackson

'You big-talkin' man.'

That clip of Johnny and June. I loved watching it on YouTube — they were so sexy together, their bodies moving, the way he looked at her, the way they grinned, that kiss at the end. They were having such a bloody good time.

I wanted a man I could dance with, have fun with.

I wanted my very own Johnny Cash.

Maybe I'd found him. 'You are my princess.'

I was driving, singing, grinning like an idiot. Just at that moment I was living on the planet of what-if-and-what-next?

Albert Road, Victoria Road. Onto Calliope Road. I parked the car and stared up. It seemed as if everyone involved with Eric Woolley lived in a Victorian mansion. Here was yet another in all its glory of stained-glass, verandas and lacy fretwork. Though this particular model had a balcony burgeoning out of the top floor as well as a turret. Isobel Woolley's Hillsborough house could have fitted into it twenty-five times.

Nice to while away a few hours in one's very own turret.

More iron gates, another stone wall. I rang the bell and a young woman opened the door. Pink checked shirt, collar up, designer jeans, fair skin, blue eyes, blonde ponytail. A younger-model Isobel. Isn't it amazing how wealthy, middle-aged men can, with neither awkwardness nor embarrassment, extract an earlier-brand woman from their homes and seamlessly ease a later one in?

Two small blond boys clutched her knees.

I held out my hand. 'Mrs Woolley? I'm Rebecca Thorne.'

'I know who you are.'

Are imperious voices allocated to these people at birth?

She shut the door but I could hear her say, 'That *woman* is here.'

Suddenly Jim Woolley stood in front of me: swollen belly, flushed, veined face. It seemed likely that this woman-model would end up financially better off than the last one.

'Rebecca Thorne.' I held out my hand.

Which he ignored. 'I told you to stay away from my family.'

'I was hoping that you might spare me a few moments to talk about your brother.'

'Get out,' he said, making a shooing motion with his hands as if I was some moth-eaten hen who'd dared to venture into his estate.

'Mr Woolley,' I said, 'I have no intention of upsetting you and your family. All I'm trying to do is my job which, in this case, means compiling an objective and accurate profile of your brother.'

'Your job,' he spat. 'Stirring up trash and knocking down decent people. That's the sort of thing you like, isn't it?'

Someone had tried to knock *me* down a flight of stairs onto a concrete floor. I'd been shown the door, insulted and threatened with dogs. And despite all of that, up until then I'd remained pleasant and calm.

Up until then.

I heard my mother's voice coming out of my mouth, ominously composed and razor-sharp. 'There are aspects of this job that I, in fact, do *not* like such as dealing with rude and vulgar people. But I presume there are also distasteful aspects to your job such as getting murderers and rapists off and representing sleazes like Denny Graham.'

He was staring at me, his face scarlet and his eyes popping. 'How *dare* you!'

'Nice meeting you, Mr Woolley. Have a pleasant day.'

Did I look behind me? I don't remember. All I remember is driving off, shaking slightly, a glutinous, murky mass of rage roiling about in my gut.

Arrogant, smug, rude, bullying

I slammed on my brakes. Give-way sign.

self-important, conceited, vulgar, boorish

The driver of the car I'd barely missed tooted and shook his head at me.

bastard.

255

I had a bag with my trainers and trackies in the boot. I'd drive along the North Shore, stop at a beach, run all this out. There wasn't anyone else to see. I had all day.

Purely out of curiosity, just before I got to Milford Beach I stopped, parked the car, got out and looked up at Denny Graham's McMansion. All those pristine gardens, all those gleaming windows. A silver sports car, and a pair of SUVs like big black beasts were parked in the large circular space outside the house. The pool glistened bright and blue. I wondered how Helen's reconciliation was going.

I looked up at the tower. I saw a blind go up, the bulk of him against the glass, the dazzle from the binoculars he had fixed on me. I saw the hand lifted in the mock wave.

I got back in the car. Along Kitchener Road into Milford Road. I thought of those cold lizard eyes staring down at me, felt a trickle of dread. I stopped at a café, sat outside in the sun and drank a coffee, then had another one and a muffin.

Stupid to let him shake me like that. Just Denny having his little bit of fun with someone looking at his castle. Hell, he wouldn't even know who I was.

I followed the road onto Craig Road where I found a carpark just up from the beach. I needed my run. I parked alongside a campervan, took my bag out of the boot and walked over to a women's changing room. Concrete floor, damp sand in the corners, block walls. Grey and bare and cold. I took off my jeans and boots, put on my trackies and trainers, changed my sweater for a T-shirt and started walking towards the car.

Another car had pulled, just beside mine, into the carpark. A man wearing a cap down over his eyes was opening the door, getting out. Then a dog hurtled towards him and he bent down, took the ball the dog had dropped and threw it. A man and a woman, both wearing shorts and red polo shirts, emerged from the track which ran down to the beach, gave us a wave as they walked towards the campervan.

'Great day.'

'Yeah. Great day.'

I breathed inwards. Opened the boot, put my bag inside, put the car keys in the pocket of my pants and zipped it up. I needed this run, alright. Warrior princess? Huh.

I stretched, started out by jogging. And then I got into it. I love the motion of running, the rhythm and connectedness as it all comes together; your legs start working hard, your arms and then your lungs get into it, the sweat is running down your face and the feeling you're right there with the sun, the wind, the sound of the sea.

I was lost in my breathing, the soft wallop as my feet hit the sand, the quark-quark of seagulls spread above the water and then I heard it. The slap of feet following. I looked around. Someone wearing a cap was twenty, thirty metres behind me.

Walking steadily. Just loping along behind.

I took another quick glance. It was the man from the carpark. He'd seemed friendly. 'Yeah. Great day.'

Out for a walk. Just out for a walk.

This beach goes on for miles.

I gained pace. Quick, over-the-shoulder glance.

The further it goes the more isolated it gets.

He was keeping up the same gap between us. So he'd sped up.

In the unlikely event he's following me, I can't turn back. So what the hell do I do?

In the distance I could see that the beach curved slightly up ahead and cut around into a bend. There would be a couple of minutes where he wouldn't be able to see me.

I slowed my pace and, though it was almost unbearable, I stopped and bent down, pretended to check my shoelace and took another look. He was gaining on me.

I started again, a slow steady jog, almost to the curve and then I sprinted as hard and fast as I could towards the scrub and rock leading up to the road.

I was bent over, scrabbling through a tangle of brush, my breath coming in short, hard gasps, moving as swiftly as I could. *Is he coming after me?* I found an overgrown track and then I was on the footpath edging the road.

There was plenty of traffic around. I was safe. I walked along the path to the carpark where I'd left my car, unlocked it, locked it behind me and started up the engine. The couple were sitting on fold-up chairs outside the campervan holding large blue mugs, a packet of biscuits on the fold-up table between them. They waved and smiled as I passed.

I drove back to the hotel, showered, drank two cups of tea and ate a sandwich. In the ordinariness of my room with sun coming in the window, traffic sounds below me and people talking outside in the corridor, the idea of anyone following me along the beach seemed preposterous. It would have been just some ordinary guy having a brisk walk along the beach.

I swam, had a long soak in the spa pool, lay on my bed reading, dozing a bit.

Something I particularly like about hotels is room service. I needed an early dinner and I needed comfort food: 'Shoestring chips with mayo. Our own specialty gourmet-burger.' After it was delivered I put the security chain across the door for extra reassurance, opened up the half-bottle of pinot gris from the mini bar and spread myself across the bed.

Skywatch. *In Their Sleep*. I didn't think so. On the other hand, I could manage *Mamma Mia* just one more time.

33

I woke with the TV on and congealing food and a half-glass of wine on the table beside my bed. I looked at the clock. 2.27 am.

I turned off the TV, filled the kettle and switched it on. It had been 7.30 when the food arrived. I'd slept a straight seven hours. I made tea, took the mug back to my bed. There was something I had to remember. Just before I fell into that dead sleep. *I have to remember that, I should write that down.* The houses, the conversations, the fear, the running. What?

Isobel Woolley. Something Isobel Woolley had said.

He was the family's black sheep.

'He was the family's black sheep so he certainly stayed right in character.'

How did she know Eric Woolley was the black lamb? *I* didn't know that. I'd looked closely at the images trying to work it out. But Eric Woolley and Caspar Stone were similar heights, similar sizes and with the costumes and those masks covering up their faces and hair, how could anyone tell?

Isobel was not smiling this time as she answered the door at 9 am. 'I've told you everything I know,' she said.

'Just one question.'

She stood in the doorway, frowning. 'I'm going out shortly.'

'Isobel, how did you know Eric was the black lamb?'

Her eyes shifted away from mine. 'You told me. That first time we talked, you said Eric was the black one.'

'But I didn't know.'

'I don't know how I knew, probably it was just a guess, but I really have to —.'

'You *did* talk to Eric, didn't you?'

'No. Well.' She folded her arms. 'Maybe you should come inside.

Just for a minute, though.'

I sat down and she sat opposite me. She looked decidedly shifty. 'All right, I did talk to him. I did know he was one of the lambs. The black one.'

'OK, that's fine, but why couldn't you have told me?'

'I didn't want to get involved,' she snapped.

I nodded. 'I can understand that.'

'It was easier to say nothing about being friends with Eric so far as the Woolleys were concerned. I suppose I just got into the habit of keeping it a secret.'

I smiled. 'They're a formidable family. I had my own little brush with them yesterday. Got thrown out twice.'

I told her about my altercation with Jim and she laughed. 'I liked Eric,' she said. 'I really loved him. I'd never had a brother and he became that, my younger brother. We wrote to each other when he was in Sydney and I went over once and stayed with a friend and went to one of his shows. He was an amazing dancer.'

'And when he was tossed out of the family you kept up your own communication?'

'He'd phone during the day when Jim wasn't there. He'd tell me what was happening and I'd tell him the family gossip and we'd have a bit of a laugh. I suppose, well, to be utterly truthful I liked the fact this was my secret, that I knew what Eric was doing when the rest of the Woolleys didn't. I don't know, I can't quite explain it other than to say it was something that was entirely mine. I loved that connection he gave me to the kind of bohemian, artistic world he lived in. All the things that had always fascinated me but I never had the courage to have anything to do with.'

'Did you see him after he moved to Wellington?'

'Yes. The Bolshoi Ballet was touring. He phoned me up and told me he had tickets and I had to come. So I organised a nanny for the weekend and went.'

'Good weekend?'

'Marvellous. I'll never forget it. I met Eric's friends and they were just lovely.'

'You met Caspar Stone?'

She raised her eyebrows slightly. 'Uh-huh.'

'You didn't like him?'

'He was the one person I didn't like so much. But, well, he was Eric's choice.'

'Why didn't you like him?' I was curious.

'He seemed superior and unfriendly. At first, I thought he just didn't like women. But he was possessive. I'd see him watching Eric. It seemed to me he never took his eyes off him.'

'Was Eric happy with Caspar?'

'I didn't ask. But happy enough from what I could see.'

'When was this?'

'The end of 1979, maybe the beginning of 1980? Somewhere around then.'

'Did Eric ever confide in you about their relationship?'

'Not then.'

I could tell by the edgy way she looked and by the way she was fiddling with the pendant hanging around her neck there was something else.

'Not *then*?'

She looked straight at me. 'Some time later Eric told me Caspar didn't like him seeing friends independently and he didn't want Eric to take dancing contracts outside of Wellington because he had enough money for both of them to live on. Eric told me he started using the money issue, saying it was his house and he was keeping Eric and so Eric should put him first, that kind of thing. In fact, Eric was getting more and more fed up. He'd get home from some dancing gig and Caspar would be waiting up, sometimes drunk and quite nasty.'

'But when you see them in the film clips together at the marches and the games — they seemed so in tune with each other.'

'It was something they both felt strongly about. Eric did love Caspar and he was hoping their involvement in the anti-Tour movement would make things better.'

'Did it work?'

'For a while. But Caspar was so incredibly possessive. He accused Eric of being involved with someone else.'

'And was he?'

'Not according to Eric. But the relationship had definitely soured for him. Listen, I've never told anyone else this but Eric was going to leave after the Tour ended. He'd been offered a dance tour in America. He had his tickets booked and friends over there. He said he needed to get away at least for a while.'

'Did Caspar know?'

'Eric intended telling him after the Tour. Oh, and there's something else I should tell you.'

'Yes?'

'Jim phoned last night. He wanted to give me strict instructions not to talk to you and he was rather cross when I said I already had. One thing, though. He did a complete rant about what you'd said about him representing Denny Graham. He said he'd never had anything at all to do with scum like Graham — his words, by the way. The thing is, he's telling the truth about that. The original firm Woolley and Barnes merged with Jacob and Frances only a few years ago. Graham was actually John Frances' client from way back.'

I drove to Newmarket, found a café and ordered a latte in a large, wide bowl. It was warm enough to sit outside and the sun was on my table.

He was possessive. Never took his eyes off him.

So what? Some people are possessive. It meant nothing. According to the police, Stone had a watertight alibi for the night Eric died. I finished my coffee. Time to shop.

One black lace overdress with a midnight blue slip underneath and the coolest soft black leather boots later, I was in my car heading back to the hotel. A browse around Fingers and a couple of dealer art galleries in Kitchener Street, a wander through Whitcoulls and Unity Books, a swim and a soak in the spa and it'd be dinner time.

My mobile beeped as I pulled into the carpark. Two texts. Margo:

'Monday on.' OK, the date to look at wedding dresses Monday lunchtime was confirmed.

The other was a number I didn't recognise but it hadn't been withheld so it must be all right. I clicked on it, brought up the photo.

Ted, Lily, Nina stare solemnly into the camera.

34

Where were they? Who'd sent this?

They weren't smiling. Those kids always smile. They always smile.

Someone's got the kids.

Anna's mobile. Nothing. No dial tone, no voice mail, nothing.

Anna and David's home number. 'Anna and David are not available right now.'

David's mobile? 'David Thorne. Please leave a message.'

Mum and Dad's. Oh thank god. Mum answered.

'Hi Mum.' I tried to keep my voice under control. 'I've been trying to reach David and Anna. Have you any idea where they are?'

'Oh, darling, hello. David's in Melbourne. I'm not sure where Anna is.'

'What about the kids?'

'So far as I know they'll be with Anna. Why?'

'It's nothing. Just, uh, I wanted to check out something with Anna.'

'Is everything all right?'

'It's fine. Everything's fine.'

Anna's mobile again. The house again. 'Anna and David are not available.' Shit. *Shit.*

Maybe she was out looking for them.

I was walking fast towards the hotel, clicking between Anna's number and the house. Anna. The house. Anna. Anna. Through the hotel doors, into the lift. Anna.

The house. 'Hello?'

'*Lily*? Lily is that you?'

'Ye-s.'

'Lily, it's Aunty Rebecca.'

'I know.'

'Is Mummy there?'

'Yes.'

'Can I speak to her?'

'Mummy? Mu-mmy?'

Of course they were there. Of course they were safe. But I was still carrying with me the image I'd conjured up in those minutes of heart-stopping terror. *The kids are gone. The kids.*

And now Anna was speaking blithely down the phone. 'Hi, did you get the photo?'

'But it wasn't your number.'

She was laughing. 'Nina grabbed my phone and it ended up down the loo so I got myself an iPhone. I really love it. What —? Rebecca, what's wrong?'

Huge, gasping sobs I couldn't seem to control.

'What is it? What's *happened*?'

'I thought. Oh fuck, this is so stupid. I thought someone had taken the kids.'

'What?'

'There was just the photo. I thought someone had them.'

'Kidnapped, you mean?'

'I just, I freaked out. I thought someone was following me yesterday. Look, I'm a bit edgy and when that photo came —.'

'Are you still getting those calls?'

'No. They've stopped. Look, I'm really OK.'

'But you thought someone was following you. Where are you now?'

'In Auckland. I'm following some things up. I think —.' I tried to laugh. 'I think I just have an overactive imagination right now.'

'Where are you staying?'

'A hotel.'

Her voice was so warm and loving I was almost crying again. 'Promise me you'll come over so we can sort all this out. David will be home tomorrow night and we'll work out what to do.'

'I'll come over.'

'You tuck yourself up in the hotel and don't worry, OK?'

I cried a bit more then I had a swim and a spa. This was crazy. There was nothing to be afraid of.

I showered, dried my hair, put on jeans and my grey silk top. There was a café just down the road, easy walking distance, everything was lit up, plenty of people about. I was perfectly safe and I had to *stop this crap.*

When I stepped outside the hotel it was much cooler than I'd thought and starting to rain. I needed a jacket. I went back inside and took the lift. The door slid open. I stepped outside. The lift shut behind me. I glanced along the corridor.

A man inserted a key into the lock, pushed open the door and stepped into my room.

35

I stabbed at the buttons on the lift and when nothing happened I started to run along the corridor. *Where are the stairs, where in hell is the staircase?*

Doors. Laundry. Cleaning. Fire escape. Emergency exit.

I shoved the door, clattered down the concrete stairs. One flight. Two. Three. Was that enough distance? I pushed the door slightly open, peered through the gap. Nobody. Nobody was there.

I ran. Along the corridor. Exit. Lifts. A lift door opened and I fell inside. Ground floor.

At reception a young woman in navy suit and sprayed-on geniality gave the impression of being visibly jarred as she looked up from her computer. 'There's someone in my room.' I'd barged through the line of Japanese tourists, my voice a hissing, wheezy gasp. 'A man. I saw a man. He's in my room.'

The Japanese tourists were staring, muttering to each other.

Lisa, who had a prominently displayed name badge, spoke soothingly, 'I'm sure this is a mistake, Miss —.'

'Thorne. No, it's not a mistake. You have to get the police.'

The mutters had become agitated. Lisa gestured to the rock-solid man in the uniform standing beside the lift.

'I want to see the manager.' My voice was bordering on a shriek.

'This way please.' She turned to the woman beside her who was gaping at me. 'Could you take over, Mary?'

Lisa spoke into a phone, took my arm firmly and guided me to a room behind the desk, the uniform following us, where we were joined by a man in a grey suit and blazing white shirt.

'John Carter,' he said, holding out his hand and grasping mine. *Trust me I'm in control here.* 'I'm the in-house manager. Please sit down. What seems to be the trouble?'

We all sat. Me between Lisa and the uniform — presumably to

keep the crazy woman under control — and John behind his desk.

Hold this together or they won't believe you. Deep breath. Composed and assured.

'I'm Rebecca Thorne. I'm a television journalist working for Zenith. I returned to my room, 714, for a jacket. I saw a man letting himself into my room.'

'You are absolutely sure it was your room?'

'Of course I am.'

'All right, Miss Thorne.' Carter darted a look towards Lisa. 'I'm not sure how this could have happened but there has possibly been a mix-up over keys. I'll have Abe here go up and check it out for you.'

'That's not acceptable to me,' I said. I was keeping my voice under control. 'If this man was intending to attack me, I don't want him to get away. I want you to call the police.'

A little sigh. He rested his arms on the table we were sitting around and brought his fingers together into a pyramid. 'I really don't think calling the police in at this point is appropriate. This most likely will turn out to be a mistake. A regrettable mistake. Abe will be able to deal with it.'

'I don't want this man to get away,' I said. The squeaky-wheel routine. Journalism 101: repetition. 'And I certainly don't want to be responsible for another woman being attacked because you people didn't act.'

Squeaky-wheel plus a teeny hint of threat.

Carter looked at me. I looked back. 'Let's compromise,' he said. 'What if we all go up to your room and take Abe and another security person with us, see what's happening, and then *if* necessary we'll call the police.'

Lisa broke in. 'John, I can handle this. Really.'

He looked at his watch. 'If you think you can manage, I do have a meeting.'

We were joined at the lifts by another hefty security guard. Lisa introduced us. Carl. I shook his hand. We got into the lift. I saw Abe wink at Carl over my head.

I might have this wrong. This could be a mistake. Can I be absolutely

*sure it was my room? Is my judgment out of kilter? So much has been
happening.*

Whoever it was could have somehow got the wrong key, might
have realised his mistake, got his wife to let him in and be, right at
this moment, sprawled on his bed one floor down, watching Sky
Sports. And, oh fuck, if I'd got this wrong I was going to look very,
very stupid.

Seventh floor. The lift door dinged. We got out, walked silently
up to room 714. Abe and Carl stayed behind Lisa as she opened the
door, stepped inside and switched on the light.

We were utterly silent and motionless as we peered into the room.

The bathroom door flew open and someone thick and heavy was
gripping Lisa, one hand over her mouth, the other around her neck.

Abe and Carl rocketed in, took hold of him, ripped his hands off
Lisa who lurched sideways and fell heavily to the floor. Carl shoved
the struggling man onto the ground, twisted one arm behind his
back and Abe knelt on top of him.

There was shouting and grunting and heavy panting and loud
thuds. I was pressed to the back wall scarcely breathing. Lisa was
sobbing and shouting into her mobile. Carter came down the
corridor at a run followed by a woman in a navy suit who bent down
beside Lisa and put her arms around her.

'Right.' Carter's face was flushed, his voice shaking slightly. 'Right.
The police are on their way. You two keep him in my office until
they arrive.'

Abe gave the man's arm an extra twist and then he and Carl
heaved him up, grabbed an arm each and turned him around.

The grey parka. The man on the beach.

'You've been following me.'

He didn't answer.

'You've been *following* me.'

His eyes were on the wall above my head. Abe and Carl marched
him towards the lift and forced him inside.

We stood close together as we waited for another lift. Carter kept
a tight hold of my arm.

He thought Lisa was me. He would have grabbed me exactly as he'd grabbed her. One hand clamped across my mouth, the other around my throat.

Someone took Lisa to A&E to get checked out. The police came. Two cars. One took grey parka away and Constable Scott from the other came into the office to take our statements. I went through the story.

'So Miss, just going over this, you were going out for a meal, you returned to your room for a jacket and discovered a man breaking into your room.'

'Yes.'

'And you believe that this is the same man who followed you yesterday when you were running on Milford Beach?'

He would have grabbed me, his hand would have been around my throat and.

'I think so, yes.'

'But you don't know him?'

'No. But —.'

'Yes?'

I couldn't do this. Because where in hell would I start? The phone calls, the photos, Rolly, the doco, Eric Woolley. I wasn't going to go through it, not with my head swimming and my body numb and starting to shiver despite the suffocating heat in this office.

I shook my head. 'I'm sorry. I just can't think.'

'That's fine, Miss Thorne. I think we've got enough for now. We have your details and we'll be in touch.'

'But you won't let him out, will you?' I clutched at his arm. I couldn't help it. 'Tonight, I mean?'

'Breaking and entering and assault? No way. He'll be safely locked away in the cells tonight and, after that, it'll be court. There's no need for you to worry, Miss Thorne.'

'I can't stay here.' *Fuck,* I was crying again. 'I can't go back into that room.'

'I'm sorting that out for you,' Carter said quickly. 'We're giving you a suite, one of our executive suites on the top floor, and I'm putting Carl just along the corridor.'

'Are you happy with that?' Constable Scott was gazing at me with the utmost sympathy.

'I don't know.' Ripples of shivers were running up and down my body.

'I'll personally escort you to your suite,' said Carter. 'You're leaving in the morning, aren't you? We'll get you to the airport in one of our courtesy cars.'

'I've got a rental in the carpark.' My teeth were chattering. I drew my arms around my body, trying to keep it still.

I could have been beaten up.

'We'll take care of that.' John glanced at Constable Scott. 'Do you think we should get a doctor to —.'

Constable Scott was nodding.

I could have been beaten up and raped.

I shook my head. I started babbling. 'I'm all right. I need something to eat. Something to drink and something to eat. I'll be all right once I have something to eat and drink.'

Carter sprang into action. 'Coffee? A cup of tea? Brandy? A brandy might warm you up, settle your nerves a bit.'

I nodded. He opened the cabinet behind his desk, poured brandy into a perfect little crystal glass, handed it to me and watched me drink. 'Better?'

I nodded.

'Another one?' He was standing over me like a mother duck ready to pounce on one of her ducklings.

I shook my head.

'Miss Thorne, would you like to go into the dining room or would you prefer to eat in your room? This is on the house, of course. Your bill, everything, is on the house.'

I closed my eyes. Dining room or room, dining room or room. It seemed too big a decision to make. I wanted to be private. But I didn't want to be on my own. I couldn't be on my own.

'Dining room.'

I sat at a table spooning cream of carrot soup with honey and ginger into my mouth. Warm bread with a crisp crust. The most expensive pinot on the list. The waiter had been eager to point out the special delicacies on the menu: oysters, lobster, carpaccio of venison with marinated, chilli-flavoured kelp, candied orange.

Soup. Soup and bread.

Were they caring for a traumatised woman or were they simply attempting to prevent a journalist disclosing unpleasant things about the hotel? Whom could you trust? Was everyone on the make, ready to pretend and lie to get what they wanted?

Shouldn't you be able to trust a man who throws a ball to a dog on a beach?

I could be lying somewhere hurt. Helpless.

Maybe they meant to kill me.

Who is doing this?

I finished my soup, drank the wine. Carter went up with me in the lift. He opened the door for me, stood back and I almost laughed as I looked around. An enormous living room with a conservatory and a spa pool. A basket of goodies, a glass bowl filled with lilies. Under different circumstances, I really could have enjoyed this.

Who is doing this?

'Everything all right, Miss Thorne?'

He shut the door behind him.

36

I picked my car up at the airport.

Drive to work. Hold it together.

Anna called and I told her I was absolutely fine but if she didn't mind I'd take a rain-check on tonight, there were a few things I needed to get done.

I want to be at home. I want to be curled up in my bed listening to the ocean. I want to huddle up and to be warm and to be safe.

And, no, I didn't mention anything about a man letting himself into my hotel room for the purposes of attacking me. I didn't want Dad, Mum, David on the phone with all the ensuing drama.

You must tell the police about the phone calls, someone has to follow this up, this is dangerous stuff, Rebecca, how did you get yourself tied up in it, Rebecca why didn't you tell us?

There was something I wanted to check out. Something that had popped into my head during the plane ride back to Wellington. I looked up the interview transcripts. From what I'd remembered it'd happened in Nelson.

And there it was:

'I saw this cop. He had his helmet down covering his face. I noticed him because of the way he was moving, real fast, holding his baton up like he intended giving someone a hiding.

He was shoving his way towards the black lamb and by the time he'd almost got to him he had his baton way up above his head and it was so bloody obvious what he was going to do with it I could almost feel that baton crunching down on my own head.'

A cop purposefully moving towards the black lamb. Targeting the black lamb. The black lamb who was Eric Woolley.

'I thought the white one would have seen the cop heading towards his mate because he was right in the way, but he couldn't have because he took off in the other direction.'

He *couldn't* have seen him? Even when he was directly in the way?

He couldn't have seen him or perhaps he removed himself when he saw the time was right.

Caspar Stone was possessive. He didn't like Eric to have friends, didn't like him to dance.

What if he'd found out Eric was leaving? It wouldn't take much, a search through Eric's things when he was out, finding letters, travel tickets. Maybe he'd had him followed.

Who was the cop?

I went over to Mike's desk. 'Didn't you tell me Denny Graham was part of the back-up team that went over to Nelson during the Tour?'

'Yep. Sat behind me over on the plane. Why are you asking?'

'Nothing important,' I said.

It was six o'clock before I could get away from work. Molesworth Street, Hawkestone Street. Driving through torrential rain, gusts of wind. I passed a house where sheets were flapping on a clothesline, pale and eerie in the darkness.

All those years of living and opportunities that had been taken away from him.

Tinakori Road. Lights on in the houses lining the street, curtains snugly pulled across the windows.

There was hardly any traffic. Much better to be inside on a night like this, much better at home with the fire blazing, the heat pump blasting. A stew-and-mash-and-pudding night. A dinner-on your-knee-in-front-of-the-telly night.

Ah, but it's Eric, I feel pity for.

I loved Eric very much.

I parked just along from the house. The gates were open but I didn't want to risk being trapped inside. I pulled the hood of my parka over my head.

One love goes away, another comes along. It's the way life is.

I opened the gate and walked up the path. I had my recorder in my bag, my mobile phone within easy reach in the pocket of my jacket.

I rang the doorbell. I heard footsteps. Caspar Stone was standing in the light of the vestibule. 'Rebecca.' He was smiling. 'I've been hoping you'd call by. Come on in.'

I stood near the door and folded my arms. 'I don't need to come inside,' I said. 'What I've got to say won't take long. I know what happened to Eric.'

'I had a feeling that you wouldn't let this go. Secrets rarely stay hidden forever. But, please, couldn't we at least sit down and talk about this?'

'I'd rather stay out here.'

He moved closer and stood there looking down at me. 'You say you know what happened to Eric. From the expression on your face I gather you believe I had something to do with his death.'

'His murder,' I said, 'and I think you had a lot more than something to do with it.'

'I'd like to talk to you honestly, Rebecca. I'm no threat to you. I'm an old man and it's time I told the truth. I only ask that you sit down and talk to me.'

God, were those tears in his eyes?

He *was* old, there was nobody else around, he was willing to tell his story and my recorder was already switched on.

'Yes,' I said. 'All right.'

The lamps softly lit the room, this room where he'd sat for thirty years beneath the painting of the lover he'd sent to his death. He was in the chair opposite me, his face flushed from the blaze coming from the fire. He stared down at his old, bony hands.

'I did love him,' he said. He gazed imploringly up at me. Did he really think I'd believe that? 'And I would never have hurt him. Not intentionally.'

'That's a rather odd statement under the circumstances,' I said, 'since you set him up.'

'I would like you to listen to my story. If you still believe I'm responsible for Eric's death after that, so be it. But, first, would you like a glass of wine, Rebecca? I know I would.'

I shook my head. He stood and went over to a cabinet, his back to me. I tucked my hand into my pocket, my hands touching my mobile. I was poised to leap up and run if he moved towards me. He took out a bottle of wine, opened it and poured a glass. His hands were trembling. 'Just a half-glass?' He turned and looked at me. 'This is an ending for me. Couldn't we mark the occasion and share a little wine while I tell you my story?'

He looked so wretched that I nodded.

'Well,' he said sitting down, reaching over and clinking glasses. 'You said you wanted the truth. Here's to that truth I've kept hidden inside myself for a very long time.'

I took a small sip of the wine and he smiled. 'It's rather good, isn't it? Eric and I used to drink it together and I kept a few bottles. Chateau Lilian Ladouys 1981. Sorry, Rebecca, you're waiting for my story.' He fell silent, as if gathering his ideas together.

'As I told you, I loved Eric deeply. I also admired him. He was extremely talented. When I first met him in Sydney I saw that immediately. I was a senior dancer in the company at the time and I did my best to ensure Eric was noticed. That was before we became lovers and after that happened I supported and encouraged him in his career. One of my concerns about returning to New Zealand was that Eric wouldn't have the choices and opportunities he had overseas but he was keen to return so —.'

'Isobel told me the exact opposite. She said Eric said you resented him dancing.'

'Please. Let me tell my story. Eric was talented and I encouraged him. That is the truth. He was also clever, creative, very good company and he was beautiful, Rebecca, very beautiful. I was, quite frankly, besotted with him.'

'So when you found out he intended leaving, you had him killed?'

He looked directly into my eyes, 'That's not the way it happened. It was Eric who arranged to have *me* killed.'

37

I shook my head. 'That doesn't make sense,' I said. 'Eric was going to leave. He told Isobel he was going to America. He already had his tickets booked.'

He was watching me, watching me intently. 'As I told you, Eric was clever. Very clever and streetwise — isn't that the description used now for people who will use any means to get what they want? He would have fed Isobel the information he wanted her to believe. Oh, I can just hear him. "Caspar is possessive. Caspar won't let me dance." Isobel worshipped Eric and she was receptive to anything he told her. In fact, Eric laughed at her. He used to call her his little hausfrau groupie.'

'What could Eric possibly have gained from lying to Isobel?'

His eyes were fixed on me. 'Can't you see? He was setting up an alibi.'

'An alibi for what?'

'For my murder. If there was an inquiry the police would question Isobel and she would tell them exactly what she told you. Eric was leaving for America and he had tickets and a job set up. A job, I may add, he had no intention of ever taking.'

'Why would he want to kill you?'

'Eric was used to an extravagant lifestyle. Even when he was ostensibly out on his own as a dancer he always had the Woolley funds propping him up. But that had dried up when he lost his temper with them and told them what he was. I think my money was why he stayed so long with me. But then the new lover came along and I rather imagine he thought, why not have both Caspar's money and my new friend?'

'Why would Eric think he'd get your money? Your relationship as a gay couple wouldn't have been recognised by law.'

'He knew I'd made a will in his favour just after Mother died.' He sighed. 'I still can't quite believe he would have gone through with it, but these are the facts. I'd become distrustful of Eric so I did some snooping and discovered he'd set up a private postal box at the local post office. I began intercepting the messages that came there. It was quite simple. I got hold of the key one day and had another cut.'

Was this the truth? The room was so hot. I was feeling almost light-headed with the heat and the intensity of his voice, all this information coming at me. I picked up my wine glass.

I picked up my wine glass and saw his eyes on me.

He spoke slowly. 'I would read the messages then put them back. My murder was to happen on the day of the test. Eric had come up with the idea of working with COST, but what he actually was setting up was the way for some thug he'd employed to get to me. He'd know exactly where I was, there'd be crowds around us to make it easy for him to put a knife into me or whatever and then slip away. The police had already predicted there'd be a fatality if things went on as they were and so it wouldn't have come as a surprise. A protester killed by a rugby hooligan.'

His eyes followed as I lifted my wine glass towards my lips.

'But that never happened,' I said.

'There was another message. Whoever Eric was corresponding with had decided killing me during the test was leaving too much to chance. The changed instructions were that a call would come through, on the face of it from COST members, that a walkie-talkie was to be picked up at a local letter box the evening before the test. Eric was to ensure I went alone. I destroyed the letter, the call came, I made excuses and Eric went.'

'You knew he'd be killed?'

'I didn't know that. I thought he'd be recognised and I hoped he'd be frightened enough to come to his senses. I still *hoped*, you see. But it was dark, they'd hired thugs —.'

'So what you're telling me is Eric was going to have you kicked to death?'

'Eric wanted all this.'

My eyes followed as he waved his hand around the room. This

wonderful, rich room, the painting of Eric softly lit by the spotlight above.

'You believe me?'

'I don't believe you.' I put my wine glass down carefully. 'You see,
I have my own theory. Eric was the black lamb. In Nelson the black
lamb almost got attacked by a cop while you, the white lamb, stood
by. And then, just six days later Eric was killed. Not long afterwards
a cop who'd been there in Nelson and was in Wellington at the time
of Eric's death came into a lot of money.'

'Really,' he said. 'I have no idea what you're talking about.'

'You couldn't bear to have Eric leave you so you had him killed.'

'Eric wasn't to be trusted, Rebecca.' His voice was low-pitched,
silky. 'You, of all people, must know people are rarely as they seem.
Connor Bligh, for example. You believed him, didn't you? And Joe
Fahey. His wife is dying, you know. You didn't know that? But you
must know about the young lawyer he has waiting in the wings. Very
pretty and very young.'

I stood up. 'I don't believe you.'

His eyes were hard, glinting. 'Didn't you say you wanted the truth?'

He came out of his chair, swiftly, menacingly.

And my mobile rang. I pulled it out of my pocket, talking into it
as I bolted across the room, pulled open the door, set off down the
passage, almost racing down the passage, talking loudly. 'Yes. I'm
here at Caspar Stone's. I'm leaving now.'

Into the vestibule and through the door, pulling it behind me and
down the steps. I looked back up at the house as I hurtled along
the pathway.

Through the window he was watching me, his eyes were black
and luminous.

38

I was in my car, breathing hard. I reset my mobile. I'd set the alarm to go off while I was in the house. Just in case I needed him to believe someone else thought I was there.

His eyes on me. On my wine glass. His eyes following as I lifted it towards my lips. The swiftness of his body. That hostility in his eyes as he sprang out of his chair.

Had he put something in my drink?

I started up my car.

Would Caspar keep a supply of Rohypnol beside his drinks cabinet? And why would he want to drug me? So he could strangle, stab or shoot me then lock my corpse in his cellar and throw away the key?

Rebecca, this is real New Zealand and not a New York crime novel.

I had an interview set up the next morning at the Central Police Station in Victoria Street to make a full statement about what had happened in Auckland. I'd tell them everything. The phone calls, the photographs, Rolly, everything. I'd give them the recording of my conversation with Stone. And then I'd leave it with them to deal with.

I drove home slowly. I turned on TV, watched as many mind-numbing, aspiring chef/model/singing-star reality programmes as I could stand and went to bed.

Up there, Miss Thorne, to the right. To the right, Miss Thorne.

The soft room, the beautiful room, the painting above the fire.

Mouths and hair and black teeth. Gaping mouths and hair and black teeth.

The painting above the fire.

Eric.

Poor Eric. He didn't get away after all.

A funeral mask, Miss Thorne.

I woke up, eyes wide open, staring into the dark, my heart juddering, my breathing rapid, shallow, all my senses alert and straining.

Where is he where is he where is he?

Soft, sure footfalls.

Where is he where is he where is he?

I am frozen, fixed. I cannot even blink as the light floods my face.

I feel the pressure of the man's arm across my chest, holding me down. I hear the man's voice filling my ears, my head. I am gazing at his face.

I know this man's face.

'Here's how we're going to play this. I'm going to give you a drink. A bit of a shame, Rebecca, you inviting a guy you didn't know into your house. A bit of a shame you had too much to drink.'

He is forcing the bottle between my lips. The liquid is fire-hot and I'm gagging, choking. I try to shut my mouth, turn away my head. He raises his hand and slaps me hard. 'Drink it. *Drink it.*'

I gag, swallow, gag, swallow.

'Good girl.'

My body is slumped, my arms are loose and his arm slackens on my chest. Though my mind is blurred and swimming with fright there is a small, small part of it which is red-hot lucid, teeming with energy and scorching with rage.

I moan and close my eyes.

That small, small part which recognises the chance and directs my arm to move slowly, slowly, so slowly. Which directs my hand to feel its way carefully beneath the mattress, so slowly and so carefully between the mattress and the base of my bed, to feel and to grasp the kitchen knife I have honed to razor-sharpness and stashed there.

To grasp the knife. To shove it in. As hard as I can. As far as it will go.

He is roaring with rage and pain and there is blood gushing over me, over him and I am shoving him, shoving him, shoving him off me, grabbing my mobile.

The bathroom. The bathroom. Lock the door.

Lock the door.

There's a man in my house. There's a man.

Jason.

39

A high white bed. Green walls.

My morning police interview was being held in the hospital.

I remembered vomiting. Retching over and over. I remembered the feeling and brightness of blood. I remembered the police and the ambulance and the doctor who shone the torch into my eyes.

'Did I kill him?' I said.

'No.' Des Horton was grinning. 'You made a right mess of him, though.'

'How did he get in?' I had a thumping headache. I rested my head back on the pillows. 'The doors were locked. I had the locks changed.'

'He got in through the skylight above the kitchen,' Des said. 'It was open when we got there and I'd guarantee when we have a look at it later the panels around it will have been removed.'

That was the noise I'd heard. That was the new sound. 'Who was he?'

'Well,' Des said, 'we've been looking into the attempted assault at the hotel in Auckland and the offender has just made a deal with police there by giving them the information he was working for Denny Graham. I'd just about bet my life this character will be linked to Graham as well.'

I closed my eyes against the light. 'Denny Graham?'

'From what we can gather, once Graham knew you intended to start fishing for information on him for the documentary you were about to do he decided something had to be done about it. Sending photos and making phone calls is a well-known Graham stunt. He's used it over and over again on dissatisfied clients who got too vocal. His intention was to spook you, scare you off.'

'But he tried to kill me.'

'We've traced a number of calls made between Graham and Caspar Stone. Graham knew you'd begun to make the links between him and the Woolley murder and when you kept going you had to be stopped. You going off to Auckland and that last visit to Stone's place. Well, let's just say it wasn't wise to keep pushing Graham like that. It wasn't wise at all.'

I closed my eyes. I felt tears trickling, slowly, pathetically down my cheeks. 'I almost got killed.'

Des patted my hand as he stood up. 'Well, you didn't and it looks like you'll be responsible for putting a couple of mongrels in prison where they belong. But next time, girl, let the police do their job, eh? It's what we're here for.'

40

*T*he year was 1981.

It was the year we lost the cricket series against Australia, but won a moral victory when Trevor Chappell bowled us his underhand, underarm bowl. Sheep outnumbered Kiwi citizens twenty-two to one, we had two television channels to choose between, gay meant happy, sideburns and knickerbockers and Lady Di hairdos were prolific. Muldoon was Prime Minister and our Rob had his government Thinking Big and told Malcolm Fraser off for the underarm bowl exactly like a bloke in charge should. Also, 1981 was Goodbye Pork Pie *year and, despite fears it would incite New Zealand youth towards lives of crime, that film made us laugh.*

Though for many *Goodbye Pork Pie* was the best laugh to be had that year. Inflation was into double figures. Unemployment figures were getting up there. And, although most New Zealanders still trusted that police would protect the good guys and go after the bad, the findings of the 1980 Royal Commission of Inquiry on the Crewe case, which had now become available for public scrutiny, demonstrated that was not always so. Which perhaps proved a foretaste of what was to come.

Because while 1981 was also supposed to be the year in which we celebrated a royal wedding, the pictures on our screens of a fairy-tale princess swathed in her yards of silk taffeta and tulle crinoline waving from a coach in London streets were interrupted by images of a very different nature.

Over here in Molesworth Street, Wellington, a bloody battle was going on as police used batons to rain down blows on the protesters they were determined to subdue.

So 1981 is most remembered for the Springbok rugby tour that provoked the worst bitterness, violence and civil unrest in our history;

1981 is the year some still look back on as the end of our innocence.

I'm facing directly into the camera. My facial expression suggests interest and concern, my voice has just about the right balance of animation and sincerity.

The short dress and long boots work OK; the image is decidedly feminine — sexy, even — but doesn't detract from the seriousness of what I'm saying. My hair looks fine, the highlights glint as I lift or turn my head.

In my last job my boss, Harry, gave me the best advice a TV journalist could have. 'Think of some bastard who'd like to see you fall right down smack on your face. Have you pissed him off or would he be laughing?'

I look hard at the young woman looking back at me. Composed and self-assured, she dips her head slightly. There is no unease in the face which now gives me a little smile.

She plays her part well. Nobody would be laughing.

The camera switches to Anna Steveley. She was one of the first former COST members I interviewed. The soft, unlined face which gazes assuredly into the camera has never, it seems, been troubled by ugliness. The impeccably cut silvery hair and feathery voice are confirmation of a life rather like an elegant yacht wheeling across temperate, untroubled waters.

'We were running away but as we came around the corner we saw more of them beating two women who were lying face down on the ground. Some of them went for the cameraman, punching him in the face, ripping the camera out of his hands and tearing out the film. Then I felt this whack to the back of my head and I fell face downwards on the road.

'I remember thinking through the shock and pain, this can't be happening. Not in Wellington. Not here.'

Tim turns to me, smiling. Thumbs up.

I am in the editing room, Mike and Tim beside me. I watch their faces watch the images I've become accustomed to. The grim-faced police, the dogs, the crouched, dazed woman with blood on her face. The protesters trying to climb fences, trying to rip them down.

The singing, the chanting, the placards. The sound of helicopters clap-clap-clappering, the plumes of smoke drifting upwards. All those sad, surreal images moving against the backdrop of familiar buildings, roads, bridges.

And now, here are the lambs. Running at the edge of the police lines, zigzagging in and out of the crowds. The white lamb wags a finger at a police officer. They turn around, wiggle their bums at a line of police, wave up at the crowded stands.

People are rarely as they seem.

MacAlister Park. The dark, dripping bush, the mud, the barbed-wire fences. The rows of protesters muffled in jackets, hats, boots. And now comes the voice-over:

But what's the defeat in five hundred men, women and kids, row on row of them, old people, young people, linking arms, singing and crying and chanting?

A rainbow of hats and coats and helmets beneath the rain.

I glance across at Tim and at Mike and the tears in their eyes match mine.

Five hundred men, women and kids, row on row of them, old people, young people, linking arms, singing and crying and chanting.

A rainbow of hats and coats and helmets beneath the rain.

Acknowledgements

I'd like to thank everyone who shared their memories of the 1981 Springbok Tour which helped so much in the writing of this novel. First and foremost was Geoff Walker, who told me his wonderful stories, read the drafts and was so generous in his encouragement and support. Thanks also to Bill O'Brien who gave me a policeman's view and helped me fill a large notebook with his recollections, and to Michael Burnside who told me about his experiences of the Molesworth Street march. Thanks to Jim and my family for, as always, their interest, support and reading.

The following books and documentaries were helpful in the writing of this novel: 'Patu', Merata Mita (NZ On Screen), 'Springbok Tour Special', *Close Up* (TVNZ), 'Try Revolution', Leanne Pooley (NZ On Screen), 'The Tour Ten Years On', Bryan Bruce (TVNZ), *Barbed Wire Boks*, Don Cameron (Rugby Press, 1981), *1981: The Tour*, Geoff Chapple (Reed, 1984), *By Batons and Barbed Wire*, Tom Newnham (Real Pictures, 1981), *The Red Squad Story*, Ross Meurant (Harlen, 1982), *Owaka Jack*, Shirley Deuchrass (Deuchrass, 2008), and *56 Days: A History of the Anti-Tour Movement in Wellington*, editors Geoff Walker & Peter Beach (COST, 1982).

Finally, so many thanks to Stephen Stratford my editor, for his careful editing, strong support and sense of humour in adversity. And thanks also to Kevin Chapman and the team at Hachette New Zealand for their belief in this novel.

About the Author

Paddy Richardson is the author of five novels and two short story collections. Her fiction has been a finalist for the Ngaio Marsh Award for Best Crime Novel and short-listed for the BNZ Katherine Mansfield Awards. She has been the recipient of the University of Otago Burns Fellowship, the Beatson Fellowship, and the James Wallace Arts Trust Residency Award. Three of her novels have been translated and published in Germany. Paddy has lectured and tutored English Literature at university level and taught on many creative writing courses. She lives on the Otago Peninsula in New Zealand.